THE
PIRATE'S CURSE

Brigands of the Compass Rose

Toni Runkle & Steve Webb

Black Rose Writing | Texas

The author grants the final approval for this literary material.

First printing

This is a work of fiction. Names, characters, businesses, places, events, and incidents are either the products of the author's imagination or used in a fictitious manner. Any resemblance to actual persons, living or dead, or actual events is purely coincidental.

ISBN: 978-1-68513-283-5
PUBLISHED BY BLACK ROSE WRITING
www.blackrosewriting.com

Printed in the United States of America
Suggested Retail Price (SRP) $24.95

The Pirate's Curse is printed in Baskerville

*As a planet-friendly publisher, Black Rose Writing does its best to eliminate unnecessary waste to reduce paper usage and energy costs, while never compromising the reading experience. As a result, the final word count vs. page count may not meet common expectations.

Early Praise for
The Pirate's Curse
Brigands of the Compass Rose

"Toni Runkle and Steve Webb's *The Pirate's Curse: Brigands of the Compass Rose* is a thrilling, emotional roller coaster of an adventure. I was hooked from the first page to the last. It's *Treasure Island* meets *The Outsiders* in a grand adventure not to be missed!"

—Haris Orkin, award-winning author of the
James Flynn Escapades

"Taking a wild turn from their unforgettable *Glitter Girl* into a new dimension of teen girl power, Runkle and Webb's new novel explodes into a world of mystery, crime, magic, family, curses, romance, and yes, piracy. From the first page to the last, a non-stop adventure of self-discovery and danger, *Brigands* delivers on everything it promises and more. Hop on board and Hold On Tight!"

—Douglas Green, author of *A Dog of Many Names* and
The Teachings of Shirelle

"A tale of teens training to battle against a menacing supernatural threat? Sign me up! Action, adventure, and heart. *Brigands* has it all! This is one boat ride you'll never forget (if you survive, that is)!"

—Kevin D. Ross, ACE. Emmy-nominated editor of
Stranger Things and *Yellowjackets*

For Julia and Katrina,
as they set sail

THE
PIRATE'S CURSE

Brigands of the Compass Rose

brigand (brig'ənd) noun c. 1400, from Italian *brigare* "to brawl, fight"

1. One who lives by plunder, especially as part of a band of outlaws
2. Any member of the secret society whose exploits, unknown to the world until now, you are about to discover within the pages of this book

Prologue

Gallows Point, Port Royal, Jamaica
November 18, 1720

The sky was painted in brilliant reds and oranges as the sun made its descent into the waters of the Caribbean. Ships bobbed in the harbor of Port Royal, all awash in the fiery glow of day's end. "Red sky at night, sailor's delight" was the ancient mariners' saying. But this night, the angry chant that cut through the thick, tropical air was anything but delightful.

"Hang him! Hang him! Hang him!" the call repeated.

A black-winged gull swooped high over Gallows Point, the highest point in all of Port Royal, where hundreds had gathered at the base of a towering Jamaican cotton tree. From its thickest branch hung a hangman's noose.

The tree was now a silhouette against the darkening sky. The chanting stopped momentarily as a hangman slipped the noose around the neck of a prisoner with black, soulless eyes. The condemned man said nothing, simply staring into the crowd that had come to taunt him.

Stepping forward on the scaffolding came a corpulent official in a powdered wig and black robes. The crowd fell silent as he read aloud from a piece of parchment.

"Calico Jack Rackham, you have been found guilty of piracy, including but not limited to, manifold acts of plunder, pillage,

murder, mayhem and general terror upon the high seas. By order of King George and Governor Lawes of Jamaica, you have been sentenced to execution this day, the 18th of November in the year of our Lord 1720. In payment for your crimes, you shall be severally hanged by the neck till you are severally dead. Do you have any final words?"

The crowd remained hushed, awaiting his response.

"You'll all be worm food long 'fore I join ye in hell!" Calico Jack spat at the crowd and the silence was shattered.

"Hang him! Make him pay for his evil deeds! No mercy for the likes of him!"

So bloodthirsty were the onlookers that they paid no heed to the muscular African man standing in their midst. The tall man wore beads and an ornate amulet around his neck, and his face was covered with a design that had long ago been cut into his flesh using the ancient technique known as scarification. And on that same face, he wore an almost imperceptible smirk.

The official stepped back and nodded to the hangman, who released the trapdoor upon which the prisoner stood. As Calico Jack Rackham plunged to his fate, his eyes met those of the African. And, just before his neck snapped, the condemned man smiled that same smirk.

At that very moment in the harbor of Port Royal, a raven-haired young woman stood at the railing of a sailing ship. She peered over the water toward Gallows Point and heard the distant cheers of the crowd.

"Jack Rackham is dead, Mistress Bonny," said a voice beside her. "You're free to leave."

Anne Bonny turned and looked upon the roguish privateer next to her.

"Thank you, Captain Barnet," Anne offered her hand but he did not take it.

"Do not misinterpret my civility," he said curtly. "Had you not made this bargain with the Crown, you might, too, be under the noose

for your part in your husband's crimes. You and your… friend, both."

He walked over to a young woman who had been watching in silence. She had stormy gray eyes, her flaming auburn hair was pulled back in a black bandana and she was dressed in a billowy shirt and breeches like a man. Barnet ran the back of his hand across her cheek familiarly. The woman glared at him but said nothing. He smiled and turned back to Anne.

"I trust never to see you in these parts again," he warned.

"You have seen the last of Anne Bonny and Mary Read," she replied.

Barnet fixed Anne with a hard stare, then walked off and indicated to the posted sentries to accompany him into a small vessel anchored next to the ship.

Anne turned and took her companion's hands. "Let us away, Mary," she urged, "as fast as the winds will carry us!"

"Aye, dearest Anne," replied Mary, then shouted to the crew. "Anchors up! We set sail for the Carolinas!"

As the crew sprang into action, a diminutive African woman appeared from below deck. She wore various beads and amulets similar to those worn by the African man at the hanging. She was carrying an infant, only a few days old.

"Seth," Anne cried, taking the child. "My sweet darling son."

"Ya can stop yah worry, Mistress Anne. The curse put into the chile be broke with the death of that mongrel," said the woman in a thick accent. "That stain don' mean nothin' now."

"Mariama. You're a blessing to me," Anne smiled gratefully.

As the schooner moved out of the harbor, Anne whispered to the child in her arms, "You're safe now, my darling Seth." She held him close to her and sobbed tears of relief, kissing the wrist of his little hand tenderly. And in the moonlight, upon his wrist could be seen a tiny discoloration, a birthmark, in the shape of an X.

Chapter 1
Bonnie Hartwright

On an oppressively hot Arizona night three centuries later, a troubled moan escaped the lips of a fifteen-year-old girl in the midst of a fitful sleep. A single bead of sweat trickled down her cheek and stopped at the silver hoop that pierced her nostril. She was in the throes of that nightmare again, where her head was being violently forced under water. She could never see the face of her tormentor in the dream. All she knew was that a hand kept pushing, pushing as she struggled for air. And on that hand, a ring—it had two tiny ruby-eyed golden skulls connected to an hourglass in the middle—the sand inside moving upward, defying gravity. Just as her lungs felt as though they would burst, she awoke with a start and a scream.

"Mmmmflllmmm!" her scream was muffled by a large hand clamped down on her mouth.

"Shut up, Bonnie! For cryin' out loud!" The voice belonged to Clint Krokel, her paunch-bellied foster father. And while he did have his hand over her mouth, he wasn't sporting a skull ring and he certainly wasn't trying to drown her. In fact, sitting in the cab of Clint's pickup parked in the middle of a rundown Tucson subdivision, she couldn't have been further from drowning.

"Get away from me, creep!" Bonnie snarled, shoving his hand away.

"Keep your voice down!" Clint hissed. "You were having another of your damn nightmares. You didn't take your meds again, did you? Jesus, Bonnie. You're gonna blow this job!" He pointed across the street to a dumpy house with a mint '69 Chevy Camaro in the driveway.

"They still up?" Bonnie asked, rubbing her eyes. "What, are they vampires in addition to being deadbeats?"

"Meth heads, more like it. Gonna be a long night," Clint said, lighting another cigarette.

"Screw that noise. I say the party's over now!" Bonnie grabbed her tools and opened the truck door.

Clint grabbed her arm. "You nuts? You go in now, that crowd, you'll end up with a gun in your face."

"Like you give a rip what happens to me!" She slammed the door and headed toward the vehicle Clint had been contracted to repossess.

With time-tested expertise, it took Bonnie less than a minute to get into the Camaro and even less than that to get it started. Despite the blaring alarm, she was soon speeding backwards out of the driveway before the car's "owners" were out of the house.

"Hey! What you think you're doin'?!!" yelled one, chasing after her, waving a pistol over his head.

"Next time, make your payments, loser!" Bonnie shouted as she fishtailed around a corner at sixty miles an hour.

"I'm so frickin' good!" she shouted, the adrenaline pumping through her veins. And in that moment, she forgot all about the horrible dreams and every other crap thing in her life. She just felt alive—very, very alive.

In fact, Bonnie felt most alive in moments like this—whenever she "acted out" as the shrinks called it. Every time she shoplifted a bottle of shampoo because the Krokels were too lazy to go to the drugstore, every time she punched a kid who mouthed off to her, or slashed the tires of some jerk who'd parked in a handicap zone, she felt this thrill run through her body, as if not only were these things *not* wrong, but they were exactly what Bonnie was *meant* to do.

Screw the dreams AND the meds, she thought.

⸺   ⸺   ⸺   ⸺   ⸺

But like every high, the feeling didn't last. Bonnie had returned to earth by the time she pulled into the driveway of the house she shared with Clint Krokel, his wife Jackie and the half a dozen other kids the state paid them to care for. The sun was up now and there was no time to catch a catnap or shower before school, so she headed right to her room to change clothes.

After settling on a pair of ripped jeans and a T-shirt, she put back on her black biker boots with chains across the front. She brushed her dark, curly hair behind her ears, revealing multiple piercings that made her single nose piercing look lonely in comparison, and then she topped it all off with a beat-up Pittsburgh Pirates cap that had struck her fancy at the Goodwill. She stood a moment, dark eyes flecked with gray, checking her reflection in the mirror, then satisfied, she headed toward the kitchen for breakfast.

Bonnie had been living with the Krokels for about a year now, the latest in a string of foster families that she'd been with since as long as she could remember. Bonnie had long ago abandoned hope of ever finding a family to call her own. Instead, she had to "make the best of it," as her case worker Mrs. Swift had constantly told her, until she was 18.

"Bonnie!" came a call from down the hall. "First bell's in ten minutes!"

"Take a frickin' pill, Jackie!" Bonnie replied, entering the kitchen.

Clint's wife rummaged through the refrigerator, a baby on her hip and two toddlers screaming at her heels.

"So you and your dad got the car?" Jackie asked.

"He's not my dad, Jackie. And yeah, *I* got it. You're welcome," Bonnie replied, pulling a jar of grape jelly out of the fridge and popping a tortilla in the microwave.

"Come straight home tonight. You're watching the kids. Clint and I are going out to the Brass Rail."

"Sheesh, if you want to tie one on, spring for a babysitter, why doncha?" Bonnie snarled over her shoulder as she walked out the front door, stuffing the last of her jelly taco in her mouth. She hopped on an old Vespa scooter in the driveway and zoomed off into the Tucson morning.

· · · · ·

The wind whipped through Bonnie's long hair as she blew through a stop sign. God, how she loved her Vespa! When she was on it, she almost felt free. Clint had repo-ed it long before Bonnie moved in, but the bank didn't want it because it had been left in such bad condition. So, it had been a yard ornament until Clint told Bonnie that she could ride it if she could get it running again. It took her about three months of hard work and strategic shoplifting to do it, but now she had it purring like a kitten.

The streets of South Tucson were quiet that morning, except for the constant hum of air conditioners that cooled the hermetically sealed adobe houses. She wished she could just keep riding. She thought about cutting class again, but she knew if she missed much more school she'd be repeating freshman year, which wouldn't look good to the pencil pushers who ruled over her life.

At least I have gym first period, Bonnie thought as she stepped into the girls' locker room. Gym was the one class that didn't fill Bonnie with dread. In fact, the opportunity to run around a track for an hour or smack somebody with a dodgeball was her idea of a fine time. Until she remembered they started their swimming unit that day.

"Crap!" she murmured, frozen at her locker.

If there was one thing that Bonnie hated beyond anything else, it was water. Her weird nightmare was to blame, she was sure of it. She was overcome with terror whenever she thought of her body being in the water, even a little. And now, her gym class was going to spend the next two weeks on a swimming unit. In the end, she was able to lie her way out of it by pleading a certain monthly "girl's health" issue, but she knew that only bought her a few days.

"Come on ladies, get on your suits and hit the water!" Sharlene Vlasic, their buff gym teacher, yelled at the locker room full of girls. "That means you, too, Hartwright. No street clothes poolside." The coach exited, leaving the girls to themselves. "Five minutes!" she called over her shoulder.

"Let's go ladies!" said Mandy Brooks, the alpha girl of ninth grade, strutting around in an exaggerated imitation of their teacher's mannerisms. "Anyone caught lollygagging will be forced to alphabetize my collection of lesbian porn!"

Bonnie tried to ignore Mandy's hateful joke and the cackles of her friends and started to change into her swimsuit. She pulled off her T-shirt and the tight collar pulled her hair up just enough to reveal—

"What is THAT???" Mandy said loudly, pointing toward Bonnie's shoulder blade.

Bonnie cringed. They'd seen "it."

The birthmark that she always tried so hard to hide. God it was ugly. Thick, a dark reddish brown like old blood—a misshapen pinwheel that looked like it had been drawn by a drunken tattoo artist.

"It's just an old tattoo," she said and quickly put her towel over her shoulders to hide it. But Mandy ripped the towel off and her minions crowded around Bonnie.

"Didn't look like any tattoo I ever saw," said Mandy, reaching for Bonnie's hair to get another look.

"Get your hands off me," Bonnie jerked away, seething.

"C-come on guys, leave her alone. It's time for class!" said Suzy Hartze, one of the cowering girls that had worked up the courage to try to protect Bonnie by changing the subject at least. "Vlasic's gonna be pissed."

"Shut up, cow! I don't remember saying this was any of your business!" Mandy hissed and turned back to Bonnie. "Let's see it again." Mandy's girls were circling Bonnie now.

"No frickin' way!" Bonnie tried to push past them. But they jumped her. "Get off me!" she yelled, as the girls held her so Mandy could get her look.

"Eeeew," Mandy screeched, "it's a birthmark! And it's sooo going on my social!" Mandy snapped a shot with her cellphone and quickly posted it to her favorite online photo sharing site.

"Like hell it is!" said Bonnie, breaking one arm free and knocking the phone out of Mandy's hand.

"Pick it up, you pathetic *foster* girl," Mandy said.

"Screw you," Bonnie elbowed a girl hard in the stomach, freed her other arm, and shoved Mandy forcefully back.

"Throw the freak in the pool!" commanded Mandy.

In an instant, the girls were on top of her. Bonnie struggled, but there were too many of them. They picked her up by the arms and legs. With Bonnie kicking and screaming, the mad procession headed out toward the pool. And the rest of the class watched in horror, with Coach Vlasic nowhere in sight.

"Toss her in the deep end!" Mandy screamed.

Bonnie panicked at the sight of the pool. "No!! Put me down!!"

"You guys are gonna get in sooo much trouble!" said Suzy Hartze, more forcefully this time.

But it was too late. Bonnie went flying high into the air over the pool.

SPLASHHHHHHHHHHHHHH! Bonnie hit the water with such force she felt the pain through her entire body. She plummeted so deep she felt her back scrape against the bottom. She flailed in the water, struggling to survive. It was her nightmare all over again. Only this time, she knew she was going to die. *Maybe it's for the best.* The dark thoughts she usually pushed away now enveloped her like the crushing weight of the water. She stopped struggling, closed her eyes and everything started to go black.

Suddenly, something ripped her from the bottom of the pool. Bonnie broke through the surface, gasping for breath, and found herself face to face with Coach Vlasic. The coach dragged Bonnie to the side of the pool, where Suzy Hartze helped pull Bonnie out.

"Are you all insane?!" Coach Vlasic screamed, looking directly at Mandy Brooks. Bonnie lay at the side of the pool, sucking in air as fast as her lungs could consume it.

"We were just having fun," Mandy replied with a practiced innocence. "We thought she could swim."

"I don't care what you thought," the coach said, climbing out of the pool. "There's NO horseplay around the pool! Hartwright, you're done for today. Head to the lockers and change. The rest of you, give me ten laps. Now!"

Bonnie shivered as she heard the splash, splash, splash of twenty grumbling girls jumping into the pool. Then she felt the warmth of a towel covering her back.

"Don't mind those she-monsters, Bonnie," Coach Vlasic said. "You gonna be okay?"

"Peachy," Bonnie shrugged Vlasic off and rushed into the locker room.

⸺ ⸺ ⸺ ⸺ ⸺

Bonnie sat on a bench and closed her eyes, taking in a few deep breaths, letting a little bit of the terror slip away with every exhale. Once her hands finally stopped shaking, she forced herself to get up and change back into her street clothes. As she started to pull on her T-shirt, she saw it had been torn at the neckline. And that little tear was all it took to change the course of Bonnie Hartwright's life forever. It was a cheap T-shirt that she'd shoplifted from the Goodwill. But it was *Bonnie's* cheap T-shirt. One of the few things that actually belonged to her.

Bonnie slammed her locker, her terror replaced with a seething and uncontrollable anger. Not quite sure what she was even doing, Bonnie ran to an old wire cart filled with basketballs. She flung the cart over, sending the balls cascading onto the floor. She yanked the cart upright and pushed it wildly past the lockers, tossing everything in sight—clothes, books, backpacks, cellphones—into the basket. She bypassed Suzy Hartze's stuff because she had at least tried to stop them. But everything else went into a massive pile in the basket.

Bonnie rifled through the pockets of the pair of jeans that belonged to Danita Mayernik, who always reeked of weed, and pulled out a lighter. At the Sports Med station, she grabbed a bottle of rubbing alcohol and doused the contents of the basket. She flicked the lighter, lit an alcohol-drenched sweat sock, and dropped it into the pile of clothes.

WHOOSH!! The contents of the basket burst into flames. With the fire in the cart dancing high over her head…

"Aaaaiiieeee!" Bonnie let loose with a primal scream as she grabbed an overhead pipe, swung, and kicked the cart squarely with both feet. The cart went crashing through the locker room doors and careened toward the pool, where all the girls screamed as the flaming mass hurtled toward them. It hit the side of the pool and went airborne… flipping, showering flaming items everywhere before slamming into the pool.

Bonnie looked over her destruction and grinned. This is what it felt like to make things right, to square the ledger.

It felt… perfect.

Chapter 2
Consequences

Two hours later, Bonnie sat in the waiting area of AzCA, Tucson's "foster kid" headquarters. She glanced over at a little girl across from her.

Definitely a foster, she silently observed. Bonnie had become an expert at spotting her "fellow travelers" in the foster system, and this one had all the signs. There was the unkempt hair and the threadbare jeans, at least two inches too short—signs that there was no "real" mom around to give a damn. And in her lap she clutched the telltale plastic garbage bag—*the official luggage of the foster child.* Whenever fosters wore out their welcome with a family, all their belongings were unceremoniously stuffed into a garbage bag just like this one, and they'd have to lug it around until they found another home.

Bonnie saw too how the little girl's eyes brightened whenever a door opened or footsteps approached. And that was the most telling sign of all. Those eyes betrayed fear and anxiety, but also a sliver of hope.

Bonnie knew the feeling all too well. How many times had she sat in that very same seat, her own garbage bag in hand, waiting to find out who her latest set of foster parents would be? Wondering would they be nice? Would they care about her? Would they maybe even adopt her? Having learned the answers the hard way, Bonnie stopped asking herself the questions a long time ago. But she could see in this little girl's eyes that she hadn't—yet.

"Bonnie Hartwright, what a surprise," Bonnie heard from the door to the inner office. The voice, dripping with sarcasm, belonged to Mrs. Swift, who had been her caseworker for as long as Bonnie could remember. Despite being 4'10" in heels, she looked pretty intimidating in the severe black suit Bonnie knew she reserved for very serious occasions. "You know the drill," Mrs. Swift gestured for her to follow.

As Bonnie got up to face the music, she paused by the little girl.

"Don't worry, it's gonna be okay," Bonnie said to the girl, whose eyes glistened at the kind words. But as Bonnie walked away, she knew deep down inside that it was a lie, a naive fantasy that she hated herself for spreading.

Bonnie plopped in the chair in front of Mrs. Swift's desk, which as usual was piled high with case files and covered with stains from her coffee mug. She stared at Bonnie's file a good long time.

"Do I look like a cheerleader to you?" she finally asked.

By now, Bonnie knew Mrs. Swift's canned speeches by heart, so she knew exactly what was coming. Bonnie didn't have many lines in this little melodrama, but she knew hers by heart. "No, ma'am," Bonnie replied, imbuing the "ma'am" with the least amount of respect humanly possible.

"Am I wearing a tight sweater with a giant red 'B' on it?" the social worker continued. "Do you see any pom-poms in my hand?"

"No, ma'am."

"So we agree that I am not in fact a cheerleader."

"Yes, ma'am."

"So then if you think I'm going to applaud, say 'rah, rah' after that stunt you pulled at school, you are sadly mistaken. Because those are the actions of a cheerleader, which we have clearly established I am not."

"They started it," said Bonnie matter-of-factly.

"You think the state gives a flying fig about who started it? I assure you it does not. Know why? Because those other girls don't have a file three inches thick on my desk. But you do. And the latest addition to that file includes such gems as destroying private property. Destroying school property. Arson. And assault with a deadly weapon."

"Assault?" Bonnie was surprised. "What deadly weapon?"

"What do you call that flaming cart of bras and panties?"

"Pretty damn cool, if you ask me," Bonnie smirked.

"This isn't a joke, Bonnie. Somebody could have been hurt! Or worse."

"Relax, nobody got hurt."

"What about the five thousand dollars' worth of designer crap you just treated to a Viking funeral?"

"Pfft. That stuff was worth maybe two grand tops," Bonnie said.

"I'm not going to be trading appraisals with you, Bonnie. Those girls' parents are screaming for restitution," Mrs. Swift said. "And the state of Arizona certainly won't be picking up the tab."

"I'll get Clint to start paying me for helping him with the repos," Bonnie shrugged.

"The Krokels? You think they want anything to do with you after this stunt? No, missy. They are done with you six ways to Sunday!"

"They didn't seem to mind the last time I caught a case." Bonnie was referring to when she got arrested for slicing the transmission belt on her neighbor's boyfriend's car after Bonnie had seen him smack her around during a block party. One of the neighbor kids ratted Bonnie out, and the jerk pressed charges, which Mrs. Swift was so kind to remind her of now.

"That punk had it coming," Bonnie said.

"Well, Zorro, that little gallant gesture of yours got you put on probation, the terms of which you just violated when you decided to torch the spring collection at Forever 21."

"If you wanted me to behave better, you should have put me with a better class of foster parents," said Bonnie with hostility.

"Beggars can't be choosers," snarled Mrs. Swift. "Families get one whiff of you, and they don't want the aggravation." At which point, she launched into a listing of Bonnie's many crimes against humanity, which included, as she put it, "a pattern of willfully destructive and antisocial behavior.

"Not to mention," continued Mrs. Swift, who was in rare form this morning, "all the psychologists and counselors you've been assigned to. How many different medications have you been on in the last ten years to deal with your O.D.D.?"

O.D.D. Oppositional Defiant Disorder. That was the fancy name that the doctors had come up with for Bonnie's "screw the rules" attitude, and the excuse they used for trying to keep her more doped up than a Russian track star.

"Well, let's see, shall we?" Bonnie replied. "First, there was Carbamazepine when you all thought I was bipolar. Then, Lorazepam, that one made me puke and gave me lovely rashes. Then, let's not forget the Xanax and Valium; those two worked just swell except for the fact that I felt like a zombie and couldn't take a crap for a week at a time."

"For all the good they did you, you might as well have flushed them down the toilet."

"Most of the time I did."

Mrs. Swift's face turned beet red. Bonnie could see she had stepped over the line.

"Well, guess what? It's not just the Krokels who are done with you," Mrs. Swift said, closing the file on her desk. "We've reached the end of the road with the state as well. You're to be labeled incorrigible and sent to Amargo Canyon until you're 18."

Bonnie felt the defiance drain from her and the panic set in. She'd heard enough about what went down inside the Amargo Canyon Juvenile Detention Center from girls who'd been on the inside to know she didn't want any part of it. It was a prison, plain and simple. Her life with the Krokels sucked, but it at least was *her* life. The little freedom that she had now would be snatched away the second she stepped inside the gate.

"Look, I promise I'll be better. I swear I'll behave with the next family. I won't talk back. I'll go to school every day and get a part-time job on weekends. Pay back all the money—"

"I'm sorry, Bonnie, but the decision is final." Mrs. Swift picked up the phone receiver and pushed a button. "We're ready," she said.

Into the office came two uniformed officers of the South Tucson Police Department.

Bonnie looked at her caseworker pleadingly. Mrs. Swift's expression wasn't even anger anymore. It was something that Bonnie couldn't quite place, somewhere between sadness, frustration, and disappointment.

"Goodbye, Bonnie," said Mrs. Swift quietly.

And with that, the door to the office shut with a painful finality.

Chapter 3
Amargo Canyon

Surrounded by barbed wire fences, Amargo Canyon "School" was every bit as awful as she'd heard: a humiliating strip search; her own clothes confiscated and replaced with a uniform of khakis and a gray T-shirt. An even more humiliating drug test, where she had to pee in a cup in front of a "trustee." Then, after confirming she wasn't on any illegal drugs, the authorities were kind enough to ram a half dozen legal pharmaceuticals down her throat to calm her down. But the worst part of the whole intake procedure was the knowledge that once it was over, she wouldn't step out the doors again for another two and a half long years.

Bonnie was led down a corridor of dorm rooms by a trustee named Officer Perez, a lean woman with a hard look. As they walked, Bonnie was barraged with shout-outs from other "students."

"Woot-woot, new meat!" "Gina! Look at this one! She think she all that." "Hey girl, you got pretty hair! Wanna hang out?"

Bonnie knew better than to show any fear. It was survival of the fittest in places like this. Just like high school, only everybody had a neck tattoo and a rap sheet. She gave her best glare into each room she passed until they arrived at a door at the end of the hall.

"What's this?" Bonnie asked when Perez flung open a door to reveal a tiny room with concrete floors, cinderblock walls, a bunk, and a metal sink-toilet combo. The only window was a slot on the door where food trays went in and out.

"Room confinement. It's kinda like solitary."

Bonnie knew exactly what room confinement was. She'd heard the horror stories from girls she knew back in Tucson. Twenty-three hours a day caged up. One hour a day to shower, stretch, and see the sky. And zero privacy, thanks to round-the-clock monitoring just in case some girl tried to hang herself with the drawstring of her sweatpants.

"I thought that didn't come unless you got in a fight or stole toilet paper or something." Bonnie looked at the tiny space and felt herself beginning to lose the battle with panic.

"State regs, *chica*, *vamanos.*" Perez clicked her fingernails impatiently on her nightstick.

"No way!" Bonnie said and made a break for the exit. In the end, it took Perez and two other guards to haul Bonnie kicking and screaming back into the cell.

"Welcome to Amargo Canyon," Perez snarled once Bonnie was finally subdued, then slammed the door shut.

"Let me out!" Bonnie pounded on the door. "I can't be here! I have to get out! I HAVE TO GET OUT!" she screamed, hurling herself repeatedly into the door—the mocking cries of the other girls echoing through the halls. "PLEASE! I'm begging you! Let! Me! Out! Let! Me! Out!" she sobbed hysterically.

She would've kept going all night had it not been for her medication finally kicking in; the lightheadedness, the disconnect with reality, the dissolution of any feeling of caring, little by little, it all overcame her. Slowly, she slid down the door and slumped into a pile on the floor. And soon the drugs mercifully plunged her into a deep and dreamless sleep.

*   *   *   *   *

Bonnie wasn't sure how many days had passed. They kept her too drugged up to know. What she did know was that she was in hell. She slogged through her days feeling like she was buried beneath a heavy, wet wool blanket. Occasionally—usually when they let her out of her cage for exercise into the fenced stretch of gravel known as "the dog run" where she was briefly reminded of the infinite sky and fresh air—she could feel her wits trying to surface. But ultimately, with her evening meds, she'd just get sucked back down again into her stupor. She'd had dark times in her life, dark thoughts that she would never share with anyone. But this was a new low.

"Hartwright!"

Bonnie slowly opened her eyes and tried to focus on the wall three inches from her nose.

"*Levántate!* Get up! Hartwright!" It was Officer Perez, who had kindly taken to kicking her cot as well. Bonnie struggled up onto her elbows. "Come on," Perez said. "They're processing you out."

Processing you out. The words hovered above Bonnie's head like a thick smoke. "They're... what?"

"Alternative sentencing," huffed Perez disdainfully as she escorted Bonnie to the administration building. "Someone's got a buddy pretty high up somewhere, I guess."

Bonnie wasn't quite able to grasp what was happening to her, especially since she didn't know anyone high up *anywhere*. But somehow, someone had gotten Bonnie transferred to a summer reform program.

"Who?" she demanded of the outbound counselor who was handling her paperwork.

"Couldn't rightly say," answered the counselor, a large-gutted, red-haired man with a matching beard that made him look like a ginger Santa Claus. He handed Bonnie a beat-up brochure about the program as he gave her a perfunctory lecture on how lucky she was to be given this second chance. He told her that if she played her cards right, she might not have to come back to Amargo Canyon in the fall. Then leaned in and whispered, "Or ever at all." As he walked her to the exit, he said. "Remember, Miss Hartwright! 'Tis the set of the sail that decides the course. Not the storm of life."

This struck Bonnie as a load of greeting card nonsense, but she wasn't about to look a gift summer camp in the mouth. Ginger Santa opened the door and gave a familiar nod to Bonnie's escort. "She's all yours."

Before Bonnie stood a brick wall of a man with a slicked-back ponytail. He had a dark beard, gold earrings in both ears, and a suit that strained against massive muscles. She blinked just to be sure he was real. He was.

"You'll be wantin' to get into the vehicle, Mistress Hartwright," he said in an Irish brogue as deep as he was tall. He opened the back door of a nondescript van with tinted rear windows.

"You work for the state, Mr. uh…?" Bonnie hesitated, glancing back toward the outbound counselor, who was already gone. This guy did *not* look like any government employee she'd ever come across, and particularly not like the kind of guy she wanted to get into a van with just then.

"Petar Devlin at yar sarvice, mistress. But you kin call me Wicked Pete," he said. The strange man gave her an oddly reverential, old-fashioned bow as Bonnie got into the back of the van. As he reached over to buckle her seatbelt, Bonnie noticed a tattoo on his wrist peeking out from the cuff of his shirt. It was unusual, a work of art really. Red and gold, full of intricate detail, and in the shape of an eight-pointed star encircled in roses.

"Mr.-uh-Wicked Pete… where exactly are you taking me?" she asked when he'd gotten into the driver's seat.

"Little place near where the Carolinas meet, miss," he replied.

"Carolinas?!" Bonnie never paid much attention in geography class, but she knew enough to know that there was a whole lot of country between them and their destination.

"Aye. Cormac's Cove to be precise."

"Cove? As in water?"

"That's generally what you might find at a cove, yes'm."

Bonnie looked down at the brochure she'd been given by the counselor—blinking past the drug haze to give it a real look. On the cover was a picture of a bunch of kids on a huge ship with lots of sails.

"W-wait a minute. It's a sailing school?!" she stammered.

"Aye," Wicked Pete replied with a wink. "That it 'tis."

Bonnie had heard that the state sometimes sent delinquents to various summer boot camps to shape them up. But sending Bonnie Hartwright, the girl who was deathly afraid of water, to a sailing boot camp? It would be laughable if it weren't so terrifying.

She thought about objecting, but the sight of the center's barbed wire fences rushing by reminded her just how miserable the last few days had been. So as they turned onto the highway toward the airport, she chose to stifle her objections. Whoever had pulled the strings, Bonnie didn't know whether to be grateful or furious. She only knew she wasn't going back.

Chapter 4
New Beginnings

"Howdy folks, we're starting our final descent into Charlotte," said a voice over the plane's sound system. After an uneventful flight with Wicked Pete seemingly connected to Bonnie at the hip, they had finally arrived at their destination.

"Follow me," the Irishman said after the plane touched down. "Stay close."

Bonnie obeyed, following him through the airport as he stayed a half step ahead of her, constantly looking from side to side. What was he looking out for? She scanned the airport as they went, but saw nothing except the usual hustle and bustle of travelers. Still, Bonnie was feeling oddly relieved when they were finally in the cab of a black muscle truck in long-term parking.

"How far away is this place anyway?" she asked.

"Couple three hours, give or take," he replied and reached over to buckle Bonnie's seatbelt.

"I know, I know. Buckle up, I got it," she said. And when she reached over to fasten her seatbelt, something caught her eye. Strapped to the back of the driver's seat was a long dagger in a sheath. An old-fashioned one, she guessed from the intricate markings on the hilt.

"Partection," Wicked Pete said when he saw her looking at it. "Kin never be too careful."

Yet again red flags started going up in her head. But again, she rationalized them away. Maybe Carolinians felt about knives the same way folks back home felt about their guns. Everyone in Arizona seemed to have a gun, which included old ladies packing heat at bingo parlors and dudes who would walk into a Wendy's to order french fries with assault rifles strapped to their backs. So what was a little hidden weaponry among friends here in North Carolina? It sure wasn't the strangest thing she'd encountered in the last twenty-four hours. Still, Bonnie remained on guard as she settled in for what was going to be a long ride.

The truck moved onto the highway and started to leave the city far behind. Bonnie tried in vain to get more information about this "school" out of Wicked Pete, but after a few more cryptic replies, she saw that any further questions would be a waste of her time. Wicked Pete seemed more focused on getting where they were going—and getting there fast, breaking about every known traffic law along the way. So, she had the rest of the drive to sit in silence and "reflect" as her counselors so irritatingly called it.

Bonnie thought back to what Mrs. Swift had said to her in the office that set this whole nightmare in motion. How upset she had been with her. She could hardly blame the woman for being at her wit's end. Bonnie had certainly put her through the wringer for fifteen long years.

For Bonnie, though, it was the only life she'd ever known. She'd been flung into the foster system when she was abandoned as a baby. She was a foundling, like out of some bad Victorian novel. Even her name was completely random. She discovered its origins one December a few years back. It was the one time Bonnie hadn't managed to outrun the tossed boot of one of her foster dads. Sporting a bruised cheek, she'd spent a long night in Mrs. Swift's office while an emergency placement was arranged.

Having been pulled away from the staff Christmas party where she had obviously been hitting the eggnog pretty hard, Mrs. Swift finally spilled the beans about Bonnie's origin story. She explained Bonnie had been found lying on the back pew at St. Brigid's Church in South Tucson by a kindly old Irish priest named Father Hartwright, who'd made sure she was safe and fed until the police arrived. By the time they got there, the trail for whoever had dumped her there had gone very cold, and there was nothing to do but make her a ward of the state. Because Father Hartwright was the one who'd found her, she was given his last name, more as a placeholder than anything else, in the hopes that soon she'd be adopted. But the adoption never came, so the name was hers to keep. Father Hartwright, in giving the baby to the authorities, had also remarked, "Have you ever seen such a bonny lass?" and so the name "Bonnie" stuck as well, and Bonnie Hartwright she remained.

Over the course of the years Bonnie had come to believe that the person who abandoned her, very likely her own mother, had actually tried to drown her. What else could explain her violent, recurring dream? It had to be linked to some kind of memory, Bonnie concluded. Her therapists all told her she'd been too young to have any such memories. But Google told her otherwise.

Bonnie looked out the window; there were now acres and acres of rolling green hills dotted with gorgeous pine trees. And the air felt damp. Not the dry air of Arizona. It was cooler and had taken on a distinct smell.

Salt. We must be close to the ocean. Bonnie shuddered at the thought.

As if on cue, the truck slowed and Wicked Pete turned from the two-lane blacktop onto an old dirt road hidden among massive ancient trees. They blocked out what was left of the sun, and the truck headlights bounced along the uneven road until they fell on a tall iron gate that looked at least as old as the trees. It was rusted in places and there was an intricate design twisted in metal that arched over the top of the gate:

Bonnie recognized the image, an eight-pointed star with roses. It looked just like the tattoo on Wicked Pete's wrist, and she wondered if he might have been a "student" here back in the day. Which actually wasn't that hard to imagine, she concluded, since she could conjure up any number of crimes a teenage version of this guy might have committed to land him here. After all, you don't get a name like Wicked Pete for volunteering at a nursing home.

The Irishman tapped the horn twice, hopped out of the cab and flung open Bonnie's door. "Cormac's Cove," he announced, beckoning her to step out. "End o' the line, lass."

It wasn't until they were within a few feet of the gate that she saw the boy on the other side, illuminated in the truck's headlights, unlocking a giant padlock.

"I can't believe you actually made it in time," the boy said. Dressed in jeans, boots, and a white billowy lace-up shirt, he spoke in a velvety Southern accent. Other than the throwback getup, he looked pretty much like an average teenage boy—probably a year or two older than Bonnie was—all legs and arms, very tall with dark auburn hair and fierce, restless gray eyes.

"Ain't you been able to count on the word of Petar Devlin always, lad?" Wicked Pete replied. He then made the introductions. "Master Reed Ballister. Mistress Bonnie Hartwright."

"Present and accounted for," Bonnie said. "One notorious underwear arsonist delivered without incident." She offered her hand to the boy but he didn't shake it.

Instead, he just sized her up with a strange, scrutinizing gaze.

"Hey, Clark Kent, easy on the X-ray vision, okay?"

He looked away. "You coming?" he said to the Irishman.

"Got that unfinished business down in the Keys. Best get back to it," he said.

"Right," Reed nodded. "I got it from here then." Bonnie saw his hand go to his belt to rest on what looked like a very long dagger of his own.

Wicked Pete did that strange little bow again and then took off down the road.

"We better hurry; they're waiting," Reed said as he locked the gate behind Bonnie.

"Who's wait—" she didn't finish her question because—

—with the CLICK of the lock, a feeling swept over Bonnie. It started in her head and spread through her body—warm, like sunlight filling her and she suddenly felt…

Safe, Bonnie thought. It was a weird thought, to be sure. But not as weird as the feeling itself, which she couldn't remember experiencing before in her whole short life.

"You okay?"

Bonnie realized that Reed was at her side, holding her steady. "Yeah," she replied, pulling away. "It's just been a really strange day."

"Hate to break it to you, but things are about to get a whole lot stranger."

"Stranger how?" asked Bonnie. But Reed didn't answer; he just flung her backpack over his shoulder and started off down the road toward a large white house in the distance.

She ran to catch up. "Hey. Dude. I'm talking to you. Stranger how? And who's waiting? And while we're at it. How the hell did I end up here in the first place, cuz the world's largest leprechaun who brought me here wasn't exactly a real talker."

"All your questions will be answered. You just have to be patient."

Bonnie was about to say that she would *not* be patient. That she wanted answers and she wanted them now. But just then they broke through the canopy of trees to reveal—set against the flaming orange-red sky of sunset—the Atlantic Ocean! Bonnie stopped short at the sight of it. Broad, deep blue, moving as if alive beneath undulating swells topped by whitecaps. Stretching north to south as far as the eye could see. Her heart pounded violently in her chest. A rush of blood roared in her ears.

Then suddenly, a frightening sensation of falling, followed by a series of dreamlike images—visions—flooding her mind's eye in rapid succession. *A blood-red sky. A huge twisted tree. A black-winged gull. A hangman's noose. An empty grave. The hourglass ring. A blood-curdling scream*!

The next thing Bonnie knew, she was running. Blindly, so driven by panic that she wasn't even aware of the brambles and thick foliage that slapped and scratched at her skin, or of the distant sound of Reed's voice calling her name. She didn't know how long she ran or how far when at last she came upon a tall, ivy-covered stone wall. She didn't hesitate. She ran straight for it, ready to scramble over. But just as her hands touched the cold stone—

ZAP! Bonnie was thrown backwards with tremendous force, landing hard on her rear end. She felt a cold buzzing in her hands and saw blue wisps of glowing smoke emanate from her palms.

"Bonnie," she heard Reed's voice and felt a hand on her arm; she jumped to her feet. She looked down at her hand to see that she now held Reed's dagger between the two of them. She was as shocked to see it there as he was. Somehow, Bonnie had managed to snatch the knife out of the boy's belt without even realizing she'd done it.

Bonnie brandished the knife at Reed and she demanded in a shaky voice, "W-what is with this place? Who *are* you people?!"

Reed held up both hands and spoke soothingly. "Bonnie. I need you to listen to me. Everything is okay. Just give me the kn—" He held out his hand and took a step forward, but Bonnie lunged at him with the knife and took a wild swipe! Reed deftly dodged the blade, knocked the dagger out of her hand, and shoulder-tackled her to the ground.

They rolled around in the dirt, each struggling for the upper hand.

"Calm down!" Reed yelled, grabbing at her arms.

"Get off me!" Bonnie screamed, clawing and punching wildly.

They wrestled through the brush. Reed finally got on top for good, pinning her down with his knees and hands. Out of the corner of her eye, Bonnie saw the dagger lying nearby. She yanked one hand free and brought it around the handle of the knife. But just as she started to bring it up… a leather boot came down hard on her wrist.

"That'll be enough!" came a gravelly voice from above her. "The both of ya."

Bonnie looked up. Standing over her and Reed was a gaunt man who peered down at her with menace. He had wiry graying hair and a craggy face, made more frightening by the eerie light from the glowing lantern he carried. A black eyepatch covered his left eye and his left ear was burned to a nub, a mangle of twisted and melted flesh.

"No more fuss," he demanded. "You'll be comin' with me, lass." And as Bonnie's eyes trailed down to the enormous jagged-edged dagger in his other hand, she knew that, indeed, she would.

Chapter 5
A Secret Ceremony

Bonnie felt a firm nudge in the small of her back, the insistent eye-patched man on her heels and the boy Reed Ballister bringing up the rear. They walked first to a cliff's edge, then down a narrow switchback toward a cove with jagged rocks and crashing waves fifty feet below. The one-eyed man was so close on her heels she could smell the rum thick on his breath, a quality you don't necessarily want in knife-wielding men.

"W-where are you taking me?" she asked nervously.

"Cave o' the Four Winds," replied the rough-hewn man, whom Reed addressed as Jonesy. At first, Bonnie couldn't see the cave at the base of the cliff because it was hidden by two enormous boulders.

"Inside," Jonesy growled once they'd reached the opening.

Hesitantly, she entered the black maw before her. The passage was narrow; a few yards in, Bonnie could see a flickering yellow glow and heard raucous voices. Jonesy nudged her forward and she stumbled out of the narrow passage. The voices inside fell silent.

Bonnie found herself in a large, dank chamber that smelled of fish and brine and the ancient world. The yellow glow came from a roaring fire around which were seated a group of maybe two dozen kids. They were all shapes and sizes and ethnicities. *The other "inmates,"* she realized.

"Found these two over by the southwest wall, Cap'n," Jonesy announced, stepping up behind Bonnie. "Nick o' time too. Relieved Master Reed of his dirk, she had. If'n I hadn't interceded, the boy might be missin' the better part of his manhood."

That last bit of news was greeted by hoots and stomping from the teens. Bonnie looked over at Reed and even in the low light of the cave, she could see his cheeks burning red.

"Silence!" a commanding voice boomed. From the shadows stepped a strapping man of about 70. He had a short gray beard with traces of red, and wiry shoulder-length hair pulled back into a low ponytail. He too wore old-style clothing—a worn leather overcoat, a crimson velvet sash and strapped to his side, a long cutlass nestled in a leather scabbard.

He walked over to her and looked at her with the same penetrating gray eyes as the Reed kid and she knew instantly that the two were related.

"At long last… Bonnie," the man whispered reverentially. "I see you've already met my grandson, but allow me to introduce myself. I am Captain Eleazer Ballister at your service. I run this school."

"School?" Bonnie asked, looking at her surroundings. "Doesn't look like any school I ever heard of."

"My apologies. We didn't get you here in time for the formal orientation. We discovered only two days ago that you were one of our number."

"A criminal?" Bonnie asked quizzically.

"No," he laughed. "Well, yes. You see, your legal entanglements in Arizona brought you to our attention, but in fact your presence here is an honor, and an invitation to claim your true birthright."

"I'm not following."

"Have you found that you have certain larcenous talents? Do you find thrill in misadventure? Do you bristle under the yoke of authority?"

Bonnie wasn't about to deny it.

"That is because you, as are all gathered here tonight, are a corsair!" He said it with a swell of pride and a cheer rose up from the others.

"What the hell is a corsair?" Bonnie demanded. He might as well have been speaking Aramaic.

"Sea raider, freebooter, marauder, picaroon?" the captain added, hoping to clarify. Bonnie shook her head and shrugged her shoulders. Still nothing.

"He means you're a pirate!" Bonnie looked over at a boy, maybe 16, who had just spoken. He was handsome, mixed-raced, with wild hair and chocolate eyes that didn't quite have the hardened look of the others. In fact, he had an unmistakable smirk on his face, as if he was amused by her in some way. Then he curled his hand into a hook shape and added playfully in a fakey pirate accent, "We all gots pirate blood in us! Arrghh!"

"We do not use that term, Mister De Luca. It is a crass word used to sell movie tickets and Halloween costumes," the captain continued. "It does not at all represent the elegance of the bloodline from whence we spring."

There was a beat, then Bonnie said, "Ooh. I get it. This is one of those 'theme' reform schools, like where they send gangbangers to a dude ranch to play cowboy."

"She don't believe it!" said a glassy-eyed kid with greasy hair and bad teeth.

"Neither did you at first, Hashpipe!" a Latina girl with a buzz cut and arm full of tattoos jabbed him in the ribs.

Jonesy cleared his throat, "Beggin' your pardon, Cap'n, but the moon, she's peakin'."

Ballister checked an ancient pocket watch with moon phases on it. "Indeed." He put it away and then put a comforting hand on Bonnie's shoulder. "I know this is difficult," the captain said. "Be assured I will explain all to you once we're done here. But for now, the edicts being very specific, I'll ask you to take a place in the Sacred Circle so we may begin the ceremony."

She shot a glance at the exit, which Reed was now blocking in a stance that told her he wasn't about to let her get away again.

Having no other choice, she moved to the fire to look for a place to sit. De Luca, the chocolate-eyed boy, moved to make room for her. "Have a seat, Curls," he said.

And with that, Bonnie found herself in possession of both a seat and a nickname.

■   ■   ■   ■   ■

BLEEEEEOOOOOOO!

A low and haunting sound echoed through the cave as Jonesy blew an instrument made from some kind of animal horn adorned with strange markings.

"Let the 275th annum Ceremony of the Compass Rose commence!" Jonesy proclaimed.

"Boy. These guys are really milking this gimmick," Bonnie whispered to De Luca, fighting back an eyeroll.

"Who says it's a gimmick?" De Luca smiled at her, and this time Bonnie gave in to the eyeroll.

"Society has names for you," Ballister said, circling the fire. "Juvenile Delinquent. Youth offender. Gangbanger. *Cholo*. But these are just the labels of an unseeing world. You simply have not yet learned to harness your gifts. At the very least, the next few weeks will teach you to do that. A few of you," the captain paused and looked at the "corsairs" one by one, "a *very* select few, in whom the corsair blood runs most crimson and true, will have the honor of becoming a Brigand of the Compass Rose."

"A what of the what?" Bonnie mumbled to herself.

"Brigands," De Luca leaned over to her. "It's what they called gangs back in the day."

"And the other thing?"

De Luca pointed above their heads. Bonnie had missed it when she entered because she simply hadn't thought to look up. But there, centered over the fire and beautifully carved into the ceiling of the cave, twenty feet in diameter, was the now-familiar eight-pointed star with roses. And Bonnie put it together.

"A compass rose," she whispered under her breath as an inexplicable feeling of awe and reverence swept over her. Confused, she shook it off.

The captain picked up a log from the fire and, using it as a torch, walked slowly with it around the perimeter of the cave. "Behold the Wall of Investiture. Here lay the names of those who have preceded you," he said.

Whispers filled the cave as the light illuminated the walls, revealing names, hundreds of them, scrawled everywhere. Some of them seemed ancient, faded by dampness and time. Names like Jedidiah and Angus. Some were newer, like Jaden and Kyle. And women's names were there too. Cora, Lila, and... Brigid?

Brigid. Bonnie was startled to see the name of the church where she'd been left. The name disappeared into blackness as the captain brought his torch down.

"You are here to see if you are worthy to join your ancestors in the service of a greater cause. To fight an evil that has plagued our line... and the world... for 300 years."

Evil? Bonnie thought. This was starting to get seriously weird. Like death cult, Kool-Aid-drinking weird.

Captain Ballister tossed the torch back into the fire and with that, blue sparks shot up violently, popping and snapping in all directions before fizzling out and leaving behind a blue haze and the smell of electricity. Bonnie noticed that it was like at the wall, except the haze didn't dissipate; it hung just above the heads of the kids, moving slowly counterclockwise in a circle. Bonnie blinked disbelievingly at what she saw (or thought she saw) within the blue haze.

Figures. Clashing Swords. An Ancient Ship. The low moan of a battle cry. Death.

A sudden rush of cool wind blew through the cave, taking with it the blue haze. Bonnie shivered and blinked back to awareness.

"D-did you see what I just saw?" she asked De Luca.

"I think we all did," he answered as she looked around the fire at the shaken faces.

Bonnie's mind was moving a mile a minute trying to make sense of what they'd witnessed, but she was coming up empty.

"Which path you take," Bonnie heard the captain say, "who you're fated to become, begins this night… with this." Ballister held up something in his hand. It was a compass.

Made of gold, it glinted in the firelight. And like everything else in this place, it looked very, very old. It was ornate, with foreign-looking symbols engraved around the outside face.

"The Compass of Moirai," whispered a runt of a Black kid with a pair of thick glasses strapped to his head in true nerd fashion. Bonnie hadn't noticed him before; he'd been blocked by the giant hulk of a kid next to him.

"Bravo, Mister Chisolm!" Ballister said. "We have at least one among us classically trained in our ways."

"Way to go, Barnaby! Remind me to copy off you at test time!" De Luca said, reaching over to give the smaller boy a hearty fist bump.

Ballister held the compass high. "Bequeathed to the progenitor of our line and imbued with powerful Gullah magic—"

Magic?! Now they're talking about magic. Okay, this is just absurd.

"—the Compass of Moirai, or Compass of Fate, indicates far more than magnetic north. Rather, anointed with special powers… it has the ability to see what lies inside you, and thus points you to those with whom you're destined to share your journey of the sea… and soul. Your crew."

He brought it close and read the words engraved around the face. "Boreas, Notus, Eurus, or Zephyrus."

"North, South, East, and West! The Greek words for the four winds," offered Barnaby, emboldened by the captain's earlier praise.

"Correct again, Mister Chisolm!" the captain replied. "And thus too we shall name our crews."

"What a *brown*-noser," murmured a pampered-looking kid who sat across the fire from Bonnie. He sneered at Barnaby in a way that made Bonnie know right away she didn't like him. Whatever else was happening, Bonnie still knew a douchebag when she saw one.

Ballister continued. "Now… the divination ritual. You will each pass the compass around the circle. When it's your turn, rise, hold it in the palm of your left hand and speak your name. The Compass will know where you belong."

"What, is the Sorting Hat at the dry cleaners?" Bonnie snorted under her breath, but her joke echoed in the cave. Everyone looked at her, and she could tell by their grave expressions that this was very serious business to them. For the moment anyway, she decided to keep her skepticism to herself and enjoy the ceremony for what it obviously was—pure theater.

"As the tradition holds," Ballister continued, clearing his throat, "we begin with the one who sits in the south position of the compass rose."

All eyes now turned to a tall Asian kid with spikey hair who sat directly below the "S" of the compass on the ceiling. "Mister Yeun, you have the honor."

Logically, Bonnie knew a compass couldn't *know* anything, but still she felt her pulse quicken in anticipation as Yeun rose to his feet.

The captain placed the compass in the boy's left hand. "Name's Kevin Yeun," the boy said, "but everybody just calls me Yeun." As soon as the words passed his lips, the needle started to move. It slowed, moved back and forth as if contemplating, then finally stopped on one of the points.

The boy announced excitedly, "Zephyrus! I'm Zephyrus!" He then thought a moment. "Uh, is that good or bad?"

Everyone laughed.

"That lies with you," replied the captain.

What followed was a mix of thrilling anticipation punctuated by wild cheers and jeers depending on where someone ended up. Even Bonnie found herself getting caught up in the excitement of the whole thing.

Brice, a chubby kid with a friendly smile, was the first to join Notus. When Barnaby took his turn, the compass stopped on Boreas. He jumped to his feet and whooped, obviously getting what he wanted. The kid didn't seem like he was too much in the physical strength department, but he seemed to know what was what in this place, so Bonnie figured his crew would be in pretty good shape. She immediately had to amend that assessment when the pampered kid—whose name turned out to be Tanner Prescott—got placed in Boreas as well.

Zion, a tough-looking kid with a boxer's build, was the first in Eurus, followed by Stevie Ray, a good ol' boy with nicotine-stained teeth and Southern drawl. Hashpipe, the guy with greasy brown hair, went Notus, which clearly scared the chubby kid. The first to go, Yeun was soon joined by the only two other girls in the group, Luz Delgado, the buzz-cut girl, and Daya Cepeda, a Dominican girl in tight braids. Tanner Prescott's eyerolls went into overdrive with the next two Boreas picks: Malachi Maguire, a hulking giant of a boy with white blond hair (*and on the spectrum*, Bonnie assumed from the way he rocked back and forth and avoided eye contact) and Micah, his pudgy brother who looked like he'd seen more Cheetos than sunlight.

A Notus, a Zephyrus, a couple of Euruses, and then finally it was Bonnie's turn.

Despite the part of her that kept insisting this couldn't be real, Bonnie felt a very real apprehension. When she took it in her hand, the compass felt heavier than it looked. It was unusually warm and emitted a slight vibration and glowed blue. She turned it over in her hand to look for an opening for a battery, but it was seamless. She said her name and waited. Nothing happened. There were whispers and all eyes were on Bonnie as the needle of the compass remained motionless. "It's not doing anyth—" she started when suddenly the compass needle began to spin wildly! First clockwise, then counter-clockwise, rapidly changing direction without a pattern.

"Wow!" said Barnaby, edging in to get a better look.

"W-What's happening?" Bonnie asked nervously, but the captain seemed to be as clueless about this turn of events as she was. The compass heated up and the vibration intensified. The needle spun faster and faster and faster. The compass felt scalding hot in her hand. She tried to drop it, flinging her arm around, but it was as if it were glued to her skin.

"Make it stop!" Bonnie screamed. There was a loud POP! She shrieked as the compass flew up out of her hand, landing face down on the cave floor. That strange blue smoke rose from it, but this time it turned to black and had a rancid odor.

Reed rushed to pick it up and did so gingerly. He brought it to Captain Ballister.

"Grandfather, that's never happened before... has it?" Reed spoke in a hushed voice.

"Nay, not in three centuries." Ballister, hands shaking, turned the compass over and brushed off the sand. The glass face was cracked and blackened. It was destroyed.

"W-what does it say?" Bonnie was almost afraid to ask. The captain wiped the black smudge with his thumb.

"Boreas. It says Boreas." The captain gave her a deeply troubled look.

Bonnie looked around at the others. Jonesy gave her an accusing look with his one good eye. She had no idea what she had done, but she knew it was bad.

"Yo! What about me?" De Luca finally said, all eyes shifting from Bonnie to him. He was seated to the left of Bonnie and was to be the last to go. She gave him a grateful look for having taken the spotlight off her, to which he responded with an almost imperceptible nod.

"I haven't gone. How am I supposed to know where I go?" he continued.

Ballister stared down at the blackened disk in his hand, the look on his face as shattered as the face of the compass. "I-I, there is no precedent, I…"

"Well. I think it's obvious," Bonnie spoke up. "Every other team has six members but Boreas. We only have five." After all she had seen, Bonnie felt she could really use an ally and she definitely thought this guy could be one. She wanted him on her crew.

"Boreas, yes, yes, all right," the captain said distractedly, still eyeing the mangled remains of the compass in his hand.

"But Grandfather!" Reed objected, then stopped when his grandfather held up a shaking hand. There was a beat of anticipatory silence.

"The fates have spoken," the captain said without an ounce of conviction in his voice.

Chapter 6
Late Night Discoveries

Just after the ceremony, while the others were being led to the crew cabins that would be their homes for the rest of the summer, Captain Ballister brought Bonnie to his office in the large white house she'd seen on the way in.

Still shaken by all that she'd witnessed in the cave, Bonnie found comfort in the room: its weathered wood paneling, leather furniture, and nautical décor had a reality to them that soothed her jangled nerves.

"The Log of the Forebears," Captain Ballister had announced upon placing on the desk before Bonnie a large leather-bound book embossed, of course, with a compass rose. She opened the volume and carefully turned its yellowed and delicate pages.

"The others have already seen this," Ballister said as he sat down behind his desk, "but it's something that you too need to be aware of—it traces our proud lineage from our founding."

Bonnie ever so gently thumbed through the book. Handwritten on every page were the most intricate genealogy trees imaginable dating back centuries. She saw some of the names she had learned that night. The Ballister family was there, of course. So too were the names Prescott and Chisolm and a couple of others she remembered from the ceremony. As were a few that were even more familiar.

"Oh my God!" she exclaimed. "Is that—there's a president in here!"

"Indeed there is," the captain said, leaning back in his chair as he lit a pipe carved in the shape of a mermaid. "In seventeen generations, a family tree sprouts more than a few unusual branches."

"So where am I?" Bonnie said, paging through the book, as secretly her heart soared at the chance that she might finally learn the details of her birth.

"Alas, you'll not find your name in there," Ballister said, shutting the book in front of her.

Bonnie felt a surge of disappointment. "Right," she said bitterly. "How could I be in there? I don't even know who my parents are, let alone my ancestors from three hundred years ago."

"Your absence from the book does not delegitimize your presence at this camp. Over the centuries, there have been literally thousands of descendants in every corner of the globe. Being a family of sailors, all of a certain lusty temperament, you understand how that might occur. Regrettably, some of our number have slipped through the cracks. So we have had to devise other methods of discovering who is, in fact, a blood corsair."

"Lemme guess. Magic?"

"Science," he replied. "Do you recall the drug test you took when you arrived at Amargo Canyon?"

"Being forced to pee in a cup kinda sticks in your memory," she replied.

"Those tests aren't simply to screen for drug use. They are DNA tested as well and then fed into a national database to see if they might connect to other outstanding crimes. Since many of our line have a habit of finding themselves in trouble with the law, we periodically 'access' that database…"

"Holy shit, you hacked the feds?"

"As I said, our ilk has certain predilections," the captain continued, "and quite simply, Miss Hartwright, your DNA sample was found to match that of our common ancestor."

The captain went to the fireplace and flipped a switch, illuminating a large oil painting that had previously been in shadow.

"Behold Mary Read," said Ballister reverentially, "the foundress of our order."

It was a breathtaking portrait of an attractive woman in colonial era attire. But instead of petticoats and bonnets, she was dressed like a man—in breeches and a billowy white shirt under a tattered blue tailcoat jacket. The woman stood on a pier, a sailing ship moored in the background behind her. A large green parrot was perched on the ship's rigging and from the mast flew a black flag with the unmistakable insignia that seemed to be everywhere—the compass rose!

Bonnie inched closer to get a good look at the woman. She had flaming auburn hair tied back with a black bandana. Her eyes, the same stormy gray eyes as Reed and the Captain, were ablaze with determination. In her right hand was a dagger with an ivory handle in the shape of a sea maiden, and just above the wrist was a compass rose tattoo just like Wicked Pete's.

"A woman pirate?"

"A woman *corsair*," Ballister corrected her. "You're related to her. As are we all. Mary Read herself lived the buccaneer life in the days of her youth. Sailed under the Jolly Roger some three centuries ago until… well, until she left the high seas for a higher calling, that of establishing the society of which you have this night become a part."

Bonnie still wasn't sold. "I give you credit for the whole feminist angle you've got going here. But I've seen enough daytime TV to know you can't match somebody's DNA to hers without something to match it *to*. And she's been dead, what, a couple hundred years?"

"Bright girl. You are, of course, correct." Ballister then walked over to a pedestal with an ornate gold and wooden case on it that stood nearby. It was a reliquary, though Bonnie didn't know the word for it yet.

"Few have been privy to what you're about to see, child, but it's vital to dispel any doubts you may still harbor," the captain said. He opened the box and revealed its contents.

There, on a red velvet pillow, was a mummified hand!

Bonnie moved toward it, filled simultaneously with fascination and dread. The hand was shriveled and wrinkled and had grown brown and leathery with time. But what held Bonnie most enraptured was what was on the wrist. There, faded but visible, was a tattoo in the shape of a star, surrounded by roses. The very same tattoo in the portrait!

"Is that—?" Bonnie whispered.

"Aye," Ballister said as pipe smoke encircled his face. "The hand of her from whom we have come—Mistress of the High Seas... Mary Read, our very reason for being... and your direct ancestor. Welcome to the family, Mistress Hartwright."

Bonnie looked from the hand to the portrait, trying somehow to connect one to the other. Her day had just gone off the track from Strange and plummeted into a huge canyon of Bizarre.

*   *   *   *   *

An hour later, Bonnie stood before the stone wall she had encountered earlier, poking it here and there with a stick. Each poke prompted a ZAP, blue hot flashes of electricity and the acrid smell of burned wood. After the events of the evening, Bonnie came to the conclusion that her initial urge to scramble over the wall might have been the right one after all.

"Forget it. You're not gonna find any wires or anything."

Bonnie turned, startled. Out from behind a massive tree stepped her crewmate De Luca. "I already checked," he said.

"Did you follow me?" Bonnie demanded.

The boy held up a lit cigarette. "Contraband. Been coming here most nights since I got here. These puppies are hard to give up. Thinking about bolting, Curls?"

"Why? You gonna rat me out?"

"And get our whole crew in trouble?" he asked. "No way. By the way, name's Wilder. Wilder De Luca. Outta Coney Island, New York."

"Bonnie Hartwright," she said vaguely, but turned her attention back to the wall. She poked it again with the stick, causing the ZAP!

"So if it's not an electrified fence, how's it work?"

"Magic."

She shot him a look. "Right. And tomorrow morning, Captain Dumbledore is gonna pass out the wands."

"Only difference is, that's just a story," he said matter-of-factly. "This shit is real."

"So you believe it? Everything they're saying. About this place. And us?"

"Not at first. I mean, who would?" Wilder took a long drag on his cigarette. "When Wicked Pete showed up after I got busted for relieving a few too many boardwalk tourists of their wallets, I didn't buy any of this stuff. Not even when they showed me my name in that book."

"Your name's in the book?" Bonnie asked with a hint of envy.

"Yeah, right next to my old man's."

"So your dad's a pirate, too?"

"Apparently. He never told me. I had to hear it from Pete. He said my old man didn't want any part of this scene. Guess you could say he joined a land crew instead."

"A what?"

"The mob," Wilder said with a shrug. "Heavy into plundering."

"The mafia? Wow. That's hardcore," Bonnie marveled.

"You don't know the half of it."

"But *you* came," Bonnie continued. "And now you believe. Just like that?"

"'Believe' has nothing to do with it. Come on, Curls. Evidence is all around us. That freaky stuff with the compass. And in the smoke? And this…" Wilder tossed a large stone at the wall, causing a HUGE ZAP. The stone rolled back and came to rest at their feet.

"How can you *not* believe?" Wilder asked.

Chapter 7
Morning Breaks

Bonnie stood staring at the stained-glass window above the altar—the cut pieces of glass harmonized to form a beautiful compass intertwined with red roses. She basked in a sense of peace as the light fell through the window, illuminating the quaint church around her.

Her eyes followed a single light beam that streamed down into a carved mahogany baptismal font before her. Inside its brass basin, the water rippled slightly, holding within it the reflection of a single stained-glass rose.

"I've come for you." A voice, low and guttural, shattered the peaceful quiet of the church.

She spun around and saw a figure silhouetted in the open doorway. And in a flash it was upon her.

Bonnie found herself struggling for air. Her head was violently shoved backwards into the water of the font by a hand she knew all too well. It was the hand with the hourglass ring! She opened her mouth and SCREAMED!

"Bonnie! Wake up!"

Her eyes flew open and she saw a figure towering over her. Instinctively, she started flailing, fighting off the figure. Hands grabbed at her wrists to restrain her.

"Bonnie! It's okay. It's me."

Bonnie blinked and took a deep breath as she realized she was in her bunk in the Boreas cabin. Standing over her was not the attacker from her dream, but Wilder De Luca.

"You were having a nightmare," he said gently.

Bonnie looked around the cabin to get her bearings. Crowded into the doorway of the room was the rest of Boreas.

"What are you staring at?!" Bonnie yelled at them.

"Okay, everybody out!" barked Reed Ballister, pushing his way into the room. "Don't you all have chores? Get! You, too, De Luca!"

"You gonna be okay?" Wilder asked, and didn't leave until Bonnie had at least worked up a nod in the affirmative.

As Boreas filed out of the cabin, Bonnie quickly replayed the dream in her mind. It was the same as always. Only this time, there was a church, a little white chapel, and a stained-glass window with a rose... *and what else*? But the rest of the dream evaporated when she noticed Reed Ballister still standing over her.

"What the hell!" Bonnie said, hiding her trembling hands under the blanket. "Isn't there any freaking privacy in this place?"

"Not a whole lot, unfortunately," Reed answered with an icy tone that Bonnie suspected might be the result of the embarrassment she caused him the night before. "But you get used to it."

"I doubt that. What time is it anyway?" Bonnie noticed the sun was just coming up outside the window.

"5:15. That must have been some dream. You slept through Jonesy's five o'clock horn."

Bonnie vaguely remembered being told by Ballister that "corsairs rise with the sun" but she'd hoped he'd been kidding. Still groggy, she sat up in bed and took in the cabin's four weathered walls that looked even more rustic in the light of day, if that were even possible. The room was essentially a large wooden box containing four bunks, three of them empty. The boys of Boreas all slept in a room on the other side of the cabin which was connected by the "Parley Room," a large common area. There was a small wood-burning stove and at the side of her bunk, a kerosene lamp because there was no electricity. There was also no indoor plumbing. Or phones she learned when hers had been confiscated. Those were reserved only for the main house. Because "the best preparation for the future is to understand the past"—again the words of Captain Ballister.

"Which way to the nearest can?" she asked, pulling her jeans on over the panties she had slept in. "I gotta take a serious pee."

Reed turned away, blushing as she pulled a t-shirt over her sports bra. "There's a chamber pot under your bed," he offered.

She looked at him blankly, then reached under the bed and pulled out a brass pot. "Dude, seriously?" She dropped it in disgust. The pot made a metallic clang as it hit the hardwood floor. "Okay… how about the *second* closest bathroom?" she asked. "You know, one with maybe a door?"

Reed led Bonnie outside the cabin, where she got a good look at the compound in the light of the morning. It was in a clearing in the midst of a wooded area. There were four identical cabins, each with a porch and one main entrance. Outside the cabins hung carved wooden signs, each bearing its own distinctive symbol. Boreas's consisted of an artistic representation of its winged mythological namesake, the Greek god of the north wind. The cabins, she noticed, were situated in the same layout as the points on a compass.

She saw that two Eurus kids were chopping wood outside the front door of the cabin to the east. A scrawny kid from Notus passed by his cabin struggling mightily with two wooden buckets of water that hung from a crude yoke across his shoulders.

"Where did you guys park the frickin' time machine?" she snarked.

"My grandfather believes in tradition. Like his father before him and his grandfather before that."

"And you too one day I suppose?" Bonnie asked.

"Yes. I suppose," Reed conceded with a shrug.

"Must blow having your life mapped out for you like that," Bonnie said. "Guess I'm lucky to be an orphan."

"Nobody's lucky to be an orphan," he answered. He said this with such obvious pain that Bonnie knew he spoke from personal experience.

"Take that path," he said abruptly. "Outhouse is just past the trees. Shower's right next door. Breakfast is in 30 minutes. Don't be late…"

And with that, he was gone.

∎   ∎   ∎   ∎   ∎

After an outhouse stop and what might have been the coldest shower in recorded history, Bonnie hustled up to the main house for breakfast. As she ran, she heard the clanging of the breakfast bell that confirmed that she had indeed managed to pile being late for breakfast onto the list of her infractions of the last twenty-four hours.

She took the steps that led up to the wraparound porch two at a time until what she saw made her stop short; there, on a distant bluff, was a little white church with a steeple. Bathed in the lovely glow of the sunrise, it looked exactly like the church in the dream she'd just had. *I wonder if there's a stained-glass window with a compass rose,* she found herself thinking.

But all thoughts of her dream and the church were quickly banished as a tantalizing whiff of frying bacon hit her nose, reminding her how long it had been since she had a full meal. The seductive aromas were coming from inside the house, so Bonnie approached a screen door to investigate. She cupped her hands around her eyes and pressed her forehead against the screen to peek inside.

There was a spacious, old-world kitchen, cluttered with pot racks, bowls stacked high. A large center island was covered in cooling pies, mounds of pancakes, and piles of bacon sitting atop grease-soaked towels. In the far corner, a gray-haired woman labored over a pan full of what smelled like apple butter. She wore a rose print dress and a ruffled apron. Her skin was fair, though slightly wrinkled with a spray of fading freckles across her nose.

Bonnie was about to enter when she heard a man's voice coming from inside the house.

"Somethin' 'bout this whole thing jes ain't right." It was Jonesy; Bonnie recognized the old sea dog's voice from the night before. She quickly pressed herself against the house so as not to be seen.

"I'm quite sure you are overreacting, Mr. Jones," she heard the old woman say.

"Ya wouldn't say that, missus, if'n ya seen what happened to that compass. Like the very fires o' hell had taken possession when that girl touched it."

Bonnie's heart leapt when she realized they were talking about her.

"Was it now?" The old woman asked, and Bonnie detected concern in her voice.

"Mark me words, it's a bad omen. Ya know of omens, missus."

"I do. Still, best to keep your superstitions to yourself, Mister Jones. If the captain—"

"Mistress Hartwright?" came the captain's booming voice. Bonnie turned, startled. So engrossed had she been in the conversation that she didn't hear him come up behind her. "What are you on about there, girl?"

"Which way to breakfast?" Bonnie said, recovering. "This place is like a maze. You guys oughta hand out a map at the entrance like they do at the zoo."

Just as the captain was about to answer, the screen door opened and Jonesy stood there, eyeing them both. He pushed past Bonnie and headed down the path toward the shore.

"Eleazer?" The woman came to the doorway, holding a tray of freshly baked biscuits. She froze when she saw Bonnie as if she had just seen an apparition. Her tray went limp, sending a couple of biscuits tumbling to the ground. "Mercy," she whispered.

"Winifred," Captain Ballister said, clearing his throat and stepping into the kitchen behind Bonnie. "Mind your biscuits, dear."

The woman quickly righted the tray. "Oh my goodness, yes," she said, gathering herself.

"This is Bonnie Hartwright, our latest arrival," the captain said, nudging Bonnie into the kitchen.

"Of course you are!" the woman replied, taking Bonnie's hand warmly into hers. "I'm Winifred Ballister, missus to the captain here. But you can call me Grandma Winnie." And then she pulled Bonnie into a big bosomy hug.

"For the love of Amerigo Vespucci, mother, let the girl take a breath 'fore you suffocate her!" Captain Ballister said, trying to pull Bonnie from his wife's clutches.

"Just welcoming our newest corsair, father!" Winnie said, finally letting go of Bonnie.

"Welcome her with a full plate then, woman!" the captain said as he pecked his wife on the cheek. Grandma Winnie led Bonnie into the kitchen and gathered her a heaping plate of tantalizing food: bacon, eggs, grits, huge red strawberries and a biscuit the size of a softball slathered in butter.

Now laden with breakfast, Bonnie stepped out a door that led onto an open-air porch. The hubbub that was the breakfast conversation screeched to a halt, and she felt two dozen pairs of eyes following her as she scanned the porch for a place to sit. It was Wilder De Luca who finally came to her rescue.

"Over here, Bonnie! I saved you a spot!" he waved and motioned for Bonnie to join him at the table that Boreas had claimed for itself. In fact, now that Bonnie thought about it, it looked like all the kids were sitting with their crews. *Just like high school*, she thought. Except unlike high school, Bonnie actually had a table where she belonged.

Wilder scooched over and made room for Bonnie. She sat down between him and the brainy kid Barnaby Chisolm. Directly across from them were Micah Maguire and his giant of a brother Malachi, the white-haired boy. In the light of day, Bonnie noticed Malachi had mismatched eyes, one blue and one gray. And at the end of the table, putting as much distance as possible between himself and the others, was Tanner Prescott, the arrogant punk that Bonnie had taken an instant dislike to the night before.

Bonnie said self-consciously. "Shit. Did everyone hear me screaming this morning?" She indicated the other crews who were stealing glances her way.

"I think they're staring at you cuz of what happened with the compass," Barnaby offered.

"That was *not* my fault!" she declared loudly, almost a pronouncement, so that the other crews could hear. "That thing was ancient. It was due to blow a gasket."

"That's not what it looked like to me," Micah said, drinking syrup straight from the pitcher. "Looked like it went freaky the second *you* touched it. You gonna eat that biscuit?"

Bonnie was about to defend her honor and her biscuit when Wilder quickly changed the subject. "So we were just talking about how we all landed in here. Apparently, the Maguire brothers here are computer hackers."

"Yeah?" Bonnie asked, grateful for the distraction. "Spill it, dude. I want names, dates, and badge numbers of arresting officers."

Micah spoke with a mouthful of Bonnie's biscuit, "We came up with this sweet identity theft racket charging comic book memorabilia on other people's credit cards and then selling the stuff on eBay. Woulda gotten away with it too if we hadn't tried to fence *Aquaman 1*… Shoulda known better than to get messed up with DC."

Tanner snorted, "Nerds…"

Bonnie looked down the table at him. "Lemme guess, you're in here cuz you and your prep school buddies knocked off a J. Crew store for that wardrobe of yours."

"Hardly," Tanner shrugged. "Got wasted one night and totaled my dad's Testarossa on the Pacific Coast Highway."

Bonnie perked up, "Testarossa, as in Ferrari? That car is a classic! Those things go for 200 grand easy!"

"220, but whatevs," Tanner replied, picking his teeth.

Bonnie snorted in disgust. "Can't believe you trashed such a beautiful machine."

Tanner shrugged. "The thing was insured so no big whoop."

Bonnie shook her head and then turned her attention to Barnaby. "What about you?" she asked. "You look a little young for this place. What's your crime against humanity?"

He hesitated. "I didn't do anything," he finally mumbled.

"What do you mean you didn't do anything?" Bonnie asked. "We're all supposedly 'pirates,' aren't we? You must have done something wrong or you wouldn't be here."

"The wimp doesn't have the guts to jaywalk on a lazy Sunday morning," threw in Tanner, looking over the top of his Ray Bans. "He's only here cuz his old man pulled some strings with the captain."

Off Bonnie's confused look, Wilder explained. "Barnaby's what you call a 'Special Admit'—he's a legacy."

"A what?"

"Legacies," Micah elaborated. "Kids of Brigands. Apparently, his dad was some kick-ass hero back in the day."

"So you actually *want* to be here?" Bonnie asked.

"Sure. I mean, I guess so. My dad was Boreas so…" Bonnie understood now why he'd been so excited about being placed in that crew at the ceremony. "Plus… well, he thought it would help me get in touch with my *inner macho*," Barnaby said quietly.

The table erupted in laughter, and even Barnaby joined in.

"That is rich!" Wilder said, patting him on the back. "Well, Barnaby my man. Stick with me this summer. I'll see to it you got macho coming out of your ears. Curls, you should have heard this kid rattling off the facts about this outfit last night! Like a regular Google for pirates!"

Barnaby brightened at the compliment.

Bonnie turned to Barnaby. "So I guess you'd be the one to ask about this so-called 'evil' the captain was talking about last night?"

"Uh-uh," Barnaby said, shaking his head. "That's a secret. Nobody's supposed to know 'til we're Brigands."

"Translation—Owl Eyes don't know shit, just like the rest of us," Tanner snarked.

"I know stuff!" Barnaby insisted.

"So keep us posted, eh?" Wilder said. "In the meantime, we can't let the morning go by without letting Bonnie kneel at the old confessional. Your turn, Curls. Fess up."

Omitting any mention of her embarrassing birthmark, Bonnie offered up the story of her own transgressions, complete with the flaming cart flying into the pool. The others found it impressive not only for the style with which it was executed, but also for the righteous retribution involved.

"That's badass!" Wilder said, clapping in appreciation. "Remind me not to piss you off!"

"You know what pisses *me* off?" Tanner interjected. "That the captain's shitty compass lumped me with you lame-asses. I been sailing since I could walk, and who do they stick me with? A chocolate-covered runt, a fat slob and his retard brother, a halfrican pickpocket…"

"Halfrican-*Italian* pickpocket," Wilder interrupted. "As long as you're being racist, you might as well be accurate."

Tanner ignored the comment, "Not to mention a worthless chick."

"You always make friends like this?" Bonnie asked.

Tanner leaned toward Bonnie. "None of you are even in the vicinity of being my friends. Especially you. Chicks are good for one thing, and it sure as hell ain't sailing."

Bonnie stared him down. "I bet you're quite the ladies' man as long as you have Daddy's money to throw around, *Spray Tan*."

"Trust me," Tanner smirked. "By the end of the summer, you'll be polishing my brass and loving it."

"I'd rather swallow an oily rag," Bonnie shot back.

"Hey stop it already! You're upsetting my brother!" Micah pleaded. Everyone turned to see that Malachi was rocking back and forth at the table and moaning in a low voice.

"Um, you gonna be okay there, buddy?" Bonnie asked.

"Save your breath," Tanner said. "The kid's a mute in addition to being a retard."

"He's not retarded! He's special!" Micah snapped defensively. "And he talks. But only when he has something important to say."

"Then I already like him better than Prescott," Bonnie said. "But seriously, Micah, I think you'd better get him his meds." Bonnie had been part of the foster system so long it had made her an expert in mood-altering pharmaceuticals, and Malachi Maguire seemed a prime candidate for *something*.

"They don't allow that here," Barnaby said. "Brigand bylaws."

"You're kidding, right? I mean, half the kids here have gotta be on meds," said Bonnie. The nightmare she'd just woken from had been so intense that for once she was actually looking forward to her daily meds to take the edge off her panic about the place.

"They think meds dull our natural tendencies and abilities," Barnaby explained.

"Well, somebody better do *something* quick," Wilder said. "Malachi looks like he's gonna blow." Indeed, the boy's moaning had become louder. Micah put his arms tightly around his brother.

"Uh. What are you doing?" Bonnie asked.

"Deep pressure touch," Micah replied, his face buried deep in Malachi's chest. "It stops the overstimulation. Don't just stand there. Help!"

Bonnie put her arms around Malachi, squeezing tightly. Soon Wilder and Barnaby joined in, encircling Malachi in their embrace.

Tanner Prescott watched the scene without a hint of compassion. "Freakshow," he murmured and left the table in disgust.

As Bonnie kept hugging the giant boy, she felt the tension in his body receding. She buried her face in his T-shirt and held on tight, wondering where exactly all this was heading. Self-destructing compasses, magic walls, weird visions, worsening nightmares, and the one thing she feared most—water—as far as the eye could see. And all this without a drop of medication to squelch the panic she felt welling up inside her. Now more than ever, she knew…

It was going to be a very long summer.

Chapter 8
The True North

Bonnie gasped when she saw it. The ship was huge. At once gorgeous and terrifying, it was surely the most magnificent thing she'd ever seen. Coming around some rocks that sheltered the cove was seventy feet of graceful lines built of teak, with two masts that stretched impossibly high into the air. Each of the canvas sails groaned against the morning winds as the elegant schooner glided across the water.

"Sweet mother," she heard Wilder say. "That thing is sick."

"Even better than my dad described it," agreed Barnaby.

Bonnie was too stunned to reply to either. Once she saw the ship, she briefly forgot that this glorious craft was afloat on billions of gallons of what scared her more than anything else. For just a moment, she too marveled at the sight and felt her pulse quicken the closer the ship got.

As it approached, Bonnie saw where Reed had disappeared to. At the wheel, he called out to Jonesy as the two men deftly maneuvered her toward the pier, where it would be moored next to the *Solstice Skye*, a small cutter, as well as a couple of rowboats already tied there. Bonnie watched Reed work the wheel, his auburn hair whipping in the wind, his handsome mouth set and determined, his actions sure and confident. A smile crossed her face, one which she suppressed the second she realized Wilder had witnessed her entire reaction.

"Dude, I can't believe you people expect us to sail that thing," interrupted Tanner, intruding on whatever melodrama Bonnie had going on in her head. "That tub must be 200 years old."

"Three hundred, more like it," Captain Ballister replied with a smile. "The *True North* has been in our service for generations. Built by the great Octavius Wallace in the Gloucester shipyard in 1714 and obtained by Mary Read at a dear price in Port Royal some years later."

Bonnie suddenly realized this was no replica; this was the exact ship she'd seen in the portrait in Ballister's office.

"And it still sails?" snorted Tanner derisively.

"Not only does she still sail, Mister Prescott," the captain beamed, "she's faster than a dockside floozie—can hit 12 knots in a stiff wind! Bring her in, lads!"

By the time the corsairs made it to the ship, it was anchored and secured. Reed lowered a rope ladder off the edge, but didn't climb down, instead jumping off the ship to the dock below as easily as if he were stepping off a curb.

"Morning," said Reed, wiping his hands on a bandana he'd pulled from his pocket. "It's a little choppy to the south," he turned to the captain. "But I imagine she'll handle this weather plenty fine if we want to open her sheets a bit."

"Aye," he replied. "I thank you for the report, Master Reed. Now, I need you to check all the windlasses for wear and make certain our turnbuckles and shroud terminations are in order."

"Aye Captain!" he said, and was promptly back on the *North*, setting to work on the captain's to-do list. Ballister then addressed the group, "Now, on board with the lot of you, so you can better make this dear lady's acquaintance."

Bonnie froze when she heard this. *On board? Now?*

Tanner bounded up the rope ladder and walked around the deck like he owned the thing. "Let's see what this piece of junk can do," he said.

A kid from Eurus named Wendell was the next on board, and was immediately drawn to the ship's port side. "Guys! There's a cannon!"

"Cool your jets, Noble, you freakin' pyro," Luz from Zephyrus called out as she clambered on board after him. "Ain't nobody shootin' no cannons today."

Wendell, a farm kid from South Dakota who'd been busted for selling illegal fireworks, looked crestfallen at the news. Even so, he continued to examine the cannon with fascination as the other corsairs joined him on deck.

"Hey, Captain," asked Zion as he boarded. "Ain't we gonna raise the Jolly Roger or something? I thought every pirate ship is supposed to have a flag."

"And this vessel does as well, Mister Campbell," replied Captain Ballister. "A flag that shall be raised when you've become a crew worthy of sailing under Brigand colors. Until then, she goes without."

Ballister's statement was met with oohs and aahs and surmises about when they might be ready for such an honor.

Still on the dock, Bonnie stood aside, more than happy to let others go ahead of her. Before long, it was just she and Wilder on the dock.

"Nervous?" he asked.

"I'm kind of a desert girl," she replied. "I-uh-never sailed before."

"Most of us haven't," he reassured her. "We'll all learn together."

Bonnie could see the others peering down at them from the deck; she couldn't put off getting on board any longer. She took a deep breath as Wilder steadied the ladder.

"You got this, Curls," he said. "I'm right behind you."

Bonnie put her foot on the first rung and started to climb. She'd made it almost to the top when her foot slipped off a wet rung. She felt herself falling but suddenly a hand gripped hers. Then, Bonnie was pulled effortlessly onto the ship and she found herself face to face with Reed, their fingers still interlocked, perhaps a bit longer than either of them had expected.

"Hey!! Cabin boy!" Wilder De Luca yelled, still hanging off the side of the ship. "Other people want to get on the boat today, huh?"

Reed stepped aside to allow him on board. "It's a *ship*," he said dryly, inches from Wilder's face.

"Sorry, I left my Human-to-Pirate dictionary in my other pants," Wilder replied. "Don't you have some turns to buckle or something?"

"Master Reed!" Ballister interrupted from the foredeck. "Fetch me my spyglass from my quarters before we cast off!"

Reed scowled at Wilder and turned on his heels. "Aye aye, Captain," he called out and disappeared into the cabin.

*   *   *   *   *

Five minutes later, Reed was back at the ship's wheel as the *North* pulled away from the dock. Bonnie stood stiff-legged and felt the ship bobbing under her. She knew she wouldn't get her sea legs right away, but she remembered what Barnaby had told her. *Bend your knees and focus on something far away.* She looked out across the calm ocean to what looked like a distant island. It was barely visible through the fog, but it seemed to be doing the trick. She felt surprisingly okay. Especially compared to Brice, who was already looking peaked, and would end up spending most of the trip heaving over the port side gunwale.

Still, Bonnie wasn't about to take any chances, so she stood with her back up against the door that led to the cabin below deck. Once she was as far from the edge of the ship as humanly possible, she returned her attention to Captain Ballister, who surveyed his new crew from the elevated quarter deck at the rear of the ship.

"Feel the ocean beneath you, corsairs! We Brigands are of a sort drawn to the sea; it's in the blood we all share. Before the Thunder Moon is full, you'll be well at home on this deck, I promise."

"Yo, Cappy!" called out Wilder. "So when's the class on mutiny?"

There were laughs from all parts of the ship, but the old captain remained unfazed.

"It's right after the seminar on walking the plank," he replied casually. "I'm making a list of volunteers, and you're already in the first three slots, Mister De Luca."

Hoots of laughter rang out across the deck. Wilder smiled and nodded in appreciation. Game recognizes game.

"But I do thank you for bringing up your, shall we say, peccant natures. Now of course, you being of Brigand blood, I expect each of you to be inclined to break rules and defy authority. We know the little boxes the world tries to cram you in all too well. They drug you up, tie you down, and only call it success when they've sucked every bit of life spark out of you. Not here! No sir, here, you shall roam free and take full ownership of your souls, ashamed of nothing, beholden to naught but the justness of our cause—living like the true corsairs you are!"

Everyone cheered. Bonnie realized it was exactly what Barnaby had said about the camp's ban on medications. And the nodding heads around her told her that many of her shipmates could relate.

As the *North* moved out into the deeper water of the Atlantic, the captain explained how the days would be organized. Each day, he said, would consist of several classes, which Ballister referred to as "experiences." After each experience, the captain would award "pieces of eight" to crews depending on their performance.

"Pieces of eight what?" asked Micah.

Barnaby jumped in to explain, "Pieces of eight were the old Spanish coins from colonial times. Each coin equaled 8 *reales*, which is where they got their name. Eight *reales* – pieces of eight!"

"Thank you, Barnipedia," Tanner applauded. "More useless information to ponder while you're wondering why you don't have a girlfriend."

Probably to spite Tanner, Captain Ballister tossed a coin in Barnaby's direction, and he gleefully snatched it out of the air, the proud recipient of the first coin of the summer. The captain explained more would be coming; if corsairs did particularly well, they would be singled out for praise and earn a coin for their crew; if somebody screwed up or broke rules, the whole crew would be penalized and a coin taken away. At the end of each week, the crew with the fewest coins for that week had the dishonor of being the "Marooners"—meaning they got stuck spending Sunday doing chores while everyone else got a day to themselves.

Bonnie looked down and saw to her surprise that she was now standing in the middle of the deck under her own power. Somewhere between here and the dock, she'd found her sea legs. In fact, as she looked out over the water and heard the sound of gulls over the splash of the waves, she felt a thrill she had never experienced in her life.

Maybe, just maybe, she thought, this summer wasn't going to be so bad.

Chapter 9
Summer Days

Bonnie thought she was going to die.

The day was sweltering, and her clothes clung to the sweat gushing out of her every pore. Bonnie and the rest of Boreas were in the midst of their first "experience"—a class mysteriously called "Anodyne Arts & Natural Survival." The location of the classroom was equally mysterious and would only be revealed after doing some serious orienteering, using a bizarre map made of some animal hide with ink faded in places. There was a hand-drawn compass rose and cryptic phrases providing clues.

Tanner Prescott had decided that it was he who was the "expert" and had taken over the navigating. But after an hour of tramping around, it was clear that Boreas was hopelessly lost.

"Okay, we've been going in circles. Time to hand over the map," Bonnie demanded.

"Take a Midol and just chill a second," Tanner snapped.

"Please, just do what she says," whimpered Micah as Malachi helped him to the ground beneath the shade of a tree. Micah was particularly suffering because in addition to having to haul his overweight frame around in the gloppy heat, he had a sunburn so bad he looked like he'd swallowed plutonium.

"Come on, Tanner," Wilder objected. "Just look at the poor kid. He's barbecued."

"Well, maybe the dude should hit the shut-down button on his laptop a bit more often and get outside."

"Just turn over the freakin' map already!" Bonnie yelled.

It ended up being Barnaby Chisolm who took the map and got them back on track. "Next time you know something, speak up," Bonnie encouraged him and he smiled sheepishly.

·   ·   ·   ·   ·

They finally arrived at their destination: a large herb garden surrounded by a low picket fence not far from the main house, but all the other crews had long been there. Boreas had to endure the jeers of the other corsairs as they made their way into the garden.

It irritated Bonnie that their squabbles had already put Boreas on the bottom of the heap, and she let her frustration out in that time-honored tradition of teenagers: pointless whining. "An herb garden? What do a bunch of stupid plants have to do with being a corsair anyway?"

"Ever try to eat a piece of rope?" laughed Grandma Winnie, rising to her feet from behind a tall tomato plant. "Although with a little rosemary, almost anything can be edible. This way."

Wearing a large sunhat and gardener's boots, Winnie led the corsairs down the hill and through a small gully. The gully ended at a knoll in which there was a large wooden door. She flung open the door and directed them down some steps.

The underground room was spacious, dimly lit, and cool: a root cellar that had long ago been converted into some kind of old-style apothecary. Bonnie looked around in awe. Oddly shaped root vegetables hung from the ceiling. Bins full of grains and powders lined the floor. Mason jars filled shelf upon shelf on the far wall. Handwritten labels showed which ailment the contents were meant to cure: *HEADACHE, TOOTHACHE, CONSTIPATION.* But Bonnie noticed odder ailments as well, like *HEARTACHE,*

DISAPPOINTMENT, and something called *INEXPLICABLE DISCOMFITURE.*

"This, my young corsairs, is Anodyne Arts, and I took it from some of the grumblings I heard outside that you are downright skeptical about its value to sailors."

Bonnie shifted behind Wilder so that Winnie couldn't make eye contact with her. The old woman paused for a moment and then continued. "Let me tell you all a story by way of an answer. In 1843, three Brigands were shipwrecked on a tiny island off Cape Hatteras. Wounded, no food, for two weeks before being found. Without this class, they surely would have perished. For ours is a world full of beauty, but just as surely the elements can conspire against us. I see some of you have already discovered that," she said, indicating Micah.

"As I've always said, it's better to learn by example. Front and center, Mister Maguire," Winnie patted a stool and Micah gratefully took a seat.

"The earth has more lessons than we realize," Winnie said as she walked down a row, eyeing jars until she found what she was looking for. The label read "Blister Banish."

"All righty," she said to Micah. "Off with your shirt."

Micah, too miserable to protest, did as he was told, revealing such red and peeling flesh that nobody had the heart to work up even one good fat joke.

Winnie doused a cotton ball with liquid from the bottle. "It'll sting a little at first…" she warned.

Micah whimpered as she moved the cotton ball across his skin. But soon the look on his face went from agony to heavenly relief.

"The Lord has provided us all we need to survive," Winnie explained as she worked. "It's only when we learn to harmonize with nature's rhythms that we can truly thrive."

Everyone watched amazed as the blisters began first to pop, then to disappear. The angry red skin faded to a mottled pink.

"Whoa!" "Holy crap!" "It's magic!" the corsairs marveled.

"What you call magic," Winnie replied, "the Gullah root workers refer to as good old-fashioned remedies."

"And what exactly is a Gullah?" Bonnie asked. It was the second time she'd heard that word, and still had no idea what it meant.

"Not '*what?*' child. '*Who?*' The Gullah are the descendants of West African slaves who settled these parts, along the low country," Winnie explained. "They may have been slaves, but in their hearts and in their homes, they clung to their old way of life. Including this little treatment I'm applying this very moment."

"But the Gullah knew magic, too, right?" Barnaby asked. "That's what my dad said, anyway. Said they called it *hoodoo.*"

"Magic is just a word used by people who don't understand the mysteries of creation. But yes, Barnaby, Gullah folk brought many practices from the old country. This very cove is thick with what you call hoodoo because of a Gullah woman who took a particular interest in our family."

"That explains that freaky wall," Wilder said.

Others chimed in about their crazy and literally painful experiences with the "taser wall" as Luz called it.

"The fact that it keeps you all on the Cove is just an added benefit." Grandma Winnie laughed. "Though it may not seem it, the Wall of Cloister was actually created to be protective in nature. It is intended to keep out certain... non-Brigand elements."

"You mean, kind of like in *Sons of the Forest* where you have to build a defensive wall to keep out the mutants and cannibals?" Micah asked.

"Dude, we seriously gotta put a limit on your screen time," Wilder said.

"There!" Grandma Winnie said brightly, applying one last dab of ointment to Micah's back. "You're right as rain! Now put that shirt back on, we've much to do!"

Winnie spent the rest of the afternoon leading them around the garden, pointing out properties of various plants, explaining how garlic juice could help with an infection and how steeping the leaves of a scented geranium in vinegar would cure a headache. But for every healing plant, there was a plant rife with dangers. The bittersweet vine could cause vomiting and convulsions. The sap of the mulberry would bring on hallucinations. The berries of the poison sumac... sudden death. There was an edge to Grandma Winnie's normally sweet tone that suggested to Bonnie that all this talk of poisons and death was more than merely cautionary, that it may very well serve a vital function one day.

*   *   *   *   *

Despite a few fascinating tidbits about nefarious properties of certain plants, the general consensus was that Anodyne Arts turned out to be a big-time snoozefest. Tanner Prescott even proclaimed that if the class was any indication, the rest of the summer would be a cakewalk. By the end of the first week, however, it was clear to everyone that Tanner couldn't have been more wrong. With each experience more physically demanding than the last, it wasn't long before they were longing to be back in the cool comfort of Winnie's root cellar.

Bonnie was amazed at how many different ways Captain Ballister could cook up to test the mettle of the corsairs. In an experience known as Guts & Grit, the captain had built a hardcore obstacle course high in the trees, and the corsairs had to navigate from station to station across narrow rope bridges while Reed and Jonesy heaved cattails and pine cones at them from the ground, forcing the corsairs to dodge madly out of the way while trying to keep their balance. They had another class called Marlinspike Seamanship, which was just a fancy name for knot-tying. But the captain spiced that one up by giving each crew a bunch of short pieces of rope and forcing them to tie them into one long rope with bowline hitches, which they'd then use to swing across a deep gully. If the knots didn't hold, somebody was bound to end up waist-deep in the muddy marshes at the bottom.

On and on the training went, from sunup to sundown, each day more challenging than the last. And just as one set of muscles would begin to heal, new aches and pains were more than happy to take their place.

Meanwhile, the captain distributed the pieces of eight throughout. Bonnie's innate abilities, Tanner's sailing skills and Barnaby's encyclopedic knowledge of Brigand lore scored Boreas a good handful of coins, but their shortcomings always seemed to result in deductions and they constantly lagged behind the other crews, a fact which Tanner managed to blame on everyone but himself.

And then there was the sailing. They only went out a few times on the *True North* that first week, usually one crew at a time, with Reed acting as the teacher and helmsman while Captain Ballister watched from a comfortable perch in the crow's nest high atop the mainmast. Bonnie had found that as long as there was something solid between her and the ocean, she could focus on her job, and not the fact that a fall into the ocean was one false move away.

But by far, Bonnie's favorite class was a nighttime experience called Celestial Navigation & Nautical Wayfaring, or as the corsairs called it, "C-Nav." Captain Ballister would take all the corsairs out on the *North*, far from the shore. They would then lie on their backs and stare up into the starry sky as Ballister pointed out the constellations they'd need to navigate by in the dark. There were jokes at first ("You guys never heard of GPS?" Wilder had asked on the first night) but eventually, the deck got quiet and the only sound was the captain's low voice over the ocean breeze and the water quietly lapping against the side of the ship. It was so dark that Bonnie could ignore the water almost completely. Lying on the deck, she felt her body almost disappear. It was only she and the star-filled night floating suspended above the dark waters. She never felt so full of bliss.

Ballister would start out quizzing the kids on the night sky but ended up telling tales of corsairs of days gone by. For Bonnie, it wasn't so much the content of his stories that appealed to her, but their tone. For the first time in her life, an adult didn't criticize or condescend. He just *talked.*

Captain Ballister saved his most reverent tones for his stories of Mary Read, the founder of the Brigands of the Compass Rose. He told of an English girl who craved adventure in a time when young women were taught to crave nothing of the sort. Desperate to escape her circumstances, Mary disguised herself as a man to join the British military, a penchant she continued well into her pirating days. After her service, Mary boarded a ship bound for the West Indies. There, she eventually fell in with a ruthless pirate named Calico Jack Rackham. It was with Rackham's wife, an Irishwoman named Anne Bonny, that Mary forged the greatest friendship of her life.

"Mary and Anne were as close of companions as any two who ever lived," Ballister remarked.

"What happened to this Anne Bonny person?" Bonnie asked on one occasion.

"Yeah," agreed Wilder. "Why wasn't she in the Brigands?"

"'Twas her husband's treachery that killed poor Anne," Ballister replied "And 'tis that selfsame treachery that brought the Brigands into being."

"What level treachery are we talking about here?" asked Micah. "Is it like the Didact in *Halo 4* kind of badass?"

"Dude, I don't think the captain speaks Xbox," Wilder offered.

"Fatboy's right though," said Tanner. "Enough with the secrecy. I think we got a right to know where all this stuff is leading."

It wasn't the first time the subject was brought up and it wouldn't be the last. But the answer from the captain was always the same:

"Some truths must not be spoken until their time. To answer you now would be to reveal our sacred purpose, which can only be made known to those who have proven worthy of the ancestral wall."

The ship fell into a hush, as everyone pondered what their secret purpose could possibly be, and who among them would be chosen to know it. But rather than drop the matter entirely, Captain Ballister went on to tell maddeningly seductive stories of other Brigands through history, of battles both won and lost, but mostly of the heroism shown by Brigands who had lain on these same decks of the *North* long, long ago.

"Where are all these Brigands now?" asked Wilder. "I only see Jonesy around here. And sometimes Wicked Pete."

Bonnie nodded her head. It did seem odd that this society had been around for centuries with nothing to show for it but a broken-down sailor and the surly Irishman who'd dropped her off.

"Oh, they're out there," the captain assured them, "scattered about, engaged in various areas at various levels. All committed to our mission and working this day towards its end. Of course there are others, good Brigands all, who we've… lost along the way." The captain cleared his throat and Bonnie thought he might have been choking back a tear.

Bonnie looked over at Reed, who stood not far from her. She could have sworn his eyes too were shimmery wet in the moonlight.

"Lost. All lost," the captain repeated. He then fell silent as he gazed out over the equally silent water.

Chapter 10
Siobhan

The padlock on the old barn door fought slightly against the key as Reed Ballister twisted it open.

"Well? What are you guys waiting for?" he said as he pushed open the heavy wooden door.

The corsairs tentatively stepped inside. It was the smell that hit Bonnie first: an odd combination of wood, leather and steel. Her eyes adjusted to the low light and she and the others stood in stone silence at what confronted them. For built on the barn's dirt floor was a life-size wooden replica of the deck of *True North*, including masts that reached into the rafters.

On either side of the deck was an immense cache of weapons. Mainly swords, but other weapons too, with names that they would soon come to know such as bucklers, boarding axes, hand fids, daggers and dirks. They hung in meticulous order on pegs around the walls. Nearby was a wooden bucket full of grapefruit-sized cast iron balls called grenadoes—smokepots designed to be filled with gunpowder, lit on fire, and hurled at an enemy. Next to them was a larger version of the same thing known as a carcass, so heavy it needed to be shot from a cannon.

"Jesus H.," marveled Wilder, surveying it all. "When do we attack Mordor?"

"Soon I hope!" exclaimed Wendell, salivating over the combustibles.

Bonnie was still not sure whether to be thrilled or terrified. "Kinda seems like the Brigands want us to be prepared for some seriously nasty stuff."

"Sure 'tis the way of it, Mistress Hartwright!" came the familiar voice of Wicked Pete, the Irishman who'd been Bonnie's escort to the Cove. Bonnie hadn't seen him since he dropped her off at the gate. And now here he was, big as a convenience store, looking much more at home in a leather vest and breeches than the ill-fitting suit he'd sported at their last meeting. But Bonnie noticed something else, too. A not-quite healed gash over his right eye made her wonder just what exactly the Irishman had been up to in his absence.

Wicked Pete strode to the weapons cache. "The true Brigand knows that danger, she lurks 'round every carner." He pulled a sleek longsword from the rack, and the sound of the steel blade sent chills down Bonnie's spine.

"No offense to you and your little cosplay fun here," Tanner scoffed, "but these days people have a little thing called gunpowder. Ask Yeun about it; his people came up with it a long time ago."

"Bruh, I'm Korean, not Chinese," Yeun complained.

"Whatever," Tanner shrugged. "Same diff."

"I'm with Hollywood over here," chimed in Luz. "The bangers in my neighborhood go in for something with a little more pop, know what I'm sayin'?"

"Guns 'taint da Brigand way," Wicked Pete replied. "Any geebag can pull a trigger. But master da blade, add a bit of cunnin' and sure you'll be able to defend yarself from anyone."

Barnaby Chisolm nervously eyed a sleek cutlass that looked sharp enough to cut firewood. "I-I don't think I'm comfortable with all this."

"Think of it as doin' yar duty by yar birthright, Mister Chisolm," said Wicked Pete. "Brigand history is crimson with bloodshed, it is. And 'tis me job to see to it that the blood spilt ain't yar own."

The corsairs looked at each other, their initial excitement now tempered by the ominous words. Bonnie swallowed hard.

"Okay, we'll start with some basic moves; everyone grab a blade!" Reed announced.

"Choose wisely yar weapons, young corsairs," Wicked Pete shouted as the kids flocked to the shimmering swords. "Make sure the steel sings to ye. It ought feel like a piece of yar own flesh."

After much debate and consideration, the corsairs had all chosen their weapons. As for Boreas, Micah settled on a short sword with a pearl-ringed pommel, and Malachi chose the largest broadsword on the rack, and even that seemed to shrink once in his huge hands. Tanner examined the choices carefully before finally picking a sleek ruby-handled rapier, while Wilder just grabbed the coolest sword that caught his eye, a scimitar with a leather-wrapped grip. For Barnaby, it seemed less a matter of what suited him than what he could actually lift without pulling a muscle. Ultimately, he chose a long dagger with a serpent carved into the mahogany grip.

One sword immediately spoke to Bonnie. She felt drawn to the very blade Barnaby had seemed so scared of when they first came in. Polished and glistening, it was perhaps two feet long, with the now-familiar rose on the pommel.

"'Tis a fine choice, Mistress," Wicked Pete said. "We call 'er Siobhan. She was the blade that Mary Read herself used in many a battle. She'll serve you well."

"Siobhan," Bonnie said solemnly under her breath, surprised at how the sword felt heavy and yet perfectly balanced in her hand. As she gripped it, she felt the same warm vibration she'd felt from the compass. She slashed it through the air to get the feel of it and with each slash she swore she heard harmonic tones.

"D-do you hear that?" she asked Wilder, who was trying out his own blade.

"Hear what?" Wilder asked, as he playfully fought off some imaginary foe with a variety of ridiculous swashbuckler poses. "I be ready to defend Brooklyn from all adversaries! Argh!" Bonnie laughed and applauded, thoroughly entertained by Wilder's antics until—

CLANK!

Reed's sword stopped Wilder's blade in midair.

"This isn't playtime, Mister De Luca," he said. "Pay attention."

"All righty, gather round!" Wicked Pete announced. "Notus and Eurus with me. Zephyrus and Boreas be with Master Reed!"

And so the training began. Though some in her group initially complained about getting stuck with Reed instead of the powerful Wicked Pete, they quickly ate their words. Because what Reed lacked in power, he more than made up for in swiftness, agility, and technique.

"Guy knows his stuff," Bonnie whispered to Wilder.

"So that's a lunge," Reed said, demonstrating a maneuver against a burlap practice dummy with a moving spring arm. "Keep your sword close to your body, otherwise you won't be able to counter and you leave yourself open. Who'd like to give it a try?"

"Back off, I got this," said Tanner, shoving the others aside.

The circle widened a bit to give Tanner some room. He lifted his blade to his face and kissed it dramatically.

"Only action he's gonna get this summer," said Bonnie, eliciting snickers.

Tanner growled in the direction of Bonnie's insult and then suddenly sprang into action. His sword sliced through the air and his feet blazed as he vanquished the dummy, leaving a pile of stuffing and wood chips on the ground, a display greeted by cheers from all sides. Reed started to work with Kevin Yeun as Boreas gathered around Tanner.

"That's some serious shit, man," Micah said. "Where'd you learn all that?"

Tanner shrugged and gave the dummy another stab. "I hung around a lot with the stunt coordinator on the set of *Blood of the Buccaneers III*."

"Wait a minute! *Blood of the Buccaneers*?!" Micah said. "Your dad's Gordon Prescott? As in *the* Gordon Prescott?!"

"That's what his star says on the Walk of Fame," Tanner said, casually doing another spin move as they watched.

"Who's Gordon Prescott?" asked Bonnie, still not willing to be impressed by *anything* about this jerk.

Barnaby jumped in. "His company produced all those pirate movies, used to be in the Brigands."

"Yeah, but he decided he had better things to do than playing pirate all day," Tanner said, brandishing his sword without a hint of irony. "Like get rich off all this B.S."

"Caught *Blood of the Buccaneers III* on cable last month," Wilder offered. "Movie sucked a bag of donkeys, man."

"Whatever. Biggest opening weekend of the spring." Tanner sliced through the air again. "Only reason I'm here is cuz my dad's punishing me for wrecking his car. End of summer I'm outta here, too."

"Sellout," Bonnie faked sneezed the word into her hand.

Tanner turned on his heels and swung the sword around so the tip was inches from Bonnie's nose. "What'd you say?"

"Get that frickin' thing out of my face," Bonnie said unflinchingly.

"Make me." Tanner again thrust his sword toward her face, this time getting even closer.

"That's quite the long sword you got there," Bonnie said, her gaze fixed on Tanner. "Can't help but wonder if you're trying to make up for other attributes that ain't quite so... ample."

Suddenly Tanner swung the hilt of his sword around and tried to smack Bonnie in the side of the head with it. Bonnie instinctively deflected the blow with her elbow. Tanner brought his sword around at her and with preternatural speed, Bonnie brought Siobhan up and slapped away Tanner's blade with such force that it sent him staggering backward.

By now, everyone had turned to see what was happening.

"Hey!" yelled Reed, seeing the fracas.

Having regained his balance, Tanner started for Bonnie and she for him, both their swords raised in ready fighting position.

THWACK! A huge longsword sailed with precision between them, stopping both in their tracks before imbedding into a beam, its hilt swaying back and forth between their noses.

Everyone was shocked into silence. *What. Just. Happened?*

As calmly as he had thrown the sword in the first place, Wicked Pete walked between them to where his blade now stuck out of the wall.

"First rule 'round here, corsairs," he said quietly, returning the sword to its scabbard. "No one engages in combat without wearing padding." He waved toward the west wall, where heavy leather protective gear was hung. "You carry live blades in yar hands, fools! Dey could cut a man's troat in a second! Reed, lad, I think it's best we separate this muck for the day. Prescott, ye'll work wit me group far da rest of da marnin'. Now, Mister Prescott!"

Tanner glared at Bonnie as he moped over to the other group.

Bonnie glared right back at him and felt a familiar rage welling up inside her. She knew herself too well to think that this would be the last time she would tussle with Tanner Prescott that summer.

And now she was armed. *Lovely.*

Chapter 11
The Marooners

"This bites," proclaimed Micah as he awkwardly pushed a mop across the teak deck of the *True North.* It was the end of the first week of experiences, and Boreas found themselves in dead last place.

So while the other corsairs were swimming or napping or, in a weekly show of mercy, enjoying an hour of precious electronics time, Boreas, the latest crew of "Marooners" as the weekly losers were known, had to do whatever the captain decided needed doing. And that week, they were tasked with polishing and cleaning the *True North* from bow to stern while Reed played overseer from the crow's nest and Jonesy handed out water and cleaning supplies.

Tanner was doing a half-hearted job of polishing a brass bell on the foredeck. "Where I come from, we have *people* to do this kind of thing. All I'm sayin'."

"Hey, Buccaneer Boy," Wilder said from the quarterdeck. "Finish up there, cuz I need you to clean the bowsprit."

"Let the special needs child do it," Tanner said, waving in the direction of Malachi Maguire. "They like that sort of thing. Menial tasks give them a sense of accomplishment."

Tanner's nonchalant cruelty launched Bonnie off on a flurry of insults. But her defense of Malachi quickly devolved into charges and countercharges about who truly was to blame for Boreas's sorry showing in the first week.

Reed jumped down from the mast. "Stop it! All of you! This is the reason you're in last place. Because you can't stop arguing for three seconds and act like a crew!"

Reed separated them to different parts of the ship and warned that if they didn't shape up, they'd start from the top and do it all over again.

"I expected more from you," Reed whispered to Bonnie as he passed her on his way to the bow of the ship. Bonnie felt her face get hot with anger.

Why was *she* the one Reed expected more from? Why not anyone else? She didn't like anyone expecting *more* from her, especially since nobody had ever expected *anything* from her in her entire life.

▪   ▪   ▪   ▪   ▪

As the day wore on, whenever someone lagged behind, Jonesy would hover over the offender and stare with his one good eye, which seriously creeped everybody out and was more than enough to get them back on task. Once, when he was safely out of earshot, Wilder whispered to Bonnie.

"How do you suppose Jonesy lost that eye?"

"Don't know," Bonnie whispered back, "but I bet alcohol was involved."

"I'd bet there's alcohol involved in about 80 percent of what that old coot does," Wilder replied. "Guy smells like he's been marinated in Bacardi."

"Heads up!" Micah shouted. Bonnie and Wilder turned toward his voice.

Malachi was standing at the bow, staring out over the water. And, for some reason, he was wearing a bright yellow hooded rain slicker that he'd found somewhere.

"What's he doing?" Bonnie asked as the others gathered to see.

"Looks like rain," Malachi announced. "Looks like rain."

"Remember when I said he only talks when he has something important to say?" Micah asked.

Bonnie nodded.

"Looks like rain," Malachi repeated, eyes fixed on the horizon.

"This is one of those times!" Micah yelled and took cover beneath a pile of canvas.

"What are you talking about?" Wilder asked. "There's not a cloud in the sky."

SQUAWK!!!

Out of nowhere came at least a dozen large multicolored birds, a whole flock in fact, flying right at the *North*! In the lead, one particularly large bird, green with a big red X on its chest.

"Aggh!" Jonesy howled from the aft of the *North*. "The fiends have returned!"

"What the hell?" Tanner said what everyone else on the ship was thinking.

"*Póg an talamh!*" Reed yelled and also hit the deck.

Barnaby immediately recognized the Irish phrase and did the same. The others looked perplexed. "*Póg an talamh!*" Barnaby repeated. "Kiss the ground!"

Bonnie and Wilder dropped to the deck beside him.

"Didn't you guys pay attention in Blades & Daggers? Jeez!" Barnaby shook his head.

"Are those… *parrots*?" Wilder asked, peeking over a barrel as the flock did a flyover.

"You better believe it! The parrots of Tuscarora Island!" screamed Barnaby, peeking out from under the bell. "My dad told me all about them!"

"What's the big deal? They're just stupid birds," Tanner said, still standing.

"Those stupid birds are coming right at us!" Wilder yelled as the parrots came back around.

"No," Reed said, "they're coming for Jonesy!"

Low, low, and lower still the birds flew as they swooped below the tree line. And straight for Jonesy, who howled at them madly, shaking his fists.

And with that, the parrots in formation like a squadron of WWII bombers unleashed a barrage of poop that hit the ship's deck like machine gun fire. RAT-A-TAT-ATATAT, forcing Tanner to dive overboard to avoid being hit. Poop spattered everything in its path. Including, and especially it seemed, Jonesy.

"Aiigeee! The devil bird has blinded me!" Jonesy yelled out, a face full of white glop.

"Oh my God, they *are* going for Jonesy!" Bonnie marveled.

"He and the birds are sworn enemies," Reed nodded.

"Better head for the hills, dude! Them squawkers mean business!" Wilder screamed out, enjoying Jonesy's predicament immensely.

Instead, Jonesy got to his feet, snatching the mop off the deck. Slipping and sliding in the guano, he made his way to the very front of the bowsprit. Jonesy brandished the mop like a battle axe.

"Don't you test me!" screamed Jonesy. "I'll make parrot pie of ye!"

"Cloudburst on the way," Malachi said. "Cloudburst on the way!"

"Look out!" Bonnie cried out. "They're coming around for another strike!"

This time it was one for the ages. PLOP! SPLAT! SPLUSH! It was a blitzkrieg of bird droppings, a firestorm of feces, a minefield of manure that poured out of the sky onto the old sea dog. If Jonesy's own mother had been swallowed whole by a shark, Bonnie couldn't imagine him being more upset than he was right now.

The corsairs hooted and howled and cheered wildly. Even the usually stone-faced Reed Ballister cracked a smile. With his one good eye semi-blinded by parrot droppings, Jonesy swung the mop wildly and futilely, hitting absolutely nothing. Until—

WHAM! In a moment of literal blind luck, the mop caught the big green leader right across the red markings on its chest. It SQUAWKED and fell stunned to the deck.

"I got ya now, ya foul fowl!" Jonesy stood over the bird, holding the mop over his head about to strike the final blow.

"No! Don't kill it!" Bonnie lunged and slid across the poop-covered deck into Jonesy, knocking him off his feet and allowing the parrot to regain its senses and fly away. The other birds joined their leader and flew off across the ocean until they disappeared over the horizon.

Bonnie surveyed the aftermath. She looked at Jonesy, glaring at her in milky-eyed fury. At Tanner, bobbing in the water below. At Barnaby and Micah, who'd both been hit by poop shrapnel, collateral damage in the attack on Jonesy. At Malachi, who was the only one clean as a whistle. And finally at the *True North*, whose deck was now utterly ravaged with parrot droppings, an entire day of sweat and toil in the blistering sun down the tubes. They would need to put in hours more of hard labor just to get the ship back to where it had been before the onslaught.

Bonnie looked at Wilder, and his broad smile told her they were thinking the same thought.

Worth it. Worth. Every. Damn. Minute.

✶   ✶   ✶   ✶   ✶

Okay. Maybe it wasn't *completely* worth it, because having to re-clean the *North* meant Boreas missed dinner. And despite Winnie's merciful appearance with some tomato and cucumber sandwiches, nobody could enjoy the meal because of the stench of bird excrement baking in the sun.

"Woulda been worse," Wilder offered, "if Malachi here hadn't warned us. That was awesome, dude!" He offered a fist bump that was left hanging by Malachi, who was busy rearranging the cucumber slices on his sandwich into a more pleasing pattern.

"How did he know those birds were coming?" wondered Barnaby.

Micah shrugged. "He just seems to know things. He's been like this since he was little." According to their Irish grandmother, it was because Malachi was a "caul baby," born fully encased in his amniotic sac—a very rare (and lucky, according to Barnaby) occurrence. Over time, the Maguires learned that whenever Malachi spoke, they'd best listen.

"If he really wanted to help, he would have been more specific," Tanner grumbled. "'Chance of rain?' How the hell were we supposed to know what that meant?" He then went on a rant about how the birds were probably a health hazard and should be exterminated like the vermin they were.

"Why didn't you just let Jonesy polish that big one off?" he complained to Bonnie. "What were you thinking, saving that crap factory?"

What Bonnie had been thinking was that she felt a kinship to the bird because she knew how it felt to go through life with a big, ugly mark. Instead, she just told Tanner to piss off.

"What the hell are they doing here, anyway?" Tanner wouldn't let it go. "This isn't the frickin' Amazon."

"They're feral parrots," Barnaby explained.

"Feral? Is that like a breed?" asked Wilder.

"No," Barnaby corrected him. "It just means they used to be tame, but now they're wild. In this case, their colony is over on Tuscarora Island."

He pointed to the east, over the water at the landmass in the distance. According to Barnaby, the island was first settled by the Tuscarora tribe, but they'd abandoned the island in the early 18th century after a bloody conflict with the English settlers. Its offshore location and secluded harbor made it the perfect hideaway for any scoundrels who needed to escape the long arm of the colonial authorities. Once the age of piracy ended, the parrots had been left behind by their pirate owners hightailing it off the island.

"So we got crapped on by the grandson of Blackbeard's parrot?" asked Wilder. "I feel so honored."

*   *   *   *   *

Apparently appreciating the fact that Bonnie had been its protector, the big parrot with the red X on its chest began showing up by itself for the sole purpose of visiting Bonnie. The first time it returned was a couple of days after the bombardment. It swooped over the side porch during breakfast and fluttered down to Bonnie's spot at the table. Then, cocking its head, it looked directly at Bonnie and dropped a twisted piece of aluminum on her plate.

"Those birds are always picking up shiny stuff here and there," explained Reed from a nearby table. "They're real scavengers."

"He's bringing you a present!" Barnaby suggested.

Bonnie looked the bird in the eye, and cautiously reached out her finger to the parrot.

"Careful, Bonnie," said Wilder. "I bet it's got a nasty bite."

"I don't think he wants to bite me," Bonnie replied. "I think he wants a friend."

The bird nuzzled up against Bonnie's finger. She took a piece of biscuit from her plate and offered it to the bird, which pecked at it eagerly.

"Hey little guy," Bonnie said, speaking more tenderly to the parrot than she'd ever spoken to any human. "You got a name?"

"Jonesy calls him Feathered Fiend from Hell," said Reed, "but I'm not sure he likes that one."

"Tell you what," Bonnie said to the bird, "I'll call you Crossbones, cuz of that pretty red mark on your chest. What do you think about that, boy? Crossbones?"

Bonnie decided to take the slight move of its head as a nod of assent.

"Crossbones it is," she said. And the bird nuzzled one more time before it flapped its wings and flew off, disappearing into the thick of the trees.

Soon the parrot would be a regular visitor to the Cove, seeking out Bonnie wherever she was. It wasn't long before Bonnie was in possession of a scratched-up spoon, a pink sequined hair tie and $1.35 in nickels, dimes and quarters. In return, Bonnie would give him table scraps or wild blackberries she'd pick from the bushes behind the cabin. Initially, Jonesy made a few more attempts at parroticide. But ultimately, he gave up when Winnie pointed out that the flock had left him alone since Bonnie befriended the bird. So whenever Crossbones showed up, Jonesy would simply disappear into the woods, cursing the bird and mumbling under his breath about Bonnie "throwing in with the devil." The old salt would inevitably return hours later, smelling of rum and eyeing Bonnie with suspicion.

Chapter 12
A Secret Exposed

It had been going so well. Despite the many physical challenges and the frequent skirmishes with Tanner, Bonnie was beginning to feel a sense of ease. And although Boreas had the embarrassing distinction of being in last place every week, Bonnie continued to outshine her crewmates in most of the experiences.

Beyond that, she felt a profound shift within herself. Where once she had dreaded early mornings, Bonnie found herself looking forward to them. She took to rising before the others to climb the wildflower-laden hill near the church, or wander to the beach and sit among the swaying broomsedge, or go to her favorite spot, the bow of the docked *North*, where she stood taking in the glory of the sunrise with the wind in her hair. *The True North.* Somewhere along the way, she had fallen in love with the venerable schooner; she had even begun fantasizing about standing tall on its teak deck, shouting orders and feeling the ship beneath her feet responding to her commands as it cut through roiling seas. Since she had mastered her fear of going out *on* the water and had gone the longest stretch of her life without a nightmare, she began to believe that maybe she belonged in this place. She should have known better.

*　*　*　*　*

It finally happened the morning after the full Thunder Moon, which Bonnie calculated was about a month into their training. She knew the day would come eventually. After all, you couldn't very well go to a sailing school without at some point actually getting *into* the water. Until then, she'd scrupulously avoided it in much the same way she had all her life. That is, through evasion, distraction, and good ol' fashioned lying. When Luz and Daya invited her to go body surfing after dinner, she said she had a stomachache. When everybody went for a swim off the side of the *North*, she conveniently decided it was then that she "needed" Reed's help to learn to tie a paracord woggle knot. Whenever there were diving contests off the dock, Bonnie would retreat to the barn to work on her swordplay. However, her aversion to water hadn't gone entirely unnoticed by the rest of Boreas. On more than one occasion, Wilder ever so indirectly asked her what was up and gave her that "look" whenever she came up with one of her fibs.

The experience that day started with a strenuous five-mile hike through dense forest and along rocky coastline. Not that Bonnie noticed. She was too busy mentally preparing for the water challenge that lay ahead. So by the time they arrived at the secluded lagoon with the stunning waterfall, Bonnie had convinced herself she could do it. After all, since she'd been on the Cove, she'd discovered she could do a lot of things she never would have believed she was capable of back in Arizona. Bonnie hoped that her corsair blood would rise to the occasion here too, and that she would miraculously discover the ability to get "into" the water without losing her mind.

The rules of the experience were simple. It was a relay. All four crews would line up at the edge of the secluded lagoon (known to the Brigands as the "Picaroon Paradise"). Jonesy would then fire an 18th century flintlock pistola into the air, signifying the start of the competition. One from each crew would jump into the water and swim out to the waterfall. There, about 10 feet below the crystalline surface, was a treasure chest overflowing with doubloons. Each corsair would gather up as many coins as they could, swim back and deposit them on the sand and tag the next person, who would swim out for their share of the booty. Whichever team got the most doubloons would be declared the winner. And since it was the last challenge of the week, double the pieces of eight were at stake, meaning there was an outside chance that Boreas could move into third, overtaking the habitually mediocre Notus, and finally getting a Sunday off.

The crews huddled up to decide their order amongst themselves. As usual, Boreas couldn't reach a consensus. Reed put an end to their squabbles by making them draw straws. Tanner was to go first, followed by Wilder, then Micah, Barnaby and Malachi, and finally Bonnie was to swim the anchor leg. On the one hand, she was relieved to be last because it gave her more time to work up her courage; on the other, it also gave her more time to totally freak out. As the sound of the waterfall splashed around them, Bonnie eyed the lagoon with steely determination while the rest of Boreas staked out their position on the shoreline. *I can do this! I'm going to do this!*

BANG! The sound of the pistola signaled the start of the race. The first four swimmers soon arrived at the treasure chest, overflowing with coins ten feet below. Then, an underwater melee broke out as each swimmer battled for coins before running out of breath and returning to the surface. As usual, Eurus and Zephyrus led the way. For a while, Boreas was neck and neck with Notus for third, but fell behind again when Barnaby, not much of a swimmer himself, failed to bring back little more than a handful of coins. It looked like Boreas was destined for last place and like Bonnie's performance wouldn't end up mattering anyway... until Malachi returned with the biggest haul of all. They spilled from his beefy fists, his pockets, and he even spit some out from his mouth as the cheers of Boreas filled the morning air.

"We've got to be ahead of Notus!" Barnaby cried out, watching Malachi's haul join the other coins in the pile.

"Holy crap," exclaimed Wilder. "We just might not suck this week!"

Boreas was back in the game. The anchors from Zephyrus and Eurus were already on their way out to the chest, but Brice from Notus was only just now swimming to shore. Bonnie heard the excitement in the voices of her crewmates as Malachi tagged her in.

"Go Bonnie!" she heard the cheers.

Caught up in the excitement, Bonnie took off running for the water just as Brice lumbered back to dry land. She just *knew* she was going to do it. She believed it with all her heart and soul... at least until the moment she came to a complete stop at the edge of the water. In her mind, she was still moving, but she looked down and sure enough, there she stood, frozen, the cool water lapping against the tips of her toes, her legs as motionless as fence posts.

She felt like the veins in her head were about to pop. The shouts of her fellow crew members to "go" and "run" were muffled by the pressure of the blood whooshing in her ears. The sound of the waterfall got louder in her head, and that bizarre feeling of falling again until—

A series of flashes: *The church from her dream. The steeple. A cracked bell. The stained glass. An old cemetery. With a gravestone! In the shape of a Celtic cross.*

And then everything went black.

∎   ∎   ∎   ∎   ∎

"She's freakin' afraid of the water!" Tanner shook his head, incredulous, as he paced back and forth in the cabin once they had returned. "So freakin' afraid she freakin' passed out! Un-freakin'-believable!"

The rest of Boreas sat dejectedly in the parley room after Bonnie's meltdown cost them third place and their Sunday off, but

Tanner Prescott was in rare form. "I freakin' knew the freakin' second that freakin' compass put her on our crew we were freakin' screwed."

"Dude," said Wilder, "you seriously need to invest in some new adjectives."

Bonnie would have normally appreciated Wilder's humor, but at the moment, she was *not* having it. Instead, she sat curled up in the overstuffed chair, her hair still wet from having passed out face first in the water. She stared at flames that danced mockingly in the fireplace as the others argued around her.

"Relax," Wilder continued. "It's not the end of the world that we have to do chores again tomorrow. Builds character."

"Speak for yourself," Tanner said. "I don't need any more character."

"Yeah. We're gonna have to agree to disagree on that one," Wilder replied.

Bonnie got up. "I'm sorry, okay? I'm sorry the water freaks me out; I wish it didn't. It's just that I…" For a moment Bonnie thought she might tell them about the terrifying nightmares and the even more terrifying recent visions—that it would all come spilling out. "I always have been. I-I don't know why," she lied. She went into her room and slammed the door. She crawled into her bunk and pulled the covers up over her head. But she could still hear the voices in the parley room.

"You're such an ass, Prescott," she heard Wilder say.

"It *is* pretty weird, when you think about it," it was Micah's voice, "that a blood corsair is afraid of the water."

"I'm afraid of a lot of stuff," she heard Barnaby pipe up in her defense.

"But you're not afraid of water, are you?" Micah followed up.

"No," Barnaby said quietly.

"What are you getting at, Maguire?" Wilder asked, but Bonnie heard no reply.

"Look, if you won't say it, bro, I will," Tanner said, jumping in. "First, there was the freaky thing with the compass. Then all the screaming in her sleep. And today. Just before she passed out. It was like she was in a trance or something. The chick's eyes were wide open, but she wasn't seeing any of us. It was like she was seeing —"

"Something else," Barnaby whispered. "Something really horrible."

"It's hella creepy shit, man," Tanner concluded. "They need to wash her out, the sooner the better. She doesn't belong here."

"She belongs here as much as any of us," Wilder snapped.

"Look, De Luca, I know you have the hots for her and all, but facts are facts," Tanner replied.

"All Tanner is saying is that she isn't like the rest of us," Micah added. "What happened today at the lagoon... There's something, I don't know... *different* about her."

"That's all I'm sayin'!" Tanner said. "There's something seriously off about that chick. And the rest of you are just too freakin' stupid to see it."

And for the first time all summer, Tanner Prescott had said something that Bonnie completely agreed with.

Tanner freakin' Prescott!

Chapter 13
Highcross

A giant reclaimed school bus, nicknamed "Moby" for its size and white paint job, bounced along a coastal road. Bonnie sat alone at the back of the bus, staring sullenly out a window as Boreas headed toward their latest marooning task. Each pothole they went over sent a jolt through her system that mocked how she felt—a dull mix of guilt and humiliation over her part in her crew's latest loss. Toss in a growing feeling that the others had been right the night before about her not "belonging," and you get a nice stew of awfulness for a Sunday morning. Her crew picked up on her vibes and steered clear, sitting up front near Winnie and Reed, who was in charge of piloting the gargantuan bus to its destination. Boreas was heading to the nearby town of Highcross to help Winnie with the monthly shopping. And nobody looked too thrilled about it, least of all Tanner Prescott, who kept shooting nasty looks at Bonnie the entire trip.

To make matters worse, Bonnie was dealing with the feeling of unease that had overcome her the minute the bus had pulled out of the main gate at the Cove. She tried to shake it off and focus instead on Barnaby Chisolm, who was, as usual, a font of information.

"Highcross was first settled back in the 17th century by Mr. Charles Eden, who went on to become governor of the whole colony."

"Lining his pockets all along the way," snorted Winnie.

Indeed, as Barnaby continued his history lesson, he explained that Eden was well known for his efforts to rid the Carolina coast of pirates, but many suspected that he had been in cahoots with them all along and actually profited off the kickbacks from the pirate booty that he let slip out of the colony untouched. Bonnie knew enough about politics to know that things hadn't changed much since pirate days.

After fifteen more minutes of Barnaby's tales of colonial intrigue, Reed steered the bus into the seaside town of Highcross. They stopped at a red light in front of the marina, where were docked the most expensive looking boats Bonnie had ever seen. The whole place reeked of old money and second marriages.

There was some kind of commotion going on at one of the slips, and the corsairs pressed against the windows to get a better look. A small police boat was anchored nearby, its lights flashing. A well-tended woman in obvious distress was talking to a man in a sheriff's uniform. The sandy-haired officer was trying to calm the woman.

"Wonder what she's so upset about?" asked Micah.

"Maybe somebody didn't cut the crusts off her sandwiches," Wilder replied.

"Nah. I bet it's that!" Barnaby pointed out a row of neon-colored signs along the boardwalk.

$10,000 REWARD

FOR INFORMATION REGARDING RECENT YACHT BURGLARIES
CONTACT: HIGHCROSS SHERIFF DEPARTMENT

"Pirates!" exclaimed Barnaby.

"Looks like somebody's trying to horn in on our territory," Micah joked.

The light finally changed and the bus pulled past the marina. The novelty of the place pulled Bonnie out of her funk. The streets of the town were lined with high-end chain stores and resort wear shops, but they were all dressed up with phony baloney wooden signs and antique-looking storefronts in an attempt to make the tourists feel like they were getting a taste of Carolina history along with their eight-dollar cup of coffee.

"All this stuff is new," Reed said, pointing along the waterfront. "They've been developing it for a while now."

"Ruining is more like it," Winnie said with disdain. "The town council doesn't realize you can't manufacture charm."

If Winnie didn't care for the town, it became quickly apparent that the feeling was mutual. As the bus crawled through the morning traffic, people on the street were staring at them. One woman deliberately guided her children in the opposite direction. *If only they knew we were all pirates*, Bonnie thought, snickering to herself.

The bus pulled into the parking lot of the farmers' market just off the town's main street. Bustling stalls lined either side of the boardwalk, which was teeming with shoppers perusing the makeshift mall for bargains and souvenirs. Winnie got up from her seat at the front of the bus and faced the corsairs. She began by handing out lists of items for them to obtain.

"You mean you're gonna trust us to go on our own?" Wilder asked incredulously. "With no fence to zap us if we try to make a break for it?"

"Well, I've got my own errands that need tending to," Winnie said as she loaded a folding cart with jams and jellies for consignment sale at one of the booths. "I can't be watching you children every minute."

"Wait. How are we supposed to buy anything without money?" asked Micah, who was clearly working an angle to get a little pocket change for the donut booth he spied across the street.

"The folks that run these here booths, they know us," said Winnie. "Been doing business here for years. Just tell them you're with Grandma Winnie, they'll put it on our tab. You'll work in pairs and when you're done, meet up back at the bus."

"I'm with my brother!" Micah called.

"Me and Curls!" said Wilder.

"No surprise there," Tanner said. "Guess that leaves me with you, then." He grabbed Barnaby's list. "Just stay out of my way, Owl Eyes." With Barnaby on his heels, he headed into the mass of people as the others broke off into pairs and dispersed.

"Stay close to each other!" Winnie called after them. "And stay out of trouble!" She then gave a nod to Reed, who nodded back in recognition of some unspoken direction.

It was immediately clear that it was going to be hard for the corsairs to stay on task. After weeks on the Cove, the novel temptations of the market were too great. Barnaby got distracted by a guy close to the parking lot selling pirate memorabilia while Tanner wandered off to chat up a covey of teenage girls at an ice cream stand. Micah, with an agenda of his own, led his brother to a booth where a guy in a striped apron was giving out free samples of kettle corn.

Bonnie and Wilder, tasked with obtaining flour, sugar and duck fat, headed in the opposite direction. But soon enough, Bonnie found herself distracted as well. Each booth was its own mini-universe, offering up delights. Homemade preserves in gingham covered mason jars. "Artisan" this and "Handmade" that. Pulled pork sandwiches and zucchini chips, deep fried okra and corn cakes with slaw, and something called "country apple sausage pie" that sounded kind of gross but looked and smelled heavenly. And all along the way, it seemed like every other store window and power pole was plastered with a sign like they'd seen near the marina warning the shoppers to be on the lookout for the yacht burglars that had been striking of late.

And just as Grandma Winnie had mentioned, Bonnie did see a few of the people she called the "Gullah," in booths with vendors dressed in African and Caribbean style garb selling traditional doodads of all kinds: artwork, sweetgrass baskets, cookbooks, seasonings and traditional healing herbs. It was quaint and colorful, but the hoodoo magic Winnie had spoken of was nowhere to be seen.

"Hey! Check it out," Wilder pointed across the way. "I think Micah is seriously jonesin' for snacks." Bonnie turned to see Micah getting an earful from the kettle corn guy for trying to sneak a second sample. Micah looked desperate. Malachi just looked like a lamppost.

"Poor sap," Wilder shook his head. "He hasn't had so much as a gummy bear for weeks."

"Processed sugar *is* the nerd's heroin," Bonnie concurred.

"Which is why we're gonna help him out," Wilder said, grabbing her arm. "Come on."

"How? We don't have any money."

"Curls. Seriously? You have to ask that question?"

Wilder smiled slyly. It suddenly dawned on Bonnie what he had in mind and she smiled in response.

"C'mon," he said with a wink, "it's pillaging time." With that, he disappeared into the drugstore at the edge of the market. Bonnie knew it was completely stupid, but she followed him into what she guessed would not be the last bad decision she would make about this boy.

Inside, Bonnie and Wilder worked instinctively as a team. They immediately began casing the joint. Bonnie found it thrilling just how in sync they were and how they communicated without words, as if they'd known each other forever. A nod of Bonnie's head indicated that they should split up and Wilder disappeared down the chip aisle as Bonnie worked quickly at the candy end, expertly shoplifting half a million dollars in 100 Grand Bars. She was fast and flawless and felt the thrill of the heist as she headed for the front door and a clean getaway. Out of the corner of her eye, she saw Wilder near the magazine rack engaged in a heated discussion with… Reed Ballister! They were busted! *How had he seen them? Had he been following them? And how—*

SMACK! Bonnie's distraction caused her to crash into a customer who was stepping out the door at the same time. The collision made the man drop his bag of purchases and sent

Bonnie's purloined candy spilling out over the pavement in front of the store.

"You clumsy—!" he growled at her.

"I-I'm so sorry," Bonnie said. She dropped to her knees to gather the spilled items and separate her candy bars from the items belonging to the man—duct tape, rope, thick zip ties and large utility knife—then she put the man's purchases back into his plastic bag.

She stood up and found herself before a very tall, sinewy man with a narrow face. He had dark, longish hair slicked back from its own grease, a thin mustache that crawled across a scowling mouth and a five o'clock shadow that was disrupted by a jagged scar that ran from his left ear to the middle of his chin.

"Watch where you're going, you little sow!" He grabbed the bag, snarling through crooked teeth that were as yellow as the pit stains on his shirt.

As he brushed past her, a sudden jolt shot through Bonnie; a sense of something sinister, foul. *A stench?* She fought the urge to vomit. The odor reminded her of the smell from the crawl space beneath the trailer of one of her foster parents. Bonnie, at the tender age of ten, had been ordered to see what was causing it and found herself on her belly, eye to eye with a dead raccoon, its body bloated and exploding with writhing maggots in the Arizona heat.

Death. The guy smells like death, Bonnie thought as she watched the scar-faced man get swallowed up in the crowd.

·   ·   ·   ·   ·

A couple of minutes later, Bonnie and Wilder emerged from the store empty-handed, Reed having forced them to put back their entire haul.

"That was stupid. We could have gotten caught returning that stuff," Wilder grumbled.

"*Now* you're worried about getting caught?" Reed scoffed. "I guess I'm going to have to babysit you until we get back to the bus."

"Like you haven't been following us all along," Bonnie said. "Come on Wilder, we have grocery shopping to do."

Reed tagged along just behind the two of them as they first stopped at Uncle Quackers, the stand that specialized in everything duck, and then at the Spice Shack for sugar. They then made their way to Ophelia's Organic Dry Goods booth. While Reed and Wilder added fifty pounds of flour to the five gallons of rendered duck fat and thirty pounds of sugar already on the cart Uncle Quackers loaned them, Bonnie noticed a tented stall across the way.

It was another of the Gullah stands she'd seen scattered throughout. Unlike the others, though, this one had a sign that touted magic:

FORTUNES by FATIMATA:
GULLAH SEER of the PAST, PRESENT or FUTURE

At the entry was a wizened old woman with almond-hued skin. She was propped up by a twisted driftwood cane. She was frail and shriveled, with thinning white hair through which her scalp was visible. Her eyes were milky with cataracts, but she seemed to stare right at Bonnie. Her lips moved as if she was saying something, but Bonnie couldn't make it out. The old woman turned and disappeared into the tent.

Despite Reed's warnings to stick close by, curiosity got the best of Bonnie. She felt compelled to follow the woman into the stall.

On the surface, it seemed like the other booths she'd seen: crammed with fabrics and artwork that were an odd but interesting mixture of Caribbean, African and Southern cultures. However, the herbs and potions sold here were more unusual, more reminiscent of those found in Grandma Winnie's apothecary. Bottles of potions lined the shelves with handwritten labels saying things like *LOVE, SAFE TRAVELS, CONFIDENCE, CLEANSING, GOOD LUCK*, and *PASSION*. Hanging all about the stall were little bags of herbs, called gris-gris, which filled the air with various unplaceable aromas and, according to the signage, could "ward off all manner of evil."

There was no sign of the old woman, but Bonnie heard voices in the back of the stall, where a curtain of thick beads made of chicken bones hung. She moved a little closer and through the curtain could make out the figure of a large woman in her 50s, dressed in a sunflower yellow print dress with huge orange ruffles around her shoulders and hips. Her hair was a mass of twisted dreadlocks that fell down her neck, and wrapped around her forehead was a black and gold band with exotic symbols engraved into it. She sat at a table, giving a reading to a tourist and spoke in some kind of pidgin dialect.

"Don' be worryin' none, missus," the fortune teller said. "Dat layabout son a your'n, he gwine find his way off dah couch inside a six munt."

"Six months?" asked the clearly dispirited tourist, a middle-aged woman decked out in overpriced resort wear.

"Er, wait, no no. Did Fati say six? Three munt! It's three munt. De connection betwixt our worl' and their'n be someteems coagulated."

Bonnie rolled her eyes at the idea that anyone would be so gullible as to pay money for such a sham. She turned to go when someone grabbed her hand. A strange electricity shot through her, like what she'd felt back at the Cove wall. She looked down, startled to see the ancient woman sitting in a corner, so small that Bonnie hadn't noticed her behind a table piled high with items.

"You in dangeh, chile!" the old woman hissed. She spoke in the same dialect as the fortune teller.

"W-what?" Bonnie asked and the woman's grip tightened so that Bonnie could see her veins bulge through her crepey skin.

"B'ware, dah man who smell like death," she said in a low ominous voice. "Evil, it seeks yah, and it ain't gwine be restin' 'til it finds yah." Bonnie felt horror wash over her as the woman's sightless eyes looked not *at* her but *into* her.

"I-I have to go," Bonnie pulled away gently from the woman, fearful she would break her in two if she didn't. But the woman gripped her hand and snatched one of the little herb bags from the table.

"Gam Gam gots sometin' fuh yah. Take dis gris-gris," she insisted, jamming it into Bonnie's hand, "fuh protection! Keep it on yah always! Promise me! Promise!" Bonnie's fingers closed around the gris-gris just as—

"What are you doing over here?" Bonnie turned to see a clearly annoyed Reed Ballister standing nearby.

"I…" She turned back to look at the old woman, but the chair was empty. "J-just looking."

"Don't go running off without telling me!" Reed grabbed her by the arm, a little too harshly for her tastes. She jerked her arm away.

"Relax. It's not a big deal." Bonnie's anger at Reed's unreasonableness made her forget about the old woman's frightening words, at least for the moment.

"I'm responsible for you! And I say it is!" he snapped at her.

"Hey, pump the brakes a bit, why don't you? We won't tell granny on you," joked Wilder, who had joined them, pulling the cart full of supplies.

"Come on. We need to get back," Reed said curtly and grabbed the wagon handle from Wilder. Bonnie looked down at the gris-gris still in her hand. She glanced back toward the fortune teller's booth, then stuffed the talisman into her pocket and hurried after the two boys.

By the time they got to the bus, everybody else was already on board, their noses pressed against the window. They were all watching Grandma Winnie, who was standing just outside the bus engaged in a heated exchange with an older man in a polyester suit with a too-short tie. Reed stopped in his tracks.

"Oh shit," he said. "Charley Eden… "

"Wait a minute," Bonnie said. "Eden? As in Charles Eden, that crooked governor dude who founded the town way back when?"

"Yep," said Reed. "His family's been running Highcross ever since."

Reed led Bonnie and Wilder around the other side of the bus so they could eavesdrop unseen.

"That's fool talk, Charles!" they heard Winnie say. "This is the first any of 'em have been off the Cove all summer! We keep a very tight leash on our charges."

"Really? Do I have to bring up the joyriding incident from last year?" Eden said with a greasy southern drawl.

"That was never proven!" said Winnie.

"Well, *somebody's* rippin' off all the damn boats in the marina, and I wouldn't put it past your delinquents for a second!" he said. Bonnie thought of the signs and the hubbub down at the marina. "I swear, Winifred," Eden continued, playing to the gathering crowd. "I'm not going to let another summer's revenue be impacted by your little band of punks!"

As the crowd nodded in assent, Bonnie looked at Reed. She saw the color rise in his cheeks.

"Councilman Eden, just put your cards on the table for land's sake," Winnie replied, clearly running short on patience. "Your family's been after Cormac's Cove since we were both in short pants. You couldn't get it then and you won't get it now, even if it is for your precious little apartment complex."

"It's a resort for your damn information and we'll just see who gets what at the next council meeting."

Reed had clearly heard enough. He stepped around the bus and faced Charley Eden. "You know you can't eminent domain us without cause!"

Eden appeared startled by his sudden appearance. "This is none of your affair, you motherless miscreant."

"Listen, old man, I'm sick of you harassing us every time we come to town."

"Is there a problem here?" came a deep, soothing Southern drawl.

Bonnie, who'd come out from the side of the bus with Wilder, looked to the man who had just approached. She wasn't in his eyeline, but he was in hers. He was the sandy-haired sheriff she'd seen earlier at the marina.

"No problem, Sheriff Maynard, we were just leaving," Winnie said, taking the quickest glance at Bonnie. "Come on, kids, onto the bus."

"Damn right, we got a problem here, Bobby!" Charley insisted, blocking the way to the open bus door.

"Councilman Eden," the sheriff said in that same calm, steady voice Bonnie had heard cops use in Arizona to break up street fights and defuse domestic disputes. "We go through this same conversation every summer."

"And every summer you take their damn side!"

"Because every summer they don't do anything!"

"You know as well as I that ain't the reason, Bobby!"

Instead of responding to Eden's spittle-laced charge, the sheriff smiled and nodded at Winnie. "Now, Uncle Charley, what say we just let these folks be on their way?"

Bonnie exchanged surprised looks with Wilder. The idea that the sheriff was somehow related to this obnoxious blowhard didn't sit right with her. She could no more link the two in her mind than she could raw onions and vanilla ice cream.

The sheriff turned to address the crowd of gawkers. "That means all of you. Let's be about our business, folks." The councilman gave one last huff and joined the crowd as they went back toward the market, badmouthing the school along the way.

"Winifred, I'm sorry," the sheriff said, shaking his head. "You know, Uncle Charley, he gets a bee in his bonnet every now and again, but nothing…" His voice trailed off as he caught sight of Bonnie. Their eyes locked. And she saw a look cross his face. Surprise? Recognition? She couldn't be sure. "… ever comes of it," he finished the thought, still looking in Bonnie's direction.

"It's fine, Bobby. Don't pay it no mind." And then following the sheriff's gaze to Bonnie, she changed her tone. "Reed! Finish loading the supplies. You two, get on the bus," she commanded. "Go on. Git!"

Wilder and Bonnie quickly did as they were told. Reed looked a little confused by his grandmother's sudden need to make a hasty exit, but he also did as he was told. When the bus pulled out of the parking lot, Bonnie looked out the window at the sheriff, who stood there immobile, his eyes fixed on her.

Bonnie faced forward, but as the bus pulled out of town, she couldn't help looking back in the direction of the ancient Gullah woman, the ornery politician, and that kindly sheriff, who made her uneasy in a way that she couldn't quite explain.

Chapter 14
The Chapel on the Hill

Bonnie stood in the middle of the Highcross farmers' market. But something was off. The same familiar stands lined the boardwalk, but the market was completely empty.

Abandoned.

She sensed him before she saw him. It started with a shudder through her spine and ended with the overwhelming stench of rotting flesh. She slowly turned and there he was at the other end of the market. The man she'd run into at the drugstore, the man with the huge scar. He reached into his plastic bag and produced the rope that had spilled out when they had collided; it was fashioned into an enormous noose! He smiled a sadistic smile.

"Run!" came a woman's strong, clear voice in her head. "RUN!"

So Bonnie ran. Blindly she ran, weaving in and out through the various stalls. Frenzied, panicked, everything a blur until she nearly ran into the old Gullah woman at the fortune teller's booth, her filmy eyes blindly staring at her.

"He's a 'comin' fuh yah!" she whispered, clutching Bonnie's arms with her bony fingers.

Bonnie yanked herself free from the old woman's grip, but tripped and fell to the ground, only to discover she was no longer in the farmers' market at all, but now back in the little chapel from her

earlier dream. Still on her hands and knees, Bonnie noticed
something on her wrist:

It was her birthmark! What was it doing there and not on her
shoulder?

"Hello, my child," came a guttural growl.

Bonnie scrambled to her feet! At first, she thought the man from
the market had followed her and was standing there in the shadows.
But no... Even though she couldn't quite make out his face, she
somehow knew this wasn't the scar-faced man.

"I've come for you," said the figure, still cloaked in shadow,
except for a slash of light that fell across his hand, revealing the
hourglass ring.

Bonnie turned to run, but the man lunged at her, knocking her to
her knees. As she staggered to her feet, the man grabbed her by the
throat with one hand and shoved her backwards into the baptismal
font. Bonnie's eyes went wide as she felt her head again being forced
into the cold water of the font. She fought ferociously, kicking and
clawing, and finally managed to break back through the surface.
Bonnie scratched at her assailant, pulling away the floral fabric of
his collar to reveal a horrific rope burn around his neck! She barely
managed a breath of air before his hand came down hard on her face,
shoving her below the water again.

"No!"

Bonnie awoke with a start. There was an instant of panic before
she realized she was in her bunk in the cabin. She rushed over to a
pile of dirty clothes and frantically dug through the pockets of her
jeans until she found the gris-gris that the old Gullah woman had
given her. She clutched it to her pounding chest as she took big
gulps of air. When her breath and heart finally returned to a steady
rhythm, two words came out of her, an involuntary whisper.

"He's close."

.   .   .   .   .

Bonnie's dreams were back; there was no getting around it. After a stretch of calm and peaceful nights on the Cove, she'd been thrust back into her nightmares. Maybe it was the shock of the blackout by the waterfall, or the general creepiness of the guy at the farmers' market, or the weird way she felt after her encounter with the old Gullah woman. Whatever the reason, the earth beneath Bonnie had shifted, and she was no longer certain of her footing. The Boreas boys had heard her scream as well. Tanner had made a snide remark about it when she'd entered the parley room. Barnaby and Micah avoided eye contact. Wilder just looked at her with unspoken concern.

Bonnie spent her morning shower trying to convince herself that the dream meant nothing. *Sometimes a dream is just a stupid dream,* she told herself. But then, on the way to breakfast, she paused on the porch of the main house to look at the little white chapel, standing solemnly against the winds, in the gold light of sunrise—and suddenly she wasn't so sure.

Being a foster kid, she hadn't been with one family long enough to be raised in any religion and had been to church only a handful of times in her life. Yet now she'd dreamed of the same church twice since arriving at the Cove, in such incredible detail that it was impossible to ignore. And she wondered if she should—

"Go there," came Malachi's voice, as if finishing her thought. Bonnie whirled around, startled to find the giant boy behind her. He pointed to the church without turning away.

"Go there," he repeated.

"The church? You think I should go to the church, Malachi?" she asked.

"Go! SEE! SEE!" he said more urgently and grabbed her hand. He looked at Bonnie with those weird mismatched eyes, and Bonnie felt like he was looking into her very soul. For his expression went from horror to sympathy and finally... anguish. Tears rolled down his cheeks.

"Malachi!"

Micah called to his brother from the side deck to hurry him to breakfast, and the moment was broken. Malachi's eyes became emotionless again. He walked away from Bonnie as if nothing had happened. But Bonnie knew something had. If there was one thing that she learned these last few weeks, it was that when Malachi Maguire spoke, he should *not* be ignored.

She was definitely going to the church.

*   *   *   *   *

Her opportunity finally came after dinner. As usual, the crews kicked back at their cabins as the summer sun began its slow descent behind the trees. Bonnie knew she had to shake Wilder, who would be sure to follow her out of concern if she just up and left. She finally was able to ditch him when she roped him into a card game with Hashpipe and Stevie Ray. Wilder was soon so wrapped up in hustling them out of contraband cigarettes that he didn't notice when she slipped away.

Ten minutes later, Bonnie dropped over the gated wall that surrounded the churchyard and took in the small chapel in front of her. Situated on the highest hill at Cormac's Cove, the church was a very old but sturdy structure. It certainly *looked* like the church in her dreams, but she couldn't be sure. She knew only one way to find out. She climbed the steps that led to the heavy wood door and turned the knob. Locked. She peeked in a window. And though she could barely make it out in the dwindling light, she saw it, the immense stained-glass window over the altar—cut into the shape of an eight-pointed star with roses—just how she'd seen it in her dream.

Her heart pounded wildly as she made her way around the church. Moving along the side, she looked up at the bell in the steeple. It was cracked! Just as it had been in the vision she had before blacking out at the treasure dive. It *wasn't* all in her head. So, she knew even before she turned the corner that the cemetery she had seen would also be there. And it was bigger than she expected, with gravestones as far back as the eye could see.

But it was the headstone closest to the church that called to her. For it was in the shape of a Celtic cross, also exactly like the one she'd seen in the vision. She knelt before it and gently pulled aside the ivy that obscured the inscription:

ANNE CORMAC BONNY

Bonnie recognized the name. Mary Read's dear friend, whose death had somehow led to the establishment of the Brigands. Why had Bonnie seen *her* grave in the vision?

"Bonnie?" a male voice came from behind her.

She jumped to her feet and whirled around. There at the side of the church were Reed and Wilder, standing shoulder to shoulder.

"What are you doing here?" Reed asked.

"What are YOU doing here?" Bonnie demanded angrily. "Can't I be anywhere without a damn babysitter?"

"I was worried about you," Reed and Wilder said simultaneously. They immediately exchanged a scowl, as if it pained them to be in agreement on anything.

"I figured out pretty quickly you were trying to distract me with that card game," Wilder explained, "so I went looking for you."

"I stopped by the cabins after I finished my chores," Reed said, "and noticed you both were missing. I found Wilder over by the north wall."

"Then we ran into the Maguires down by the beach," Wilder continued. "We asked if they'd seen you. Malachi kept saying 'church, church'..."

Great, Bonnie thought. *The one time the big guy decides to talk and he rats me out!*

"Well, you found me. So now you can leave."

"Bonnie," Reed said, "this church is off limits. That's kind of the point of the wall and the big lock on the front gate." He held up a ring of keys from his pocket.

"What is this place anyway?" Bonnie asked, indicating the graveyard.

"We call it the Field of the Fallen," Reed replied.

"Whoa. Our family plot," Wilder remarked, exploring the area. "Hey! Check this out. Another De Luca. We must be related."

"Look, you guys," Reed said. "You need to get back to your cabin."

But Bonnie wasn't listening. "Did everyone here die in battle?"

"Come on," Reed insisted, heading back toward the gate. "If Grandfather finds us here, you'll be marooning the rest of summer."

Wilder started to follow, but Bonnie remained at the foot of Anne Bonny's grave.

"Reed. Did Anne Bonny… drown?" Bonnie asked.

"What? No, why?" Reed stopped in his tracks.

"She wasn't drowned inside the church in one of those things with the holy water?"

Bonnie saw a look of surprise flash across Reed's face and then instantly disappear. "The baptismal font? No, she wasn't," was all he said in reply.

"Okay, Curls. That's a weird and oddly specific question," Wilder stated.

"But there *is* a… baptismal font in there, right?" Bonnie said pointedly.

"Most churches have them," Reed replied, his face now expressionless.

"Is it brass with a wood pedestal?"

Reed looked stunned.

"Uh, what's happening right now?" Wilder asked.

Bonnie looked at Reed, her expression full of challenge. "I'm not leaving here until I go inside that church." She headed back toward the building.

"You are not going in there!" Reed blocked her way.

"Why can't I?" she demanded. She then snatched up a rock and eyed the stained-glass window. "Either you let me in or I'll find my own way in."

"Whoa! Children! Let's de-escalate a bit before we all lose our playground privileges," Wilder said to no effect whatsoever.

Bonnie and Reed squared off, steely-eyed, neither one of them budging.

Finally… a change came over Reed's face, perhaps because he could see she was not going to be denied. He sighed and tossed her the keys.

"Make it quick," Reed said.

*   *   *   *   *

A few moments later, Bonnie stepped into the darkened church, the two boys close behind. When her eyes finally adjusted, she saw it. There at the front of the church was the mahogany baptismal font, identical to what had appeared to her in the dream! She moved toward it and stood over the brass basin, now empty, but for a single droplet of water at the bottom, a remnant of the evening mist. Bonnie hesitated, but then reached out her hand. She extended one trembling finger into the font and the instant it made contact with the water droplet, her mind was assaulted by a tumult of images.

The hand. The hourglass ring. The rope burn on the neck. The water. A scream!

"Bonnie? Bonnie!"

Bonnie heard the voices as if they were far away. Her vision slowly came into focus and she found the faces of Reed and Wilder, both staring at her, very concerned. She slumped in a pew, trembling.

"Bonnie. Can you hear me?" Reed asked. "Say something."

After a pause, she spoke.

"I've been here before… in my dreams."

And without even trying, everything came out of her, the whole story. Like a dam bursting, it came in a torrent of words in no particular order. She told them about how she'd been abandoned in a church much like this one as a baby, and about the nightmares she'd had her whole life. And of the visions she'd had since coming to the camp. She even went as far as to tell them about her birthmark, which had started showing up in her dreams.

"I'm gonna say something I've never said to anybody out loud," she said quietly, staring at her shoes. When the boys nodded assent, she continued, "I always thought that maybe the dreams weren't dreams at all, but a memory. That someone really tried to drown me before I was left in that church in Arizona. That maybe that person was my own mom."

She wiped a tear from her cheek. She cleared her throat and continued, "But now I don't know what to think. How do I explain that I've seen all this before? Unless I've actually been here before and, how could that even be possible, I… unless…" Her voice trailed off.

"I dunno," said Wilder. "There's so much whacked out about this place, nothing would surprise me at this point."

Bonnie turned to Reed. "What do *you* think? Could there be something to all this?"

Reed looked at her, and Bonnie thought she saw something in his expression. Like maybe he wanted to tell her something, something important, but instead he said…

"I think you got handed a raw deal the minute you were born. I think that'd mess with anybody's head."

Bonnie looked from Wilder to Reed and back again.

"Oh God," she moaned and covered her face. "I should never have told you guys!"

Bonnie rushed from the church, furious with herself for baring her soul to these boys, not long ago strangers! She had opened up, trusted them, and now they thought she was some little pathetic wretch of a thing. It made her feel vulnerable and weak and she HATED it.

When Wilder and Reed caught up to her, she was leaning against the side of the church, her face turned, trying to hide the fact that she was sobbing.

"Bonnie," Reed said gently, placing his hand on her shoulder.

"Don't touch me!" Bonnie pulled away from him. "I don't need your pity!"

Reed looked at Wilder, unsure what to do. For a moment, the two boys just awkwardly stood there. Finally, Wilder was the one who broke the silence.

"You know. When it comes down to it, we're all pretty f'd up. Remember when I told you about my dad being in the mob?" Bonnie didn't respond. "What I didn't tell you was that he got murdered about a year ago. Bullet to the back of the head. It was me who found him, in the trunk of his car."

Bonnie uncovered her face and looked at Wilder, who continued, "After he died, my mom, she pretty much lost it. Got really depressed. Stopped going to work. I couldn't even get her out of the apartment. She'd been in love with my dad since she was 15. And since both their families cut them off cuz they were from opposite ends of the crayon box, me and him were all she had. Mom just couldn't handle losing him," Wilder said, and Bonnie nodded. She did know about hurting. What she didn't know about was loving someone that much. She wondered if she ever would.

"A couple of months ago, she finally left the house. Went out one night and never came home. Cops don't know if she's alive or dead. I guess I just wasn't enough to stick around for…" Wilder's voice cracked as he said the last sentence.

"That is messed up," Bonnie said, her heart going out to him.

Reed had been looking at the ground throughout Wilder's confession. Finally, he spoke as well.

"Come with me," was all he said, and led them toward the back of the graveyard.

Moments later, the trio stood before one of the newer markers. Two names were engraved on it: Daniel and Caitriona Ballister, both with the same date of death. Immediately, Bonnie knew she was looking at the graves of Reed's parents.

"My mom and dad," Reed said, confirming her intuition. "They both died in battle. When I was around two. All I have of them is stories my grandparents tell me and flashes of memories. Except I don't know if the memories are real. Because you know how when you hear about something that happened to you a long time ago, you don't really know if you're remembering the thing, or just remembering the story? And my grandparents, I love them more than anything and they've given me this great life and taught me so much, but, you know, they're not *them*. They can never be them."

"Guess that makes us all orphans," Wilder said somberly after a moment of silence.

"Yeah. I guess it does," Bonnie agreed.

Bonnie looked at the two boys on either side of her and realized that they hadn't been pitying her at all. Rather, they understood her, in a way she had never been understood before. Just like her, they were all messed up; they all had gotten handed a raw deal in their lives. And in that moment, Bonnie realized another thing: that opening up to the boys didn't make her weaker. It allowed them to open up as well, and in doing so, they were telling her that they trusted her too. A word popped into Bonnie's head. Out of the blue and as strange as the night itself...

Friends.

Chapter 15
Jonesy's Lair

There was a change in the air in the days that followed Bonnie's visit to the church. It was subtle, barely perceptible unless you really took the time to notice, which most people at the Cove did not. But Bonnie noticed it. She, Wilder, and Reed had become a unit. A trio. A "clique" even. Whenever there was downtime, the three of them gravitated toward one another. They'd talk about nothing and everything. It didn't matter because it felt comfortable—a new feeling for Bonnie. In fact, once she'd "let it all out" to the boys, she hadn't had a dream or vision since. They didn't talk more about what they had shared at the church, but they didn't need to. Bonnie felt that on some level they believed her. More importantly, Bonnie believed herself. She finally knew in her mind what her gut had been telling her all along, that there was something to it all, though she didn't know what. And frankly, she didn't feel a burning desire to find out just yet. Something told her that once she did, there would be no turning back. So instead, she focused on the best part to come out of the episode for her—that Reed and Wilder understood her and accepted her, and that was enough for Bonnie.

"Any luck?" Bonnie asked Wilder as the two rummaged through a clump of brush on their hands and knees during Grandma Winnie's latest attempt to get the corsairs to commune with nature.

"Nope. The only thing I think I found is poison oak," Wilder replied, scratching his arm and eyeing a suspicious leaf.

If Blades & Daggers and C-Nav were two of Bonnie's favorite experiences, Anodyne Arts had to rank as one of her least. While she enjoyed being among the local flora, when it came right down to it, identifying plants was pretty much a thankless chore, and none of Grandma Winnie's pep talks could change that. But that's exactly what she and the rest of Boreas were stuck doing this afternoon.

"We've been at this all day!" whined Tanner, vastly overestimating the hour or so since they'd been dispatched into the woods.

"Wait, what's 'feverfew' supposed to look like again?" Micah asked Malachi, who showed him the stunning picture he had drawn and inked of the ruffled-leaf plant with its delicate white flowers, one of dozens of intricately detailed pictures in his sketchbook.

"That is some awesome drawing there, Malachi-angelo," Wilder said in appreciation.

"Yeah. He's gonna win this one for us, for sure," Barnaby excitedly agreed.

"Wilder's lame puns certainly won't," kidded Bonnie, and nudged Wilder with her elbow. Malachi handed the sketchbook to Bonnie, who flipped through the many pages of photo-like renderings of plants. "This is just… spectacular, Malachi! You don't say much with your words, but you manage to say plenty just the same, don't you?" She patted the boy's arm. Malachi didn't exactly smile, but he didn't pull away from her either.

"It's cute and all that the Jolly Dumb Giant can draw, but pretty pictures won't keep us from running errands again this Sunday," Tanner said as he followed Barnaby. "Let's just keep moving."

"Whoa!" Barnaby's voice rang out from beyond a line of trees. "Look what I found!"

The others rushed up to see. They came to a clearing where the thick underbrush had been patted down and cut away. It was some kind of encampment next to a running stream, where somebody had stacked a half dozen water buckets. A large tarp strung eight feet high between trees provided shelter from the rain and sun. There was a hammock for a bed, and apple crates served as furniture. At the center was a rock fire pit with a small pot blackened from years of use. Men's clothes hung from a clothesline, and beneath it was a large basin with a washboard.

"Hey, check it out!" called Tanner, examining a steamer trunk under the hammock. "A treasure chest!"

"Yeah, that looks *real* promising," replied Wilder, eyeing the worn chest, its brass corners tarnished, its leather straps scratched and frayed.

"Leave that alone; that stuff doesn't belong to you," warned Bonnie.

"Like that's ever stopped any of us before," Tanner sneered, jimmying the lock.

"I wonder who it *does* belong to," said Barnaby.

"It's Jonesy!" Tanner announced, pulling an old photo out of the chest.

Bonnie had never thought about where Jonesy went at night. He just seemed to show up every morning to teach his classes.

"You gotta see this stuff!" Tanner said as he sifted through the contents of the chest.

"Put it back," Bonnie said, but the others had already rushed over and she found herself curiously drawn as well.

At first glance, it was full of junk. Faded plastic flowers. Stacks of yellowed newspapers. A long-stemmed cherry wood pipe. There were some documents, too, pretty old by the looks of them. And a picture in a tarnished silver frame. In the photo was a young Jonesy on a fishing boat, smiling happily, his arm around a beautiful young woman. Bonnie noted that in the photo Jonesy still had both his eyes... *and from the clear look in them, his sobriety.*

"Oh man, look at the knobs on *her* console," Micah drooled. "Wonder who she is."

"Says here the arm candy's name is Elsie," Tanner said. "And get this, she was his wife!" He held up a marriage certificate.

"Wonder what happened to her?" Barnaby said.

"She died in a fire," Bonnie said, having pulled a death certificate from beneath the plastic flowers, "like a year after they were married... Oh my God. And she was pregnant, too." Suddenly she was ashamed at what they were doing. It was horribly wrong and she was about to say so when—

"The hell yer doin'!?"

Jonesy burst out of a thicket of trees. He practically tackled Tanner away from the box, violently ramming his shoulder into the boy's chest.

"I got so little in this world!" the old man yelled, snatching the certificate out of Bonnie's hand. "And ya have the cheek to go mucking through me personal affairs!"

He fell to his knees and collected the mess of papers and mementos that had scattered onto the ground, muttering to himself as he did, "... taking liberties with a man's belongin's—it jes' ain't right..."

Bonnie could barely watch. She knew she'd invaded the privacy of a poor, broken soul in the most obscene way she could imagine. Boreas looked at one another, not quite sure what to do next. Finally, it was Jonesy who broke the silence, speaking in a slow, deliberate voice.

"'Twas to have been a boy..." he said in almost a whisper, his one good eye fixed on the death certificate still in his hands. "They burned our house to the ground that night, they did, with nary a care 'bout the woman with child therein, filthy savages. I swore from that night, I'd never sleep under roof again."

"Is that how you lost your—" wondered Barnaby.

"Me eye?" said Jonesy, rising to his feet, and wiping the dust off his hands. No one had the nerve to look at him directly. "What's this, then? All a sudden too ashamed to look upon me now, are ya? Don't think I ain't seen yer starin' at me time to time, at this mangled hunk of flesh that passes fer me ear. At me eye— speculatin' on what lies beneath and how it come to be.

"Well, take a nice good look then." Jonesy lifted up his eyepatch, turning in a circle for all to see the scarred socket beneath, midnight black and vacant as an empty grave.

"So now yer questions be answered," he said, flipping down the eyepatch. There wasn't anger in his voice anymore. It was simply a bottomless pit of pain that Bonnie knew the old man would never climb out of.

"Well, ya all had your bloody laugh now, haven't ya?" he said with resignation. "Be off, the lot of ya." He wiped a tear from his good eye with his sleeve and knelt back down to finish putting his belongings back in order.

Boreas silently backed away, exchanging looks of mortification as they retreated into the woods. As Bonnie walked by the pile of empty liquor bottles at the edge of the camp, she turned to look at Jonesy, still slumped unmoving over the chest.

As she did, one last thought insistently popped into her mind: *If he didn't drink, he'd surely go mad...*

. . . . .

Thirty minutes later, Boreas sat huddled around the fire in the parley room, deep in conversation. Particularly, they discussed the horrifying revelation about how Jonesy had come to be disfigured and trying to figure out who exactly the "filthy savages" were that murdered his family.

"It's gotta be this 'enemy' of the Brigands we're supposed to be training to fight," Wilder concluded, supplying the air quotes with his fingers.

"Whoever the hell that is," Bonnie added.

"Who cares who it is," Tanner said. "Not like I'm ever gonna have to deal with them."

"Yeah, we know, Tanner," Bonnie sneered. "You don't give a crap about any of this. You're outta here at the end of summer. Blah, blah, blah."

"Why am I even talking to you morons?" Tanner asked himself. He rose and headed to the boys' bunk room.

"Hey, what you got there, Prescott?" Wilder said, noticing something in the pocket of Tanner's cargo shorts.

"I don't have anything," shrugged Tanner.

"Liar!" Bonnie said, blocking his way to the door. "In the pocket of your shorts. Come on. Let's see it."

"Since when are you so interested in the contents of my pants?"

"You're such a pig," she said, disgusted. "Give it."

When Tanner refused to budge, Malachi stood to Bonnie's defense and towered over him, fists clenched. Finally, Tanner backed down. "Fine. Call off your pet gorilla," he said and produced a flask of rum from the pocket and waved it in her face. "Puerto Rico's finest."

"You stole that from Jonesy!" she declared.

"It was an act of mercy," he said, changing course and heading for the sofa across from the fireplace. "The old guy's liver could use the rest." He flopped down on the sofa, opened the flask, and took a big swig.

"Ah!" he said, smiling. "Now that's what I'm talking about!"

"You take that back to Jonesy right now!" Bonnie demanded.

"Dude, don't bogart the stuff!" Micah exclaimed, grabbing for the flask. "We gotta pool our resources for the good of the crew. It's like pirate code."

Tanner reluctantly gave up the booze to Micah, who took an experienced swig.

"Yes, mama!" Micah yowled and held out the flask to his brother. But Malachi was too entranced by the roaring fire to pay much attention to the goings-on among the rest of the crew.

"Bonnie's right," said Barnaby. "Jonesy's gonna be mad when he sees it's gone."

"The guy barely knows what day it is half the time. He'll never miss it," Tanner replied, taking another gulp. He held out the flask to Barnaby.

"Don't give him that. He's just a kid," Bonnie stepped in.

"No, I'm not," Barnaby protested. "I'm almost thirteen!" He grabbed the rum and took a pull from it. He then hacked loudly from the bitter alcohol.

Tanner laughed, but then nodded in approval. "That's the Boreas spirit, Owl Eyes!"

"Pass it here," Wilder spoke up, coming to Barnaby's rescue.

"Wilder!" Bonnie said admonishingly.

"Spray Tan's right. We're doing the guy a favor." Wilder took a pull, and then he held it out to Bonnie. "Whattaya say, Curls?"

Bonnie hesitated. She'd gotten into plenty of trouble in her day, but she wasn't a drinker. She'd seen too much destruction and mayhem in her foster homes where the booze was flowing to have any interest in going down that road.

"Pass," she said.

"Of course she does," Tanner said, taking the rum back from Wilder. "She can't sleep through the night without screaming bloody murder, she's afraid of getting in the water, AND she doesn't drink. You *sure* you're not here by mistake, *Curls*?"

Bonnie hated to be goaded into doing something she didn't want to do, but her status in Boreas was on the line. She felt bad judgment, insecurity, and rage boil up in her all at once.

"Gimme that." Bonnie grabbed the flask from him.

She lifted it to her lips. The rum burned going down. Every fiber of her being wanted to gag, but she resisted. Instead, she only smiled broadly, as if she'd just drunk a glass of Grandma Winnie's sun-brewed tea.

Bonnie's grin widened and she held out the flask triumphantly. "Who's next?"

Before long, Bonnie was drunk, all thoughts of Jonesy's tragic past having been extinguished three shots ago.

Bonnie lay flat on her back and stared at the ceiling. The entire room seemed to be moving one way while her body moved the other.

"Thish rum is soooooooooooooooo delishious," Bonnie said, slurring her words. "I like this rum. I like it a lot. I think I want to marry it."

"Sorry, De Luca. Looks like Hartwright's found herself a new boyfriend," snickered Tanner, who was about two inches to Bonnie's left. Or so she surmised from the sound of his voice, although her powers of orienteering had gone out the window along with her balance about thirty minutes earlier.

"You know," Bonnie said to no one in particular, "we never *talk*. Don't you want to just talk sometimes? You know, like really *talk*?"

Micah laughed as if Bonnie had just said the funniest thing in the history of mankind.

"You're drunk," Tanner said matter-of-factly, sullenly examining a frayed thread on the sleeve of his shirt.

"So are you," Bonnie said.

"I can hold my liquor," Tanner said.

"If you could hold your liquor so well, you wouldn't've gotten into an accident with your dad's car," Bonnie said.

"Who says it was an accident?" Tanner replied, his eyes still on the errant thread.

"Wait a minute," Wilder sobered up for a moment. "You're not saying you wrecked that beautiful car *on purpose,* are you?"

"What's it matter if I did?" Tanner replied, taking the flask and going in for another gulp. "My dad's got plenty of dough anyway."

"Yeah, yeah, we know," said Micah. "He's a big, rich producer. Whoop-de-do."

Tanner stared at the flask in his hands.

"He's rich all right. He likes to buy things. Buys cars, buys friends, rents wives 'til they get sick of him, like my mom did. Thanks for the birthday card, Mom, by the way. Oh, that's right, you forgot. It's okay. Dad forgot, too. That car wreck? Ha! I coulda taken that curve in my sleep if I wanted to... only mistake I made was not finishing the job."

The corsairs looked at each other, speechless. All Tanner's defenses had dissolved into the rum. He wasn't just joyriding that night; he had actually tried to take his own life. For the first time, Bonnie didn't see him as the arrogant, pompous, spoiled ass he'd been since Day One. Instead, she saw he was just a mixed-up kid like the rest of them. Shit, like the rest of the world. Bonnie felt the urge to get up and comfort the boy, and she would have if she'd been able to move.

"BOREAS FOREVER!" Bonnie yelled in lieu of a hug.

"Hear, hear!" The others banged loudly on the nearest hard object and called out their agreement in an effort to rouse Tanner out of his funk.

"We better take it easy," Barnaby warned. "Somebody might hear us."

"And what if they doodlie do?" said Bonnie. "We're pirates, aren't we? We're supposed to get drunken from time to time, amirite?"

Bonnie pushed herself up and stood precariously in the center of the group. "You know what elsh pirates have? An earring!" She batted at her own ears to emphasize the point. "See? Like this."

Bonnie teetered a bit. "And you wanna know a secret?" she whispered conspiratorially. "Ta-daaa!" She pulled up her T-shirt to reveal a belly button ring. A tiny pearl pendant hung from Bonnie's navel. She shimmied her hips to make it move and nearly fell over.

"That is totally, totally, to-ta-lly cool!" said Micah, clapping wildly.

"I am definitely a fan of that," Wilder said with a huge grin.

"Oh hell yass," slurred Tanner, the flash of exposed midriff rousing him from his self-pity.

"Yeah. So, don't you be saying I'm here by mistake! Cuz if we go by piercings, I'm more pirate than any of you!" She pointed around the room in a circle and nearly toppled over from dizziness.

"She's got a point," Wilder agreed.

"Damn straight I do. Fact, I think it's *you* guys who need to prove to *me* you're real pirates. Every one of you needs to get a piershing!" She touched Wilder's nose. "Including you." Even in her drunken state, she felt a little electricity when her finger met Wilder's skin.

"Yeah, right. I'll get right on that next time I'm at Tiffany's," said Wilder.

"Screw that noise!" said Bonnie. "I'll give you guys a piercing for free. Right here, right now. I got enough earrings for all of ya."

"And just how are you going to do that?" Wilder asked.

Bonnie smiled slyly.

Chapter 16
An Initiation

After a daring stealth raid of Grandma Winnie's apothecary, Bonnie returned to the cabin with the requisite supplies: a needle from her sewing kit and witch hazel to prevent infection. Once Bonnie commandeered the cork from Jonesy's flask to use as a base to put behind the boys' ears, they were ready to begin.

"Okay!" Bonnie said, rubbing her hands in anticipation. "Who's my first valiant warrior?"

The room got quiet. The boys, who had been all bluster and bravado when Bonnie first suggested it, suddenly became skittish when faced with the reality of a piece of sharp metal puncturing their flesh. Wilder finally stepped forward.

"I'm 99 percent corsair, Curls," he said. "Let's make it a hundred."

Bonnie clapped gleefully. "Yay! I was hopin' it'd be you."

Bonnie wobbled over to the fire and heated the tip of the needle. Then she turned to Wilder, took his left earlobe in her hand and secured the cork behind it.

"This'll probably hurt," Bonnie warned.

"I ain't afraid," said Wilder. "Drunk and on the verge of puking, yes. Afraid, no!"

Bonnie swayed as she went in. Wilder watched with concern as the needle seemed to be headed straight for his eye. He adjusted his head and Bonnie miraculously hit her target, sinking the needle deep into Wilder's earlobe. She could feel him tense up, but he said nothing, smiling through gritted teeth.

Once Bonnie removed the needle, she wiped the blood and pulled out one of the half dozen hoops she had in her right ear. She slipped it into the fresh hole in Wilder's ear, clicking the clasp shut. Boreas erupted in a cheer.

"This is the shit!" Wilder grinned, checking his look in the mirror. With his unruly hair and tawny skin, he definitely looked the dashing pirate. Bonnie felt her cheeks flush and had to look away. "Next!"

Bonnie did the other corsairs in rapid succession, planting an earring in each of them. Barnaby was the last to go. He put on his bravest face, sat down on the floor, but as Bonnie was about to pierce him, he jumped up.

"I c-can't!" he burst into tears. "I'm sorry," Barnaby sniffled. "I guess maybe it's me who doesn't belong here."

"There's a news flash," Tanner said.

"Shut up, Tanner! It's not that you're afraid, Barnaby," Bonnie said, draping a comforting arm around his shoulder. "You're just not there yet. I didn't get my first piercing until I was 14."

This was a complete lie, but it made Barnaby feel better. Bonnie turned back to the rest of Boreas. There they were. All potential Brigands of the Compass Rose, looking very pirate-y and fierce with their fresh piercings.

"If Mary Read could see us now," Bonnie said once they all had had the chance to admire each other's earrings.

"Bet ol' Mary had her share of piercings," Wilder speculated. "And a tat or two, I'd imagine."

Wilder's comment mixed in Bonnie's head with just enough alcohol to create a cocktail of a really bad idea.

"Want to see something cool?" she asked with a sly smile.

　　　　　✦　　　✦　　　✦　　　✦　　　✦

Ten minutes later, Boreas stood silently in Ballister's dark office, lit only by the single lantern they'd brought with them.

In front of them, on the red velvet pillow in its gold and wooden box, was the relic of Mary Read's mummified hand. Bonnie had just opened the lid to reveal it in all its creepy, fascinating glory.

"Whoa. I've heard of lucky rabbits' feet," whispered Wilder. "But this is some next level superstition right here."

"Gnarly! Is that really Mary Read's hand?" asked Micah.

"Yep," Bonnie said. "Ballister showed me on the first night."

"That is disgusting AF," said Tanner, turning away to root around Ballister's liquor cabinet. "You look at it all you want. But I could use me another swallow…"

"This thing rocks!" Micah said, enjoying the gruesome view of the hand, "And look at the way it's all curled up. Like it used to be holding something."

"You're right. It definitely used to be holding something," said Barnaby.

"Probably the nadsack of some scrawny know-it-all, eh Chisolm?" said Tanner, returning to the group, a bottle of scotch now in hand.

"I wonder if it got chopped off in battle," Wilder surmised.

"More likely the Brigands removed it themselves after she died," said Barnaby, pushing his nose closer to the box.

"Get outta here," Wilder scoffed.

"I'm not kidding. Check it out." Determined to prove his point, Barnaby circled the container. "Look at the way it's been cut. And it's sewn on the end, see? Lots of tiny, perfect stitches. This is for sure a relic. And the thing it's in is called a reliquary."

"Why would they want to stare at some dead lady's hand all day?" Tanner asked, already on his third belt from the whiskey bottle.

"Actually, it was pretty common in the olden days to save the body parts of a saint or somebody for veneration."

"So there are people who went around worshiping dead guys' fingers?" Wilder asked. "And people say *our* generation's messed up!"

"Not worshiping," said Barnaby, "remembering."

"Makes sense. To remind us of our purpose," nodded Micah.

"Which we still don't know, by the way," Bonnie said, stepping back from the reliquary. "Why can't Ballister just level with us? Who killed Jonesy's wife?"

"Yeah, Barnaby, what's the deal, little man?" Wilder asked. "Your pops must've told you *something*. He's way high up in the Brigands."

"No, like I said before, i-it's not allowed. Brigands are sworn to secrecy," Barnaby explained. "We'll find out when the captain thinks we're ready."

"I think Owl Eyes knows more than he's been letting on," said Tanner.

Barnaby averted his eyes.

"He does know something!" Micah said.

Barnaby felt the eyes of the corsairs boring into him. He looked at Bonnie for support, but she seemed just as curious as everyone else. He breathed deeply. "Okay, but you got to promise not to tell ANYONE!"

The corsairs each made the most solemn oaths their alcohol-addled brains could concoct and then crowded around him. Barnaby looked over his shoulder to make sure they were still alone and then leaned forward conspiratorially.

"Remember when the captain told us about Calico Jack Rackham?" Barnaby asked.

"You mean the dude whose treachery we're supposedly fighting to this day?" Wilder asked. "That kind of little factoid is pretty hard to forget."

"What the captain didn't say was how it all went down back in the day," Barnaby said, as drunk on the newfound attention as the others were on the alcohol. "Apparently, Jack, Anne, and Mary were pirating around the Caribbean together and were wanted by the authorities. Only Anne and Mary managed to get off."

"How?" Bonnie heard herself ask.

"Anne was pregnant with Jack's baby, but for the sake of the baby, she and Mary cut a deal with the British Navy and gave up the location of their ship. That's how they caught him. Jack got hanged a few weeks later."

"Wait," Bonnie said, grasping a straw of logic that had cut through her drunken stupor, "I thought Ballister said Calico Jack was responsible for Anne Bonny's death. How can that be if *she* got *him* hung?"

"There's a curse." Barnaby finally said in such a quiet whisper that everyone had to let it sink in for a moment to make sure they'd heard it right.

"What do you mean a curse?" Wilder asked.

"I mean a curse. I heard my dad talking about it one night on the phone with the captain."

"What kind of a curse? On who?" Bonnie asked.

"I didn't hear that part."

"Awww!" the corsairs moaned in drunken disappointment. Barnaby could sense he was losing the room.

"But I did hear something else," he quickly added.

"What, Barnaby?" Bonnie asked. "What else?"

"I heard him say…" Barnaby relented, "that… Calico Jack is still alive."

A low moan escaped from Malachi, who had up until then been sitting quietly in a corner. The others were startled, having forgotten he was even there. Boreas looked around at each other in the lantern light.

"So you're saying the Brigands' enemy is… a 300-year-old pirate?" Micah asked.

Barnaby nodded seriously.

Wilder suddenly howled and practically doubled over with laughter. "Woo! You had me going there for a minute!" Wilder said, slapping Barnaby on the shoulder. "You tell a mean campfire story, Barnaby!" And then everyone joined in the laughter. Even Bonnie, whose dread evaporated.

"This isn't a story," Barnaby objected. "I heard it!"

"Sure you did," chuckled Tanner.

"A zombie pirate!" Micah said. "That's rich!"

"I propose a toast!" said Wilder, passing out shot glasses he'd secured from Ballister's bar. Once the glasses were full, he raised his own.

"To Bonnie, for these kick-ass piercings!"

"To Bonnie!" and they clinked glasses and took a sip.

"To Jonesy, for providing tonight's refreshments!"

"To Jonesy!"

"To Mary Read and her totally dope mummy hand!"

Clink!

"To Anne Bonny for putting down the scurvy dog Jack Rackham!"

Clink!

"And," Wilder said, lowering his voice to a spooky whisper, "to Calico Jack Rackham, wherever you are!"

Clink! And they laughed hysterically and downed the last of the whiskey bottle.

Interlude
Resurrection

Just outside Port Royal, Jamaica
December 1720

On a cloudy night lit by a full moon, a single spade was driven into an overgrown mound of dirt on a godforsaken spit of land along a beach. A shovelful of hardpack tossed onto a pile nearby sent dirt and bits of sand flying, carried by a wind that howled mercilessly over dozens of similar mounds along the desolate beach—unmarked graves all.

A hulking figure peered over a gaping hole in the sand.

"Are you sure this is the place, Mr. Salifu?" said the voice of a man up to his waist in the hole, his face lit by the lantern held by the other.

"Yes, the very spot, Mr. Kincaid," said Salifu, bringing the lantern closer to his shovel-wielding companion. "I saw them who buried him myself." Salifu was the same huge African man with the facial markings who'd been in attendance at the hanging of Calico Jack Rackham in Port Royal forty days earlier.

"Don't know why we're doin' this," said Kincaid nervously. "Seems mighty unholy, disturbin' his eternal rest."

"There be no rest in the hereafta for the likes of Jack Rackham— just you keep to diggin'."

Even in the darkness, Kincaid could see from Salifu's steely glare that he was not a man to be trifled with. He turned back to his shovel.

Clunk! It hit something hard. It was a plain pine coffin, wet and black with rot that had already set in. At Salifu's behest, Kincaid set to digging double-time, as the outline of the coffin became visible.

Once the coffin lid was fully exposed, Salifu reached into a bag and pulled out an ornate amulet, putting it around his neck; it was the same amulet he'd worn to the execution. He then pulled out a little leather pouch as well. From inside he grabbed a handful of white powder.

He slowly turned in a circle, whispering to the powder as he did.

"Oh dark majesty! Hear our plea… Fi oju rere wo awa iranṣẹ rẹ bi a ti nṣe iṣẹ rẹ nihin lorile Aye. Jẹ ki ẹmi rẹ ṣokalẹ s'ori wa."

He tossed the powder high into the air. It ignited into flames that floated above their heads.

As the flames danced in the air, Kincaid stared up in stunned disbelief and made the sign of the cross. "Jesus save us!"

"Your savior, he not welcome here. This be a transaction with the darker spirits."

Salifu waved his hand and the dancing flames overhead disappeared. He held his hands over the grave and moved them in circles over the coffin.

Salifu clapped his hands three times. "Jẹ ki o wa laaye! Jẹ ki ara yii wa laaye!!" chanted Salifu over and over as he circled the grave. A cloud moved in front of the moon, turning the night to pitch blackness.

"Jẹ ki o wa laaye! Jẹ ki ara yii wa laaye!!"

A gale force gust of wind came off the ocean, whipping sand into the faces of the two men.

"Jẹ ki ara yii wa laaye!! Make this body live!!!!!"

The coffin shook violently. Kincaid scrambled out of the grave just as the heavy cover of the coffin flew into the air, ripping the hinges off the wooden base. It hovered over them for a second and then catapulted itself into the ocean.

The wind stopped suddenly. There was silence.

A broad smile came to Salifu's face.

Even though every morsel of his sense was telling Kincaid not to, he peered over the edge of the grave into the coffin below. There lay Calico Jack Rackham, dead as the day he was buried. Maggots crawled all over the corpse; a good twenty were busy gnawing at his face. The flesh of his cheek had already been chewed away, and more maggots milled about in his open mouth. The face of the corpse was twisted in terror. Suddenly…

PTHEWWW!!

Maggots went flying as Jack spit them out into the air. Kincaid recoiled in horror.

"Agggh!" came a blood-curdling scream from Jack's mouth. The pirate writhed in agony, decaying limbs flailing about in the coffin that still encased his body. Salifu stepped forward and raised his hands over the grave.

"I reclaim this wicked soul for thy purposes!" he cried out with authority.

Slowly, Calico Jack sat up, the rot of his face healing as if by magic, the milky gaze of death draining, replaced with eyes fiery and black as coal. He shook his head, and shuddered, as if he'd just awakened from the worst nightmare imaginable.

Kincaid gasped, "Calico Jack lives again!"

. . . . .

Later, the moon much lower in the sky than when this dark adventure began, Calico Jack and Salifu sat before a roaring fire on the beach; the broken and fileted body of Kincaid lay face down near the grave.

Calico Jack ravenously ate meat from a spit.

"Kincaid, you say his name was?" Jack asked, his sharp teeth ripping more meat from the bone. Salifu nodded. "Well, he's helped in more ways than one this night, he has! Shame his kin will never know just how good he turned out!"

The pirate let loose a hearty laugh, which turned quickly to stone silence when he saw what the shaman had taken from his bag.

It was a ring of almost unimaginable craftsmanship.

"Is that—?" Calico Jack said, reaching out greedily, suddenly forgetting his hunger.

"The Ring of Adokan, aye, Jack Rackham, 'tis none other," Salifu said. "Just as we agreed."

Jack leaned in close, lustfully, to examine it. It was large, decorated with two golden skulls connected to an hourglass in the middle. The rubies in the skulls' eyes danced with an unholy glow in the firelight.

"Every grain in this hourglass represent a day in your life, Calico Jack Rackham. When the sand be gone, so be your days on this earth. But seein' as you've struck a bargain, here you may remain, on but one condition."

"Yes, yes," said Jack impatiently, "we've gone over all this before!" He reached for the ring, but Salifu snatched it away.

"The one condition is this; you must pay for your time here on this side of the veil with the lives of your kinfolk, your flesh and blood, the joinin' of your blood and that of the betrayer Anne Bonny. Every generation, startin' with the babe she now clutch to her breast, there be one of that generation that bear the Stain of Musangu, a mark on their body to match the blackness in your soul, Jack Rackham. Only when that of your line be drowned by your own hand does you gain the years your descendent woulda have."

"And I shall go straightaway to find that infernal betraying harlot Anne Bonny and get what be mine, the years that child does owe me!"

"No, Jack Rackham," corrected Salifu. "You must wait. Wait 'til the next marked one in the line be born. Otherwise, your line be wiped from the earth, and Darkness shall collect its debt. Your child be taken to the Carolinas by Anne Bonny and her companion. We have eyes upon them. They won't get beyond our gaze. But you must wait."

"I will abide. I will abide," Jack said.

"And if you fail, you understand the eternal price."

"I'll never go back there. Never!" Calico Jack threw a haunted glance at the gaping grave.

Salifu fixed a hard gaze upon Calico Jack. Then put the ring on the tip of Jack's middle finger. The pirate's eyes were aflame with a ravenous passion not of this earth.

"Do it! Do it!" he whispered. "Make me immortal!"

Salifu rammed the ring down the length of Rackham's bony finger. As the ring reached its destination, Jack shuddered. A sheet of lightning crashed over their heads, and rain poured from the sky. Jack kept shaking until he let out an involuntary cry.

Then his body went limp. His legs could barely hold his weight. He shook his head and gathered himself. He looked at Salifu. The African said but one thing.

"It is accomplished."

Chapter 17

The Morning After

Bonnie felt the impact of a foot introducing itself to her ribcage as she lay sleeping on the floor of the dining porch. She blinked against the excruciating morning sunlight until she could finally make out the form of Kevin Yeun standing over her.

"What happened, Hartwright?" he asked. "You guys forget to put the bread away and get invaded by ants again? So Boreas!" There was raucous laughter from the other corsairs just now arriving for breakfast, and Bonnie felt a bolt of pain shoot through her head.

She still hadn't quite grasped where she was or what was happening. She sat up and looked around to see Wilder passed out right next to her. Like literally snuggling beside her. Tanner snored on top of one of the dining tables to her left. Barnaby and the Maguires had somehow found a crocheted blanket and huddled together underneath it, dead to the world, looking as if they'd just had an audition for a multicultural commercial for baby shampoo.

"This looks like my kinda slumber party!" Luz called out. "Check out what I found!" She held up the empty whiskey bottle for all to see.

That triggered memories of the night before to pop up randomly in Bonnie's mind. She remembered Tanner stealing the rum, and the drinking, and then there was a vague recollection of something in Ballister's office, something disturbing that Barnaby had said. *But what was it?*

Bonnie looked over just in time to see Micah's eyes fly open as he bolted out from under the blanket and tore to the side of the porch, hurling a magnificent shower of vomit into the bushes below. The other corsairs laughed and cheered, and some even held up their fingers to score Micah as if he were in the Olympics competing for the gold medal in competitive puking.

"What's going on here?!" Bonnie looked up to see Reed standing over her, the empty whiskey bottle now in his hand. He stared at Bonnie and at Wilder's close proximity to her, especially at how Wilder's hand was still resting on Bonnie's hip as he slept. Bonnie immediately scooched away. This woke Wilder, who shot up and rammed his head into the edge of the nearby table.

"We, uh," Bonnie started to explain, but then realized the hole she was in with him was probably deep enough and her voice trailed off.

"We mighta done a bit of plundering last night," Wilder answered for the speechless Bonnie, rubbing his head. "It's kind of hard to remember."

"Dang, dude. What's that in your ear?!" said Daya, pushing past Yeun. "Hey, everyone! De Luca's got himself some bling!" she shouted, and the crowd moved in to take a closer look.

Wilder reached up to his ear, just now remembering that Bonnie's earring had been deposited there the night before. Bonnie groaned as it all came back to her.

"Oh," Wilder said. "I guess that happened, too."

"A bunch of us got 'em," Micah jumped in, acting as cool as the drying puke on his shirt would allow.

"Yeah. Thanks to Bonnie, we're real corsairs now," Wilder smiled at the shared memory and gave Bonnie a nudge.

Brice quickly asked if Bonnie could pierce his ear as well and others joined in on the begging.

"There'll be no more piercings!" Reed yelled, then turned back to Bonnie, his eyes boring into her. "And don't think I'm running interference for you guys with my grandfather on this one!" Reed said loudly, unleashing all his firepower on her even though he was supposedly reprimanding all of them.

"Dude, indoor voice," said Tanner who, along with Barnaby and Malachi, was just now waking up. "My head is frickin' killing me."

"Your head is gonna be the least of your problems!" Reed said deliberately loudly. "Cuz when the captain sees this—"

"Oh, I see it alright." Ballister had just arrived, Grandma Winnie right behind him. Everyone got silent as the captain took the empty bottle from Reed.

"Look at this, mother. Boreas seems to have had a bit of a frolic last night… Who's responsible for all this?"

Boreas was silent. Bonnie looked at Tanner, who was clearly not going to fess up to his part in their escapades.

"It was me," Bonnie finally spoke up. "I take full responsibility."

Bonnie braced herself for the worst. Ballister scratched his whiskers. Finally, he reached into his pocket and produced some coins.

"Fifteen pieces of eight for Boreas!" he proclaimed.

"You're *rewarding* them?!" Reed was stunned. Boreas was stunned too. They had never won fifteen coins for anything all summer.

"Aye. For coming together so splendidly as a crew. And the first to do so, as well!" Ballister explained, "Are the rest of you paying attention? This kind o' bonding is what I've been talking about all summer!" And he placed a handful of coins in Bonnie's palm.

"We're not in last place anymore!" marveled Barnaby, now wide awake and doing the math in his head.

Boreas expressed as much excitement as they could with their still throbbing hangovers.

"And," Ballister held up a hand as a hush fell over the crew, "for being out of your cabins after lights out, minus two coins!" Ballister held out his hand to Bonnie, who reluctantly gave back two of the coins. He then continued, "*And*, for unauthorized use of Grandma Winnie's medical supplies, I'll be needing three pieces of eight." Boreas looked at one other, surprised that Ballister knew about that one.

"You all may prove excellent corsairs, but you're a sorry bunch of burglars," Winnie said. "The apothecary was a fright this morning." Bonnie counted out three more pieces of eight into the captain's hand.

It didn't end there. "*And*," Ballister continued, "for breaking into the main house and entering my private study, another five coins. *And finally*, there need be a deduction for your partaking of the spirits, which has been the ruin of many a fine corsair… TEN pieces of eight."

"Wait a minute," said Micah. "That puts us…"

"Five coins down from when we started," Barnaby said glumly. Groans all around.

"Imagine that!" Ballister remarked. And the other crews burst out laughing. "Now, we've a very long, very hot day ahead of us. So eat your breakfast, those of you who can, and meet on the beach in thirty minutes." The captain smiled and headed back into the house toward his office. Reed followed him, without so much as a look at Bonnie as he passed.

As the other crews followed Winnie into the kitchen to be served, Boreas just sat, trying not to puke from the smell of food or from the heat that was already on its way to sweltering.

"Well," said Wilder, "that kinda blew chow, didn't it?"

"Kind of?!" groused Tanner. "It means we're freaking marooners this week… again!"

"We were already gonna be marooners, Tanner," Micah said, still holding his throbbing head in his hands.

"Look on the bright side," Barnaby piped up with an enthusiasm that could only come from someone who hadn't gotten completely wrecked the night before. "We're a crew now!

Shipmates! Buddies! Amirite?" He emphasized his point by putting his hand familiarly on Tanner's shoulder.

"Screw off," Tanner said, jerking away. "I'm not your freaking buddy."

"But we got pierced. We had an adventure. We shared feelings—"

"*You* shared feelings. I got wasted and talked some shit that *you* were stupid enough to believe."

"Whoa, Tanner. Chill," Bonnie said.

"Look. If you're worried about us saying anything—" Barnaby started.

"I said it was bullshit!" Tanner spit. "So shut the hell up about it, you little wuss!" And he shoved Barnaby, causing him to fall onto the porch.

"What the hell, Tanner!" Bonnie interceded.

"Relax, dude. No harm. No foul," Wilder added. "We were drunk."

Bonnie shook her head and stared at Tanner. The vulnerable boy from the night before who only longed for connection with his dad had completely evaporated. She helped Barnaby up,

"And to think I actually felt sorry for you last night," Bonnie said to Tanner.

"*You,* pity *me*? More like the other way around, *foster girl,*" Tanner hissed.

Bonnie felt the heat rise in her face. It was the first time anyone had called her that since she arrived. She was surprised by how much the label still stung.

Tanner wasn't done. "And I'm not in your little pussy sorority, ok? So you can have your damn pledge pin back." He pulled the earring out of his ear, threw it to the ground and crushed it.

That was it. Bonnie snapped. She lunged at him with all her might, sending her shoulder into Tanner's stomach. It knocked the wind out of him and sent him flying.

A crowd quickly gathered. "Fight! Fight!"

Bonnie started pummeling Tanner, but he was blocking the punches with his arms.

"Crazy bitch! Get her off of me!" Tanner screamed.

"Hey! Stop it!" Reed came running.

Ultimately, it took both Wilder and Reed to pull them apart, but Bonnie still kicked at Tanner as they dragged her away.

"By the wounds of Magellan, that's enough!" cried Captain Ballister, finally arriving at the fight. He shook his head. "Well now, looks like the Boreas camaraderie was not long for this world," he said.

"Is that all you're going to say?" Tanner whined. "That frickin' psycho attacked me!"

"Not at all, Mister Prescott," replied the captain. "It's time we settled this once and for all. Mistress Hartwright, Mister Prescott, gather your wits together. We reconvene in the barn in ten minutes to resolve this the corsair way…"

Bonnie was shocked. "You mean..?"

"Aye," Ballister replied. "With a blade."

A cheer went up from the others.

It. Was. On.

Chapter 18
A Battle for Supremacy

Ten minutes later, Bonnie stood in the barn clutching her sword, Siobhan. Across from her, a seething Tanner squeezed the hilt of his ruby-handled rapier. They were surrounded by their fellow corsairs who'd crowded in to witness the match.

Bonnie had known this day would come; it was inevitable from the moment the supposedly infallible Compass of Moirai sentenced them to the same crew. She blinked and took a deep breath, willing her pounding hangover away so she could focus on the task at hand.

"Protect your left side," Wilder coached Bonnie as he fastened her heavy leather vest. "He favors that direction."

Bonnie nodded. She wasn't worried about getting hurt. Her protective padding would see to that. No, her concern was far more profound than physical injury. This was a fight for the very heart and soul of Boreas.

"We are here to irrevocably conclude the disputes between these two corsairs," Captain Ballister proclaimed from the middle of the mock deck. "I expect all enmity to end here within these walls. The first corsair to disarm their opponent will be declared the winner. Prepare for battle." He then stepped back into the crowd of onlookers.

Bonnie and Tanner brought up their blades. The crowd went crazy. Though most of the corsairs seemed in Bonnie's corner, Tanner too had his share of supporters among the onlookers.

"You got this, Curls," Wilder encouraged, making the final adjustments to her padding.

"Be careful!" warned Barnaby.

"Commence aggressions!" Ballister commanded.

Bonnie and Tanner circled each other, looking for an opening. Ballister had earlier explained the rules of engagement: strikes to anything but protected areas were forbidden and would result in disqualification. Wicked Pete served as referee and held a long pole to separate the fighters if necessary. Grandma Winnie stood by with her medical bag at the ready and Jonesy hovered nearby as well.

As she circled her opponent, Bonnie glanced over at Reed, hoping maybe he'd give her a nod of support. Her heart sank a little when he deliberately avoided eye contact. That little break in concentration was all the distraction Tanner Prescott needed. He sprang into action, swinging his blade savagely right to left! Bonnie retreated, backpedaling and deflecting Tanner's sword as she gave ground.

"Damn, he's good!" Micah marveled.

"Using the Antonelli Lunge right out of the box," Ballister said to himself. "Clever opening."

Bonnie finally took refuge behind the giant mast in the middle of the deck as Tanner acknowledged the cheers of his partisans.

Tanner turned back around, his sword at the ready.

Bonnie advanced with her sword held high. Tanner pointed his blade at her chest as she approached.

Crash! Bonnie slashed at Tanner, who parried the blow.

"Nice block, Tanner!" yelled Stevie Ray.

She swung again. Another perfect parry!

Bonnie planted her foot and spun around, her blade whizzing through the air.

"The Diluvian Whirl," Captain Ballister remarked to Grandma Winnie. "Lesson Three."

Bonnie's sword headed straight for its target when… Clang! Tanner did a spin of his own and blocked the move with the tip of his weapon, sending Bonnie's sword violently whipping back over her shoulder. She winced in pain as she struggled to maintain her grip on the hilt, knowing that the second the sword hit the ground, the match would be over.

Bonnie regained her balance, and she and Tanner began to circle each other again. She knew her only hope was to corner him in a place where she could press her advantage.

She looked for an opening in her opponent's defense. Tanner decided to break the standoff and advanced first.

He swung at Bonnie with an overhand swing.

Parry!

He swung again with a backhand toward Bonnie's shoulder.

Deflection!

Bonnie countered the blows and advanced herself, starting an offensive of her own. And as she did, the low hum she'd become accustomed to hearing from the sword grew richer, more harmonious. Though she knew no one else could hear it, it strengthened her as she swung at Tanner with growing confidence and precision.

Tanner blocked the first two of Bonnie's strikes, but only just barely.

"Come on, Bonnie!" Reed shouted, then caught himself, remembering he was still upset with her.

Tanner swung his blade wildly now as he advanced, but Bonnie was in a groove of her own. She ducked and the blade zipped over her head, lodging itself in the wood of the mast.

"Hey Tanner! We got plenty of firewood in the cabin!" yelled Wilder.

Bonnie barrel rolled out of the fight zone as Tanner yanked his sword from the mast.

"I can't watch!" winced Barnaby as he buried his face into Malachi's enormous chest.

"She's doin' all right," said Wilder. "She's figuring him out."

"She better do it quick," said Micah. "Tanner's getting mad."

Indeed, Tanner Prescott marched forward full of piss and vinegar. Slash from the left! Slash from the right! Thrust straight toward Bonnie!

"The Wiederhold Gambit," said Ballister, nodding. "Classic."

"He's totally exposed! Get him Bonnie!" yelled Wilder.

Bonnie saw the opening. She dropped to her knees and let Tanner's blade sail harmlessly over her head. She swung at Tanner's breastplate with a backhand strike and felt the vibration of the satisfying whack of steel to leather.

"Ahhh! Dammit!" screamed Tanner.

Cheers from Bonnie's side!

Bonnie tossed her sword from hand to hand in anticipation of Tanner's next advance.

And advance he did. The fury he'd shown before was just overture to this new flurry of thrusts and slashes. Steel striking steel!

Bonnie retreated. Desperate parries! No counterattacks possible!

And she was backed up against the mast. Tanner had cornered her in exactly the same way she'd wanted to corner him.

"She's a goner," said Micah, shaking his head.

She'd stuck her foot in it, for sure. Bonnie's desperation grew as she fended off thrust after thrust from Tanner. Siobhan's blade crashed against the hard steel of the rapier as she fought for survival.

Then it came to her. An inspiration at the moment she needed it most.

She dodged Tanner's sword and pulled her own sword up toward Tanner's blade in a sweeping backhand motion, throwing Tanner off balance.

"Holy—!" gasped Reed. "The Palermo Maneuver!"

Bonnie now had the advantage. With Tanner on his back foot, Bonnie was able to hack back at him and start a counterattack of her own.

"Impressive," commented Ballister. "You've taught her well, Reed."

Bonnie's blade was barely visible in the blizzard of metal that she was unleashing on Tanner.

"Grandfather, that's just it," replied Reed. "I haven't taught the Palermo Maneuver yet! She just... *knew* it."

Ballister and Grandma Winnie exchanged a quick look at this news.

Tanner had lost all advantage. Now he was the desperate one. Bonnie lashed blow upon blow on him, using techniques that came to her out of nowhere.

Fifteen years of life kicking Bonnie in the teeth began spewing forth with every strike. Every last bit of it coursed through her veins and came out of Siobhan, which was by now just an extension of her own body. And oh, how Siobhan sang! Glorious harmonies only she could hear.

Tanner was helpless against it. He made one last desperate maneuver with his sword, but Bonnie slapped at it as if she were slapping the hand of a child who wanted an extra cookie. Tanner's sword went flying from his hand.

"What happened?" said Barnaby, finally able to pry himself out of Malachi's T-shirt.

"Bonnie just kicked some major ass!" Wilder replied, whistling and hooting all the while.

Tanner cowered on the wooden deck, utterly helpless.

Bonnie lowered her sword until it was an inch from Tanner's throat. Every impulse in her was screaming, "Do it!" Tanner stared at the sword, wide-eyed.

Everyone went silent as they watched the motionless Bonnie, her jaw clenched, her nostrils flaring, her eyes wild and dangerous.

It was Ballister who finally came to her. He gently put his hand on hers. "It's over, child. You can put the sword down now."

Breathing hard, blood pounding in her temples, Bonnie had to muster all her inner strength to force herself to stand down. She finally dropped Siobhan on the deck and turned around as the barn erupted in cheers over the clanking of the blade on the wooden floor.

"Match to Mistress Hartwright!" Wicked Pete called out.

Captain Ballister marveled, "Amazing. Simply amazing."

Tanner lay on the floor of the barn, humiliated. Bonnie walked slowly back toward her crew, fully aware of how close she'd come to something really, really awful. Wilder came to her first; he gave her a warm embrace, and her tension started to recede. Soon, all of Boreas got in on the congratulations. Even Reed gave her a hug.

In the midst of the celebration, nobody noticed Tanner get off the deck. Nobody saw him retrieve his sword. And nobody witnessed him approaching Bonnie, whose back was turned.

Nobody noticed, that is, until Bonnie felt the cold steel of Tanner's blade rip into her shoulder just beyond the protection of her vest. She screamed in pain.

Blood had been spilled at last.

Chapter 19
A Late-Night Rendezvous

Bonnie stood before Winnie in her apothecary, the stab wound from Tanner's blade still bleeding from her shoulder. "It's nothing. Really," she said.

"It's deep and if I don't stitch it properly, it'll get infected. Now, take off that shirt and let me look at that shoulder," Winnie said.

Bonnie hesitated to let Grandma Winnie stitch her wound because it was so close to her birthmark.

"Not to worry," Winnie assured her, misunderstanding her hesitance. "I've got a numbing salve of arnica and black cohosh; you won't feel a thing."

The determined look on the old woman's face told Bonnie that this wasn't a battle she would win. So, she did as she was told, pulling off her T-shirt and taking a seat on the stool in front of her.

"I'm going to need you to hold your hair to the side whilst I do this," Winnie said. Bonnie pulled her hair over to the side, revealing the mark on her shoulder blade. The distinct hitch in Grandma Winnie's breathing told Bonnie that she had seen it. She braced herself, expecting the old woman to comment on it.

But Winnie said nothing. Instead, Bonnie could feel the cold needle enter her flesh. True to the old woman's word, the herb anesthetic almost completely deadened the pain.

"You know," Winnie said, pulling the stitch, "you really oughtn't to have turned your back on that boy."

"That was a dirty move Tanner pulled!" Bonnie objected.

"Child, did you *really* trust Tanner Prescott to suddenly become a man of honor?"

"So it's my fault?" Bonnie was annoyed that Winnie seemed to think *she* was to blame for getting hurt, and not the jerk who'd done it.

"It's not about blaming anyone. It's about learning who to trust, and who not to."

"And how am I supposed to know who they are, if nobody will even tell us the reason we're here? Unless, maybe, you can tell me?"

Bonnie cocked her head back hopefully. Winnie was still a moment as if she were considering it.

"It's not my place to tell," she said finally, pulling another stitch. "These Brigands, they have their way of things." There was an edge of bitterness in her voice.

"Wait. You mean, you're not… a Brigand yourself?" Bonnie asked.

"Nay," Winnie said. "I was just another wide-eyed girl at the Highcross Spring Social until I caught the captain's eye. But in these fifty-three years since, I've certainly been schooled in the Brigand life, only too harshly at times," she said sadly and Bonnie knew she was talking about Reed's father Daniel.

Bonnie felt Winnie's warm fingertips touch the birthmark, ever so gently. They lingered the briefest moment and then she pulled away, patting Bonnie's shoulder.

"There you are. Right as rain," her voice now lilting and pleased. "Oooh. There's even going to be a scar."

"Uh. And that's a good thing?" Bonnie asked as she pulled her shirt back on.

"Every scar, *every mark*, has a story to tell, child, not only to the world, but to yourself," Winnie replied. "That too is something you'll learn ere long."

.   .   .   .   .

By the time Bonnie finally joined the other corsairs, they were already three experiences into the day. And that day proved to be a particularly trying one, as the excitement of the sword fight in the barn did little to lessen the throbbing headaches that pressed down on Boreas like a bag of barbells. Immediately after the fight, there had been talk of sending Tanner home right then and there. But in the end, Captain Ballister decided that the greater punishment lay in making him stay, so he announced that the boy would be peeling potatoes every night for the rest of the summer, and left it at that.

Both Tanner and Bonnie did a good job of ignoring each other for the rest of the day, but no one else could ignore what had happened in the barn. All day long, Bonnie was inundated with fist bumps and attagirls from the corsairs who'd witnessed her virtuosity with the blade. But as delicious as it was to see Tanner humiliated in the eyes of the others, those matters were not what occupied Bonnie's mind as the day wore on.

Instead, she kept thinking about what Winnie had said in the apothecary about having to learn who to trust. That had always been easy for Bonnie. Most of her life, she simply chose to trust no one. But that had changed since she came to the Cove. She began opening up in little increments. She felt she *was* getting better at knowing who to trust and who not to trust. And one person she knew in her heart she could trust was Reed Ballister.

Only at the moment, he wasn't talking to her. After the swordfight, he had reverted to the sullen and evasive behavior he'd shown when finding her passed out on the porch. She tried to talk to him several times, but he kept avoiding her. It took her a while to realize that Reed wasn't acting mad, but was in fact acting hurt.

And once she figured that out, it wasn't a stretch for Bonnie to figure out why. And she decided she needed to remedy it right away.

So, after lights out, Bonnie sneaked up to the main house, where she now stood in the bushes waiting, watching Captain Ballister on the porch, taking the last few draws on his evening pipe. When Ballister finally retired to his room, Bonnie sprang into action. She climbed the trellis to the upper porch and quietly rapped on the doors she knew led to Reed's room. After a moment, the door opened. Reed stood there, in pajama bottoms and no shirt, his eyes heavy with sleep, his hair disheveled.

"Bonnie. What are you doing here?" he whispered in a voice that Bonnie couldn't quite decipher.

"I was in the neighborhood, thought I'd drop by," she said, attempting humor and doing everything in her power not to look directly at what was most definitely a six-pack of well-defined muscle.

"You're supposed to be in your cabin."

"Well, it's been established that I am not always where I'm supposed to be," Bonnie said, then asked, "So… Are you gonna ask me in or what?"

"You know I'm not supposed to," he said.

"Right. And it's been established you *always* do what you're supposed to," Bonnie said teasingly, a half-smile on her ruby lips. Reed hesitated, torn between wanting to let her in and knowing better.

The choice was made for him when they heard someone stumbling up the path below. It was a drunken Jonesy. Reed pulled her in, quickly closing the door behind them. He put a finger to his lips, and they were silent until they heard Jonesy's footsteps cross the porch and fade away.

"That was close," she whispered. "Thanks."

"How's the shoulder?" Reed asked perfunctorily as he stepped back from her.

"Better… I don't think I'll be entering any shotput competitions any time soon, but other than that…"

"What do you want, Bonnie?" Reed asked more pointedly, moving a less intimate distance from her over to a bedside table, where he turned on a desk lamp. Bonnie blinked. After living so long by the light of oil lanterns, the brightness of the electric light seemed odd to her, disconcerting.

"I came to apologize," she said as she slowly walked around, taking in the bedroom. She had always been curious about his room, but like Ballister's office the private quarters were off limits to the corsairs. Now that she was in Reed's inner sanctum, she couldn't help but drink it in. His shelves were lined with books about sailing and weaponry and history… and the history of sailing and weaponry, with one shelf devoted solely to about two dozen leather-bound black books which bore handwritten labels with dates in ten-year increments starting with 1746-1755.

Above the desk was a world map from which protruded fifty or sixty stick pins in various locations: the Horn of Africa, Belize, the Florida Keys, to name a few. Above the map was a handwritten label: "CONFIRMED SIGHTINGS" it read. On top of the desk was a serious computer set-up with three separate monitors, the only distinctly teenage boy things in the room. Next to the keyboard was another leather-bound book in which were pasted news clippings, with current headlines about distressing issues like "Blood Diamonds" and "Human Trafficking." Notes in Reed's handwriting were scrawled in the margins. She moved in to make out what they said, but Reed quickly closed the book, startling her back to the present.

"I said, apologize for what?" Reed repeated a question she had obviously tuned out.

"Oh… about last night," Bonnie said as she picked up a framed photograph of a beautiful strawberry blonde woman and a handsome auburn-haired man standing at the helm of the *North*, "Are these your parents?"

"Yes," he said.

"You look like your dad. Same serious expression."

"Look. I appreciate you coming," he said, taking the photo and returning it to his desk. "But you don't have anything to apologize for. My grandfather obviously didn't have a problem with your little bonding adventure. He and I don't see eye to eye about a lot of things. Nothing for you to be sorry about."

"That's not why I'm here," Bonnie said, turning to look at him. "We should have included you... *I* should have," she said sincerely. "I'm sorry."

"That's ridiculous. I'm your teacher," he said with absolutely zero conviction.

"You're more than my teacher. You're my friend," Bonnie said as she reached out and took his hand. "And I haven't had many of those in my life."

Reed didn't say anything. Nor did he remove his hand from hers.

"And, as one of the very few members of the super exclusive Bonnie Hartwright inner circle, you must be initiated." Bonnie produced from her pocket a folded bandana. She opened it and revealed her makeshift ear-piercing kit. Reed looked at her.

*   *   *   *   *

A couple of minutes later, Bonnie sat across from Reed on his bed, "disinfecting" the needle with a match.

"I don't know about this," Reed said.

"Come on. Everyone knows any decent pirate has an earring," Bonnie replied. "I can't believe you haven't got one already."

Reed shrugged. "I guess I feel like I haven't earned one yet," he said.

"What are you talking about?" Bonnie replied. "I've seen what you do around here. You practically keep this whole place running all by yourself. Nobody's more pirate than you."

"Maybe," Reed said, and Bonnie caught a secret smile at the compliment.

"Not maybe. *Absolutely*. Now brace yourself," she said, "Cuz being a pirate hurts sometimes." And she went in for the kill.

"I think I can handle a little needle—OW?!" he yelled as she pushed the needle into his lobe.

"Shush!" Bonnie warned, and they sat quietly for a moment to make sure nobody had heard them. Once they knew they were safe, she removed a two-inch hoop earring from her ear. It was one of her favorites, so parting with it was a little painful. But she knew this earring was the only one worthy of being worn by Reed Ballister.

"Okay," she said, "here we go." She slowly stuck the post of the earring through the hole in Reed's lobe. There was a little blood, but it entered the ear clean and came out the other side. Bonnie squeezed it to clip it closed.

"It stings!" Reed said in a hoarse whisper.

"Big baby. Here… let me blow on it," she laughed and began blowing on his ear. At first it was purely medicinal. But then Bonnie became aware of his closeness. So close she felt the heat radiate from his cheek onto hers. Saw the flush of it in the lamplight and became aware of the flush of her own. She realized her shoulder was leaning into his bare chest and his body felt strong, safe and warm. Very, very warm.

She glanced to the side, followed the strong line of his jaw, then looked up to see that he was looking at her. Her heart skipped a beat. He had fixed her with those intense gray eyes that were so deep and dreamy she felt in terrible danger of falling into them forever.

She slowly turned to face him. Her lips millimeters from his. His breath hot on hers. She felt a pull, ancient and primal, drawing her to him.

"Bonnie," Reed said, suddenly pulling back, "you should get some sleep. You didn't get a whole lot of that last night as it is."

"Right," Bonnie said flustered, at once grateful and a little hurt that he had backed off. "You are so right. I'm super tired. I mean last night was, wow, yeah, I didn't get a lot of rest. So, yeah, I definitely need to get some sleep."

She collected her supplies and got to her feet. She opened the French doors.

"Bonnie…" Reed said and she turned. "Thanks for including me."

She playfully flicked his earring as her handiwork reflected the lamplight. "It suits you… Cabin Boy," Bonnie pronounced, and smiling, she quietly closed the doors behind her.

Chapter 20
A Mysterious Visitor

Bonnie's heart was racing. And it wasn't from the fifteen-foot drop from the porch to the ground that she'd just made. No, it was the close encounter she'd just had with Reed in his bedroom. *Dumb, dumb, dumb*, she scolded herself. Wiping the dirt from the hand she had used to steady herself when she landed, Bonnie was about to resolve to never, ever let stupid teen hormones and emotions get the better of her again, when she saw it.

Down the gravel drive by the entrance gate was the sudden glare of the headlights of a large SUV. They flashed twice in rapid succession, then the lights disappeared. Bonnie knew that she couldn't just let a mysterious late-night caller come and go without doing a little sleuthing.

Moving toward the gate, Bonnie could just make out the unmistakable silhouette of Grandma Winnie greeting an unknown man who emerged from the vehicle. The locked gate was between them as they became involved in conversation. But Bonnie was too far away to see who the visitor was or to hear what they were saying. So she got closer.

The moon was obscured by the trees, so as long as Bonnie stayed out of the moonlight, she could approach without detection. Taking refuge behind a large sycamore tree about twenty feet from the SUV, she noted the telltale light bar of a police vehicle on the roof. She still couldn't see who the man was, but she could now make out the conversation he was having with Winnie.

"You shouldn't have come here," said Winnie in a hushed voice that could not hide its annoyance.

"I came to warn you," Bonnie heard the man say. She immediately recognized his deep Southern drawl. She'd heard it before, at the Highcross farmers' market. It belonged to the sheriff who'd been so kind to them. But she also remembered the weird vibe she had gotten from him.

"Just got out of the council meeting," he continued. "Uncle Charley called an emergency session. They're talking about getting a search warrant for the Cove. Judge Murdock is locked and loaded to sign. They're just itching for a reason to pull the trigger."

"And thus has it ever been," Grandma Winnie replied. "You could have sent me a postcard in 1998 and accomplished the same purpose... Look, Robert, we both know the real reason you're here."

Bonnie could see the sheriff shift from one foot to another in the silence that followed.

"Interesting group of kids you got on the Cove this year," he finally said.

"And I'm going to stop you right there. I wish I could help you, but you know the lay of the land as well as I—"

"What in the name of Sir Francis Drake are YOU doing here?!"

Bonnie whipped her head around and there stood Captain Ballister, peering in her direction with a lantern in his hand. She was busted!

But then she watched in amazement as the old captain marched right past her without so much as a glance in her direction. He hadn't seen her after all! The captain continued on toward the gate with a head full of steam. "Calm down, Eleazer," said Winnie as he arrived at the gate.

"I've told you, Mr. Maynard, that you were never to set foot on this cove!"

"I think I got a right," Maynard said.

"Any right you had, you lost a long time ago. Now, I am giving you ten seconds to turn that vehicle back toward Highcross or you and I will settle this with a blade!"

"Eleazer!"

Bobby said nothing at first. Then finally, he put his hat back on and tipped it to Mrs. Ballister.

"Grandma Winnie, my apologies for keeping you out so late," he nodded. "Captain… this isn't over." He got into the SUV without another word. Five seconds later, he was disappearing back up the dirt road.

Captain Ballister stormed back toward the house and Winnie followed, calling after him. "Even if you believe Bobby doesn't have a right, the girl certainly does!"

"Not a word of this to Mistress Hartwright!"

What?!

Bonnie's knees felt weak for a moment at the sound of her name and she had to steady herself against the trunk of the sycamore.

What in the world did *she* have to do with any of this?

.   .   .   .   .

The encounter at the gate gnawed at Bonnie all the next morning, so much so that she brought it up to Reed that afternoon at lunch.

"So, I saw the weirdest thing when I was coming back from your room last night."

"Whoa!" Wilder's ears perked up. "*Room*? You were in his room last night?!"

"What'd you see?" asked Reed, completely ignoring Wilder.

"Well, I saw headlights over by the main gate. So I went to check it out. That sheriff guy, Maynard or whatever, was talking to Grandma Winnie. This was like 1:00 a.m."

"Hold the phone. You were in Cabin Boy's room at one o'clock *in the morning?*"

"Did they see you?" Reed asked, suddenly concerned.

"Uh, excuse me, what exactly were you doing in his room at 1:00 a.m.?" Wilder asked, insistent.

"No, I was careful," Bonnie answered Reed. "But I heard what they were saying. The sheriff was warning Grandma Winnie about what that Charley Eden and the council were up to. That's when the captain showed up, and man was he *pissed* that the Sheriff was there."

"It's weird he came out here in the middle of the night. But it's no secret around here my grandfather hates him."

"Dude. What's that in your ear?" Bonnie and Reed both turned to Wilder, who had been staring in the direction of Reed's earlobe.

"If you must know, I pierced his ear last night." Bonnie was irritated. "Now don't be such a dweeb about it." She turned her attention back to Reed. "Why does your grandfather hate him so much? It seems like he's just trying to help. It's weird."

"Also weird that nobody mentioned this little after-hours party before now," Wilder mumbled under his breath.

"Wilder! Shut up! I'm trying to figure this out here. Reed? Thoughts?" Bonnie turned to Reed, who had just put down his fork with some portent, and looked over his shoulder to see that their conversation wasn't being overheard.

"Okay," Reed said, lowering his voice. "I'm not supposed to tell you this, so don't tell anybody, especially my grandparents."

"Cross my heart," Bonnie said, leaning forward conspiratorially.

"Sheriff Maynard used to be a Brigand."

"Whoa! Plot twist! What happened?" Wilder asked, returning to Planet Earth for a moment. "I thought joining the Brigands was like a lifetime deal, like when swans mate or you marry an Italian chick."

"Usually it is, but sometimes corsairs just aren't cut out for this kind of life. The way Grandfather tells it, he had great hopes for Sheriff Maynard, but he just up and quit after the induction ceremony, ended up being a cop instead."

"Maybe he preferred the exciting life of busting keg parties and writing parking tickets," offered Wilder.

"I don't know," shrugged Reed. "But Grandpa just won't let it go."

"That makes what happened next even weirder," said Bonnie, still puzzling over the odd encounter. "When the captain was walking back to the house with Grandma Winnie, he said something about not telling *me* about the whole thing," she added, saving the juiciest bit of information for last.

"Are you sure that's what he said?" Reed asked.

"'Not a word of this to Mistress Hartwright,' that's what he said."

"Why would he say that?" Wilder wondered aloud. "Why should you care about it?"

"Yeah, Reed. Why should I care?" Bonnie gave him a scrutinizing look.

Reed looked deep in thought, like he was trying to put together the pieces of a really confusing riddle. Bonnie thought for a moment that Reed had come up with the answer, but ultimately he just shook his head. "I-I'm not sure." And she believed him.

In the end, Bonnie came away with more questions than answers and it frustrated her terribly. The answers would come soon enough, but for now, there was only uncertainty and a gnawing feeling that something about the young sheriff was... off.

Chapter 21
The Triquetra Challenge

Whatever questions remained about what Bonnie had overheard had to be set aside, for the very next day was the day they had all been buzzing about since the beginning of summer: Origination Day, the commemoration of the day Mary Read had founded the group so long ago. It was to be celebrated with a mystery challenge, followed by a huge bonfire and party down at the beach. More importantly, it marked the end of their first phase of training, which meant they would soon announce the cuts. To Bonnie, the day felt an odd combination of great excitement and profound dread.

When they reported to the dock after breakfast as instructed, they found Captain Ballister, with Reed at his side holding an intriguing velvet bag.

"Corsairs! *Maidin mhaith*!" Ballister greeted them, a gleeful twinkle in his eye. "Welcome! Welcome! As you know, today is Origination Day. A day that symbolizes a beginning and, for some, an end."

The crews looked around and Bonnie knew they were all wondering who would be left standing after this day. She, for one, did not hold out hope for her own crew.

"In honor of this auspicious day, and as a last opportunity for some of you to redeem yourselves, you will embark on one final challenge. An age-old experience which your forebears have participated in for three centuries: the Triquetra Challenge!"

On cue, Reed reached into the velvet bag and pulled from it a beautiful golden disc.

"Behold the Triquetra Star Taker!" Ballister took the disc from Reed and turned in a circle so that all could see the intricate celestial designs engraved upon its face. The crews stared in awe as it reflected the sunlight.

It was an astrolabe, what the Brigands called a "star taker." They had learned of such devices in C-Nav—it was an early navigational instrument that was a handheld model of the constellations. This particular one, according to Ballister, had belonged to the O.G. pirate himself, Sir Francis Drake, who had used it to circumnavigate the globe in the 1570s, collecting glory for his queen and booty for himself along the way. In the ensuing centuries, it had guided generations of sailors to the ends of the world and back home again.

"Mary Read liberated this priceless treasure from its previous owner back in her plundering days," Ballister explained as the kids crowded around him for closer inspection. "When her dear friend Anne Bonny passed," he turned it over to reveal the reverse side, "Mary had it engraved with this triquetra in the Irishwoman's honor."

The corsairs knew exactly what a triquetra was; Wicked Pete had spoken of it often. It was the Celtic interlaced circle representing the sailor's trinity of sky, wind, and sea.

"The winners of today's Triquetra Challenge will have the honor of displaying this precious disc in their cabin for the remainder of the summer," Ballister announced to a general murmur of great excitement.

"Wait. How can that be if some of us are getting sent home soon?" asked Daya.

"Because, Mistress Cepeda, in addition to that honor," the captain added with great flourish, "the victorious crew will also be granted unlimited immunity from the upcoming cuts."

A roar burst forth from the crews!

Immunity. Bonnie's heart soared at the thought. She wanted so badly to stay.

"So what's the challenge?" Yeun shouted over the hubbub and the other corsairs all joined him in asking excitedly.

The captain walked down the dock to where the smaller cutter the *Solstice Skye* was moored just beyond the *True North*. "This year's Triquetra Challenge is simple, but it will test your mettle as men and women of the sea. Each crew must sail this cutter out into the ocean, well beyond the safe waters of the cove. There, if you navigate correctly, you'll find Mr. Jones, who'll be waiting in a dinghy, tethered to a buoy. He'll have for you a flag emblazoned with your crew emblem. Your job is to retrieve that flag, run it up the mast, and as quickly as possible, make your way back home again… here to the dock. The crew that completes the challenge the fastest will win this glorious prize and all privileges which accompany it."

With that, Bonnie's heart sank. Boreas was a shambles of a crew. Any semblance of unity had evaporated with Tanner's act of cowardice after the sword fight. The chances of their completing the task *at all*, much less faster than the others, seemed remote at best.

"Remember, there is no strength without unity! You're a crew. Behave like one," Ballister said, putting his hand on Bonnie's shoulder for emphasis. "Choose your captain carefully, and divide your responsibilities accordingly. The races begin in two minutes!" Crews had already started buzzing with strategy, so that Ballister needed to shout his last words above them.

The looks Boreas exchanged with one another fell somewhere between sheer panic and utter hopelessness. Finally, Tanner spoke up, "Okay, De Luca, you got the wheel; the Maguires are my trimmers, Chisolm—"

"Hey!" Micah objected. "What makes you think you're the captain?"

"Isn't it obvious?" Tanner replied. "Third place in the America's Cup trials last year in San Diego. Hello?"

"And you stabbed Bonnie in the back... literally," Wilder said. "You're crazy if you think we'd trust you with this. Or anything. Ever."

"Yeah!" said Micah. "I say we have a vote. And we vote for Bonnie." Micah raised his hand and his brother's as well.

"Me, too. I vote for Bonnie!" Barnaby spoke up.

"Ditto!" Wilder agreed. "Looks like we've got our captain, Curls," Wilder concluded.

Bonnie hesitated. She desperately wanted to win, and Tanner was the better sailor.

"Time's up!" Ballister called out, ending any possibility of further discussion. "Let the races commence!"

"Looks like you're it," Wilder said to Bonnie, who looked like a deer caught in the navigation lights.

"You idiots just blew your only shot to win this thing," Tanner said, turning his back on them.

The crews cast lots to determine the running order, and appropriately enough, Boreas came in last in that, too. As the first crew prepared to launch, Bonnie took her nervousness out on her cuticles.

Reed shot off the pistola signaling the start of the race and hit the stopwatch he wore around his neck. One by one, the crews went out and made their way back to the Cove. Through the course of the morning, familiar patterns emerged. Eurus, sure of themselves almost to the point of cockiness, established an early lead, but Yeun had his Zephyrus crew in fine form as well. Thanks to a slick maneuver coming out of the turn, they were able to trim valuable seconds off their time, and crossed the finish line a full six seconds ahead of Eurus. Notus fumbled their start, struggled to catch wind, and finally crawled across the finish line nearly four minutes off the pace.

"Boreas! You're up!" called out Captain Ballister. "Zephyrus is still the one to beat with…?" he looked to Reed, who was keeping track of the times.

"27 minutes, 7 seconds!" Reed replied.

Taking a deep breath, Bonnie pushed down the anxiety that was slithering up her throat and turned to rally her troops. "Okay. We can do this, you guys," Bonnie told her crew, trying desperately to sound confident.

Nobody looked too confident, least of all Bonnie. But determined to at least play the part, Bonnie was the first on board and immediately started barking out orders. Micah and Malachi, the mainsheet trimmer and trimmer's mate for the race, did as they were told and immediately took to their halyards. Crew boss Wilder headed to the foredeck and started prepping the lines on the spinnaker. Bonnie assigned Barnaby to Navigation and Tactics and told Tanner to take the wheel.

"Hard pass," Tanner snorted. "I forgot for a minute that I didn't want to be here." And he flopped down into the boat and lowered his Ray-bans over his eyes, signifying that he had absolutely no intention of doing *anything*, much less minding the helm.

"You are such an—" Bonnie started furiously.

"Boreas, how's it coming?" Captain Ballister shouted out.

"Just about ready, Captain!" Bonnie turned to Barnaby. "Barnaby, I need you to take the wheel," she commanded.

"Wait. What? I-I don't think I can do this," he said, panicked.

"Relax, my man," Wilder said, untangling a mess of rigging that Notus had left behind. "Nothing's gonna happen. We've only seen a few sharks in these waters all summer, and most of them didn't look all that hungry."

Somehow, Barnaby didn't see the humor in Wilder's assurances.

"Barnaby," Bonnie said to him, grabbing him by the shoulders. "I won't let anything happen to you. I promise."

It was what the boy needed. Once he finally took the helm, Bonnie went over to Tanner.

"And you," Bonnie said to him in a hushed tone so no one else could hear. "If you screw us over or try to sabotage this rig, I'll freaking toss you overboard like I'm chumming for sea bass."

Tanner sneered at her and pushed his sunglasses higher on his nose.

"All hands ready, sir!" she shouted in the best show of confidence she could muster.

"Top Notch!" Ballister replied. "We'll see you all in a bit then!"

"Aye aye, Captain," said Bonnie. "Mister Maguire, cast off!"

Micah released the boat from the dock and Reed fired the pistola, whose report rang out across the Cove. Boreas was now officially on the clock.

"We are away!" said Micah.

"Very good. Mister Chisolm! Set course for east-northeast!" Bonnie shouted.

"Aye! Aye!" yelled Barnaby nervously.

"All for Boreas!" yelled Bonnie.

"For Boreas! For Boreas!" the others screamed, caught up in the excitement of the moment. Except, of course, for Tanner, who glared spitefully as the boat started to glide across the glassy water.

"Looking good so far," Bonnie shouted five minutes into the journey and gave Barnaby a reassuring pat on the back. "A little more trim on the mainsail and we'll be right on course!"

Everyone was feeling pretty good about the course of their run. The Maguires high-fived each other. Barnaby, growing more confident by the moment, let out as manly a whelp as he had in him, and Wilder started hooting and hanging off the side of the boat.

"Is this all you got, Ocean?" he said. "You gotta come with more than this to take us down! Woo!"

"Yeah! Cut her loose, Bonnie," shouted Micah over the wind. "Let's win this mother!"

Bonnie smiled. "Wilder!" she called out. "I need the draft of that foresail to be a skosh closer to 30 degrees!"

It took Wilder a bit to process the command, but finally he had the foresail maneuvered into position. They cut through the water at high speed now and Bonnie marveled at how well they were working together.

After another few minutes, they saw the dinghy in the distance, and a communal cheer filled the air. Then Micah, watch in hand, yelled, "Hey! We're ahead of Zephyrus!"

"Are you kidding me?" Bonnie asked.

"By seven seconds!" Micah replied, recalling the split times that Zephyrus had reported back on the dock.

At this news, Tanner got to his feet.

"Hey! What do you think you're doing?" Bonnie said defensively.

"Helping us win this thing!" Tanner replied. "De Luca! Let's pull in the ring backstay!" The exhilaration of a possible win was too much for the racer in him to resist.

High spirits filled the cutter as the crew approached their target. Until they noticed that Jonesy wasn't standing at the ready to hand off their flag at all, but lying in the bottom of the dinghy.

"Oh man!" said Wilder. "Dude's asleep!"

"I hope he capsizes and drowns!" Tanner said angrily.

"Slow down and let Malachi nudge him with the pole," Micah suggested.

"No! If we have to slow, we'll never beat Zephyrus!" Bonnie shouted, swept away in her desire to win. "JONESY!" she called out.

The others joined in, yelling the old sea dog's name. Except for Malachi, who stood silently at the bow with an arm outstretched, ready to grab the flag if Jonesy could ever be roused in time.

"JONESY! JONESY! WAKE UP!" the others screamed at the top of their lungs.

Finally, Jonesy startled from his drunken sleep. He seemed confused for a moment, then fixed his gaze on the cutter that was coming up fast. He scrambled to his feet and looked around frantically for the flag.

The cutter was already on its way past when Jonesy found the flag and held it out. It seemed like it was too late, that all was lost, but Malachi held onto a rope he'd somehow tied to the mast, then kicked himself off and swung wide across the side of the cutter, his free arm reaching back toward the rapidly receding dinghy. As he flew out over the water, the cutter pitched violently starboard, nearly capsizing from the boy's massive weight. Malachi's fingertips strained until they just managed to grasp the very edge of the flag! They closed tightly around it as he swung back to his spot on the *Skye*, taking the banner on board with him and tumbling onto the deck in a heap.

EVERYBODY CHEERED! Malachi promptly scrambled to his feet and ran the Boreas flag up the mast for all to see.

"Time?" Bonnie shouted.

"Fifteen seconds ahead, Captain!" Micah replied, checking his watch. "We actually *gained* time on the exchange!" Boreas all sprang into action. Victory within reach, they quickly maneuvered the boat around and started the return trip to Cormac's Cove.

"We can win this! Mister Chisolm!" Bonnie commanded. "Find the edge of that no-go zone! Let's bring this craft back to the Cove."

"Putting the keel five degrees leeward!" Barnaby responded with growing confidence.

"Perfect angle of attack, Barnaby! I knew you had this!" Bonnie yelled out from the edge of the boat, where she and Wilder hiked out over the side to aid in the turn.

"Woooo!" screamed Bonnie, leaning out even further over the edge of the boat.

But even before they'd completed their turn, Malachi spoke out as he surveyed the horizon.

"Dead ahead, dead ahead," he said in warning.

"What's dead ahead?" Bonnie, who'd learned to listen when Malachi spoke, was suddenly on high alert. "Micah, what's he dead-aheading about?"

"Beats me. The parrots maybe?" he replied.

They all scanned the blue skies and saw nothing until… appearing on the horizon—not birds, but a mass of clouds—jagged flashes of lightning at its center. And it was moving across the water—fast.

"Squall line!" called Tanner.

"Holy crap!" yelled Bonnie, eyes fixed on the fast-approaching storm. "And we're right in its path!"

"What the hell's a squall line?" asked Micah.

"I remember hearing something about it in Clouds & Climate," Wilder replied, "but who pays attention in that class?"

"It's a flash storm, idiots," Tanner said, running to secure the foresail. "This bitch catches us, we're screwed!"

The wind blew stronger, swirling and pulling hard on the sails.

"Crap, what are we gonna do?" Micah asked.

"Let's just head out to open sea, outrun the bastard," suggested Tanner.

"No. There's no time, the way that thing is bearing down on us. It'd run right over the tail end of us," Bonnie said.

Lightning flashed again, this time followed by a huge sonic boom of thunder so violent Bonnie felt her internal organs vibrate. The sky was now filled with black clouds and heavy rain fell in the distance.

"Micah, make sure the lazy sheet is ready to run! We may have to drop the foresail!"

"You shitting me?" Tanner asked.

Bonnie didn't want to pull the maneuver, and everything they'd learned in their classes told her not to. It was a tough one, even for an experienced crew. But Bonnie sensed that the last thing she wanted to do was to hit this squall head on with full sails. A sudden gust could easily capsize the boat.

"Hartwright! This bunch of losers can't pull that kind of play out here in this wind!" Tanner repeated his objection.

"Bonnie's got this!" Wilder yelled at him, then turned to Bonnie. "Uh, you *do* have this right?"

"I've got this!" she shouted over the wind. And for the moment, she seemed to. Micah's maneuver momentarily steadied the boat despite the increasing wind. Boreas looked at one another, relieved. Then—

WHOOSH!! A tremendous gust of wind blew across the boat, sending a wave over all on board, smacking Bonnie in the face with a slap of salty water.

And that was all it took. Bonnie froze. It was as if every bit of confidence that she'd amassed over the summer had dissolved the second the wave smashed into her face. She was suddenly the scared girl at the bottom of the pool back in Tucson again.

Wilder was yelling something but Bonnie couldn't hear a word. She felt every muscle in her body tense up. All she could register was pounding in her head pierced by the indistinct yells of her crewmates. The rain pelted her as she dropped to her knees.

It was all moving too slowly and too fast at the same time. Bonnie threw up all over the deck. The chunky vomit ripped her throat on the way up, and some of it lodged in her nostrils and burned.

Breathing open-mouthed, she stared into the wooden bottom of the boat and watched her own spittle as it dropped out of her mouth and formed a little pool of liquid only to be washed away by another wave of water over the side of the cutter.

"Bonnie! We need you!" Wilder called to no effect. "Someone! Mind the spinnaker!"

"She's worthless!" yelled Tanner. "We go on my call from now on!" He ran to Barnaby's post at the wheel. "You hold this tub tight, you little twat, or you'll kill us all! Maguire! De Luca! We're baring the poles!" he said, not even noticing that he had just given the very order that Bonnie had made herself not two minutes earlier.

Wilder ignored the order and ran to Bonnie's side. He knelt next to her.

"Bonnie! You've got to move!" yelled Wilder, putting a hand on her shoulder.

Bonnie didn't move. Couldn't. She was frozen with fear.

"We can't hold this bitch upright much longer!" screamed Tanner. "De Luca! Get back to your post and drop that sail!"

"That's *your* post, assbag!" Wilder screamed. "And Bonnie is still captain of this vessel!"

SNAP! Suddenly the knot on the mainsail gave way in the harsh wind, and the boom arm began swinging wildly across the width of the boat.

"Malachi!" Micah yelled after his brother, who was chasing the boom around the deck. "We gotta secure this thing ASAP!"

Wilder ran to help the Maguires corral the boom, but Tanner stayed next to Barnaby at the wheel. The boom caught the wind and whipped across the boat again, forcing the three boys to dive to their stomachs to avoid the pole.

With the mainsail unsecured, the cutter pitched wildly in the ocean, veering on the edge of tossing the entire crew into the water.

Bonnie, still on her hands and knees, became vaguely aware of the danger the entire crew was now in. Every part of her mind wanted to go help them, but her body was unwilling to move even an inch.

"You're gonna get us all killed!" Tanner yelled to Barnaby, who was struggling to keep control of the wheel. "Give me that!"

"I'm not abandoning my post!" Barnaby said. "Not without an order from Bonnie!"

Tanner wrestled control of the wheel away from him. He shoved the boy, sending him reeling across the deck. WHAP! The unsecured boom caught another gust of wind, whipped across the boat, and hit Barnaby squarely in the stomach.

The boom picked up the boy like a rag doll and flung him over the side of the boat!

"Barnaby!" Malachi called out.

"Man overboard!" Wilder yelled. "Tanner! You did this, you piece of crap!"

Time stood still for a moment. Bonnie couldn't hear anything but the whoosh of the wind. Then, in the midst of the water cascading down on her, she heard the little boy's voice and her mouth became bone dry.

"Help!" called Barnaby from off the port side of the boat. Out of the corner of her eye, she saw him struggle to keep his head above water and knew he wouldn't last long in the surging waves.

Bonnie felt something come over her. What, she couldn't say, but it felt like an unnatural calm. As if all the fear inside her had doubled up on itself and become something different, something pushing her forward. Something fierce and powerful.

She sprang to her feet, and for reasons she couldn't explain, found herself drawn into the very thing she feared more than anything else in life, the unforgiving water.

"Bonnie, no! You can't swim!" she vaguely heard someone yell. Maybe Wilder. But she didn't hesitate at all. She catapulted herself over the rail head first.

Deep, deep, deep she dove into the water, as she felt the power of the ocean engulf her.

She pushed back through to the surface and was within a couple of feet of Barnaby. As she reached out for him, for a moment she believed she could actually do this.

"Hold on Barnaby!" she shouted as her hand was about to grab his shirt. Then a wave pounded over her and drove her beneath the water. She struggled to find her way to the surface. But in the relentless, churning water, she couldn't tell which way was up. She panicked!

Then the visions came.

Gallows on a craggy point. An empty grave on a moonlit beach. A drowned man in a baptismal font. Black eyes filled with rage. And finally, a hand with the hourglass ring, pushing her down, down, down.

She felt the huge crush on her lungs as she used up the last molecules of oxygen. She stopped struggling as the light of the world around her narrowed into a pin dot of a tunnel and the blackness of oblivion started to take its place. But in that minuscule circle of light that was left, she saw something else. It was a face. Not a face with rage-filled black eyes. It was the face of a boy, eyes filled with terror, slipping beneath the surface, reaching to her in desperation.

Barnaby! She screamed his name in her head, her consciousness exploding back to life and with it her will. She propelled herself toward him. Before she knew it or knew how she had done it, she broke the surface of the water and brought Barnaby with her.

"I got you!" she said. "Just hold on!"

And despite the fact she had never swum before in her life, Bonnie swam with all her strength toward the cutter, dragging Barnaby behind her.

"Over there!" she heard a shout from Wilder, who was hanging off the edge of the cutter, pointing her out.

She got Barnaby to the side of the boat and to Wilder, who took the boy from her grasp and pulled him onto the deck. Wilder went to grab Bonnie but a swell had moved her out of his reach. Just as another swell threatened to move her further away, Malachi's long arm reached out and yanked her onto the deck as if she were made of feathers.

Bonnie, on her back, lay gasping for breath on the deck of the cutter, the rain coming down hard on her face. Then the rain stopped. The black clouds parted, revealing a patch of blue sky. As suddenly as it had hit, the squall left them. It would pick up strength until it hit Tuscarora Island in the distance and then eventually break up over land.

"Safe for now," Malachi said, staring into the distance. "Safe for now."

Bonnie looked at Barnaby lying next to her, who somehow had managed to open his eyes. She smiled at him.

"I told you I wouldn't let anything happen to you."

And Barnaby returned her smile. A brilliant sun broke through the clouds, and it felt warm on Bonnie's face.

It felt… perfect.

Chapter 22
Origination Night

The rest of the day was a whirlwind of sheer bliss. As long as Bonnie lived, she would remember it as one of the best of her life. Maybe they hadn't won the race, but Bonnie had won something far more valuable—the battle over her debilitating fear of water, the war with herself. There was no longer any doubt in her mind that she was a true corsair, regardless of what might happen next. She had proven it in legendary fashion that day.

When the cutter finally hobbled back into the Cove with Boreas's storm-tattered flag still flying from the mainmast, everyone gathered round to hear the story of their narrow escape.

"It was Bonnie!" yelled Barnaby to the assent of the rest of Boreas. "It was Bonnie who saved us!"

Winnie pulled Bonnie into her trademark hug, complete with tears and kisses. Captain Ballister patted her back, proclaiming he couldn't be prouder of her. The others high-fived her and told her how amazing she was. So complete was the adulation of Bonnie that the corsairs barely noticed when Jonesy rowed his way back to the pier in his dinghy, the squall having somehow miraculously avoided the old sea dog altogether.

It was Grandma Winnie who finally broke up the love fest and demanded that Boreas report to the apothecary for a thorough going-over for injuries prior to the evening's festivities. By the time

Winnie had finally finished examining them from head to toe, the sun was starting to disappear behind the trees. Bonnie left the apothecary just as the horn blew signaling everyone to head to the secluded beach where their celebration was to take place.

Bonnie rushed to her cabin to get out of her salt- and sand-encrusted clothes before heading to the banquet. She had just torn off her T-shirt and tossed it toward her footlocker when she saw it. Lying across her bunk was a lovely white eyelet sundress and a long black velvet ribbon, presumably for her hair. Pinned to it, a note:

For tonight. xoxo Grandma Winnie

Not really being a "dress" sort of girl, Bonnie took a while to talk herself into wearing it. But she finally put it on, mostly out of fear she would hurt Grandma Winnie's feelings if she didn't. She could tell from the delicate stitching that it was no store-bought dress. Then there was the matter of how to do her hair. The dress was too nice to just go with her usual wild tangle of curls. She ultimately decided to wear the ribbon as a headband, using it to frame her face.

Before letting the rest of her hair fall over the birthmark, she paused in the mirror to take a good, long look at it. It occurred to her that if not for that ugly thing on her shoulder, she would never have discovered who she truly was. Bonnie thought about this a moment. Sometimes the things we hate most about ourselves, the things the world tells us are ugly, end up leading us into new and better places that we can't even imagine. For a second, she even thought about tying her hair up and letting the whole world see it, but in the end, she decided she wasn't ready to be quite that exposed just yet.

*   *   *   *   *

As she came to the end of the narrow footpath that led to the cave, she saw that everyone else was already on the beach there and the partying had begun. Bonnie looked around. She got a little self-conscious when she saw she was the only girl wearing a dress. But her feelings of self-consciousness were instantly swept away when she took in the absolute splendor that awaited her.

On the sand were the tables from the dining hall; they'd been hauled down there and set up in a circle. They were decorated with the loveliest lace tablecloths that Bonnie knew Winnie had to have made herself. At the center of each table, mason jars spilled over with all manner of Carolina wildflowers in vibrant pinks, yellows, purples, and blues. Hundreds of candles and dozens of torches made the scene simply magical.

Captain Ballister stood in the center of it all, dressed as he was on the night of their solemn induction ceremony with his sash and ceremonial sword. Winnie was at his side in a pink gingham dress, and the glorious last rays of the setting sun brought out the rosiness in her cheeks even more, if that were possible.

Just over Winnie's shoulder, Bonnie saw Wilder by a buffet table, talking a mile a minute to a small gathered crowd while he stuffed shrimp in his mouth so fast you'd think he was about to make a break for it. She laughed to herself when he dripped something on his shirt. Then quickly crinkled her brow when Daya stepped in to wipe it off for him, getting a little more familiar than was warranted by a splash of cocktail sauce, in Bonnie's opinion.

But it was Reed who first spotted Bonnie. He had just arrived at his grandmother's side when he saw her. He took her in: the white of the dress against the light golden hue her skin had taken on in the summer sun, the black velvet ribbon that framed her face and rosy lips, her fiery dark eyes flecked with gray. Bonnie couldn't hear what he said, but she read lips well enough to figure it out.

"Wow."

Winnie followed Reed's gaze to Bonnie.

"Bonnie!" Winnie said, waving her over. "Let me get a look at you in that dress." She took Bonnie by the hand and twirled her. "Why, it fits to perfection!" she pronounced. "I can still find my way around a needle and thread despite these old eyes. Take a gander, Eleazer!"

"You look beautiful!" the old captain exclaimed.

"This was Grandma Winnie's doing," Bonnie said a little defensively, blushing and looking down at herself.

"We women can't all the time be warriors," Winnie replied, a conspiratorial wink thrown Bonnie's way. "We must sometimes remind ourselves that we are also ladies." Winnie turned to Reed, "What say you, grandson? Isn't she lovely?"

"Uh, yes," Reed said. "She looks… nice." Even in the dwindling light, Bonnie could see that he was blushing too.

"*Nice*, Cabin Boy?" Wilder had come up. "You maybe wanna check your thesaurus on that one. Nice is what you call your third grade teacher! This… this is scorchin'!"

"I think you've been nipping at Jonesy's rum again," Bonnie said self-consciously.

"Bonnie!" Barnaby called out, running up to her with an unimaginably broad grin and grabbing her hand. "C'mon! Everybody's asking for you!" And with that, she was dragged toward the party.

Immediately the talk went to Bonnie's heroics during the squall. Having been interrupted earlier by Winnie's examinations, everyone was now eager for more details. Boreas were beside themselves repeating the tale again and again of their adventure at sea. Even Tanner appeared to be more than happy to bask in the glory of Boreas's heroism—though undeservedly so. Perhaps it was because no one wanted to ruin the celebratory mood of the evening that Boreas didn't call Tanner on it. No one had an ounce of animosity left in them after their ordeal.

After about 30 minutes of mingling, the sun had completely set. Captain Ballister picked up a mason jar from the table and tapped it with his pipe. A silence fell in the twilight.

"Corsairs, as you may have gathered by now," Ballister explained, "for the Brigands of the Compass Rose, keeping the tradition of the old ways is paramount. For not only on this night do we celebrate the present, but we also honor those who have come before us, valiant Brigands all. Let us have a moment of silence to remember those who sacrificed themselves to the mission for which so many of our ancestors have toiled."

All bowed in silence. Bonnie thought of the sea of gravestones in the churchyard, of Reed's mom and dad, and wondered if any of them were destined to meet the same fate.

Once all had raised their heads again, the captain continued. "Since your arrival, I have watched your own sacrifices as you grew together as crews. Watched you grow into fine corsairs, able to battle the elements, your enemies, and in some cases, the enemy within yourself."

Bonnie thought he glanced specifically at her when he said the last line.

"As you should realize by now, you all are special. You are the chosen, regardless of what may come after tonight. And tonight, as has been tradition lo these many centuries, the time has come to award the cherished prize of Origination Day, the Triquetra Star Taker!"

The corsairs cheered as Ballister shouted, "Zephyrus, front and center!!"

Yeun led the Zephyrus crew to where Ballister stood at the head table. Taking the prize from the captain, he sheepishly grinned as the rest of the corsairs chanted his name in unison.

Boreas exchanged bittersweet looks, knowing how close they had come to beating their time had fate and weather not intervened. Still, Zephyrus had won fair and square. Bonnie had to hand it to Yeun; he had shaped up to be a pretty fine corsair. And Bonnie loved the fact that Daya and Luz, the only two other girls in camp, were on the winning team as well. Bonnie got to her feet and led everyone in a standing ovation.

Daya nudged Yeun as the cheers subsided. With the star taker still in hand, he whispered something in Ballister's ear. Bonnie watched as the captain furrowed his brow.

"This is highly irregular," she heard the captain say in hushed tones. She exchanged a quick glance with Wilder, not quite sure what to make of this turn of events.

The captain looked at the rest of the Zephyrus crew. "Are you all sure about this?" he asked. "You know full well what it may portend."

There were enthusiastic nods of assent from Daya, Luz, and the rest of Zephyrus.

Captain Ballister shook his head. "In all my days in the Brigands, I thought I'd seen everything, but you young people teach me something new every summer," he said. "Very well, then... so shall it be. Mister Yeun, you may proceed."

Yeun held the golden disc aloft victoriously one more time. When the cheers died down, he spoke. "All day long," he began, "we've been talking. And while we are totally stoked that we had the fastest time today, we think there's another crew who deserves this more than we do."

Yeun walked to Bonnie and held the prize out to her. An audible gasp rippled through the gathered corsairs.

"No. Yeun. We couldn't—" Bonnie started to protest.

"We all agree," Yeun said with a nod back to the rest of his crew. "You guys were the real corsairs today. You deserve it more than we do."

"But you'll lose your immunity," Bonnie said.

Yeun shrugged. "It's not like we need immunity," he said and held out the star taker once again. "Now take it before we change our minds."

Too stunned to speak, Bonnie took the disc from Yeun and gave him a big hug.

Now it was Yeun's turn to lead the others in an ovation. Everyone cheered, stomped, and whistled, showing their hearty agreement with the decision.

Boreas hugged. Except for Tanner, who stood motionless in the center of the embrace, shocked. Bonnie began to cry. Tears of happiness and disbelief commingled as they ran down her cheeks. She was going to get to stay. She was a Brigand. She *belonged*.

"Now!" shouted Ballister over the hubbub of the crowd, breaking the moment. He raised his cup. "Let us celebrate Origination Day like our ancestors, with feasts and bonfires! *Sláinte!*"

"*Sláinte!*" everyone yelled, repeating the Gaelic toast they'd heard from the captain at every meal.

"*Sláinte!*" he called out again. "Let the feast begin!"

▪   ▪   ▪   ▪   ▪

And a feast it was. What followed was the most delicious dinner Bonnie had ever had in her life. There were shrimp and lobsters and oysters. There were homemade chicken pot pies the size of pizzas. With crusts so golden and flaky, chicken so plump and juicy and peas, carrots and potatoes straight from Winnie's garden. They drank sparkling lemonade and peach flavored iced tea. For dessert, blackberry cobbler.

It was a blur of food, laughter, and camaraderie. Once the dinner had been consumed and the seconds and thirds on cobbler had been exhausted, Ballister again tapped his pipe on his glass for attention.

"To the fire circle!" He commanded everyone to move to where, encircled by stones, there was a mound of wood that had been strategically arranged to achieve maximum combustion.

In contrast to their other meals, which were on a strict schedule, Ballister had allowed their supper tonight to run on to its natural conclusion. So by the time the corsairs gathered around the fire pit, the sun was long gone and the stars sparkled overhead.

Wicked Pete, carrying a torch, made his way through the gathering until he stood in front of the fire circle. "Long live the Brigands of the Compass Rose!" he called out and put flame to wood. WHOOSH! The flames leapt so high that the heat forced everyone to take a few steps back for fear of being singed. Except Wendell, who took a step forward and reveled in the blaze.

There were cheers and whoops that died to stunned silence with the appearance of Jonesy, an old Irish button accordion strapped to his chest!

Wilder leaned over to Bonnie and said, "Now this, I did *not* see coming."

"Well, he plays that horn thingy," she replied. "Maybe he's a musician at heart."

"Trust me," said Wilder. "Nobody who plays the accordion is a musician at heart."

But to their surprise, they discovered Bonnie was right; Jonesy *was* a musician. And a damn talented one at that. Because the sounds he managed to coax from that little squeezebox were nothing short of miraculous.

He began with a rousing little number they had learned in Lore & Chanties, called the "Star of County Down," to which Ballister lent his rich tenor voice. Winnie and Reed clapped along, and soon everyone joined in the clapping. Jonesy moved on to the familiar lullaby "Too-Ra Loo-Ra-Loo-Ral," which Winnie sang solo in a sweet, girl-like voice. As Jonesy nursed the delicate melody from his instrument, Bonnie couldn't help but think of his late wife Elsie and the unborn child they'd never had the chance to serenade to sleep.

After the lullaby, Reed insisted they pep things up and Jonesy complied with a series of Irish jigs. The corsairs were in fine spirits by the time he began playing the lively folk song called "The Black Velvet Band." And everyone sang together on this one, with Wicked Pete supplying some harmony for good measure. The song was a ditty about a hapless lad who comes across a roguish young woman who proceeds to lure him into criminal activity and then leaves him holding the bag. Her distinguishing characteristic was she tied her hair in a black velvet band.

"Hey, just like you have, Bonnie!" It was Barnaby who pointed it out, and it made her almost involuntarily touch the velvet band in her own hair. Swept up in the moment and the fellowship of it all, Bonnie joined in on the chorus:

Her eyes they shone like diamonds
I thought her the queen of the land
And her hair, it hung over her shoulder
Tied up with a black velvet band

Captain Ballister and Winnie began dancing around the fire and Bonnie marveled at the love the two still had for one another after all these decades.

To everyone's surprise, Micah jumped up and started dancing a crazy, spastic-y jig. People laughed but he didn't seem to mind. It only spurred him on. Joining in the fun, Brice and Hashpipe locked arms and did crazy Rockettes-style kicks around the fire. Yeun asked Daya for a dance but before she could answer, Luz pulled her away and the two girls began dancing as well.

Overhead, a streak of bright light lit up the sky.

"A shooting star!" Wilder exclaimed. "Make a wish, Curls!" Bonnie thought a moment, trying to imagine anything that would make life more perfect than it was at this moment. Wilder grabbed her hand. "Wish granted!" he laughed and pulled her out to the dance area.

"No way! Wilder!" Bonnie vehemently shook her head. But the others egged her on and Malachi surprised her by nudging her in the back toward Wilder.

"Come on, child!" Winnie motioned for her to join. So she reluctantly accepted her fate.

She and Wilder began dancing. Wilder hooked her arm and spun her and tried his best to mimic the elder Ballisters' movements, but it was hopeless. So he started dancing wildly, singing the chorus to her at the top of his lungs. Bonnie blushed but she was really enjoying herself, reveling in the infectious enthusiasm of her partner. Soon, they were whirling around the fire to the approving hoots of the other corsairs. Bonnie laughed and played along and she swung her hair back and forth in rhythm with the music. As the song hit its third verse, Wilder tried to spin Bonnie around, but the couple was moving too fast for such a precise move. Bonnie went twirling out of his grasp and stumbled a bit, only to land in the arms of Reed Ballister, who deftly stepped in at the last moment to prevent her from falling.

Wilder held his hand out, clearly expecting that Bonnie would be returned to her rightful partner. Instead, Reed smiled at Bonnie and slipped his arm around her waist.

"Sorry, pal. Finders, keepers!" Reed said, and proceeded to dance her around the fire.

"Hey!" Wilder protested. "I had dibs!"

Reed ignored Wilder's pleas as he and Bonnie danced in perfect time to the music. Unlike Wilder, there was no awkwardness in Reed's dancing. Before long they were moving so perfectly together that everyone stopped and watched. Reed hooked her elbow, spun her one way and then another. Then he took her hands and they turned in circles on the sand, her dress twirling in a perfect arc. Bonnie looked up at the stars, brilliant in the sky, and marveled at the warm night. She wanted it to go on forever. But soon the song ended and Bonnie, disrupted from her enchantment, abruptly stopped spinning. She felt dizzy and staggered. Reed caught her, their faces so close. And she became keenly aware of the heat from the fire and the fact that her pulse was racing. The moment only lasted a second but seemed like an eternity. She then pulled away and smiled. Reed bowed and Bonnie responded with an over-the-top curtsy.

Just then, another shooting star crossed the sky. Then another and another. Until the sky was filled with them.

As she stood there beneath heaven's light show, out of breath, laughing, in her perfect white dress, celebrating a perfect victory, surrounded by perfect friends, for a moment Bonnie, just like the lass in the song, felt like the queen of the land.

⌁   ⌁   ⌁   ⌁   ⌁

Later, Bonnie lay in her bunk, staring at the ceiling. The Triquetra Star Taker sat on the clothes chest next to her bed. But it wasn't the cherished prize that occupied her thoughts. Instead, she replayed moments from that night in her mind. The moment when Wilder offered his hand, and the electricity that coursed through her. They were so much alike. And with him she felt alive and fittingly wild. There was an unpredictability to it. Even in how they danced, crazy and out of sync, yet completely attached by some magnetic force. There was a danger to it. A giddy craziness that held promises of unexpected adventures and spontaneity. And she liked it. It excited her.

But then, equally insistent in her thoughts was the moment Reed had stepped in and taken her into his arms. That moment, there was a shift down in her core. And the two of them danced as one. In perfect rhythm and step. As if they had rehearsed a lifetime. She zigged and he was there to meet her; she zagged and he effortlessly greeted her, as if he'd anticipated her moves, her very thoughts. There seemed a connection between them borne of some kind of previous history. Or maybe it was future in nature. Perhaps it was destiny. And while there wasn't the giddiness she had felt when dancing with Wilder, there was a deep and satisfying safety and comfort that she had never known before.

As she pondered these things, Bonnie, who had never loved anyone in her entire life, wondered if it was possible to be in love with two people at the same time.

Chapter 23

Tuscarora

Bonnie awoke the next morning with a sense of calm. Her sleep, untroubled by dreams or visions, was hours of blissful rest. And, while everyone else snoozed in their bunks, she stole away to the *North* to watch the sunrise. Crossbones, who regularly joined her in this morning ritual, was perched on the railing at her side. As she softly stroked the parrot, she felt the ancient ship bobbing with the morning tide, and knew with satisfaction that she was staying.

Her sense of peace was disturbed when she heard a hubbub coming from up near the cabins. By the time she got there, the other corsairs were crowded around the giant oak tree in the center of the clearing. She saw her Boreas mates at the back of the crowd and walked over to join them. "What's going on?" she asked.

"They've posted the cuts," Wilder said.

Bonnie watched as Brice, his round cheeks streaked in tears, broke from the crowd and rushed past her, obviously having received bad news. She saw the crestfallen faces of several of the other corsairs as they walked away from the tree and was overwhelmed with guilt.

"Trade ya!" Tanner said to one.

"Don't be an asshole," Bonnie snapped angrily.

"I'm serious. I wish they'd cut me right outta this crap hole! Then I could be back in Newport Beach. Sipping a cold one and taking a jacuzzi."

"Why don't you just quit then?" Bonnie said dryly.

"I might as well hang around until I find out whatever this so-called secret is. Then it won't be a totally wasted summer."

Boreas joined the other corsairs to discuss who had made it, who had not, and why; and to celebrate or commiserate accordingly. Besides Boreas, who all got through by virtue of their gifted immunity, there were six more names on the list. There was the burnout Hashpipe from Notus. And from Eurus, the big guy Zion who seemed to know his way around the deck of a ship pretty well, and the budding pyromaniac Wendell, who had somehow made it through the program without burning down the entire camp. And finally, from Zephyrus, Yeun, Luz, and Daya. That last bit of news eased Bonnie's guilt a bit; the core of Yeun's crew had made the cut anyway.

Amid the celebration and commiseration, Captain Ballister appeared to address the group. Reed and Winnie were with him. Upon seeing Reed, Bonnie shot him a beaming smile, which he returned with a perfunctory nod before looking away. Odd behavior for such a joyous moment, she thought, but she figured as part of the Brigands' inner circle, he couldn't very well be happy for some corsairs when there were others who were in the midst of heartbreaking disappointment at that very moment.

"Corsairs," Ballister began, taking a position in front of the tree. "This day is always the hardest one of the summer, but one that must occur nevertheless.

"To those of you leaving us today, I say you shall never be forgotten. Every one of you," he explained, "has touched us in ways we may never know. And worry not, though you may be going home, you shan't be going back empty-handed. You return with the resources you have learned here. Use those resources to change the course of your own lives and know that we will continue the fight in your name."

And with that, he announced that the corsairs who were leaving should return to their cabins directly after breakfast to prepare to be escorted home by Wicked Pete.

"The rest of you," he continued, "meet at the *True North* in ten minutes."

·   ·   ·   ·   ·

By the time the remaining corsairs gathered on board the *True North,* the air was thick with anticipation. "I begin by offering my heartiest congratulations," said Ballister as they milled about on deck. "However, having earned that place, you now carry the most heavy burden of our ancestral cause. And for that," he paused, then said solemnly, "I offer my sincerest condolences."

The corsairs looked at each other, suddenly uncertain as to how they should be feeling about making the cut.

"To that end," the captain continued, mustering enthusiasm, "we sail today to Tuscarora Island!"

"This is it!" Barnaby whispered to his crewmates. "This is the day that the captain tells us our secret mission. I just know it!"

Bonnie glanced over at Reed, who stood off to Ballister's side, hoping to find in his expression whether or not Barnaby's hunch was right. But he would not meet her eyes. Instead, he strode to the forecastle deck and assumed command of the ship.

"Mister Noble! Weigh anchor! Mister Yeun! Set course for east-southeast! Mistress Hartwright and Mister Chisolm, man the foretop for navigation!"

·   ·   ·   ·   ·

By the time the island came into view, excitement had overcome apprehension. They all sensed that something big was in store for them. As the ship approached the island, Ballister purposely had Reed follow the shoreline closely as they made their way up from the south. They sailed toward the small harbor on the protected western side, passing a sandy inlet surrounded by lush woods.

"This is the infamous spot known as Corsair's Lair," the captain announced as they sailed by the inlet.

"*The* Corsair's Lair?" Barnaby asked when he heard the name. "Where the old pirates used to lay in wait for merchant ships?"

"The very locale," nodded Ballister. "Many a bloody battle took place here and at other such hidden holes along this coast. These waters are graveyard to more than their share of bones of ruthless men sent to their maker by the great corsair hunter, Lieutenant Maynard of the Royal Navy."

"Maynard was the guy who killed Blackbeard not far from here," Barnaby explained to Bonnie as they climbed down from the foretop and moved to the forecastle deck to get a closer look. "Cut off his head and put it on a pike as a warning to other pirates."

"So cool," marveled Micah, leaning over the bow and reveling in the gruesome history of it all. "It sucked for him I suppose, but still cool."

Bonnie's ears perked up at the name of the lieutenant. "Maynard?" she whispered to Reed as she and Barnaby took up a position next to him. "Like that sheriff guy from Highcross?"

Reed nodded. "Highcross has always been a small town," he said. "Especially way back then."

"Master Reed!" Captain Ballister called out. "Shall we bring her into port?"

Bonnie looked up. During her conversation with Barnaby and Reed, she hadn't noticed that the entire port of Tuscarora was now in view.

*   *   *   *   *

The main harbor village of Tuscarora had once been a charming place but now was crammed with little businesses. Many of the shops capitalized on the area's pirate history to attract the tourist dollar which, as far as Bonnie could see, was the only kind of dollar to be had on the entire island. There was a pub called the Grog Blossom, a stationery shop called Letter of Marque, and a place that sold handmade wicker rocking chairs that was called, yep, Davy

Jones' Rocker. The Village Pillager was across from Pirate's Plunder: purveyors of —according to their signage—"piratical pirate-phernalia."

Inside the Pillager, Tanner picked up a pewter mug featuring a buffoonish-looking pirate character and showed it to Wilder and Bonnie. "Check it out. From one of my dad's movies."

"Real authentic," Bonnie huffed, looking at the "made in Malaysia" sticker on the bottom of the mug. "All this stuff is insulting." Somewhere along the way, she had started taking pride in her corsair heritage and actually got angry at the joke that was being made of pirate lore.

Wilder picked up a knockoff of a colonial tricorn hat and put it on. He twirled around, modeling his find for Bonnie. "How do I look?" he asked.

"Like Martha Washington and Bruno Mars had a baby," she said dryly.

"That's a good thing, though, right?"

Bonnie couldn't help but laugh. She shook her head and walked off.

Back out on the street, Captain Ballister stopped and gathered all the corsairs in front of the entrance of a big old house that had been converted into a museum. A sign read: "Tuscarora Maritime Museum."

The captain addressed the group, "What you've just witnessed, in all its, ahem, glory, is what the world thinks of the corsair. But the real story is not that of Robert Louis Stevenson novels or big budget Hollywood movies." He shot Tanner a look. "Rather, as you are about to discover, it is far more amazing, and terrible, than any writer of fiction could ever imagine."

Barnaby whispered excitedly, "This is it, told ya."

"Follow me, corsairs, and prepare to meet your destiny," said Ballister ominously, and opened the heavy door to the museum.

The second the corsairs stepped inside, they were accosted by an overwhelmingly musty smell: the smell of old basements and attics that haven't been aired out in a generation. Working at the front counter was a rail-thin old man.

"Lemuel!" said Ballister, gently shaking the man's frail hand. "Good to see you again."

"That it is, Eleazer, that it is! I see you've got yourself a fine bunch of young people again this summer!" the old man said.

"As always," Captain Ballister replied. "Everyone. This is Lemuel Carmody. A finer sailor I have never known."

"There was a time, Eleazer, there was a time. Life's a bit quieter now."

"How's business by the way? Not the lines I remember from a few summers back."

"Hard to get kids to come in since they opened up the laser tag place over by the lighthouse."

"That's a shame," Ballister said, plunking down cash for the kids' entrance to the museum. "And here's a little extra for the Historical Preservation Society."

"So generous, Eleazer, so generous. Maybe I can finally get that extra room set up," Lemuel said, eyeing the cash in front of him. "Would you be wanting the tour today?"

"Not today. Just the key."

"Oh, of course. You would need that, wouldn't you?" Lemuel pulled open a drawer and covertly handed Ballister a single silver key.

"I thank you, Lemuel. And let's raise a pint next time you're in Highcross."

Ballister led the group inside.

▪   ▪   ▪   ▪   ▪

Though the museum was showing its age, Bonnie noted that it at least had an authenticity about it. All the displays had been put together with obvious care and seriousness, with many of the rooms intended to be respectful shrines to various fierce Carolina pirates: among them Stede Bonnet, Captain Kidd, and the notorious Blackbeard himself, Edward Teach.

"As we've discussed, Tuscarora Island was the stompin' grounds of many a corsair of the day," explained Ballister as he led the kids through the dingy museum, passing by an elderly couple, the only other visitors who seemed to be in the building.

Ballister elaborated on the exploits of the Carolina pirates while Bonnie examined the contents of one dusty case: some old coins, a compass, some tattered letters, and an odd-looking dagger with an ivory handle in the shape of a sea lion. She couldn't look at anything too long, though, for Captain Ballister moved at a brisk pace through the room, paying little heed to the exhibits. Bonnie lingered a moment, trying to read some of the historical information on the walls, but Micah called her into the next room.

When Bonnie finally caught up with the others, the captain was standing before a life-size diorama of a captain's cabin of a ship. In it, mannequin representations of Carolina's most infamous pirates sat playing cards around a wooden table, the center of which was piled high with booty—jewels, gold coins, silver frames—as well as half-empty bottles of rum.

"As you may have guessed, we have not come here today for a lesson about the infamous marauders like those featured in this display," he said with a dismissive wave of his hand. "No. We are here today to learn about what is *not* written in history books." His eyes scanned the room to make sure the other visitors were nowhere in sight. He then nodded to Reed, who unhooked the velvet rope from its post. The captain walked past Reed into the display.

Walking over to the "cabin door" at the back of the diorama, Captain Ballister slipped Lemuel's silver key into the lock, turned it and CLICK! To everyone's surprise, it opened to reveal not an empty museum wall, but an entryway with a steep wooden staircase that went into a basement.

"Follow me. Quickly," he instructed and disappeared down the stairs.

Reed held the velvet rope as the corsairs followed in single file. Wilder went down just ahead of Bonnie and as she started to follow him down, Reed put a hand out to stop her.

"There's something I need to tell you before you go down there."

Bonnie could see that Reed was troubled. "What?"

"Reed!" Captain Ballister had come back up the stairs and interrupted them. He looked from his grandson to Bonnie and back again, grave concern on his face. "Let's move along now!"

Ballister stepped aside, making way for Bonnie to go down the stairs. She had no choice but to do as he instructed. "I'm sorry," Reed said to a puzzled Bonnie as she stepped through the doorway.

Followed closely by Reed and the captain, Bonnie negotiated the narrow staircase and emerged into a dimly lit room. On the walls hung various old maps, there were stacks of ancient ships' manifests, and in the corner were the wooden remains of a mermaid figurehead from the front of a ship. Unopened boxes were everywhere. Bonnie saw that all the other corsairs were standing by the far wall, crowded around a huge painting that hung there. Bonnie moved closer and could see over the tops of the heads of the others that this painting featured a fierce-looking man holding a long cutlass. Wild eyes sunken deep in his head stared out at the kids as they pressed up against each other to get a look.

"Behold," said Captain Ballister after the room had quieted down a bit. "Our enemy. Calico Jack Rackham."

There was a silence that bordered on reverence. The villain of many of the captain's stories now stared down at them from the canvas with utter contempt.

Bonnie took in his image. Ballister pointed out the jacket he wore, covered in a tiny black and gold floral print. Calico, as the pattern was known, was Jack Rackham's favorite, which accounted for his nickname.

"What I am about to reveal to you does not leave this room," said Captain Ballister gravely.

Bonnie's mouth went dry and she and Wilder exchanged a look. What could the big secret possibly be?

"Calico Jack Rackham started off as quartermaster of the *Ranger*, a corsair ship under the command of the villainous Charles Vane," the captain began, "but Jack led a mutiny, assumed control of the ship, and never looked back. For years, he and his crew terrorized the Caribbean, which is where he met his wife Anne Bonny and where he first encountered our foundress, Mary Read. It was only after Rackham had a falling out with Mistress Mary and Mistress Anne that the Brigands of the Compass Rose came to be."

"Falling out? I heard they turned him over to the British Navy and got him hanged!" said Micah, recalling what Barnaby had told him the night they'd sneaked into Ballister's office.

"'Tis true, lad, but they acted only in retaliation for Rackham's own treachery, most vile and malevolent."

Everyone looked at each other as if they were wondering if there'd been a part of the story that they'd missed.

"Hold on," Yeun said, struggling to keep up. "You told us before that he was responsible for Anne's death. How can that be if *she* was responsible for *his*?" Bonnie nodded her head. It was the very question Bonnie had asked Barnaby in front of the reliquary.

"Yeah. And if the guy died at the gallows centuries ago, how the heck is he *anybody*'s enemy, much less ours?" piped in Hashpipe, now thoroughly confused.

"He must mean the dude's descendants," said Wilder. "Kind of like how Aldo Tornatore took over his old man's operation back in South Jersey."

"No, Mister De Luca, it's not like that at all," Ballister replied gravely. "I mean what I said. Rackham himself is our enemy… because he lives to this day."

"I told you!" Barnaby said out loud to Boreas.

"You're just yanking us!" said Tanner, shaking his head in disbelief.

"If only I were Mister Prescott," the captain replied.

Bonnie heard herself saying, her soft voice clear and distinct in the wake of the shocked silence, "I-it can't be."

Rather than answer with words, the captain pulled a cloth off another frame on the wall. It was a photograph taken with a telephoto lens, but its subject was unmistakable. It was Calico Jack Rackham!

"Whoa!" came the communal cry from the other corsairs. In the photo, though Jack Rackham was wearing modern clothing, his shirt bore the same unmistakable calico print.

"This is the only picture of Rackham in existence," Ballister explained. "It was taken off the coast of Argentina by one of our Brigands who infiltrated his inner circle almost twenty years ago."

A ripple of murmurs moved through the corsairs, some of awe, some of fright. They looked from the photo to the painting of Rackham and back again, as if they were watching a tennis match.

There was no denying it. It was the same man.

As for Bonnie, her head kept insisting it wasn't possible, but the knot in her stomach was saying otherwise. She looked over to Reed, who glanced back at her with an expression even more troubled than before.

"So Barnaby was right. Our enemy really is a 300-year-old pirate dude," said Wilder, shaking his head.

"I didn't say he's 300 years old, Mister De Luca," said Ballister. "I said he's *lived* 300 years."

"But… how?" it was Tanner, posing the question that was on everybody's mind.

"Rackham made a pact with dark forces, bargained for his life with a power of immense evil, allowing him to live forever."

"So he got hanged, but… he didn't die because of, what, some kind of deal with the devil?" Zion asked, a quiver in his voice.

"Evil goes by many names," said Ballister, nodding. "Call it what you will. But that darkness invaded Rackham's soul and hasn't let go nigh on three centuries. There's hardly a black deed in our world today that doesn't bear Rackham's fingerprints in one way or another. The Brigands have made it our sacred task to bring Calico Jack Rackham's evil reign to a merciful end."

"Dayumm," marveled Luz. "I've heard of being pissed at your ex, but holding a grudge three hundred years!"

"Suffice it to say, Mistress Delgado, that both Mary Read and Anne Bonny had ample reason to want Rackham dead, and we even more so today. Questions?"

There erupted so many questions from the corsairs that Ballister's answers became a jumble of noise in Bonnie's brain. Her attention was drawn back to the portrait in front of her. She was standing at the back of the crowd so she could only see the pirate from the shoulders up. But it wasn't his black soulless eyes, or the leering smirk on his face that had caught her eye. It was the calico pattern of his jacket that Bonnie had found so familiar. And she suddenly knew why. She had seen it before in her dream where she was being drowned in the baptismal font of the church.

Bonnie felt compelled to get a closer look at the painting. She elbowed past a couple of corsairs and came face to face with the giant portrait. Her eyes moved from the fabric at his neck of his calico jacket to the exposed skin near his shirt collar. And her heart skipped a beat when she saw peeking out from beneath the fabric, embedded in the flesh there, what looked like scars from a rope. Just like in the dream! Filled with an ever-consuming dread, she forced herself to take in the rest of the painting. Her eyes moved haltingly, reluctantly, down his arm to his hand. That's when she saw it.

The ring! It's the ring from my nightmares! The thought exploded in her brain so violently she thought for a moment she may have screamed it out loud.

She looked more closely to confirm what she saw. It was the ring alright, with the intricate design of the ruby-eyed skulls and the hourglass inlay. No two rings could be like that. The man in her nightmares was real. And he was Calico Jack Rackham, enemy of the Brigands of the Compass Rose.

That's when she turned to Reed Ballister and saw his guilty look. He had known all along that the man in her dreams was Calico Jack. And he had said nothing. A building sense of utter and unforgivable betrayal began gnawing at her like an animal.

She felt herself getting dizzy, her heart pounding so rapidly she could feel the blood pulsating through her body. A sickness in the pit of her stomach. She had to get out of there. Now!

She turned and headed for the stairs.

"Bonnie…" Reed rushed to her, grabbing her hand.

"Let go of me!" She yanked free and fought her way through the rest of the kids.

"Bonnie!" Reed called after her, but she'd disappeared up the stairs. Reed gave chase, taking the steps two at a time. Back in the museum, he leapt over the velvet rope of the exhibit and hustled through another gallery where he ran into Lemuel.

"Hey!" said Lemuel. "What in tarnation?"

"Did you see the girl?!" Reed demanded. "With the dark hair?"

"Headed down the hall, towards the restroom."

Reed rushed to the restroom at the back of the museum and threw open the door, revealing not Bonnie, but the elderly tourist woman they'd seen earlier. She looked at Reed strangely, but he pushed past her and checked the stalls.

Empty!

Reed grunted in frustration and ran out the front entrance of the museum. Crowds of tourists filled the sidewalk in every direction. He looked frantically for any sign of Bonnie.

There was none.

She was gone.

Chapter 24
Fatimata's Shop

Bonnie gripped the sides of the rusty trash barrel and vomited violently into it. Again and again the convulsions came, until finally there was nothing left but bile. Trembling and weak, eyes swimming with tears, she finally pushed herself to an upright position. She looked around to see if anyone saw her. But she was alone in the gloomy alley behind the museum. Taking a deep, steadying gulp of air, she felt the burn and bitter taste in her throat. She tried at once to shake off and somehow understand what she had just seen inside.

Reed! Her thoughts flew back to him. He knew about this whole thing—the ring, the painting, everything! She'd seen it in his face before she ran from the basement. That was why he had been acting strangely, why he'd tried to stop her from going downstairs. Because he knew! And he just let her go on thinking she was crazy!

What kind of friend would do such a thing? And why? Unless… he was hiding something from me, something… bad, she thought, feeling a chill go down her spine.

"Dat he wuz, chile. Sometin' very, very bad."

Bonnie startled at the sound of the voice and looked around to see where it was coming from. She saw a figure move behind the screen door across the alley that was the back exit of one of the shops on the next street. The screen door creaked open to reveal the ancient-looking Gullah woman from the fortune teller's stall at the Highcross market, the one who'd given her the gris-gris.

"I-I don't know what you're talking about," Bonnie said nervously, making a move back toward the museum.

"Sure yah does. Best yah knows dah truth 'bout it, too, chile, 'fore the one with dah hourglass on his ring find yah!"

"H-how do you know about that?" Bonnie turned back.

"Cuz Gam Gam see evertin', I does," the woman replied, her milky cataract-filled eyes shone an opalescent blue in the dim light of the alley.

Bonnie shuddered.

"Yah seekin' answers, ain' dat right? Well, dis be dah place tah find 'em." The old lady pointed a crooked finger inside. "Me gran'baby, Fatimata gwine be wid ya'll right presently."

"Why can't you just tell me?" Bonnie asked nervously, still wary to set foot inside the place.

"I is too close to dah grave mahself to be summonin' spirits," the old lady replied with a laugh. She beckoned Bonnie with the bony finger again and hobbled into the shop.

Bonnie hesitated. She had been convinced that fortune tellers were nothing but a bunch of scammers, but she wasn't so sure anymore. Despite an overwhelming feeling of dread, Bonnie followed the old woman inside.

As the elderly woman sat silently on a stool outside a beaded doorway, Bonnie took in the shop. A larger version of the stall she'd seen at the farmers' market, it held the same exotic and hypnotic blend of sights and smells, only more of them. There were potions and gris-gris, but also many other items stacked from floor to ceiling. Bowls of bones belonging to various animals: chickens, black cats, and even raccoon penis bones. There were badger teeth, whole dried hearts of bats, and strings of twine from which hung dozens of dried chicken feet. On the counter, there was even a cooler of pimento sandwiches for sale, and a large glass jar of pickles floating in a murky liquid.

Just then two women in colorful shorts and sun visors emerged from behind the beaded curtain that separated the front and the back of the store. They giggled like teenagers as they crammed dollar bills into the tip jar on the counter.

"Fati ready for y'all now," the old woman said, pushing the beads aside for Bonnie, indicating she should go back.

Bonnie followed the old woman into the back.

Standing before her was the same woman she had seen telling fortunes at the farmers' market.

"Well! Greetin's, chile!" she said in the same pidgin English as before. "My name's Fatimata! Descendant of Gullah blood and gifted of dah sight. Whatcha lookin' tah see? Dera boy yah wonderin' on? Hmmm?"

Bonnie looked at Gam Gam, uncertain.

"Dis young lady got some dark spots in her story dat need some… clearin' up," the old woman offered.

"Dat right? Well, set yahself down. Fati gwine give yah a look at dah black holes what plague yah, young un'."

Gam Gam nodded encouragement and Bonnie took a seat at a small round table in the center of the cluttered back room where she had been led.

"I loves lookin' inta dah soul a young people," the fortune teller smiled as she pulled away a brightly colored cloth that lay across the middle of the table, revealing an exotic-looking wooden bowl. Around the outside were little carved skulls. The fortune teller filled the bowl with dried twigs, herbs and assorted bones. "So much life an' light. So much tah look forward tah," she winked and set the contents of the bowl on fire.

Black smoke rose in a thin line to the ceiling. Bonnie thought it smelled acrid and lovely at the same time. Like lavender and charred wood and something she couldn't quite put her finger on.

"Now, gives Fati yo hands, chile," said Fati as she reached across the table, "and we see w'at we kin see."

Bonnie put her hands out and the fortune teller took them. As their fingertips touched, there was an electric shock followed by the faintest flash of blue light, startling them both. The fortune teller instantly pulled back, a troubled look crossing her face.

"How wuz it yah come tah be here taday?" she asked, a hint of suspicion in her voice.

"Uh… She brought me in." Bonnie turned toward Gam Gam but the old woman was gone, the beaded curtains swaying gently in the wake of her sudden departure.

"M-maybe this wasn't such a good idea." Bonnie rose from the chair.

"Sit. Yah already here. Let ol' Fati show yah whatcha come fer."

Bonnie reluctantly sat back down and the fortune teller again took her hands, this time without incident.

Fati closed her eyes and hummed, low and deep in her throat. Then she said, "I conjure dah spirits of dah Gullah Geechee dis day, askin' for dem tah see not only through dah eyes at dah front of dey head, but also dem what is in back. I conjure and ask yah look deep in dis chile's soul for dah memories dat come from dah blackness!"

It happened so suddenly that Bonnie didn't have time to react. Fati's hands clamped firmly around Bonnie's wrists. Bonnie panicked and tried to pull away, but the strength of the woman was almost superhuman.

The woman's eyes fluttered then flew open and, staring into the distance, she let out an agony-filled moan.

"Oooooh! Water! I see water! I… cain't breathe! Dere fear. Great fear, and so much water, no air, no air," Fati gasped.

Sparks shot up from the bowl, startling Bonnie as the edges of her vision went gray. Bonnie felt herself falling. She tried catching her breath but couldn't. Then, the visions began again!

All the old ones. But new ones too. *She was under water. There was the hand with the hourglass ring. Suddenly, a woman's scream! A woman running. And a rope. A noose, swaying in a tropical breeze. Then a loud snap and feet hanging and struggling, then still. A baby. With the mark on his wrist. And the silhouette of the man inside the church. A slash of light illuminating the rope burns around his neck.*

A man drowning in the baptismal font. Bonnie watching in horror as the grains of sand in the hourglass ring change direction, falling up, defying gravity… the gray fades to black and…

Bonnie opened her eyes wide, taking in a big gulp of air. She looked across at the fortune teller, who seemed to be in some kind of trance.

"You! You are dah cursed one! Dah bearer of dah stain!" The woman's voice was deep, otherworldly. She let go of Bonnie's hands. But Bonnie didn't move. She was transfixed as she watched the woman put one thick thumb into the ash of the bowl and, without looking down, began drawing a shape on the white tablecloth with the ash as she spoke, "Dah bearer of dah stain is in grave danger. He comin'. Dah man wit' dah ring. Dah man dat craves tah regain dah sands of time. He close. So, so close…"

Bonnie stared in abject horror at what was drawn on the tablecloth. There, scrawled in ash, was the shape.

There was no mistaking it. The woman had just drawn Bonnie's birthmark in the ashes.

"Get out!" yelled Fatimata. Whatever trance she had been in was gone and she looked at Bonnie with genuine fear.

"You saw it too! The vision. What does it mean?!" Bonnie asked.

"I didn't see nothin'!" The woman was visibly shaking and not doing a very good job of covering it up. "O-our session is over!" the fortune teller said without a hint of an accent as she pulled Bonnie to her feet.

"No, wait, please. What do you mean, I'm cursed? Why does he want to drown me? The man with the ring?" Bonnie pleaded, digging in her heels. But Bonnie was no match for the large and powerful woman who dragged her into the front of the shop.

"Y'all have a nice visit on Tuscarora. Take a pickle on your way out!" Fati said with a forced grin and disappeared back through the beads.

"Please, ma'am, I'm begging you!" Bonnie started after her, but the old blind woman blocked her way with her cane.

"Bes' tah leave her be, chile. It's dah vision of dah curse—done vexed her," Gam Gam said calmly.

"B-But I have to know! What does the mark mean?" Bonnie was desperate.

"Ask dah boy wid dah gray eyes," Gam Gam said, leading her out the door. "Meantimes, hang on tah dis, yah'll gwine be needin' it." She put a piece of paper into Bonnie's hand and slowly closed the door. The sign went from OPEN to CLOSED and the curtain was drawn.

Bonnie stood for a moment, blinking and dazed in the bright sunlight. When her eyes adjusted, she looked down at the paper in her hand. Scrawled on it was an address:

Fatimata Robinson
1634 Watercress Place
Highcross

Bonnie took wild, uneven steps as she hurried away from the shop, still in shock and just starting to process what had happened to her. She whirled on her heels and tore through the streets of the village, looking down every side street. Reed, the boy with the gray eyes, had the answers, according to Gam Gam. *Of course he does,* Bonnie thought. And she was going to get those answers one way or another.

*   *   *   *   *

As fate would have it, it was Reed she encountered first. She saw him on the crowded boardwalk that fronted the marina. He was with Wilder and he looked worried, downright frantic in fact. Reed didn't see Bonnie until she was almost in his face.

He started to speak, relieved. "Bonnie! We've been looking—"

Bonnie shoved him hard, surprising him. "Why didn't you tell me?"

"Whoa, Curls, chill!" Wilder tried to get between them but she pushed him away, not taking her eyes off of Reed.

"You knew it was him in my dreams. I described his ring to you! Why didn't you say anything?"

Reed looked down at the pavement. "I wanted to. I tried, I—"

"Liar!" Bonnie was livid. "You never tried! You've all been lying to me since I got here!"

"Lying about what, Bonnie?" asked Wilder. By now the other corsairs had gathered around and were watching with concern. "What are you talking about?"

"Ask him!" Bonnie said, pointing at Reed. "He knows. Don't you, Reed? I'm talking about Calico Jack, right? I'm talking about that creepy hand in your grandpa's office! I'm talking about how you guys magically plucked me out of nowhere even though I'm not in that stupid book! I'm talking about THIS!"

Bonnie pulled back her hair, finally revealing the birthmark for all to see. The look of shame that flashed across Reed's face told her that the fortune teller had been right. She *was* in danger. And Reed had known about it all along.

"You knew I had this mark. Even before I told you about it. And you knew what it meant. You knew he wanted to kill me. And you said nothing! NOTHING!"

"Mistress Hartwright! That's enough!" Captain Ballister's voice boomed across the marina; its authority froze Bonnie's rage for a moment. The captain approached them amidst a general murmur from the kids.

"S-she found out," Reed explained to his grandfather.

The captain nodded gravely. "Was only a matter of time with a girl as bright as she, I reckon."

Bonnie glared at Reed and back again at the captain.

"Who the hell are you people?"

Interlude
The First Victim
Cormac's Cove, North Carolina, 1746

Anne Bonny, now living under her family name of Cormac, beheld the all-too-familiar mark on the forehead of her newborn granddaughter and breathed a sigh. What a difference twenty-five years had made. When she had first seen that same mark on the wrist of her son Seth back then, it meant unspeakable horrors for him and every one of his descendants who had the misfortune to be born with the affliction. Now, on the little girl's head, about to be doused with the holy waters of baptism, it was nothing more than a minor imperfection on an otherwise perfect baby. Nay, thought Anne, it was a badge of honor. A little reminder of how she and her dear friend Mary Read had traded the life of Calico Jack Rackham for their own freedom so many years before. Anne held the baby in her arms and approached the baptismal font at the front of the church atop the hill, with Mary Read at her side who, still true to her nature, was dressed in her Sunday best trousers and vest.

Father Flaherty spoke to Seth and his lovely bride Elizabeth, gathered at the font.

"What name have you chosen for your child?"

"Mary Colleen Cormac," the couple answered, beaming with joy, and Seth kissed the crucifix that hung from the end of a string of rosary beads he held in his hand.

Anne looked from the baby's angelic face out across the chapel at the new life she had built. Seated in the pews were Seth and Elizabeth's three other children, Keira, Conor, and Rory. Next to them, Mary Read's twin sons, Aidan and Ronan, now vigorous young men of 25.

The only vestige of Anne and Mary's forgotten life of piracy was Anne's faithful servant Mariama, who had been so instrumental in their escape from Port Royal all those years ago. She now looked on through cataract-ravaged eyes from the front pew.

Anne watched as the holy water trickled over her granddaughter's birthmark and splashed into the brass basin of the baptismal font. Her smile widened as the priest continued to bless the girl in the Latin words of the rite.

"In nomine Patris et Filii et Spiritus Sancti."

There was a bit of levity when Mary Read momentarily forgot her line when the priest asked her whether or not she, as godmother, rejected Satan and all his works, but eventually she gathered herself enough to say the one word in Latin that she knew: "Abrenuntio. I do renounce him."

Anne and Mary exchanged a knowing look. They had literally done that very thing years before in the harbor of Port Royal. Renounced evil and swore to make a new start of it in the colonies. They had been true to their word. And this beautiful baby that she now held in her arms was their reward, Anne was sure of it.

＊　　＊　　＊　　＊　　＊

A great cheer echoed in the chapel when the ceremony was complete, and the entire party filed down to the family house to begin the celebration that promised to continue late into the night. Only Seth lingered in the church. As the man of the house, he felt the responsibility to make sure that the chapel was secure, as lately there had been signs of someone squatting in the church when no one was around. The town of Highcross was always teeming with vagabonds and drunken seafaring men, and Seth wasn't keen to leave the doors open in case it had been one of these unsavory sorts who'd been taking refuge there.

He collected a few of the hymnals that had been used in the service and began stacking them on a low shelf when there came a voice from behind him.

"Ahoy, son!"

Seth turned to see who had interrupted his work. Standing in the doorway was a man of about 60. Gray hair, gray goatee. Slightly bent at the waist, a hump at his shoulder, he wore the clothes of a man of the sea.

"If you've come for the christening, 'tis done," said Seth, rising to meet his visitor, but instinctively taking a step back.

"The babe is not my concern... as yet. 'Tis ye I be here fer. And long I been awaitin' this moment."

The man approached the baptismal font where Seth now stood. Despite his advanced age, there was something quite dangerous about him. His eyes were hard, black, with no light reflected there.

"D-do I know you?" Seth, who was afraid of no man, felt unnerved at the sight of this old sea dog.

"Ye should, fer I am yer father."

"My father is long dead, dear friend. Died at sea during a storm."

"Is that what yer mam been sayin' all these years? 'Tis but a half truth," laughed the man. *"Aye, I was dead indeed, but I died by the betrayal and treachery of yer own mam and that mangy tomcat Mary Read. Hung by the neck, I was."* He moved the collar of his calico shirt, revealing around his neck what looked like a rope burn.

"'Tis too much rum what's got into ye. Be off, old man, I've little time to jaw about nonsense," Seth shoved past the stranger, who clamped his hand onto the young man's shoulder. It was a strong, painful grip, much stronger than his advanced age should have

allowed. That's when Seth saw it. On the old man's middle finger. A gold ring with skulls and crossbones inset with an hourglass. And Seth saw that the sand had nearly run out. Only a few grains remained.

"Nay. 'Tis I, Calico Jack Rackham, who have little time," smiled the old sailor and with one move grabbed Seth's wrist harshly, revealing his birthmark:

Seeing it exposed, the old sailor's mouth curled into as evil a smile as ever was. He snatched the rosary beads out of Seth's hand and pulled them forcefully around the younger man's neck. The Bible Seth held dropped to the ground as he struggled to break Rackham's deathly grip around his neck.

The chain of beads snapped from the pressure and Seth gasped for air. The crucifix on the end of the chain fell to the floor and the beads scattered.

Seth made a break for the front door of the church. Before he got to the steps, the older man grabbed him and drove him backwards toward the baptismal font.

Then, Calico Jack shoved his son's head beneath the water and held it. He watched with crazed fascination as the sands of the hourglass began moving upwards, defying gravity, refilling as the very life of Seth ebbed from his body. And as the sands of the hourglass were replenished, so too was the old bent body of Calico Jack Rackham, replenished with the vigor of youth. As bubbles escaped from Seth's nostrils, Jack's vision began to sharpen. As Seth's eyes bulged, the gray hair of Jack's goatee turned a lustrous black. As Seth's clawing hands finally went limp, Jack's hunched back lengthened and broadened with rippling muscle. Jack stepped back, looking exactly as he had the day he was hanged. Time had reversed itself, just as had been promised.

He looked down at his victim, whose shriveled face now looked every bit as old as Jack Rackham's had when he'd walked into the church. If there had been a remorseful bone in Jack's body, it had been dulled by the feeling of power, of life, of youth that coursed through his veins as he siphoned off the remaining years of his son.

"The curse is fulfilled," he said with satisfaction as he stepped away from the lifeless body slumped at the foot of the font. "I am free!"

"For now, Jack Rackham, for now."

A voice reverberated through the church. It was Salifu, the large African man draped in beads who had been present at Jack's hanging. He looked as ageless and vibrant as he had on the day of the pirate's resurrection.

"Damn yer curse, Salifu!" howled Jack, looking at his ring. He saw that, indeed, there was more sand in the top of the hourglass, but there was still much in the lower part. "You must tell me now! How many years have I gained?"

"But twenty-eight years, Jack Rackham. That is all the boy had left in him. You know the provisions of the curse as well as I," Salifu said. "You only gets the years your victim woulda lived on this earth, no more no less."

"If only I could take the babe!" Jack, eyes afire, drunk with the power from his newly gained youth, took a step toward the door. "So many years would I gain!"

"Aye. And lose eternity." Salifu placed a firm hand on Calico Jack's shoulder, stopping him. "Kill her now and your chance to live on dies with her, for the next stained one is yet to be born. No, Jack Rackham, all you have bought this night is more time. But fear not; next time they be more years left and more grains to be had," said the shaman, "but 'til the moment come to collect again, you must bide."

"Let it come quickly!" Jack snarled.

"With patience, immortality come," Salifu said gravely.

Jack held his ring up to the light that fell from the stained-glass window.

"I shall not rest until it is full," said Jack, his voice black as his soul. He threw back his head and let out a lusty laugh that rang through the empty church, out the door and seemed, as if by magic, to be carried on the wind.

.   .   .   .   .

When Anne found her son Seth's lifeless body slumped beneath the baptismal font, she sensed the horrifying truth. When she turned him over and saw the wrinkles on his once youthful face and the bloody, jagged patch on his wrist where his mark had been cut from the flesh, she knew it for a fact. Calico Jack Rackham had come back to collect his debt.

She screamed and screamed. Screams of such anguish that they were heard down to the big white house, and everyone gathered there came running to see what was the matter. By the time they arrived, the guests found not only the murdered Seth on the floor, but lying next to him his mother Anne, collapsed and barely clinging to life.

.   .   .   .   .

Three hours later, the shake of the doctor's head told Mary and Mariama that there was nothing to be done. "'Tis her heart," he whispered as he left the bedroom where Anne lay, ashen, frail, unconscious. Mary closed the door behind the doctor.

"It be my fault, missus Mary. I done thought he was dead. Poor Mista Seth! After all these years. Kilt by he own father. Lord a'mighty," sobbed Mariama.

"No, Mariama. We all believed Jack had long been moldering in the grave. How he is still alive is... is some sort of miracle," Mary replied.

"Nah, missus. As fer from a miracle as can be. It be dark magic! The darkest o' magic. All the way from the old country. Oh, I's to blame."

"The blame is mine," came the faint whisper from Anne, "for laying in with the devil." Mary went to her friend's side.

"Hush, dear Anne." Tears rolled down Mary's cheeks.

"Dearest Mary. I have asked much of you in this life. And before I go, I must ask more."

"For you. Anything."

"Baby Colleen. Anyone else who may bear that cursed mark. Protect them. I beg ye… do not let him destroy us. Do not let his evil win," Anne said as the last breath of her life escaped her lips. And her eyes went still, looking at nothing but perhaps the void beyond.

. . . . .

Later that night, a shooting star streaked across the sky high above the Atlantic. Then another and another, followed by hundreds more, all joined together in the performance of a spectacular fire show in the heavens. On the Cove below, Mariama walked the perimeter of the land she knew by heart, bags of bones and herbs in each hand, chanting old world hoodoo incantations. In a nearby cave, Mary sat staring into a roaring fire. Dressed in the pirate garb from her previous life and flanked by her sons, she turned something over in her hand.

As dawn was breaking and the fire was dying, Mariama, exhausted and looking older than her 80 years if that were possible, stood at the mouth of the cave. "It be done, missus. The gris-gris done helped," the old woman said, holding up the herb bags in her hands. "It is accomplished."

"Ironclad, then? Against him?"

"Against him and all in league with his evil. Long as this land be home to any of Reads, it gwine be a safe place for those what got the Stain o' Musangu on they bodies."

Mary nodded. "Then you have done your part. It is time for the Reads to do theirs." She turned to her sons, opened her hand, revealing to them what she held. It had been given to her by Anne, a gift from their first plunder together. A symbol of an everlasting friendship that would never lose its way. It was a necklace, a thin, gold chain.

On the end of the chain, a pendant in the shape of a compass rose. Aidan and Ronan considered the necklace and nodded. They understood what was to be done.

Mary rose and looked past the boys, and past Mariama into the darkness beyond her. "Dearest Anne. I make you this promise," she said quietly, her fist clenched and jaw set in fury, showing for the first time in years the fierce pirate she had once been. "As long as Read blood runs through veins, I vow to the heavens that Calico Jack Rackham will not win."

Chapter 25
The Cold, Hard Truth

"Of course!" Bonnie said, then burst into laughter.

After Captain Ballister had convinced Bonnie to calm down, they sailed back from Tuscarora and he had brought her directly into his study. With Reed and Grandma Winnie at his side, he laid out the entire history of Calico Jack Rackham and how the Brigands had come to be.

Having told Bonnie everything, they now stared dumbfounded at the laughing teenager in front of them.

"Of course, I'm marked for death by some damn zombie pirate!" she said, still engulfed in a paroxysm of laughter. She buried her face in her hands, her shoulders convulsing, and soon her laughter morphed into uncontrollable sobs.

Reed put his hand tentatively on her arm. "B-Bonnie, are you okay?"

"No I'm not okay!" she pulled away harshly, tears now streaming down her face. "How could you not tell me? I hate you!"

Reed shrank back, deeply hurt.

"I beg you to forbear a bit, dear," Winnie jumped in to defend her grandson. "The boy was under strict orders from us not to say anything. You needed time to adjust to your truth."

"Great. So… what? That whole story about finding me by chance was a big lie? You've known about me all along and left me in that shitty foster system for no reason?"

"Well, we *have* known about you," admitted Ballister, "but unfortunately, we lost track of you shortly after your birth."

"*Lost track?* What am I, a set of keys? How do you lose track of a whole person?"

Ballister and Winnie exchanged glances.

"Tell her," Reed interjected forcefully. "If you don't tell her, I will."

The captain finally spoke up. "The truth is, Bonnie, the reason we know about you is that we knew your mother, a girl who was not much older than you when you were born, and just as headstrong, I might add."

"What?! You knew my mom? How?"

"Because child, you were born right here on Cormac's Cove," Winnie replied. "This, Bonnie, is your home."

Winnie nodded to Captain Ballister, who reached into his desk and produced a snapshot of a teenage girl, and showed it to Bonnie. The girl looked as if she could have been Bonnie's older sister, standing between younger versions of Winnie and the captain.

"Her name was Brigid," he said. "Brigid Byrne."

Brigid. Of course. The name she'd seen on the cave wall on that first night. Bonnie could feel her hands shaking as she took the photograph from the captain. She looked for the first time in her life at the face of her mother—a face that held the clues to her—the large dark eyes, the heart-shaped mouth, and on the girl's left forearm, a mark just like Bonnie's!

"She's marked, too?" Bonnie said in wonder.

"Yes," the captain said. "She too bears the Stain of Musangu. You are the seventeenth of Anne Bonny's line to be so marked."

"But not just her line. Seth was *his* son too, right? He cursed his own son?"

"Aye. 'Tis hard to fathom that a father would do this to his own flesh and blood," Winnie spoke up, "but he seduced Anne and fathered the child for the express purpose of carrying out his dark pact with the underworld. The poverty of such a man's soul…" She shook her head.

Bonnie shuddered at the sheer evil of it.

Since that first murder, Ballister explained, Calico Jack had been on a methodical hunt for marked persons—"stained ones" he called them—extending his own life while at the same time amassing fortune and power across continents and centuries.

"Which is why it is incumbent on the Brigands to protect the bearers of the mark," Ballister said. "For as long as he collects years and there are sands in the hourglass, Calico Jack will live and his reign of terror will continue."

"But obviously you *haven't* protected them. I mean, he's still alive."

"We have protected a good number," Ballister said defensively. "And others, we have prolonged their lives so that the years Rackham would gain were minimal."

"But not all of them," Bonnie said. "You couldn't save all of them, could you?"

"You must understand, our task has not always been easy," Ballister explained. "In the beginning, yes. When the family tree contained but a handful of branches. But over time, with more and more branches, the bloodline scattered to the winds. But you must take heart, child," Ballister said. "If you listen and do as you are told, we can save you."

"What about my mother?" Bonnie finally asked the question she feared the answer to most. "Were you able to save her?"

"The last murder we know of," the captain explained, "was 28 years ago off the coast of Argentina, a nonbeliever who refused Brigand protection."

"So that means my mom's still alive?" Bonnie felt a surge of hope amid the bleakness.

"We don't know that for sure, Bonnie. But if anyone could survive, it would be she," Winnie said encouragingly. "Right, Eleazer?"

"Indeed!" the captain nodded and went on to explain that the Ballisters had taken Brigid in after her parents were killed in a mysterious accident. "By the time she was your age, she had become one of our fiercest warriors. We have high hopes for her survival," Captain Ballister explained.

"So we're not Brigand by blood, my mom and me. We're just marked ones you were training to be *like* Brigands?"

"Well, yes and no. Your ma, *she* was not of Brigand blood," Ballister said. "Your father, on the other hand, was one of the Brigand boys who was at the Cove. Brigid admitted as much, but refused to identify him."

Bonnie was stunned. "So, I'm a marked one *and* a Brigand?"

"Aye, a Bonny and a Read. The first one ever so born," said Captain Ballister.

"Maybe that's the reason for what happened with the compass," offered Reed. "And why you've been having those dreams."

"Dreams? What dreams?" asked the captain.

"Bonnie," Reed said, "has been seeing Calico Jack in her dreams."

The captain looked deeply shaken. "T-that's never happened before."

"There hasn't been a marked one born of a marked one since the line began, either. But as the Gullah taught us from the beginning," Winnie explained, "these things are often portentous. In any case, your being born with a mark absolutely terrified your mother. Because while she was not fearful for herself, she was afraid for you. So, shortly after you were born, your mother took you from here. From us."

"I-I don't understand. Didn't that Gullah woman put some sort of enchantment on the Cove? Why would she leave if it's safe here?"

Winnie hesitated to answer as she glanced at Reed. Bonnie saw that Reed was now looking at the ground, arms crossed.

"There was an incident," it was Ballister who spoke up. "Some Brigands were killed, two of our most formidable fighters in fact, at the hands of Calico Jack and his men. Not here on the Cove, of course. Far away. But..." his voice trailed off.

"But Brigid was close to them," Winnie continued. "Best friends, in fact. It devastated her... frightened her."

Bonnie could see Reed was trying hard to hold back emotion, and she knew in her heart that the Brigands Ballister was talking about were Reed's parents.

"Your mother lost faith, Bonnie," Ballister said, clearing his throat. "She became convinced we couldn't protect you. So she took you and ran. We've been searching for years, but every lead we've followed has come up empty."

"We were always looking for a young mother and her daughter," Winnie continued. "We never thought that she'd gone off on her own."

"Some mom, huh?" Bonnie said bitterly.

"Actually, it makes perfect sense," Ballister said.

"It's what I would have done," Winnie agreed, putting her hand tenderly on Bonnie's cheek. "What any mother would do. Don't you see, Bonnie? Giving you up was the only way she could truly protect you. You became like a needle in a haystack to Calico Jack."

"Aye," agreed the captain. "Thousands of miles away, no name, no papers, no connection to the Brigands at all. It almost worked too. We're just lucky we found you."

Bonnie didn't feel lucky. In fact, she felt the opposite of lucky. And she was afraid. More afraid than she'd ever been.

"But you *can* protect me, right? If I stay on the Cove, like you said? He can't get to me here. I'll be safe."

"No!" Reed jumped in. "They can't guarantee it, no matter what they say."

"Reed!" Ballister said angrily. "That's not true!"

"It is! It's time we look this thing straight in the eye, Grandfather!" Reed said, equally filled with anger. "The truth is, Bonnie, there's hardly any of us left. That's why you haven't seen many of us doing the training. We're not as powerful as we used to be. Our bloodline is diluted. And so is the magic around this place." He turned to the captain. "Everybody's noticed it getting weaker by the year, Grandfather. They just don't say anything in front of you."

"And why not?!" Ballister demanded to know.

"Would it have made a difference?" Grandma Winnie asked pointedly. His silence was his answer. "I know you don't want to admit it, my love, but you *must* see it. For the sake of us all," she continued. "The magic. It's... different. I feel it. And I fear the Brigands are on the verge of something terrible..."

After a long beat, Ballister finally spoke.

"'Tis true. We are not what we once were," he said wearily, staring at his hands on the desk, bony and wrinkled with age.

Bonnie couldn't believe what she was hearing. They were essentially admitting that for all their so-called tradition and commitment, the Brigands couldn't guarantee her protection.

"Yeah, well, screw this noise!" Bonnie said, bolting up out of her chair. "I'm out of your little pirate cult. I'll take my chances back in Reality Land!"

Ballister grabbed Bonnie's arm with a grip so powerful it put an end to Bonnie's retreat. "I'm afraid we cannot allow that, dear," he said, his tone deadly serious. "You must understand this is much bigger than you. Than us."

Winnie stepped in. "Eleazer, you're hurting her."

Ballister realized his grip was too strong and quickly let Bonnie go. "I'm sorry. But I must make you understand. You see, most evil men are limited in the evil they can do by their mortality. When an evil man dies, his villainy dies with him, but…" A shadow of fear eclipsed the captain's face and his voice dropped to a hoarse whisper, "… do you know what evil a man can do when there is no expiration date on his soul?"

Bonnie felt gooseflesh spread over her body like falling dominos. She tried to wrap her mind around what a truly evil person could do in three hundred years. Especially someone capable of killing his own child.

Then, only one thought came to her head as it banished all others from her mind. That thought was as clear and insistent as any that she'd had in her life:

I'm dead.

Chapter 26
A Plan of Action

"This is seriously messed up," Wilder said as Bonnie held up her hair, allowing her crewmates to inspect the mark more closely.

Tanner shook his head. "I got to hand it to you, Hartwright. You officially win the prize for the suckiest life in this place."

After the Ballisters told her everything, she had stormed out, even refusing Winnie's offer of her herbal "inexplicable discomfiture" potion. The way she saw it, her discomfiture was *very* explicable. Burdened with this new knowledge, she wasn't going to do to her friends what the Ballisters had done to her. She felt she owed at least her crewmates the truth. So she went back to the Boreas cabin and told them everything. Down to the last detail.

"They lied to me about everything. There was no DNA test! They made the whole thing up!"

"Slow down!" Wilder struggled to keep up with the blizzard of information coming at him. "Why would they do that?"

"Because they didn't want to tell me that they really found me from a picture of my birthmark!"

"How is that even possible?"

"Remember Mandy, that girl whose stuff I torched?"

"That bitchy chick who threw you in the pool?" Wilder asked, remembering Bonnie's story of how she'd ended up there in the first place.

"Yeah, what I didn't tell you was what started the whole thing. She took a picture of my birthmark and posted it on social media. That's why I got so pissed at her. Anyway, apparently Reed developed some algorithm to alert them whenever the mark comes up anywhere online."

"And Reed knew about this the whole time?" Micah asked.

"Yeah. The whole thing. And he didn't tell me. Asshole."

"I kinda don't blame him, though. I wouldn't wanna be the bearer of that kind of news," Wilder mumbled.

"Okay. So he's not an asshole," Bonnie replied.

"Well, I didn't say *that.*"

Bonnie couldn't even bring herself to smile at Wilder's joke. "Whatever he is, no way I can trust him anymore." Bonnie was furious at him, but she was even angrier at herself.

"Look," Micah said, "there's gotta be something we can do about this whole thing. It can't just be set in stone."

"Sure it can. That's why they call it a curse," Tanner said.

Bonnie felt the doom close around her and it choked her. "Oh, God. That Gullah lady was right. He's coming for me. He's going to drown me, just like in my dreams." Bonnie began to hyperventilate.

Wilder reached out and put his hands on her shoulders. "Curls. Listen to me. That's not going to happen. I swear on my life."

"Yeah. We'll protect you, Bonnie," Barnaby said.

"We all will, right Malachi?" Micah said. Malachi sidled up next to Bonnie in a show of support.

"No! I won't let you risk your life for me. Any of you!!" Bonnie said, her cheeks burning.

Just then, all eyes turned to Tanner, who had gone to the boys' side of the cabin and pulled a suitcase out from under his bunk.

"The hell you doing?" Wilder asked.

"What's it look like?" Tanner replied, stuffing clothes into the open suitcase.

"You're just gonna abandon her?" Wilder asked.

"I got plans for my future and it doesn't include risking my ass to protect some skank from Arizona. First thing tomorrow morning, I'm outta here."

"Coward, just like your dad," snarled Barnaby.

"And he's lived to tell the tale," Tanner snapped his suitcase shut.

"Forget him," Wilder turned to Bonnie. "Look. That Mandy may have done you a favor. You're the marked one. And that totally blows. I get it. But you're also a Brigand! That means something. Means we're your family… Really, really distant family," he hastened to add. "Besides, isn't it worth it to know that your mom abandoned you not because she didn't love you? That she left you in that church… because she *did*."

Bonnie thought on this. Wilder was right. Crazy as it sounded, knowing that little scrap of good in this dung heap of wrong made it all almost worth it.

"You're right. It is better knowing," Bonnie said rising to her feet, her fear pushed aside by a sudden determination.

"Wait! What are you doing? Where are you going?"

"To find out if my mom is still alive," Bonnie said and went out the front door.

*   *   *   *   *

Ten minutes later, Bonnie was down at the dock where the cutter was moored. Wilder, who had followed her when she stormed out of the cabin, watched as she quietly prepped the boat to sail.

"Why don't you just tell the Ballisters you want to see that fortune teller lady again and forget this cloak and dagger stuff?" Wilder whispered.

"Uh-uh. I'm the cursed one, remember?" Bonnie said as she prepared the vessel for night sailing. "No way they let me off this cove unless the place is on fire, and maybe not even then."

"And they'd be right. It's dangerous for you to go out there."

"I refuse to live in fear. Especially knowing my mom might be out there somewhere. And she's in just as much danger as me, maybe more, and she might need my help."

"Bonnie. Hold on," Wilder said. "Let's just war-game this for a second. Let's say you get to Highcross without getting caught and the address that blind old lady gave you was actually real *and* that they are home and will let you in at this hour… What makes you think this fortune teller lady, Fatty…"

"*Fahhti,*" Bonnie corrected.

"Fati, Fatty, whatever. What makes you think she can tell you anything about your mom?"

"She knew I was cursed, didn't she? She knew about my mark."

"I dunno, Bonnie."

Bonnie stopped working for a moment and turned to address him directly. "Think if you were in my shoes and you had a chance to find out what happened to your mom, you'd go to the ends of the earth to chase it down, too! Wouldn't you?" Bonnie saw Wilder's eyes go sad at the mention of his own missing mother and she immediately regretted bringing it up.

"Look," she said in the most reasonable voice she could muster. "I need to do this. If it turns out Jack has already killed her, I swear, I'll do whatever the Ballisters tell me. But I have to know. I just have to."

Wilder bit his lower lip and shook off the sadness.

"You win, Curls. Let's do this…" Wilder stepped onto the cutter.

"You're not coming with me!" Bonnie said.

"There's a badass undead pirate out there who wants to drown you! No way am I letting you go out there alone!"

Bonnie fumed for a moment. But the look on his face told her that Wilder took his newfound role as her protector very seriously.

"Fine, cast off the stern line and take the helm. I'll trim the sheets."

Wilder went to remove the line from the cleat when suddenly a boot stepped down hard on the rope. He looked up to see Reed standing on the dock over them.

"Where do you think you're going?" he asked.

"I don't suppose you'd believe it if we said we'd heard the mackerel were biting?" Wilder offered.

Reed let out an unamused snort and turned to Bonnie.

Ultimately, she had no choice but to tell him the truth. When she was done, Reed stood silently contemplating for a moment.

"You guys are not going to Highcross in that boat," he finally said.

That was it. Bonnie snapped.

"I don't care what Wilder says, Reed Ballister, you *are* an asshole! A total and complete asshole! I thought I could trust you. That maybe you finally had the balls to stand up to your grandfather and make a decision on your own. But no! You're still your grandpa's little cabin boy, aren't you!" Bonnie railed on about Reed's betrayal and shortcomings and as she did, Reed attempted to interrupt her.

"Bonnie… Bonnie…! Bonnie, will you just shut up for a second!" Reed yelled, which finally silenced Bonnie's tirade. "I said you're not going to Highcross in *that* boat. I didn't say you're *not* going."

*   *   *   *   *

"The *Solstice Skye* is too recognizable," Reed explained a few minutes later to Bonnie and Wilder as he dragged the dinghy from the boathouse onto the beach. "Last thing we want is to draw attention to ourselves. We don't need any of those Highcross busybodies telling my grandparents where we are."

"We?" Bonnie asked.

"You'll get caught without me," he said matter-of-factly. "I know where we can go ashore just outside of Highcross and hide the dinghy." He put the boat into the water and handed each of them a paddle. "Now, let's go."

The trio rowed in silence, giving Cormac's Cove a wide berth until safely past it, then bringing the dinghy in closer to shore and hugging the coast. Once they were far enough past the Cove and the point where the wind could carry their voices, Bonnie finally broke the silence.

"So, I'm uh, you know, all that stuff I said back there…" she started as the dinghy bobbed forward in the water. "I didn't really mean it."

"Sure you did. And you were right," Reed said. "I should have spoken up sooner. The old Brigand ways aren't working anymore and they haven't for a long time. We gotta try something different. Too many good people have died already."

"You mean like your mom and dad?" Bonnie asked. "That's who your grandparents were talking about back in the office, the ones who got killed and sent my mom running?"

"Yeah," Reed answered after a beat in a voice so quiet that it was only just audible. Wilder and Bonnie exchanged sympathetic looks.

"They must've been pretty tight with my mom," Bonnie said, the remains of her anger dissolving away.

"The way Grandfather tells it, as close as any three friends could be," he replied, looking steadfastly ahead. He went on to explain how his dad, Daniel, and his mom, Caitriona, had been killed on a secret mission to Sumatra shortly before Bonnie was born. Reed was about two years old at the time. Having grown up on the Cove, Brigid saw Daniel as an older brother. And Caitriona was her best friend… They were not only bound by their fates as Brigands, but by their deep and abiding friendship.

Bonnie looked out across the dark waters.

Sort of like us, she thought.

Chapter 27
Contact from Beyond

When the lights of Highcross came into view, Reed guided the dinghy to a secluded rocky shoreline several hundred feet from the marina. On Reed's signal, Bonnie and Wilder hopped out and together they dragged it out of sight behind a thicket of trees.

"This way," whispered Reed as he led the way up the embankment and into the woods. They stayed under cover of the forest until Reed thought it safe for them to emerge into the town proper.

It was pushing midnight by the time the trio made their way through the back streets and alleys to the address that Bonnie had received from the old woman at the shop. Watercress Place was smack dab in the middle of Marina Crest Estates, the new high-end townhouse development that Charley Eden had helped bring to Highcross.

"Wow," marveled Wilder, surveying the property. "Pretty swanky."

"What? They don't have koi ponds in Brooklyn?" Reed asked.

"Dude, on Coney Island, fancy fish like that wouldn't last ten minutes before they were lunch for the alley cats."

They made their way through the complex and soon found themselves standing in front of the fortune teller's door, looking up at the two-story townhouse. There was no sign of life.

Wilder stepped up to push the buzzer when Bonnie stopped him.

"Don't ring the bell!" she said a little too loudly.

"Why not?" Wilder asked.

Bonnie hesitated, lowering her voice again, "She, uh, might not be that thrilled to see us."

"I thought she invited you," Wilder said.

"That was her grandmother," Bonnie said. "The fortune teller herself didn't *exactly* invite me."

"Not exactly? Well what *exactly* did she say?" Reed asked.

"I'm paraphrasing here, but it was something like 'Get out, and darken my doorstep no more, you spawn of evil!'"

Wilder turned to Reed. "Remind me the next time I vow to protect somebody to first be sure they aren't a lunatic."

"So, what was your plan here, Bonnie?" Reed asked.

"My plan is we get into her apartment, then she'll *have* to talk to us."

Reed and Wilder looked at each other, it dawning on them what Bonnie was suggesting.

"What are you going to say?" Wilder asked. "Sorry for breaking into your house in the middle of the night. Before you have us arrested, would you mind giving us a complimentary seance?"

"That's pretty much the size of it," Bonnie replied. "Now let's pick this lock and get in there."

Nobody moved toward the door. "Well, *I* certainly can't do it," Bonnie explained. "My expertise stops at anything with four tires."

"If only there were someone who knew how to break into a house," Reed said, and simultaneously he and Bonnie looked at Wilder.

Wilder sighed and set to work. "And I'd made it two whole months without committing a felony."

Two minutes later, Wilder pushed the door open silently.

"Okay. Follow me," whispered Bonnie. "She's probably upstairs in bed."

Bonnie took one step inside the townhouse when—

FLASH! All the lights went on simultaneously, revealing in the center of the room, pointing a long-barreled shotgun directly at them, the fortune teller Fatimata!

"Hold it right there!" she warned.

The friends' hands went straight into the air.

Except for Wilder, who instinctively grabbed the nearest thing off the stand in the entryway and pointed it at his adversary.

"Son," said Fati, aiming at his head. "Don't be a fool. Put. The ceramic frog. Down."

Wilder looked down at his weapon. As his eyes adjusted to the light, he could see that Fati was right. In his right hand, he held a hand-painted frog with glazed eyes that looked at him disdainfully.

"You ain't gonna do much damage with that, boy," said Fati, shaking her head.

"Uh, yeah," shrugged Wilder as he put the curio back on the stand, "but I left my high-caliber frog at home."

Fati had to chuckle in spite of herself. She pointed the barrel away from him for a moment. "You're all right, kid. It'd be a shame to have to shoot ya."

Reed spoke up. "Ma'am. Miss Fati. Please. I'm Reed Ballister from out on Cormac's Cove. We're here because —"

"I know about all ya'll on the cove. And I know damn well why you're here!" she said, fixing a harsh stare on Bonnie. "I'm a psychic, remember? Which is why I also know what'll happen if you don't get your boney asses off my carpet and out the door in three… two…"

"Please! There's something I need to know." Bonnie took a pleading step toward her. Fati turned the gun on Bonnie.

"I done told you all you need to know. I'm not messing with the dark spirits!" Fati's voice sounded angry, but underneath, Bonnie could tell it was nothing but scared.

"You don't have to mess with any dark spirits," Bonnie said, standing her ground. "All I want to know is if my mom is still alive."

"Girl. You've got dark spirits coming out your pores!" Fati scoffed. She saw the desperate look on Bonnie's face and seemed to soften for a moment. "It's nothing personal. It's just that I have an affinity for, you know, being alive. So… GIT!"

"Dey'll do no such ting!" A frail but insistent voice came from the top of the staircase. It was the old blind woman from the shop.

"Gam Gam! This doesn't concern you," said Fati, still pointing the gun at Bonnie.

"No. But it concern YOU!" she said with more authority than Bonnie thought her fragile body could muster. Wearing her nightgown and a robe, she took hold of the banister and started down the stairs. "Dis be 'bout yo destiny, Fatimata, and dah fate a all dese yung'uns. Which be 'xactly why I tole dah girl tah come round."

Gam Gam moved across the living room to where Fati stood. "Now, yah put dat fool weapon down dis second and obey what it is I'm sayin' to yah." Despite her poor vision, she quickly found Fati's ear and gave it a violent twist.

"Yowww!" the fortune teller yelped, but the old woman's grip only tightened. Fati lowered the gun.

"Now. Y'all gwine offer our guests a refreshment, or I hafta do everyting by mahself?"

*   *   *   *   *

Fifteen minutes later, they sat in Fati's ultra-modern kitchen eating biscotti and sipping on espressos that she'd whipped up with an obviously expensive coffee maker.

"Mmm. Now that's what I'm talking about!" said Wilder, sipping the espresso appreciatively. "Is that a Lavazza I'm tasting?"

"Well now. Mr. Frog knows his beans," Fati smiled appreciatively.

"Use a coaster fuh yo drink, boy!" snapped Gam Gam, "Dis ain't no pizzeria!"

"Oh sorry." Wilder quickly complied, having grown rather fond of having both ears intact. "But wait, how did you know…" His voice trailed off.

"This is a real nice place you got here," said Bonnie, looking around at the fancy surroundings. "Judging from your shop, I thought it would be a little more… uh…"

"Rustic? That's just part of the illusion," Fati replied.

"Like the accent, huh?" asked Bonnie about the Gullah accent that had completely disappeared.

"If you give white folks a show, they tip better."

"And how do we know that anything you tell Bonnie tonight isn't all just part of the show, too?" Reed, who had been quietly scrutinizing the whole scene, finally spoke.

"Don't believe me? There's the door, honey," Fati said.

"Reed!" Bonnie shot him an angry look. "Apologize!"

"No disrespect, Miss Fati," he said, "it's just that the way I heard it, there weren't any Gullah left with the sight."

"Oh, there's some. Scattered about. Most are deep underground, keeping their gifts inside the community. You're looking at the only two Gullah I know of with the shine in these here parts. A family thing. Runs deep with our women. My grandmama here, and my mama, too, may she rest in peace. They could see things that nobody else could, see things that people were aching to hide, even from themselves."

"Y'all see plenty yo'self, Fatimata," Gam Gam said.

"Yeah. But I don't often share what I see. The last thing folks want is the truth. I just try to figure out what it is they want and give it to them. But when you came into the shop, girl. There was nothin' fake there. I felt something so powerful coming off of you, so… so dark I didn't want no part of it. And I still don't."

"You done panicked," Gam Gam said matter-of-factly, sipping her coffee, "Ain't no shame in it. Many a seer do it dah first time dey encounter powers o' true unrelentin' evil."

"Look, can we do this already?" Fati said, collecting the espresso cups, which tinkled against each other, giving away her serious case of nerves. "Sooner you're outta here and outta my life, the better."

◦　　◦　　◦　　◦　　◦

A couple of minutes later, the group had moved to the dining room, but not until Fati had gone around and closed all the shutters tight, looking up and down the street before she did. In the center of a round, glass dining table, Fati placed a very old-looking wooden bowl and filled it with herbs and bones. Bonnie felt both hope and apprehension take hold of her core.

Fati sat at the table and took a deep breath.

"I'll do this," she said. "But as long we're clear, this is the last reading I'm doing for you."

"Absolutely," Bonnie said, "I swear. I'll never ask you for anything again."

"Okay then, let's begin…" said Fati as she lit the contents of the bowl. "Everyone, gather round. Sit."

Bonnie and Gam Gam sat. Reed and Wilder stepped back, clearly thinking that they wouldn't be part of it.

"No, boys. You too," said Gam Gam, offering Reed her bony fingers. "We cain't have no souls outside dah spirit circle or none o' dis kin work." The boys took their seats.

"Hold hands," Fati ordered.

Reed took Gam Gam's hand. Wilder took the hand of Bonnie, who held on to Fati's hand as if it were a precious thing. Fati held her grandmother's hand and the circle was complete.

Well, almost. There was a noticeable gap between Wilder and Reed. The two boys shifted awkwardly, each with one arm at his side, neither willing to make the first move to do what they both knew was going to be expected of them.

"Guys. Seriously?" Bonnie scrunched her face.

"Don't worry," Wilder grinned at Reed. "You can still see other people."

"Okay, if we're done with the childishness, let's be on with things," Fati said. "Everyone, close your eyes."

The visitors quickly obeyed.

Fati rotated her head back and let out a throaty sound. It was a strange and primal noise that gave Bonnie chills.

"Name of God most gracious, master of the day of judgment, show me the straight way. We summon all the power of the Almighty Spirits to our circle."

Bonnie closed her eyes tightly. She'd never wanted anything more than what she wanted now.

"I'm seeing flames, a fire," Fati began. "Tendrils of smoke. Rising. Up. Up. Names on a wall, a cave wall…"

"That's the grotto at Cormac's Cove!" Wilder whispered excitedly. Bonnie nudged him to shut up.

"I see a name… Beginning with B… B-Brigid," Fati mumbled.

"That's her!" said Bonnie, and her eyes flew open.

"I see a stolen kiss. A boy. Eyes filled with passion. A circle within a star, a star of six points." Fati's eyes fluttered.

"My dad! You see him?" Bonnie asked hopefully.

"I see—I see… a baby girl. It's you, Miss Bonnie. Oh, how she loved you. So very, very much," Fati said, her voice husky with emotion. "You were her joy. Her world."

Tears welled in Bonnie's eyes. "Mom," she said under her breath.

Fati's voice became urgent. "Wait. I see water. Blood spilling. Fear, great fear."

Bonnie looked frightened and Wilder squeezed her hand for strength.

"Is she dead? Is my mom dead?" Bonnie was frantic. "Did he kill—?"

Suddenly Bonnie felt a jolt and her eyes rolled back in their sockets. She wasn't seeing black. It was… colors. Vague and muted at first, but then getting more vivid. Blues and pinks and purples danced in front of her just out of reach. Then they slowly materialized into something concrete.

A face. A woman. Peaceful. Her eyes closed as if dead. Then suddenly they open to reveal almond-colored eyes with dark circles beneath them. Wild curly dark hair, with a single streak of white. It was her mother, only older than the picture Bonnie had seen. The woman's peaceful look turns to panic. Horror in fact. She seems to look directly at Bonnie and yells! "NO!"

Another jolt shot through Bonnie. She was flung backwards and landed on her back on the floor.

"Bonnie!" called Wilder and Reed, rushing to her aid.

"Don' touch dah chile!" yelled Gam Gam. "It be too soon after dah vision!"

"Get her water! Now!" said Fati.

Reed did as he was told and returned quickly, but when he moved to give it to Bonnie, Fati held him back. "Not just yet. She has to come back on her own."

Slowly Bonnie regained consciousness. As she did, Fati instructed Reed to give her the water. Bonnie drank and coughed. She looked at the faces as they slowly came into focus. Gam Gam knelt next to her.

"It's okay, chile. Yah among friends." Gam Gam stroked her head as if she were a kitten.

"My mother!" said Bonnie when she finally was able to form words in her mouth. She sat up. "I saw her!"

"We saw her, too," Reed said, amazed. And Wilder nodded in agreement.

"Easy now. Yes, what you saw is true," Fati confirmed. "She is alive."

Bonnie wept with joy and relief. "Reed! Wilder! My mom's alive. Calico Jack didn't kill her! She's still alive!"

"Bonnie, that's awesome!" Wilder said.

"I'm so happy for you," Reed added, and they both hugged her.

"Do you know where she is?" Bonnie turned to Fati.

"That I can't tell you. There was magic. Hoodoo. Deep. Strong. Preventing me from seeing. And there was something else." Fati furrowed her brow. "Something coming from you," she pointed to Wilder.

Everyone looked at Wilder, who looked surprised. "Me? What did I do?"

"Somethin' about your own mamma," Fati replied. "Something so sad. So deeply sad."

"His mom is missing, too!" Bonnie chimed in.

"Ah, that's what I felt," Fati said and looked at Wilder sympathetically.

"I'm sorry," Wilder said sheepishly. "I-I didn't mean to get in the way of the reading…"

"It wasn't in the way, boy," Fati said. "Just… there, off to one side."

"Hey!" Bonnie said, excitedly. "Maybe Fati could tell you about your mom, too! I mean, while we're here."

"Unh-uh!" Fati said. "This ain't buy one, get one free night! Sorry, babies, I kept my part of the bargain. Now, keep yours and get out!"

"But his mom's been gone a while now," Bonnie pleaded.

"Please, ma'am," Reed chimed in. "Give the guy a little peace of mind?"

Fati was about to begin on a fresh round of refusal when Gam Gam gripped her arm.

"Do it," she said. "Boy need tah know."

Fati looked at Wilder, saw the hopeful, desperate look in his eyes.

"So much for 'I won't never ask you for nothing ever again,'" she groused, then held out her hands. "Go on. While the power of the spirit circle still lingers in the air."

This time Wilder took Bonnie's place next to Fati and they all joined hands again.

"Now focus on your mother, son," Fati said. Wilder looked at Bonnie, who squeezed his hand, this time to give him strength. Wilder took a deep breath and closed his eyes.

Fati began again with two guttural moans. Then she rocked back and forth. In a high, sweet voice that clearly was not her own, Fati started to sing:

Fa la ninna, fa la nanna
Nella braccia della mamma
Fa la ninna, bel bambin
Fa la nanna, bambin bel
Fa la ninna, fa la nanna
Nella braccia della mamma

As she sang, Wilder gripped Bonnie's hand hard. Bonnie opened her eyes and saw a tear trickle down Wilder's cheek.

"What? What is it, Wilder?" Bonnie whispered.

"It's an Italian lullaby. She used to sing it to me when I was little. She learned it from my dad," Wilder said. As Fati continued to sing, Wilder translated, smiling—

Here is a lullaby
In the arms of your mother
Here is a lullaby, beautiful child
Here is a lullaby, child so beautiful
Here is a lullaby
In the arms of your mother

It was the way he preferred to remember his mother. Before everything fell apart. Before heartbreak and depression consumed her. Back when she was just the mother of a perfect little baby boy. Then Wilder's smile faded. There were flashes of visions.

A bridge high above a river. Water's edge. Overgrown foliage. Underneath, out of view: a woman's body lies cold and stiff. Her lips blue, eyes unseeing.

Just then, Fati spoke, still channeling his mother, her voice tinged with sadness. "I'm sorry, baby boy. I'm sorry. I will see you again in paradise."

Wilder opened his eyes and knew. His mother was dead. He looked around at his friends and saw in their faces that they had seen it and knew too. Bonnie was silently weeping. Reed stared at the ground, jaw clenched to try to keep from crying. Even Gam Gam wiped the back of her hand across her eyes.

Wilder, overcome with emotion, buried his face in Fati's neck and wept. Fati recoiled a bit at first, not quite sure what to do. Ultimately, there was only one thing she could do. She put her arm around the boy and pulled him close. One by one, first Bonnie, then Gam Gam, then Reed moved in and joined in the hug. And for the longest time, no one let go.

*   *   *   *   *

A few moments later, Fati stood at the open French doors watching as the kids disappeared into the darkness. Gam Gam came up behind her.

"You done good, mah baby Fatimata," Gam Gam said. "You done real good."

"Then why do I feel like a bear ate me up and spit me out?" Fati's voice was fatigued, drained. Gam Gam put a comforting hand on her granddaughter's shoulder. Fati turned to her. "The other thing. About the boy. Did you... see it?"

"Yep. I seen it," Gam Gam sighed. "Wuz clear as daylight it wuz."

"Should I have told him?"

"It ain't make no difference. Dey on destiny's path now. Ain't no exits."

Fati shook her head. "God help those poor babies." And with that, she closed the doors and drew the blinds.

Chapter 28
Busted!

Bonnie, Reed and Wilder walked through the dark, empty streets just outside Marina Crest Estates, still in shock from what had just happened.

"Wilder," Bonnie was the first to speak, "I shouldn't have pushed you so hard to find out about your mom."

"No. It's okay," Wilder shook his head. "I'm the one who said it's better to know the truth…"

"I'm sorry, man. I know how it feels." Reed patted his shoulder.

"Hey. Don't forget what else you said." Bonnie put a comforting arm around Wilder. "We're family, and we're here for each other."

Wilder wiped his eyes and smiled gratefully. The three walked in silence for a time before Reed spoke.

"Bonnie," he said, "something's bugging me about that thing Fati said about the star…"

"What about it?" Bonnie asked.

Before Reed could answer, SIRENS BLARED all around them. WHEEEEEEEEEOOOOOOOOOO!

"Cops!" Wilder blurted out as the trio instinctively dived into a pitch-black alley for cover.

"It's coming from the marina!" Reed whispered, peeking around the corner. "Sheriff's boat."

"Not just the marina, all over town," Wilder replied with the studied ear of an expert on all manner of police pursuits. "There's police car sirens, too. Something's definitely going down," he said.

"We're gonna have to go into the woods further up from where we came in and double back to the beach," Reed said. "If we get separated, meet at the dinghy."

Reed led them through back alleys and small streets, always careful to avoid streetlights and security cameras. Finally, they came out in an alley behind an auto parts store. The trio looked out across the street that ran alongside the shop and could see a fenced-in vacant lot and the woods just beyond that. For the moment, the street was dark and quiet and they were in the clear.

Reed looked at Bonnie and Wilder, nodded his head, indicating for them to make a run for the woods. And just as they started across the street—

WHOOP! A SIREN gave a single blast. A police car flew around the corner, its lights flashing. Instinctively, the trio scattered, the boys going for the vacant lot while Bonnie doubled back into the dark alley. She watched as the cop car skidded to a stop and two officers jumped out and ran after the boys. Bonnie glimpsed the boys scramble over the fence and disappear into the woods.

By the time the police got to the fence and flashed their flashlights into the woods, the boys were long gone. Bonnie knew she'd have to find her own way back. She crept stealthily, hiding behind dumpsters, trees, and cars for several blocks until she found a spot where she felt safe to cross over into the woods. She knew she had a lot of ground to cover to catch up to the boys, so she went as fast as she could in the thick undergrowth and darkness.

It was hard for Bonnie to see and when she finally emerged from the woods, she found she'd overshot the mark and was now well south of the dinghy. There was a fifteen-foot embankment leading down to a sliver of beach below. Planning to backtrack along the water, Bonnie started down the embankment, holding on to exposed tree roots as she went. She had almost made it to the sand when she froze.

There were voices! Unfamiliar, and coming from down on the beach!

Bonnie pressed herself flat against the embankment, using some of the foliage for cover. She peeked through and saw the silhouettes of three men standing at the edge of the surf—a small motorboat beached on the sand near them. One was short and stocky, another tall and muscular, and third thin and wiry. They were talking heatedly, though with the wind and the sound of the crashing waves, Bonnie couldn't make out the words. But she could smell something putrid…

Death. It smells like death. Before he turned to reveal his face in the moonlight, Bonnie knew exactly who the wiry one was… She had smelled that same stench before, that day at the farmers' market. It was the scar-faced man! Seeing him there again in the darkness terrified her.

Bonnie held perfectly still, waiting for them to go, when all of a sudden, a rock jutting from the embankment that she had been balancing herself on came loose and rolled to the beach below.

The men turned at the sound. Bonnie clung with all her strength to the tree root, burying herself further into the surrounding foliage, her feet dangling. She dared not move or even breathe for fear they would make her out. She could almost feel their eyes boring into her as she hung there in the darkness. Just when she was sure she couldn't hold on a second more, there was another WHOOP of a siren in the distance.

Turning away, the men scrambled into their boat. The outboard motor roared to life and as the boat headed out to open water, the scar-faced man looked back one last time at the spot where Bonnie was hidden. And though she knew he couldn't possibly see her, the feeling of terror shot through her once more.

When they were out of sight, Bonnie let go and dropped to the beach. She took a deep, steadying breath and was overcome with the feeling that somehow she had just averted something truly diabolical.

.   .   .   .   .

When Bonnie finally made her way back to the dinghy, she found Reed and Wilder anxiously waiting for her.

"Bonnie! Thank God!" Wilder exclaimed. "We were just about to go back for you!"

"I got stuck. There were some guys on the beach!" she said, rushing toward them.

"We gotta get out of here! Now!" Reed urged. He waved an arm toward the patrol boat heading out of the marina.

Once they had finally scrambled into the dinghy and set off along the wooded coastline, they swapped stories of their narrow escapes. Though they should have been scared, they were instead buzzing with the adrenalin rush of it.

Suddenly a bright light flooded the dinghy! They froze, blinded by the overpowering glare. A voice on a loudspeaker penetrated the sound of wind and ocean.

"Sheriff's Department! Put your hands where I can see 'em!" a voice with a Southern drawl commanded. Bonnie spun around and looked at the boys, and she could see they too were working in their heads some way out of this.

But then a different voice came over the PA. This one with a softer twang. "Reed Ballister, is that you?"

Bonnie could see Reed's whole body tense up at the sound of his name. No two ways about it. They were busted. The trio put their hands in the air in defeat.

*   *   *   *   *

Moments later Bonnie, Reed, and Wilder stood on the deck of the sheriff's patrol boat before none other than Sheriff Bobby Maynard. Their dinghy, tethered to the boat, was being searched by the sheriff's chunky deputy.

"What the hell are you kids doing off the Cove?" the sheriff demanded.

"Joyriding," Bonnie said quickly, with the smoothness of a practiced liar.

"Joyriding? Are you out of your minds?"

"Haven't you heard?" said Wilder. "North Carolina is a boater's paradise."

Bonnie elbowed Wilder hard. This was no time to be a smartass.

"That's bullcrap, Sheriff!" snarled the chunky deputy as he rejoined them on deck. "We got a report from HPD of juveniles running 'round in town. Dollars to donuts it was them!"

"What were you thinking coming out here?" the sheriff said harshly to Reed. "Do you kids know how dangerous this is?" And even though his words were addressing them all, Bonnie got the feeling that they were meant especially for her. "Do you?!" He grabbed her and was almost yelling now.

"Hey!" Bonnie said. "Get your hands off me!"

"I think you're a little out of line here, Sheriff," Reed said.

"Yeah!" Wilder said angrily. "No need to go all rogue cop on us here!"

"My apologies," Sheriff Maynard said, letting go when he realized everyone was looking at him, even the deputy. He took a step back. "It's just… not a good idea for you kids to be out here so late, that's all."

Bonnie stared at Sheriff Maynard. She was unnerved by his reaction and wondered just exactly how much this ex-Brigand knew about her.

"You're right, Sheriff Maynard." Reed's tone was overly placating and conciliatory. "It was stupid and I take full responsibility. If you'll just let us go back, we swear it'll never happen again."

Wilder nodded. "I agree, Sheriff. What we could really use right now is a strongly worded warning."

The sheriff shot them a final angry look then turned to his deputy. "Deputy Wayne, set a course for Cormac's Cove. We'll be escorting these young people back to where they belong."

"What? You're just letting them go, just like that?" The deputy seemed surprised.

"Did you find anything in the dinghy?" asked Maynard, more than a little annoyed with his deputy.

"Nope," Wayne responded, grudgingly. "But don't mean they didn't toss it overboard."

"Toss *what* overboard?" asked Bonnie.

"Like you don't know," Deputy Wayne snarled.

"Another yacht got hit tonight," Sheriff Maynard explained.

"Jewelry and lots of cash," the deputy chimed in, "but then you prolly know that already, doncha?"

"That's enough, Wayne!" Sheriff Maynard said to his deputy. "Now bring the boat around like I told you."

"But your uncle said—" Deputy Wayne started.

"Well, guess what?" the sheriff jumped in. "Last time I checked the chain of command, Charley Eden was *not* the sheriff of this jurisdiction. I am. So, do as I say!"

Fuming, the deputy sulked into the pilothouse of the boat. "Your uncle's right. You're too damn soft on these Cove kids," he muttered and started up the engine.

"Thanks, Bobby, we really appreciate it," Reed said with relief.

"I wouldn't be spiking the football on this one just yet, Reed Ballister," he said, taking a seat across from them. "This whole mess here is a good bit from over. Your grandparents and me are gonna have a real good parley of our own once we get you back home."

This shut them all up pretty quickly. Even the smart-mouthed Wilder knew enough to hold his tongue. In fact, all three of them sat in silence for the rest of the trip back to the Cove, a trip back to face the music with Captain Ballister. And as Bonnie knew better than anyone, it wasn't a tune they'd be likely to enjoy.

Chapter 29
From Bad to Worse

The sun was coming up as Bonnie, Reed, and Wilder arrived back at Cormac's Cove. The chaotic scene that greeted them on shore made it obvious that their absence had been discovered during the night. And as the boat got closer to the dock, Bonnie could see the remaining corsairs gathered on the beach. Captain Ballister and Winnie were there waiting too, and the look of fury on the captain's face was unmistakable.

"What in the name of Vasco da Gama—!" Ballister started in immediately once they were secured to the dock.

"Caught 'em 'joyriding' up off Highcross," Maynard explained, and Ballister looked at the kids doubtfully—he believed that lame excuse about as much as the sheriff had.

"In the vicinity of another big yacht heist," Deputy Wayne said pointedly from the deck.

"Somebody hit the *Atlantic Chief* tonight in Slip 42," the sheriff explained.

"It wasn't us," Reed said defensively.

Ballister took an angry step toward him. "What were you thinking?"

"It's my fault," Bonnie stepped between them. "The whole thing was my idea."

"I don't give a tinker's damn whose idea it was!" Ballister turned back to Reed, furious. "Damn fool boy! Do you realize what you've done? What peril you've put us all in?"

Winnie got between them. "That'll do, Eleazer," she said, casting her eyes in the deputy's direction. Ballister backed off.

"Captain, you've every right to be angry, but not to worry," Bobby stepped in. "There'll be no report." The sheriff gave the captain a reassuring look.

Ballister's anger deflated a bit. "Fine then," he said curtly. "Since your business here is complete, best you be on your way."

Winnie interjected. "We're much obliged Bobby, thank you."

The captain snorted and turned to the kids. "Hartwright, De Luca, to your cabin," he ordered. "Reed, the house. NOW."

They headed off the pier, but were halted by the sound of a speedboat motor. They all turned and saw it, white and sleek and piloted by none other than Councilman Charley Eden.

"Oh shit," said Wilder, looking at the approaching boat, "there go my brunch plans."

Eden pulled up to the dock, waving a piece of paper over his head. Apparently, Deputy Wayne had tipped off the councilman to the opportunity to finally weasel his way onto the Cove. And Eden was ready, rubber-stamped search warrant and all.

Captain Ballister tried to argue that they had no right to set foot on the property, let alone search it. Sheriff Maynard was livid that his deputy had gone behind his back, but after studying the warrant, he had to admit that it was all proper and legal, and he had no choice but to execute it.

▪   ▪   ▪   ▪   ▪

"This is all my fault," Bonnie said to Wilder and Reed. They were standing with Boreas and the other corsairs in the clearing while the sheriff and his deputy searched the cabins under the watchful eye of Councilman Eden. Captain Ballister was holding the arm of Grandma Winnie in the shade of a towering oak by the path.

"Not all your fault," said Reed.

"We all had something to do with it," Wilder agreed. "But if it helps any, we could blame Reed. He really should have known better."

As the two lawmen entered the Boreas cabin, Wilder tried to assure Bonnie that whatever their sin had been in leaving the Cove, Eden's fishing expedition would turn up a big fat nothing. "Relax," he said. "Worst thing they're gonna find is some contraband, a pack of smokes or two, maybe a bottle of rum."

Even though she knew it wasn't likely they'd close down the school for Wilder's cigarettes or some stolen hooch, still she had a bad feeling. And for some reason, Tanner, who never gave a crap about anything or anyone, seemed suddenly concerned about the outcome of the investigation.

"Well, what d'ya know?" they heard Deputy Wayne call from inside the cabin. "Looky what I found!"

"Shit," Tanner muttered under his breath.

Two minutes later, everyone stood on the boys' side of the Boreas cabin, but all eyes were on Tanner Prescott. On Tanner's bunk, the suitcase he had packed for his imminent departure was open, its contents scattered across the mattress. Deputy Wayne held up the expensive watch he'd found inside.

"Yeah, so?" Tanner shrugged insolently. "It's my Rolex, bubba, what of it?"

"So you're sayin' it's yours?" Deputy Wayne replied with a hint of cross-examination in his voice. "So maybe you'd like to explain why the inscription says 'Thanks for 25 wonderful years, Love Myrna.'"

"I bought it at a pawn shop in L.A.," Tanner shrugged.

"That's interesting," Deputy Wayne said, consulting a list of stolen property he'd pulled out of his pocket, "cuz there was a Rolex answerin' to this very description taken from a yacht two weeks ago at the marina. Insurance company supplied us pics and serial numbers, too!"

A murmur rippled through the room.

"Fine, it's not my watch," Tanner admitted. "But I didn't steal it. I found the thing in the woods, which the last I heard isn't against the law."

"Lying is not your best play here, son," said Bobby firmly.

"I swear I found it!" Tanner, panicking, turned to Captain Ballister. "It was over by that big-ass poplar where we eat lunch sometimes. I was gonna sell it when I got back to California."

"Right," Deputy Wayne smirked. "And maybe that timepiece just sorta fell out of the sky! No sale, kid. Where you got the rest of the stolen property?"

"What the hell do I need with stolen property!?" Tanner scoffed. "I'm already rich!"

"I want every cabin turned upside down!" barked Charley Eden. "If this punk has got so much as a stolen corkscrew hidden on these grounds, I want it found!"

With only twelve corsairs left living in the cabins, it didn't take long to conduct the search. In the Notus cabin, they turned up nothing but some tiny bottles of airplane booze and a tin of smokeless tobacco, and Deputy Wayne emerged from Zephyrus with only two half-smoked cigars and a porn magazine. After the search of the Eurus cabin had come up equally empty, Sheriff Maynard wondered out loud if maybe the kid had actually found the watch after all, a suggestion that was quickly dismissed by Charley Eden.

"Fat chance!" snorted Charley. "I know he's got the stuff somewhere. Maybe a few hours in lock-up will refresh this punk's memory."

"You can't throw me in jail. I'm a minor," objected Tanner.

Eden snorted out a laugh. "Maybe that's the way of things where you're from, boy. But here, 17 and you're an adult in the eyes of the law. Cuff him."

Deputy Wayne moved forward, put the handcuffs on Tanner, and began to recite his Miranda rights.

"This is bogus! I want a lawyer!" Tanner yelled, struggling against the cuffs. "I'm not sayin' shit without my dad's attorney!"

That's when all hell broke loose and the accusations flew. Ballister accused Eden of playing fast and loose with the search warrant and that this all was a pretext to seize the land. Eden accused Ballister of running a crime ring off the Cove. Tanner cursed at Bonnie, Reed, and Wilder for bringing the cops to the Cove in the first place. Wilder yelled back that everything would have been fine if Tanner hadn't been looking to fence a hot Rolex. And they *all* vehemently denied that they'd had anything to do with any burglaries or crimes. "This summer, anyway," Wilder added for clarification.

In the end, none of it mattered. Sheriff Maynard finally yelled for everyone to "COOL IT!" Then, he said that given the situation, he had no choice but to bring Tanner down to the station to book him on possession of stolen property. Bonnie and the others could do nothing but stand on the beach and watch as Tanner was marched onto the patrol boat, with Ballister accompanying him to act as his guardian until Tanner's father could dispatch his lawyer to Highcross.

What none of them had seen during the search, however, was the surprised look on Charley Eden's face when Deputy Wayne discovered the Rolex, or the fact that as soon as the deputy stumbled on the watch, Eden surreptitiously stuffed a diamond necklace he'd brought along with him back into his jacket pocket.

Chapter 30
Guidance from Above

"What are we even looking for?" asked Barnaby as Boreas and Reed Ballister combed through the dense brush near where the giant poplar tree stood.

"This is where Tanner says he found the watch," replied Bonnie. "We need evidence that proves he was telling the truth."

"Come on, you don't believe Tanner, do you?" asked Micah.

"I believe that a whole lot easier than believing he's a yacht burglar," Reed said matter-of-factly.

"Cabin Boy's right," Wilder agreed. "That douche is too lazy to mastermind a run to a donut shop, much less a string of jewelry heists."

"So he *had* to have found it like he said; otherwise, how did the watch get into *his* stuff?" Bonnie sighed.

Just then they heard a tremendous SQUAWK!

"Your pal's back, Bonnie," Micah said, pointing out over the water.

Bonnie saw Crossbones flying toward them. He swooped in and attempted a landing next to her.

"Sorry bud," Bonnie said. "No treats right now."

Crossbones circled and swooped near Bonnie again, clearly trying to get her attention. "Not now, fella!" She waved her hand at him.

Crossbones fluttered away and came to rest on a branch above her.

"So if Tanner found the watch, how did it get here?" Barnaby asked.

"Well, the watch got here somehow," said Bonnie. "It didn't miraculously just fall out of the sky!"

And just as she said this, something dropped onto Bonnie's head from above.

She jumped, at first thinking that the bird had bombed her.

"Hey! Crossbones! Watch it, will ya?" she said, wiping her head. But then she saw something glittering on the ground next to her foot. She bent and picked it up.

"Uh, guys," she said. "I think I know how the watch got here."

Bonnie held up a diamond earring that had just dropped at her feet. It was easily two carats in size and glinted in the sun. And in unison, the kids looked from the earring up to Crossbones.

"The bird?" asked Micah.

"Why wouldn't it be possible?" Bonnie asked. "Crossbones has been bringing me stuff all summer. Why couldn't he have brought the watch, too?"

"So what, are we going to have the parrot testify on Tanner's behalf?" asked Wilder.

"No. But maybe he can lead us to the real criminals," Bonnie continued off their puzzled looks. "If the parrot is bringing this stuff over here, he must be getting it from wherever it's stashed."

Just then Crossbones took off and flew out over the water straight for Tuscarora Island in the distance.

"The parrot's colony is out on Tuscarora Island, right, Reed?"

"Near Corsair's Lair," he nodded, "just inland a bit."

"Which would be *perfect* for stashing stolen stuff," Bonnie said to the others. "You remember what the captain told us about the history of that place—bunch of grottos and caves, plenty of potential hiding places."

"No easy access from the land, either," Reed agreed. "And far enough away from town not to cause any suspicion."

"Reed. Do you think you could lead us to the colony?" Bonnie asked.

"The terrain's pretty rough but yeah, I'm pretty sure I could find it."

"I dunno. Sounds like a wild parrot chase to me," Micah said.

"It's our only shot," Bonnie said, getting up with determination. "We'll take the cutter. Be there in an hour."

"Not likely," replied Reed. "Jonesy is down on the docks guarding all the boats. No way we're getting off the Cove today."

They were all so busy plotting that they didn't notice Malachi had gone off into the woods and returned with something. He held it out to them. It was a white trumpet-like flower and a purplish wild orchid. Jimsonweed and Ladyslipper!

"Malachi, buddy, Anodyne Arts isn't 'til Wednesday," Wilder objected.

Bonnie's eyes widened. "Micah. I. LOVE. YOUR. BROTHER!" And, taking the flowers, she gave Malachi a huge kiss full on the lips and disappeared into the woods.

Wilder turned to Reed. "What the hell just happened?"

Chapter 31
Den of Thieves

What had just happened was that Malachi Maguire had shown Bonnie the precise plants that grew naturally on the Cove, which also had sedative properties powerful enough to knock out a grown man like Jonesy. After a quick grinding job, Micah and Malachi had turned the plants into a fine powder, and Barnaby was dispatched to the dock. He was able to slip the powder into Jonesy's flask during one of the old drunk's frequent visits behind the boathouse to relieve himself. Before long, Jonesy was slumped over, fast asleep against one of the dock pilings.

After retrieving their swords, Reed, Bonnie, and Wilder were soon racing across the sound on the *Solstice Skye.* Standing near the bow, Reed held onto the rigging and leaned far back to balance the weight of the pull of the sail by the strong winds.

"Faster!" yelled Bonnie, running a spinnaker sail up the mast.

With the foresail up now, the cutter picked up speed, moving like a rock skipped across a glassy lake. They made the trip to Tuscarora in a quarter of the time it would have taken on the *True North.* An expert in these waters, Reed piloted the cutter toward the south end of the island, just down from the town of Tuscarora itself. Weekend sailors usually avoided this end of the island because of its dense woods and rocky beaches, but Reed was steady and sure in his piloting and soon they had the boat in the waters off Corsair's Lair.

Bonnie and Wilder hopped out of the cutter and helped push it to shore. Bonnie took a steadying breath and fingered the gris-gris that she had made sure to wear around her neck.

"Okay, Cabin Boy," said Wilder once they'd gotten out of the water, "where do we find this parrot colony?"

"It's somewhere in there." Reed pointed vaguely past the thin strip of white sand to the dense overgrowth of woods.

"That narrows it down," Bonnie sighed.

*   *   *   *   *

Bonnie could feel the sweat pouring down her back as she used Siobhan to hack through the dense undergrowth that lay in front of her. The trio had walked for over an hour but the going was slow. Despite it being almost noon, the thick canopy of trees barely allowed any sun to penetrate and everything had a murky, gray look to it. Though they wouldn't admit it to one another, they were all feeling pretty jumpy. And when something—it turned out to be a rabbit—skittered by, Wilder actually yelped.

"No wonder the old pirates hid out here," Wilder said. "You gotta be outta your mind to come to this place."

"Yeah, not with all those killer bunnies running around," taunted Reed.

"Don't pretend like you didn't nearly crap a brick, too, wuss."

"Shut up!" said Bonnie. "You want to scare off the parrots?"

"I've got news for you, Curls," said Wilder. "I'm not seeing any parrots."

"But I'm hearing them," Reed said, stopping abruptly ahead of them. "Listen."

Bonnie stood still and became aware of a high-pitched sound, which seemed to swell and fall in a kind of rhythm. It was coming from beyond a massive deadfall up ahead.

They walked toward the deadfall and saw there was no way to the other side but over the top of it. So, one by one, they carefully climbed up the mass of tangled brush and fallen timber, hoping it wouldn't give way beneath them. As they reached the crest, they stopped. They'd come upon an area where the trees weren't as thick, so the sun found its way through in places and the entire area was much brighter.

Bonnie was the first to step through. She had to lean down to make it under the branches but when she finally raised her head, she had to catch her breath. There, in the canopy of trees overhead, as far as the eye could see, were numerous roundish, wreath-like structures made from twigs. In each, an almost perfect circular hole.

"Nests!" Bonnie said, as she watched parrots, dozens of them, moving in and out, fluttering back and forth from branch to branch. And then she realized that the high-pitched sound they'd heard wasn't a single sound, but a wall of sound created by the squeak, chirps and peeps of the large colorful birds.

"Told ya I could find the parrot colony," Reed smirked to Wilder.

"Even a blind squirrel can find a nut once in a while," Wilder replied.

"Well, we did find you," Reed shot back.

"If the burglars are holed up someplace, I doubt it's right here," interrupted Bonnie, wiping the sleeve of her T-shirt with a large leaf after she failed to dodge a huge blob of parrot poop. The others nodded.

"Then it's got to be someplace nearby," said Reed, looking around.

"Yeah, but which way do we go?" asked Wilder.

At that very moment, Bonnie's old friend Crossbones swooped down among them.

"Crossbones!" Bonnie shouted over the racket. "Where did you get the sparklies?"

The parrot made a circle and came back around several times.

"I think he wants us to follow him," Bonnie said.

"Oh really?" said Wilder skeptically. "And then maybe after that, we can have it give us the point spread on the next Giants game."

Suddenly the parrot took off. *Voom!* Like a rocket it sped through the trees.

"Come on!" yelled Bonnie, the first to give chase. "Before we lose it!"

And the crazy game of follow-the-leader was on. Bonnie was able to keep up better, as the boys constantly had to slow down to dodge low-hanging branches.

"He's just taking us back the way we came!" Wilder exclaimed between labored breaths.

"No, we're going further south!" Reed and Bonnie said in unison.

"He's heading toward those rocks!" Bonnie called behind her. "Keep up!"

"Look, no offense, but if that green crap-o-matic is leading us over a cliff, I'd prefer not to be first in line," called Wilder from the rear.

"It's not going to lead us over a cliff," said Reed.

"How do you know what it's doing? You Dr. Doolittle all of a sudden?"

"I know cuz there are no cliffs on the island, just stony beaches." Reed yelled behind him.

With his eyes fixed on Crossbones, Reed ran ahead of Bonnie and led the group, Wilder close on his heels. They broke through the overgrowth and all scrambled to come to a stop as they realized the ground suddenly dropped out in front of them to some jutting rocks a dozen feet below. Reed almost went over and would have if Wilder hadn't grabbed him by the collar and pulled him back from the precipice.

"Whoa!" Reed said, looking down. It wasn't a cliff, but hitting the hard rocks at top speed would have been good for a broken leg or a concussion at the very least.

They watched as the parrot circled overhead a couple of times, floating on the ocean breeze.

"It's bad enough he taunts Jonesy, but I think that feathered freak was trying to break our necks for good measure," said Wilder. "You owe me one, by the way."

"Whatever," Reed responded grudgingly.

"Wait, look!" Bonnie exclaimed.

They watched as the parrot circled downward near where the drop met the beach. Then he flew straight for it and disappeared. The trio strained to look over the edge.

"Where did he go?" asked Reed

"Looked like he was going to smash right into the slope down there," said Wilder.

Bonnie grabbed hold of some roots that were sticking out and used them to steady herself as she slid down the dirt slope to the beach. The boys followed her. Puzzled because there was no sign of the bird, they walked over and looked closely at the slope, which was covered with overgrowth from the woods. Then Bonnie spotted it. She pulled back some of the overgrowth to reveal an opening to a cave.

The entrance of the cave was so small that when they entered, they had to walk single file. As the entrance dipped downward, it took them deeper underground before opening up into a bigger cave—maybe thirty or forty feet wide. It was dim, with shafts of light here and there from small cracks up above. The parrot sat watching them from a jutting rock ledge near the back of the cave.

"Hey there, boy. Is this where you found the watch?" asked Bonnie, speaking gently to the bird.

"Well, *someone's* sure been here lately," said Reed. He pointed to the corner, where there were a couple of bedrolls, a camp lantern, and some fast-food wrappers with a half-eaten burger on the ground.

"All the crap they put in fast food, that burger could be from two years ago," Wilder informed them.

"Yeah. But this isn't," Bonnie held up a newspaper. *The Highcross Herald*. The heading in bold letters read:

MODERN-DAY PIRACY:
TOWN ON EDGE AFTER LATEST YACHT BURGLARY

"This is from today!" Bonnie said. "Somebody's been here this morning!"

"Or they could still be here right now!" said Wilder, nervously. "I say we get the hell outta here before whoever it is comes back. From what I know, criminals get a little testy when they catch you poking around their shit."

Reed grabbed the paper from Wilder. "Lot of good this does us. Today's paper and a half-eaten cheeseburger don't get Tanner off the hook."

"No. But this does!" Bonnie's voice echoed from somewhere at the back of the cave. She had been watching the parrot and noticed it flutter and disappear through a dark corner that had at first appeared to be a dead-end alcove. She followed the bird and soon was standing in the middle of a second, larger cave. The boys joined her.

"Sweet Baby Jesus!" marveled Wilder.

He was staring at a large rock that was covered with items: watches, jewelry, electronic devices, iPad tablets, and piles of cash. There was even a 50-inch smart TV. Sitting proudly atop it all was the parrot.

"There must be over a hundred grand worth of stuff here!" Wilder reached over to pick up a wad of cash and Bonnie slapped his hand away.

"No fingerprints, man!" she warned.

"We need to let Sheriff Maynard know about this place right away," Reed said. He pulled out a cell phone and looked at it. "Damn. There's no service out here."

"Hey! You've had a cell phone this whole time?" Wilder said indignantly.

"I'm a corsair, not a monk," Reed replied as he began snapping photos of the booty.

"The hell are *you* doing?!" Bonnie snatched the phone away from him.

"I was getting photographic evidence," Reed objected.

"You mean *incriminating* evidence!" she said as she started deleting the photos. "All these pictures will prove is that we know where the stolen stuff is. What's wrong with you two?"

"Okay. You're obviously the pro here. What do you suggest?" Reed asked.

Bonnie thought a moment. "Hide out up in the tree line. Get video on your phone of the thieves when they come back. Text it to Maynard as soon as we get a signal."

"I love it. In fact, let's do it right now, *before* they come back," Wilder said. "So maybe a little less plotting and a little more leaving."

"You coming, Crossbones?" Bonnie asked the bird. But it stayed where it was, nuzzling a fur coat that was on top of the pile of loot.

"Forget it, Bonnie. He's in love," Wilder urged, pushing her toward the exit.

Bonnie led the way back toward the cave opening. But then she stopped in her tracks, causing the boys to stumble into her.

"You bloody moron!" they heard a gruff voice say. Bonnie peeked through the overgrowth that hid the mouth of the cave. She could see a modern-day sailing yacht anchored out in the water. Bonnie could make out the name of the vessel inscribed on the port side despite the beat-up hull and peeling paint. *Dark Star.* Bonnie looked around for its occupants, seeing a couple of figures busy at work on the deck. Suddenly a man appeared right in her line of vision, not fifty feet away, near a rowboat on the beach. He turned and started coming toward her. It was the scar-faced man.

Bonnie motioned for the others to back up. Fast! They retreated back into the cave.

"You guys!" Bonnie whispered in a mad panic. "It's the guy I saw on the beach last night. The same one I ran into at the farmers' market!"

"Crap! I told you we should have left sooner!" Wilder's voice rose a bit.

"Shhhh!" Bonnie clamped her hand on his mouth.

She led the boys onto the rock ledge where Crossbones had been perched earlier just before the men entered the cave. They scooched back into the shadows.

"What the hell were you thinking, using a stolen credit card instead of cash? You know how easy it is to track that!" said the gruff voice again, this time echoing in the cave.

"The outboard was low on gas," came another voice in reply to the first man.

"Crap, there's two of 'em," whispered Bonnie.

Bonnie lifted her head slightly to get a look over the ledge and saw that in addition to the scar-faced man, there was a second man, shorter and stocky with bulging biceps, who was currently on the receiving end of his companion's foul-mouthed critique of his spending habits.

"Yer always ridin' me," complained the stocky guy, snapping on the camp lantern. "It's shameful what I got to put up with in this job!"

"Nobody cares about your bloody opinion, Clegg!" the scar-faced man growled viciously, waving a jagged knife at him. "Now grab that cash, and let's get back to the ship. The others are waitin'."

In the glow of the lantern, Bonnie glimpsed his scarred face, and the familiar odor of death penetrated her nostrils. She recoiled and when she did, she elbowed Wilder in the gut, causing him to let out a little involuntary grunt. He looked at Bonnie, horrified. They all slid back as far as they could into the shadows. The two men wheeled around and peered into the darkness.

"The hell was that?" growled the scar-faced one.

"Came from back there, Maks," Clegg said.

"Go check the stash; I'll look in here," said Maks. Clegg disappeared deeper into the cave.

Maks lifted the lantern and looked around, his eyes staring into the dark corners. The friends held their breath, not daring to move at all. Slowly, he advanced toward the area where the sound had come from, lantern in one hand, his knife in the other.

Bonnie and the boys were in shadow. The arc of the lantern light moved closer and closer. Bonnie could feel her heart beating hard in her chest, and she was sure that the scarred man could hear it, too.

A few feet from them, Maks paused; his nostrils flared and sniffed at the air like a dog. His eyes narrowed and they seemed to look straight at Bonnie through the darkness.

Maks took another step closer. Bonnie wrapped her hand around the hilt of Siobhan, muscles taut, ready to spring into action.

"Just you come out now, whoever you are," he said in a raspy voice. "I know you're there." And just as the lantern light was about to reveal the three of them—

SQUAWK!

Crossbones came flying out of the shadows. The kids were almost as surprised as Maks as the parrot flew straight at the man's face, clawing him and drawing blood. He moved swiftly back and took a swipe at the bird with the knife.

"Aaaaarrrrrrr!" he bellowed in fury, wiping blood from his eye! Clegg came running to see what the commotion was.

"What the—?"

"It's that damn bird again! That bloody scavenger's stolen from us for the last time! Kill it now!" yelled Maks.

The bird flew around the cave with the two men in hot pursuit.

"Don't let that infernal thing get away!" yelled Maks. The bird swooped down and led the thieves back into the cave where the loot was stashed.

"Run!" Reed whispered and grabbed Bonnie by the arm, pulling her down. Wilder followed and the trio rushed for the cave opening.

"There's someone here!" they heard Clegg yell and knew that they had been spotted.

"Go! Go! Go!" shouted Wilder.

The trio burst out of the cave and scrambled up the slope. Clegg emerged seconds later and grabbed at Wilder's ankle. He started to pull Wilder back down to the beach until Reed smacked the guy in the head with the heel of his boot, freeing Wilder from his clutches.

"We're even!" Reed yelled as he followed Bonnie to the top.

"Whatever!" Wilder replied, right behind him. At the top, Bonnie paused to look back over her shoulder for Crossbones. But she was yanked forward by Reed and Wilder and they all hit the ground running.

Once they reached the woods, Reed turned northward in the direction of the *Solstice Skye*. Bonnie was right behind him with Wilder bringing up the rear. Wilder looked back at one point to see where their pursuers were—Clegg was closing in—and he turned back around, too late to see a low-hanging branch. It caught him in the head and he went down.

"Wilder!" Bonnie screamed when she realized they had lost him. She and Reed ran back toward Wilder. Just as Clegg reached their friend, Bonnie jumped, grabbed a branch, swung like an Olympic gymnast, and kicked the guy square in the chest. Clegg staggered and Reed finished him off with a healthy smack in the forehead with the hilt of his sword.

Bonnie and Reed rushed to Wilder, who moaned with pain.

"Help me get him up!" Bonnie said and grabbed one of Wilder's arms while Reed got the other. They hoisted him to his feet. Wilder hobbled as Bonnie and Reed pulled him through the woods as fast as they could.

Bonnie spotted the cutter through a break in the trees and felt a sense of relief wash over her with a clean escape just fifty yards away. Her relief was short-lived as suddenly—

ZING! Bark from a tree nearby splintered! She realized they were being shot at! With guns! She saw the scar-faced guy Maks in the distance, his face twisted in rage.

ZING! Another bullet whizzed past the trio. ZING! ZING! Then another and another. They picked up the pace when suddenly something yanked on Bonnie's neck, causing her to lose her grip on Wilder and fall to her knees. As she did, a bullet whizzed just above her and harmlessly struck the trunk of a tree where she had just been standing. Bonnie looked down at the broken gris-gris necklace on the ground. It had gotten caught on a branch, jerking her out of harm's way. She felt a wave of goosebumps; the gris-gris had protected her, just as Gam Gam had promised. She reached to pick it up when—

"Go go go!" Reed yelled and pulled her to her feet. Bonnie grabbed Wilder and the trio double-timed it across the beach, leaving the talisman behind. They dragged Wilder to the cutter, bullets flying overhead the whole way.

"Let's get him on board!" Bonnie yelled.

They hoisted Wilder onto the cutter, and Reed pushed it out into the water. With the *Solstice Skye* now afloat, Reed leapt on board. Bonnie was about to join him when Maks burst through the woods, running headlong toward the surf.

Bonnie looked back just as Maks leveled his gun at her. She braced herself for the bullet. But just as he pulled the trigger, Crossbones came swooping down at him, striking his hand so that the shot missed its mark and only grazed Bonnie's arm, ripping her shirt. The gun dropped into the surf and Maks savagely backhanded the bird, sending it fluttering backwards until it landed motionless on the beach.

Reed rushed over to Bonnie as she clutched her now-bleeding arm and started to help her on board. She was almost completely on the boat when suddenly Maks grabbed her by her hair.

"Gotcha, ya little bitch!" he growled.

It was a tug of war between Reed and Maks as Bonnie struggled wildly between them, twisting, writhing, and punching backwards at the scar-faced man. But Maks had the advantage of weight and gravity and soon pulled her off the back of the cutter. Just then Crossbones, having regained his senses, swooped back down and attacked Maks's hand again, this time clamping down hard on his finger. Maks howled in pain as the parrot's powerful beak clipped him through to the bone. Crossbones yanked its head to the side and violently ripped the bony digit from the rest of the hand—the bloody severed finger falling into the water!

Maks pulled his hand back, finally releasing Bonnie's hair from his grip, revealing for just a moment her shoulder blade—and her birthmark—through the rip in her shirt. His eyes went wide.

Bonnie clambered on board at just the moment a gust of wind caught the cutter's sail and it lurched forward, pulling just out of Maks's reach.

We're safe, Bonnie thought, falling back onto the boat, clutching her wounded arm and taking deep gulps of air as Reed maneuvered the cutter rapidly into open water. She looked back and watched as the scarred man stood strangely motionless in the waist-high surf, his hand hanging at his side, blood spewing from where his finger used to be. That same severed finger now bobbed next to him in the water. But Maks seemed not to notice it at all. Instead, his eyes were fixed on Bonnie. And Bonnie could swear she saw a smile appear at the edges of his mouth. Bonnie felt a shudder from somewhere deep inside her spine.

Someone just walked on my grave, she thought.

Chapter 32
Recognition and Reunion

After their narrow escape from Tuscarora Island, Bonnie, Reed, and Wilder made it back to Cormac's Cove in record time, if someone had actually gone about keeping records for the fastest time for crossing the sound in a small cutter with a three-person crew when weighed down by an injured parrot. For the parrot Crossbones was on board as well. After finally freeing itself from Maks, the bird had managed to fly out to the cutter but then fell like a sack of pennies onto the deck, its wing too damaged to fly any further. As they got closer to land, Reed finally was able to grab a signal for his cell phone from one of the Highcross towers and called Sheriff Maynard as they approached the Cove.

"He was pretty pissed," said Reed, finally hanging up, "but agreed to check out the cave."

"Let's hope he gets there before those guys clear out," Bonnie said as she tended to the injured Wilder.

As the boat skipped across the water, Bonnie looked back and forth between these two very different boys that destiny had put into her path this fateful summer. Wilder. As charming as he was goofy and as loyal as he was unpredictable. And Reed Ballister. Cool. Implacable. But somehow distant, even when he was close to her. During the encounter with the yacht burglars, she felt like both of them really *would* have died to protect her, if it had come to that.

For the first time in her life, she felt like she was truly in the company of heroes.

■   ■   ■   ■   ■

"Bonnie, you're truly in the company of idiots!"

Captain Ballister had returned by the time they got back to the Cove, and sure enough, there was plenty of hell to pay. From the moment they set foot in the main house, the captain and Jonesy, who had just awakened, railed and bellowed despite Winnie's insistence that they back off so she could at least tend to the wounded. While Winnie performed first aid, Ballister assured Bonnie that, far from being heroes, Reed and Wilder were in fact two of the most reckless simpletons he'd ever laid eyes on for acting so foolhardy, knowing full well that she was the bearer of the mark. And that Bonnie herself was incredibly selfish to go along, given the global implications of her losing her years to Calico Jack. Not to mention the personal inconvenience that being dead would be to her.

Reed's assurances that these were just garden-variety criminals that they'd tussled with did nothing to calm the captain's fury.

"Well, these so-called 'garden-variety criminals' came this close to blowing her head clean off!" Ballister snarled.

"Uh, hey," Bonnie complained to the captain, "I'm like right here, dude."

"Well, father, if you trusted the boy a bit more," Winnie offered as she finished up a splint on Crossbones's wing, "perhaps he wouldn't have felt like he had to defy us."

"The boy is letting his affinity for the girl cloud his judgment!" declared Ballister.

"That's ridiculous! He just did what any Brigand would do!" Bonnie said, secretly hoping that wasn't entirely true.

"And since when does my judgment matter about *anything* around here?" Reed yelled. "You were in Highcross, and I had to do *something*!"

"You'll do nothing that I don't tell you to do!"

The Ballisters' argument was escalating out of control. Charges and counter charges flew across the room. Jonesy continued giving the kids an earful for their part in drugging him and had a few choice words for Crossbones, which set the injured bird to squawking loudly over the din of voices.

Amid the uproar, Yeun arrived out of breath and shouted over the noise, "Excuse me. EXCUSE ME! Sheriff Maynard is at the dock asking permission to come ashore!"

*   *   *   *   *

"I can't believe it!" Bonnie exclaimed, as she paced the dock, frustrated. Everyone on the Cove had rushed to the dock to hear the news that Sheriff Maynard's search of the cave had come up empty.

"There wasn't any evidence left?" Captain Ballister asked, as if his mind hadn't quite accepted it yet.

"Some food wrappers, parrot feathers," Sheriff Maynard answered. "But there were a bunch of shell casings on the beach. I—wait, were you shot?" He noticed Bonnie's bandage on her arm.

"It's nothing, just a graze," she brushed it off.

"Just a graze?!" the sheriff went off. "These were dangerous men you were messin' with, Bonnie! How could you have been so reckless?! Have you been taught nothing all summer?!"

"How dare you insinuate that I have not done my duty by these young folk," the captain said, his voice full of indignation. "And for you, of all people, to use the word 'reckless' on this Cove is beyond—"

"Enough! Both of you!" Winnie cut them off. "This isn't the time to pick at old wounds. We got plenty of fresh ones to tend to. Now, what are our options at this juncture?"

The sheriff clenched his jaw, looked from Bonnie to Winnie. Then he continued, a bit calmer now. "Unfortunately, Grandma Winnie, there isn't much we can do at this point. The Prescott boy's got to stay put for now. However, now that we have the description of the men Reed gave me and the name of their ship, I'll put out an APB. We're also going to be checking all local hospitals for anyone coming in with a finger injury. Meantime, since strong advice doesn't seem to have any impact around here, none of you leaves this cove without my say-so until we get to the bottom of this."

"So what, are we supposed to just sit around here telling sailing stories while Cormac's Cove is on the verge of being stolen from us?" Reed said angrily.

"That's bullshit!" agreed Wilder.

All the corsairs, silent until now, began shouting in defiance.

Bonnie huffed indignantly at the sheriff, "You don't have the authority to tell us what to do!"

"See this badge?!" Maynard yelled above the din, pointing to the star on his chest. "This badge means I DO have the authority."

And that's when Bonnie saw it.

She looked down to the badge on his shirt pocket. It gleamed brightly in the sunlight, and something at the back of her mind tugged at her. Something the fortune teller had said the night before. And Reed had mentioned something, too. *What was it?* The sun reflected off the star again. And she found herself saying under her breath, "It has six points."

"What is she talking about?" the Captain asked Winnie.

Bonnie turned to Reed as if it were revelatory. "It has six points!"

"Oh my God," Reed said, suddenly understanding. "Of course."

"We're done for today." Ballister quickly stepped between the sheriff and Bonnie. But Winnie grabbed his arm to stop him. He jerked it away but it was too late.

Bonnie reached out her hand toward the badge on the sheriff's chest. The moment her finger made contact with it—

LIGHT EXPLODED in her head! Visions. Flashes. *A full moon. A secluded beach. A secret rendezvous. A stolen kiss. Two pairs of eyes filled with passion. The Cave. Lit by a roaring fire. A name scrawled on the ceiling. Brigid. Another next to it… R-O-B…*

Bobby caught her before she fell. "Bonnie! Bonnie, are you okay?"

"You!" Bonnie said, regaining her senses and pulling away from the sheriff—the visions halting the moment his hand left her arm. "It's you!"

"Who?" asked Wilder. He looked from Reed to Winnie to the Captain, who, from the looks on their faces, all seemed to have some understanding that he did not. "Will somebody tell me what the hell is going on?"

"The star Fati told me about," Bonnie stated, "it wasn't the compass rose at all. Our compass rose has eight points. Six points was what Fati said. Like… like that," she pointed at Bobby's badge.

"Holy shit…" murmured Wilder. "You mean…"

In a split second, Bonnie did the math. The sheriff looked to be in his early thirties, so fifteen years before that… Add to that the strange but familiar way he looked at her. How he had behaved toward her, all protective, like he was more to her than a complete stranger. *It was definitely him.*

"… he's my father," Bonnie finished the sentence.

Everyone stood in stunned silence. After a moment, the captain attempted to deny it, but a look from Winnie silenced him. Bobby Maynard just stood there, his steady gaze fixed upon Bonnie. But Bonnie knew it was him. And she could tell that he knew she was his daughter.

The truth of it just hung in the air like the humidity of the Carolina afternoon.

Chapter 33

Heart to Hartwright

Bonnie sat on the end of the pier, arms crossed tightly, about as far away as she could be and still be within the sound of the sheriff's voice. That's how she still thought of him. The sheriff. She couldn't yet get her mind around the fact that he was her father.

Bonnie stole glances at him during the course of their conversation but stared mostly at the water, the way she always avoided eye contact whenever she was nervous.

Except she wasn't only nervous. She was also angry. Angry that she had been lied to yet again. Angry that there was yet another secret that had been kept from her. Reed was angry too when he realized the truth, for it had been withheld from him as well. Against the captain's objections, Reed insisted, no, *demanded* that Bonnie be given the chance to speak with the sheriff privately when she requested it. It took Grandma Winnie shooing everyone off the dock to allow father and daughter to talk. When they were finally alone, Bonnie knew she had to push back the anger to make room for all the questions that cried out for answers.

"When did you know it was me?" she asked first, only because there were so many questions in her head she didn't know where to start.

"When I saw you at the market," he answered softly. "You look so much like your mother. There was no question."

"But you didn't say anything."

"I wanted to, I really did, but the captain wouldn't have had any of it. I'd burned that bridge with him long ago when I was banished from Brigands."

"Banished? I thought you quit."

"Is that what they told you? No, Bonnie, I loved the Brigands. I never would've quit."

"Must've been something pretty terrible. Ballister's still crazy pissed."

"I fell in love with a mark bearer," he said with a hint of sadness. "The one I had vowed to protect. In the Brigands, that's not just breaking a rule; it's like violating a commandment."

For a moment Bonnie's thoughts flew to her own blossoming feelings for both Reed and Wilder, but she immediately pushed them away.

"So you were in love with her, my mom?"

"From here to hereafter and five miles past that. I remember the first time I saw her. Me and the rest of the corsairs had come down to the water after breakfast. The *North* came around the rocks and there she was at the helm. Those dark eyes flashing all wild. Her hair a mess of tangles in the wind… even wilder. Lord. She was the most beautiful thing I ever laid eyes on. Wasn't just how she looked, either. She was… something else."

Sheriff Maynard continued, losing himself in the memory. "Independent. Smart. But with a temper, too. I remember when Captain Ballister told her she couldn't put her name up on the cave wall, her not being of Read blood and all. She was fit to be tied. Felt she'd earned it, no matter what the bloodline said. So she snuck into the cave in the middle of the night and put her name up there anyway. I helped her. You didn't tell her no. Not that I ever wanted to."

"If you loved her so much, why'd you let her run off?" she demanded.

"I wouldn't have if I'd known what she was fixin' to do. She was real secretive. Didn't even tell me she was expecting for the longest time. She hid it. From everyone. She knew I'd be sent away if anybody found out about us."

"But you stepped up, right?"

"Not right away. She insisted I keep quiet. She didn't want to get me in trouble."

"But you got *her* in trouble," Bonnie said resentfully. "And you didn't care about doing the right thing. Being a Brigand was more important to you than taking responsibility!" She got to her feet. Suddenly, he was not the father she had hoped for at all. He was just another reckless teenager, afraid of the consequences of his own bad decisions.

Bobby Maynard jumped to his feet as well and followed her down the dock. "No!" he said forcefully. "I wasn't afraid of responsibility. I was afraid of losing her! Because if I did, I wouldn't have been around to protect her… and you. And I wanted so much to be with her. I loved her so much." Bonnie saw the sincerity and though she believed him, it didn't make her any less angry.

"I don't get it. If you two were so madly in love, why'd she leave you to run off to Arizona?"

The sheriff walked to the edge of the pier. He put his hands in his pockets and she saw his shoulders slump as if the weight of a distant memory had been placed upon them.

"You're still young," he said. "Maybe you don't know what it's like to lose someone you truly love. How it rips you apart from the inside and changes what the world looks like to you. But that's just what happened to your mom when Reed's folks were killed."

He went on to tell the story that she knew bits and pieces of from the Ballisters and later from Reed.

"Word came of their murders and Brigid just… it hit her real hard," Bobby continued. "Daniel was like a big brother to her. They grew up together. You weren't due for another month, but the shock of the news… Brigid went into labor. It was long, too. Hard.

I remember. Night of a bad storm. You finally came. Then she saw the mark on you and she flipped out. Wouldn't let anyone near you. Not even me. She stayed holed up in her room with you. For weeks. Slept with her sword at her side… if she slept at all. Only let Grandma Winnie in to feed her, and even then she'd barely eat. It was awful.

"That's when I knew I had to come forward. I told Captain Ballister the truth, thinking I could be the one to talk her off the ledge a bit and that maybe she'd come around by and by. They were plenty angry, but they were desperate, too, so they let me see her. But it didn't matter. It was like talking to a ghost. In her mind, she'd already left the Cove. The next day, she was gone… I should have known what she was planning when she refused to give you a name."

"I don't understand. Why didn't she name me?" Bonnie wondered.

"I guess she thought if she did, she'd never be able to give you up. She believed you could never be safe here. Figured if the Brigands couldn't protect warriors like Reed's parents, there was no way they could protect a helpless little baby like you. She didn't believe that *I* could protect you, either. Heck, maybe I couldn't. But she never even gave me the chance. That's the part that still eats away at my insides." He turned and looked at Bonnie and she could see the devastation on his face as if it had happened yesterday. *He did love her*, she thought. *He still does.*

"Did you even try to look for us?" Bonnie asked.

"I did, Bonnie. For years. After I was kicked out of the Brigands, just after she left, I lived on the road, followed even the tiniest scrap of a lead wherever it took me."

"Obviously it didn't take you very far."

"I didn't wanna give up. But I had to. You gotta understand, me and the Brigands, we weren't the only ones looking for you. Calico Jack was out there, too. Many's a time I had run-ins with his men out on the road." He rolled up a sleeve to reveal some terrible scars from several slash marks. Bonnie was taken aback. "Just a few of the souvenirs they left me… Anyhow. Pretty soon, I caught on that these run-ins weren't accidental. They were followin' me. Hoping I'd lead them right to you both. That was a chance I couldn't take."

"So you just left us out there alone."

"I know it's hard for you to understand. But you didn't know your mama. She may have been young, but she had a head on her shoulders. Plus she had an advantage on all of us. Because not only could she think like a Brigand, she was also thinking like a mom doing whatever it took to protect her child. So, I came back to Highcross and hoped you two'd find your way back here someday. But even then, I didn't totally give up. I became a cop so that I'd have access to the tools to keep looking, just in case. But now that I know she abandoned you, and that you had such a rough go of it, I-I should've done more." Bonnie heard the catch in his throat and the thickness in his voice and she knew as he turned his face away from her that he was on the verge of tears.

"I'm here now," was all she could think to say.

"Yes. Yes, you are," he said.

Bonnie knew she should go to him, to tell him it was okay. That she forgave him. It's what a daughter would do. But she wasn't there yet.

Instead, she gave him the only comfort she was ready to give. The news that Brigid was still alive. She explained excitedly what Fati had told her. She was met with the hopeful but guarded look of a man who'd been disappointed too many times to believe in the assurances of a cut-rate swami without suspicion. Still, he promised that he would help Bonnie look for her mom. That they'd find her together. But in the meantime, Bonnie had to promise to stay safe, to stay on the Cove, and not venture off again.

"Now that I've found you, if anything happened to you, I couldn't live with myself," he said, his voice cracking with emotion. "So promise me you'll stay put. That you won't leave the safety of the Cove for any reason. Promise."

"I promise," Bonnie said. And it was as solemn an oath as she'd ever made in her life.

The sheriff went to hug her, but she instinctively took a step back. So he backed off; he could see that she wasn't ready for it. Not yet. That it would take time to earn her trust and her love. And his nod told her that he was willing to wait.

The sheriff pulled away in his patrol boat, determined to find the man with the scar and save the Cove, so his daughter could stay on it, safe and protected. *I guess it's what fathers do*, was Bonnie's thought as she watched the sheriff take off across the water, smiling and waving at her happily, maybe even proudly. She would remember how he looked in that moment for the rest of her life.

Chapter 34
The Nine-Fingered Man
Gains the Upper Hand

Tanner Prescott sat staring at the vomit stain on the concrete floor of the cramped jail cell of the Highcross sheriff's office. All the dirtbags and burnouts at that camp, he thought bitterly, and *he* was the one who got hauled off in handcuffs. He couldn't believe how long it was taking even to post his bail. He'd been sitting in the cell for almost eight hours; more than enough time for his dad's executive assistant to dispatch the family attorney to Highcross to spring him. He was thinking maybe this was another of his father's "lessons" when Deputy Wayne appeared at his cell door.

"Okay, kid, let's go!" the deputy said, and swung the cell door open. "They're waitin' on ya downstairs."

"It's about time!" huffed Tanner. "Nice place you got here, dude. How about putting people somewhere that doesn't smell like piss and three-day-old hurl?"

"Oh, what a shock, Mr. Hollywood don't like the accommodations," said the deputy dryly, motioning for Tanner to follow him.

"Where I'm from, cops know their place," Tanner continued, trailing the deputy down the stairs. "Don't think my father isn't going to hear about this. You don't know who—" Tanner stopped when he saw Charley Eden standing at the front desk signing papers.

"Uh, wait, where's my lawyer? Where's Mr. Rosenthal?" Tanner asked.

"You *would* have an attorney named Rosenthal," sneered Eden. "But see, thing is, you don't need a lawyer when the charges are dropped." He handed the paperwork back to the desk clerk. "We're letting you go, champ."

"Finally wised up, huh?" said Tanner, papering over his relief with attitude. "Now you can go back to harassing immigrants or whatever the hell you rednecks do."

Charley Eden chuckled. "You got quite the mouth on you, kid. How about you zip it 'til we get you outta here, huh?" And with that, the councilman motioned Tanner toward the door, urged on by Deputy Wayne's nightstick poking him in the back.

*   *   *   *   *

The deputy and Charley Eden drove Tanner to the marina, where they got on a sheriff's boat and headed out. After what he'd been through, Tanner actually found himself glad to be returning to Cormac's Cove. But then he realized they were not heading south toward the Cove at all, but instead out to a secluded estuary a few miles north of the marina. They approached a sailing ship that was waiting at the mouth of the estuary. As the sheriff's boat sidled up next to it, Tanner saw the ship's name on its deep blue hull: the *Dark Star.*

"What the hell is this?" asked Tanner.

"Git out," Deputy Wayne said, shoving Tanner toward the rope ladder.

Moments later, Tanner, the deputy and Eden stood on the deck of the ship before the scar-faced man Maks, who was with two others, Clegg and a ruddy-faced ruffian with a gold tooth known as Santiago. All three men were heavily armed. Several others scurried about the ship as well, unfurling the sails and preparing for open water sailing.

"I thought you said the charges were dropped? I want to see my lawyer! Now!" Tanner demanded.

"Do these guys look like they give a rat's patoot about your rights?!" Eden bellowed, and the deputy cuffed Tanner hard across the back of the head to emphasize the point.

Eden then turned back to the scar-faced man. "Actually, I'd like to know myself, Maksymillian," Eden said. "What gives? Why am I not back in a Highcross courthouse throwing the book at this little pustule?"

"Like I told you on the phone. There's been a change of plans," Maks replied.

"But everything's working out according to *our* plan," Eden objected. "Are we just tossin' out a summer's worth of work here?"

Tanner looked from Eden and the deputy to the other men. He suddenly put the pieces together. "Holy shit! You're the ones who've been robbing the yachts! To make it look like it was us! Like it was me!"

"Well, now. Pretty boy here's smarter'n he looks," Maks sneered.

"Wait, but how'd you know I had the watch?" Tanner asked.

"Maybe not so smart," Clegg clucked.

"You didn't!" Tanner realized. "You were gonna plant something. But then you found my watch—the watch I found on the Cove…"

"And you served it up to us on a silver platter, you entitled little peon," smiled Eden.

"It's important to have a plan," growled Maks. "But sometimes fate gives you a wee nudge in the right direction."

CRASH! Maks was disrupted by a violent sound from below deck. Suddenly Bobby Maynard burst up through the doors, hands bound, mouth covered with duct tape!

"What the —?" Eden stammered.

"Bartholomew! Mind your prisoner!" yelled Maks, clearly perturbed. A lanky crewman scrambled onto deck.

Tanner spun around wild-eyed, no idea what was going on.

"Chris'amighty! You got the sheriff!" gasped Deputy Wayne, just as surprised as Eden.

The sheriff tried to speak but the tape on his mouth wouldn't let him.

"Get him back below! NOW!" Maks growled, and Santiago kicked Sheriff Maynard hard in the solar plexus, sending him hurtling back below deck. Bartholomew followed and then slammed the doors behind them. The dull thud of a man being beaten was heard inside the cabin.

"What in the hell are you doing with my nephew?" the councilman demanded.

"You weren't supposed to see that," Maks said and offered no further explanation.

"Well, I have, and I think I deserve to know what's going on!"

Tanner took a slight step backward. Whatever the beef was between these two guys and the sheriff, he knew his input was not required.

"Let's just say we found somethin' valuable on the Cove," Maks said threateningly to Eden, "and your nephew's gonna help us retrieve it."

"No. This was not part of the plan. I don't care how much cash you wave in front of my snout, I won't be party to it!"

"Yeah, well. You don't have a choice in the matter, now do you?"

"I do," Eden said. "And I'm putting an end to this right now. We're taking Bobby and the boy with us." He grabbed Tanner by the elbow. "Deal's off! C'mon Wayne."

"We'll just see about that," growled Maks. "Santiago, if you please."

ZIC!

Tanner looked up in shock to see Deputy Wayne with his mouth agape, blood gushing from his neck. Santiago had just run a jagged blade across his throat.

Charley Eden watched in horror as Wayne clutched at his throat, air sucking in through the open wound. The deputy staggered backward.

Maks smacked him hard with the butt of his rifle, sending him reeling over the rail. There was a SPLASH, then SILENCE.

"Holy shit," gasped Tanner. He turned to look at Charley Eden, who was still frozen in fear.

"W-what did you have to go and do that for?" Eden asked.

"I needed to get the attention of the class," said Maks, turning menacingly on him. "And if you don't wanna end up like the deputy there, you'll do as you're told for the duration of our acquaintance. Savvy?"

Eden "savvied" all right, gulping agreement and putting his hands high in the air for fear of being next.

Maks then turned to Tanner, "Now, as for you."

▪   ▪   ▪   ▪   ▪

A short while later, Tanner could see Cormac's Cove in the distance and it had never looked so good. The yacht burglars had already sent Charley Eden packing back to Highcross in the sheriff's boat, so now Tanner was alone on the *Dark Star* with Maks and his cronies. He'd been relieved when they told him that his only role in whatever this twisted plot was, consisted of delivering a cell phone to Bonnie once he got to shore.

The instructions were clear and punctuated with the waving of Santiago's blood-smeared blade in front of his face. The phone was to go to Bonnie and to Bonnie only. Tanner was to tell her to prepare for a video call at precisely 10:00 p.m., and that she should make sure to answer with no one else around. Tanner nodded assent to each of their demands.

About a half mile from the Cove, the ship came to an abrupt stop. It was jarring, almost as if it had bumped against something big and hard, like a reef. But during the course of the summer, Tanner had learned the waters off the Cove as well as anyone, and he knew there was nothing but sea out here.

"It's as far as she'll go," Clegg announced.

Maks nodded and turned to Tanner. "Here's where you get off. You'll have to swim to shore." He pointed off the side of the ship to the swirling waters below.

Tanner started to object, but the memory of the blood-soaked deputy now sinking to the bottom of the estuary kept his mouth shut tight. He took the waterproof pouch containing the cell phone, placed it around his neck, and walked toward the bow of the ship.

"What, no plank?" he couldn't help himself.

"Just be along with you," Maks snarled, "'fore Santiago needs another neck to wipe his blade on."

When Tanner stared down at the water, he understood what had stopped that ship so abruptly.

Magic, he thought. *Gullah Magic.*

He marveled at how the waves surrounding the ship were moving in the opposite direction of the surf, defying the tides and all the laws of nature. He had seen it on the Cove with the wall. But this was the first time he'd seen the protective magic at work in the waters. And in that moment, Tanner knew this wasn't about some real estate deal or a crooked politician greedy for power.

As he hit the water after being shoved overboard by Clegg, only one thought filled his mind.

This is about Calico Jack.

Chapter 35
A Bargain Is Struck

9:59 pm. One minute to the call. Bonnie felt the nerves bunching up in her gut as she sat in the parley room of the Boreas cabin. She stared at the cell phone as if willing the time to go by until the call from her father's kidnappers. At her side, Reed and the rest of her crew provided silent but palpable moral support.

Tanner Prescott had sneaked back to the cabin a few hours earlier, soaking wet, out of breath, and seriously freaked out. Despite instructions to the contrary, Tanner had blurted out his whole harrowing experience to all of Boreas. Listening to the story, Bonnie could feel the blood draining from her face. Tanner was right. These were no ordinary criminals. They were actual pirates. The man who smelled of death was in league with Calico Jack Rackham. Tanner was still at a loss about what part the sheriff played in the whole thing until Barnaby told him that Maynard was Bonnie's father.

"Shit, Bonnie. That's harsh," said Tanner in an uncharacteristic display of sympathy.

It was. It was rougher than Bonnie had imagined. Being on her own so long, she never realized how *connected* she could feel to someone, even if she'd only just discovered the truth of their relationship that day.

"What I don't get is how'd they figure out that Maynard was Bonnie's dad? I mean, I thought nobody knew but Reed's grandparents," Wilder asked.

"Probably the same way Bonnie found out about her mom," Reed speculated. "Rackham's surrounded by powerful dark magic."

"He had plenty of run-ins with Jack's men when he was looking for me and my mom," Bonnie said. "I saw the scars."

It seemed like an eternity for the digital display on the phone to go from 9:59 to 10:00. When it finally did, Bonnie held her breath. Then nothing. Bonnie looked nervously at the others as the seconds ticked on.

Then, the phone rang, piercing the silence, causing everyone to jump with a start.

Bonnie looked down at the vibrating phone in her hand, the electronic glow from the screen bathing her face in an eerie light. It rang yet again.

"I think it's for you," Wilder said, trying to lighten the mood. Everyone had bunched up in the corner of the room, well out of camera range.

"You got this, Bonnie," said Reed before he joined the others. "Just like we discussed. Calm. Steady. No fear. And don't look at us. They'll know something's up if you do."

It rang again. She looked at her crewmates one last time and then answered the phone.

An image appeared on the phone's screen. It was the face of Maks, the man with the scar. From what Bonnie could make out, he was inside the cabin of a ship.

"There's a good lass!" the scar-faced pirate said. "Was startin' to worry that little tosser didn't make the delivery like I told him. Are you alone?"

"Yes," she lied.

"Good girl," Maks said, his mouth twisting in a snarling smile. "I got someone here who'd like to say hello."

There was some jiggling and noise while the phone's camera was being adjusted for the best view, and then the picture settled and the image became alarmingly clear.

Bonnie felt her stomach flip when she saw her father's face. He was slumped in a chair, bound with his arms in front. His left eye was swollen shut, a gash stood out inflamed and angry, dripping with blood from his forehead. Bonnie had the feeling that it'd be bad, but Tanner's description hadn't even come close to preparing her for what she stared at on the screen. Barely conscious, her dad's head was being held up by Maks pulling on his hair.

"Bonnie," Bobby said weakly; his voice was raspy and wet with blood.

Bonnie felt the horror of it all rushing over her like a tsunami. She fought the temptation to look up at her friends for the support she so desperately needed. Instead, she stared at the screen, determined not to betray the turmoil she felt inside her.

"This is none but your father, lass," snarled the pirate. "He's looked better, don't you think?!" And he let out a vicious laugh.

The hand let go and her dad's chin fell to his chest, a moan escaping his lips as it did. Bonnie felt her knees start to buckle. Wilder instinctively took a step toward her, but Reed held him back and put his finger to his mouth. Wilder relented and shrunk back.

Bonnie finally was able to summon her voice from somewhere under all the fear. "So? What's that supposed to mean to me?" Bonnie said, bluffing. "I barely know the guy."

"That right? Deadbeat dad, is he? Well then," the pirate said calmly, "perhaps we can collect some back child support for you." He turned so that his back was to the camera and his hand reached back and drew out the serrated hunting knife from his belt. He moved to the chair, his body still blocking Bonnie's view of Maynard. Then there was a howling scream of pain that came from her father.

She recoiled as the pirate turned around and walked back to the camera. He held up his hand and Bonnie could see that he held a severed finger.

"Wouldya look at this," he said, putting Bobby's bloody finger where his own was missing. "It almost fits!"

Filled with rage, Bonnie was no longer able to heed Reed's advice. "You piece of filth!" she spat.

"'Piece of filth' sounds oh so formal, don't it? Just call me Maks. And I'll call you Bonnie. So now that we're friends, I got a proposal."

"What do you want?" Bonnie demanded.

"At midnight tonight. A trade. You for your father. I got somebody very interested in makin' your acquaintance."

"Where?"

"Don't do it! Don't come—" It was Bobby, trying through hoarse breath to warn her off.

Maks hit Bobby Maynard savagely with the back of his hand. Bobby's head snapped back and blood dripped from his mouth. He crumbled to the floor and the pirate turned to face the camera.

"We meet at the cave. Where you and your mates visited before," he snarled. "No cops, no adults, no weapons, and definitely none of those bloody punks I know are listenin' in on this call. But do bring that infernal bird with you. We got a score to settle, him and me. Those're the terms. Non-negotiable. And if you violate a one of 'em, your father's a dead man."

The screen went BLACK.

*   *   *   *   *

The second the phone went dead, Boreas sprang into action. There was no discussion about what would happen next. Only how. Because it went without saying that Bonnie *was* going to meet the pirates at midnight, and they *were* going to make sure that she and her dad both came home alive, and that was all there was to it.

In order to do that, it was going to take not just Boreas, but *all* the corsairs. Reed sent for Luz, Daya, Yeun, Hashpipe, Zion, and Wendell and told them what was going on. There wasn't a moment's hesitation on their part either; they were in.

There was little time, so Bonnie and Reed quickly hatched the plan and laid it out for the others. As instructed by the pirates, Bonnie would sail the cutter to Tuscarora alone. Meanwhile, everyone else would take the *True North* far to the south end of the island where they'd drop off the dinghy containing Reed, Wilder, Hashpipe, and Luz, the four best fighters from among the corsairs. They would row ashore and covertly approach through the forest to the rendezvous point at Corsair's Lair, ambush the pirates from the rear, and rescue Bobby and Bonnie. In the meantime, Tanner would assume command of the *North* and with the remaining corsairs position the ship in the inlet between Tuscarora and nearby Cuffee Island to the south, just in case the island rescue didn't go as planned and the pirates tried to pass through and make for open water with Bonnie, her dad or both.

"Whoa! Dude! Time out!" Tanner protested, backing away. "I'm just the messenger here. I don't want any part of this suicide mission."

"Typical," said Micah angrily.

"Tanner, you have to be part of it," demanded Reed. "If Bonnie's on the cutter by herself, and I go on shore with Wilder, we'll need our most experienced sailor at the helm of the *North*. That's you by a long shot."

"Did you not hear anything I said?" Tanner snapped. "These dudes murdered the frickin' deputy and he was working *with* them. What do you think they'll do to us?"

"It's what you've been training for!" Reed said seriously. "It's what we were born for!"

"What *you* were born for, maybe. I quit, remember?"

"You're such a selfish dick! *Pinche cabrón!*" yelled Luz. And the shouting began as the others laid into Tanner for his cowardice.

"Stop it, all of you!" Bonnie's shout finally silenced everyone.

Bonnie went to Tanner. "I don't blame you for looking out for yourself. I'd probably do the same. It sucks that you guys got thrown into this shit. None of you should have to do this. And it's all because of me. I'm responsible. But if the sheriff dies, that's on me, too. Which is why I'm asking you for help, Tanner. Please," she said softly. "We need you. *I* need you."

Tanner was taken aback by Bonnie's tone. Never in his seventeen years had anyone ever really *needed* him. He thought about his father, who never needed him, let alone wanted him around.

"Fine," he said finally. "But if we have any shot at making this happen, we better get moving. Winds aren't great right now."

Once Tanner was on board, the corsairs set out to put their plan into action. All except Barnaby Chisolm. It was decided that he would have to "hold down the fort" as Reed put it. He explained that while Barnaby had much to contribute to the Brigands' cause, he was *not* ready for battle conditions, not just yet. Though Bonnie was secretly relieved that the boy wouldn't be put into danger, the hurt in Barnaby's eyes as they left him behind in the cabin was almost too much for her to bear.

*   *   *   *   *

"No. You're NOT going!" Captain Ballister shouted at the corsairs, his night clothes flapping in the strong ocean breeze. On orders of Reed, he and Winnie had been roused from their slumber by Zion and summoned to the dock. They had been met by a chaotic scene of the corsairs busily loading arms and supplies onto the *North* while Jonesy, who had been standing sentry at the *North*, was being held at swordpoint by Malachi Maguire. Reed brought them up to speed on what had transpired and the captain, not surprisingly, nixed the plan.

"Absolutely not!" he repeated. "I forbid it!"

"I'm not asking your permission, Grandfather," Reed said. "I'm telling you... out of respect." He turned to the others and barked out a few more commands.

Ballister was aghast. "Insubordination more like! Looks like you corsairs didn't need a class on mutiny after all. You're doing just fine on your own!"

"I assume you're determined to take Bonnie with you," Winnie said.

"I have to go," said Bonnie as she carefully placed grenadoes from a wheelbarrow into canvas rucksacks. "If I don't show, they'll know something's up and they'll kill Sheriff Maynard for sure."

"Your father understands what it means to be a Brigand!" Ballister objected. "Brigands die in defense of the cause. I've got a churchyard full of 'em. It's heartbreaking, but it's a cruel fact of our shared destiny."

"That's a destiny I refuse to accept!" Bonnie said bitterly. "Just because you couldn't protect my mom; or your own son, doesn't mean that we stand by and just let my dad be slaughtered on a beach. No! I say it's time we took the fight to them!"

"Bonnie!" Tanner's voice called out, breaking the standoff. "We gotta go!"

Bonnie turned away from the Ballisters and rushed over to the side of the *North*, handing the rucksacks up to Wilder. Then she went over and started prepping the *Solstice Skye* for its own launch.

Ballister began to speak when Winnie silenced him with a hand on his arm.

"The things that have happened this summer, Eleazer," Winnie said quietly, "the broken compass, Bonnie's visions, all of it... maybe the fates are trying to tell us something."

"Are you taking their side now?" Ballister asked, sensing his final defeat.

"No, my love." Winnie softened up a bit and stroked her husband's hair. "I'm saying the winds have shifted. You've done all you can for them. Old men send the young off to war. It's been the way of the world since the days of Hannibal."

"I know. I know. I just wish…" his voice trailed off.

"You've done your part. And Daniel's too for that matter," Winnie said. "It's not our fight anymore, husband."

Captain Ballister watched the hustle and bustle on the deck of the *North* in silence for a moment, and then a change came over his face. Gone was the look of defeat, and a steely-eyed look of determination took its place.

"Eleazer!" yelled Grandma Winnie after the old captain as he clambered on board.

"Grandfather, you can't stop us—" Reed protested, but Captain Ballister walked right by him and disappeared into the ship's cabin.

The corsairs looked at each other blankly, not quite sure what they should do next.

Then Ballister re-emerged, carrying something under his arm. He bounded to the foredeck and loosened a line from the mainmast.

"You won't be going anywhere without this," he said, and then with one fluid motion, he revealed what he'd retrieved below decks. The corsairs watched proudly as a flag made its way up the mast of the *North*. As it reached the top, it unfurled in the wind, revealing—centered on its black background—a golden compass surrounded by red roses.

"This vessel sails tonight for Tuscarora Island!" Ballister yelled out. "Let none who mean her ill darken her path!"

And with that, all the corsairs let out a mighty whoop that echoed across the waters of Cormac's Cove.

From the decks of their respective crafts, Bonnie exchanged a look with Reed and Wilder, a look filled with shared destiny.

For good or for ill, the night belonged to them now.

Chapter 36

First Encounter

Bonnie stood on the deck of the *Solstice Skye* as it cut through the waves on its way to Tuscarora Island. There was no moon above, so she couldn't make out her destination in the misty distance. Her hand on the tiller, she adjusted the rudder, guided by that magnetic inner sense and just trusted that it would deliver her to her rendezvous spot by the appointed hour.

As the wind rushed through her hair, Bonnie's thoughts went to the *Truth North*. She knew it was out there somewhere in the dark and it gave her a sense of security. Still, she felt a knot of fear in her stomach, not for herself, but for everyone else who was being put in harm's way because of her. A few weeks ago, she mattered to no one, affected no one. And now... *Now people could die because of me*, she thought. And she didn't know which was worse: not mattering at all, or mattering this much.

Bonnie looked over at the wooden cage containing Crossbones, secured to the rail with a bowline knot. The parrot fluttered futilely against the confines of the cage.

"Yeah, I know just how you feel, buddy," replied Bonnie. "I'm sorry for dragging you into this. But, look, I didn't have a choice either. Extra treats once we get through this, 'kay?"

The parrot let out an unimpressed squawk.

The winds had picked up considerably and before long, Bonnie was close enough to make out the black, uneven outline of Tuscarora Island. She took the cutter to the southern end of the island and then brought it back in a northerly direction, hugging the coast in search of the meeting spot.

Maks had seen to it that Bonnie couldn't miss the rendezvous point, for just ahead about a quarter mile, she could see a small fire burning on the beach. And even at that distance, she could make out a lone figure illuminated by the firelight.

As she got closer, the man on the beach came into clearer view. He was not standing, but on his knees in front of the fire. Bonnie's heart lurched—it was her father, hands still bound. He swayed slightly, struggling to stay upright. Bonnie's eyes darted up and down the beach. There was a small dinghy with an outboard motor on the sand and though no one else was around, she knew *he* was there… She could sense him. The question was: were Reed and Wilder? Had the ambush team made it to the island and gotten into position in time? There was only one way to find out.

Bonnie ran the cutter up to the shore and jumped off.

"Sheriff Maynard!" she shouted, slogging through the water.

From the beach, Bobby Maynard lifted his head and saw Bonnie through the one eye that wasn't completely swollen shut. He began shaking his head. "No," he croaked. "NO! Go back!"

But Bonnie kept coming. When she finally reached the beach, a GUNSHOT rang out, hitting the sand just in front of her, and forcing her to stop in her tracks.

"Don't come any closer, sow!" a gravelly voice came from just beyond the first line of trees. Bonnie's blood ran cold. It was him. She instinctively felt for her sword, then remembered she'd had to leave Siobhan behind as part of the terms of the deal.

"You alone?" Maks called out.

"Do you see anyone else?" Bonnie spit back, a burning anger quickly replacing her fear.

Another shot rang out, this one kicked up the sand right next to her father.

"I'm alone!" she confirmed. "Check out the cutter yourself if you want. I'm here, like we agreed. Now let the sheriff go."

"All in time. Put your hands up slow. And keep 'em there."

Bonnie raised her hands into the air. Once she did, the pirate she knew as Maks came out along with two other men. One was the same man she'd seen at the cave and the beach, the barrel-chested one that Maks called Clegg. The other, she assumed from the gold front tooth, was Santiago, the man Tanner had described as the murderer of Deputy Wayne.

All three pirates had pistols at the ready and headed toward her. *How did we ever think we had a chance against these guys?* She thought, her heart sinking.

Maks stopped next to the sheriff. The other two pirates continued to Bonnie and when they reached her, the gold-toothed one held her while Clegg roughly frisked her.

"She's clean," Clegg announced to Maks, who nodded for them to bring the girl over to him.

"Why did you come?" the sheriff said when she got near. "I told you not to come."

"I wasn't going to leave you here to die," Bonnie said.

"I'm already dead," he said, too weak even to hold his head up.

"Shut your smack!" Maks backhanded him hard.

"Stop it! I'm here. Don't hurt him anymore!" Bonnie screamed, kicking furiously, but was held in place by the gold-toothed pirate.

"Ain't she a wildcat!" laughed Clegg. "Loads o' spirit in this one, aye-eeee!!!!" His laughter turned into a howl of agony as her foot caught him hard in the groin. Furious, Clegg brought his hand up to strike Bonnie. Maks grabbed his arm and stopped him.

"Don't touch the girl!" he said, twisting Clegg's arm behind his back until he squealed in pain. "Do I have to remind you who she's meant for?"

Maks finally let go and Clegg tumbled back, clearly frightened. Obviously, he knew exactly "who" she was meant for. Bonnie swallowed hard. Looked at her father, who was dazed from the blow. She reminded herself of the corsairs who right now *should* be in the dense cover of the forest awaiting the signal. She pushed through the fear and proceeded with the plan.

"Look. I kept my end of the bargain. Now let him go," she said.

"Ah, but you ain't kept your bargain in full, have you?" said Maks, holding up his hand with the missing finger. "I don't see the accursed bird."

And there it was. It had been part of the plan to "accidentally forget" the parrot on the *Skye* in the hopes of separating the pirates.

"I-I brought him! I did!" Bonnie pretended to remember. "Sorry. I left him on the boat. In a cage. I'll go get him." Her offer was also part of the plan, anticipating Maks's response.

"I ain't stupid! Clegg, fetch the bird. Santiago, bring the girl over here, closer to the fire," Maks commanded. Santiago shoved Bonnie toward the fire. As he did, she watched Clegg out of the corner of her eye walk down toward the beach, the distance between them growing. *Anytime now, Reed.*

"Closer," Maks said. Then he grabbed Bonnie by the shoulders and turned her around, so her back was to the fire. Maks lifted the hair off her back, pulled aside her shirt and revealed the birthmark, visible in the firelight. A soft breath escaped his lips.

Santiago watched lasciviously as Maks moved in closer to examine the birthmark, so close Bonnie could feel his hot breath on her neck and she shuddered in revulsion. She glanced out toward the tree line for a sign of movement. She saw nothing.

"So simple, yet beautiful in its power, it is." Maks licked his lips, running his thumb across the rough texture of it. "Just think, Santiago, this ugly stain upon this otherwise pure, untainted flesh holds the secret to eternal life." Bonnie felt a drop of wetness hit the back of her neck and roll down her back and under her shirt. She looked over her shoulder and saw the spittle hanging from the corner of his mouth. She held back the urge to vomit as he pressed intrusively against her. Beyond him, she saw Clegg with the birdcage already heading back. She knew then the other corsairs hadn't made it in time. She was on her own.

"Get your hands off my daughter!" The words penetrated the black pit of despair that had engulfed her. It was the sheriff. He had somehow found the strength to get to his feet and was charging Maks. Santiago, roused from his stupor and momentary surprise, brought the butt of his gun to Bobby's head just a second before he reached Maks. The lawman fell sprawled onto the ground at Maks's feet.

"Bobby!" Bonnie shouted and started for her father. Maks grabbed her by the hair and jerked her back hard, so that she fell to her knees next to him.

"If… you hurt her. I'll kill you," Bobby said hoarsely.

"Now that'd be quite the trick. A right failure you are, ain't you though? Fifteen years ago, you couldn't protect her. You certainly ain't gonna start now! You're right about one thing though," Maks said. "She shouldna come. Cuz now you're both dead."

Maks kicked him hard in the ribs, brought up his gun, aimed it at Bobby's face and started to pull the trigger.

It all happened quickly. So quickly Bonnie barely saw it coming herself. Still on her knees next to Maks, she used one hand to knock the gun, forcing him to misfire wildly. Then, with the other hand, she snatched the knife from the sheath on his belt, all in one fluid and almost imperceptible movement.

"What the—?" Maks exclaimed, and saw Bonnie, now on her feet, standing between him and Bobby, holding the knife firmly against her own neck.

"Put down your weapons or I'll cut my own throat," she threatened.

Everyone stood frozen, taking in Bonnie's threat. Even Clegg, who was now just a few yards away with the birdcage, stopped in his tracks.

"Well, ain't this an interesting turn?" Maks said.

"I mean it. Unless you let my father go, I'll kill myself. And I don't think your boss'll be too happy with you if I did." It was all Bonnie could think of to save her father. She knew Calico Jack needed to kill her himself to get her years. She saw how afraid they were of him and was counting on that fear.

Santiago dropped his weapon, clearly terrified by her threat. But Maks held onto his, bemused.

"Oh my, such the heroine!" sneered Maks as he moved in ever so slightly, a predator moving on its prey. "Think you'll get me cowerin' with your little floorshow? I don't think you got the guts," he said.

"Don't come closer. Or I swear to God I will!" she said, pushing the knife to her throat and drawing a trickle of blood.

"Go ahead then," Maks said, a smirk on his face as he slowly closed the distance between them.

They were locked in a game of chicken. The knife trembled in Bonnie's hand. She hesitated. Something was off. Why was this guy suddenly so eager to push her into suicide? When he'd just ordered the others to not hurt her? It didn't add up.

"Don't. It's what he wants," her father managed to croak. "Suicide of a marked one gives Jack immortality!"

Bonnie spun around, confused.

Maks let out an exasperated groan. "And we were so close to the perfect end to the evening!" Furious at the revelation, Maks lunged forward, shoved Bonnie out of the way, and went for the sheriff when—

BOOM! Bonnie felt something like a giant invisible hand lift her off the ground and slam her back into the sand with such force that it knocked the wind out of her. She lay a moment, desperately sucking in air before she finally struggled to sit up. Dazed and confused, her ears ringing, she looked around, blinking, trying to make sense of the chaotic scene that surrounded her. It all appeared as if in slow motion to her. Smoke was everywhere; the fire had blown apart and there were pieces of burning wood all over.

She heard a groan from a few yards away. She turned to see Santiago writhing on the ground, eyes blinded by black ash, clutching at his shoulder where a piece of firewood was sticking out, hot embers glowing. Then… BOOM! There was another explosion down the beach. Sand again rained down on her head. She saw Clegg stumbling in the distance, bloodied and disoriented, the birdcage on its side on the sand. And suddenly Bonnie realized what was happening.

Grenadoes! *The others are finally here!* she thought, though she wasn't sure exactly where in all the smoke and mayhem.

Everything sped up for Bonnie, and she whipped her head around, remembering. *My father! Where is he? Is he okay?* She strained to see him through the swirling black smoke. When she finally spotted him, lying a few feet from where she had seen him last, her heart lurched. She thought he was dead at first, but then his eyes fluttered open and she felt relief sweep over her. The feeling was short-lived; through a break in the smoke, she saw Maks, on his hands and knees. He was reaching for his gun, which he'd dropped in the sand from the force of the blast. Despite still being woozy herself, Bonnie sprung to her feet, and just as Maks put his hand on the weapon, she kicked it from his grasp. It spun across the sand and disappeared into the burning logs that remained of the fire.

Maks roared in fury, but to no end; his weapon was gone. Bonnie ran over to her father, helping him to a sitting position. He coughed, spitting sand. Maks rose and pulled a machete from his belt. He rushed at them. Bonnie's eyes went wide, when suddenly from the billowing black smoke—

Reed and Wilder appeared, swords drawn! They leapt between her and the advancing pirate just as Maks brought his machete down. Reed expertly deflected it with his sword. Maks brought his machete back around at double the strength, and again Reed met it with swift precision. This set off a sword fight between the two the likes of which Bonnie had never seen on the Cove: with blade-on-blade fury so fierce that blood was sought with each blow.

"You guys okay?" asked Wilder, who had run over to Bonnie and the sheriff.

"Only barely. You're late!" Bonnie said, helping herself to the dagger from his belt and using it to cut the sheriff's bonds.

"Tanner was right. Winds were a bitch."

Just then, they heard an unearthly yowl of pain and fury! They turned to see Santiago standing. He had one ash-filled eye open as he pulled the huge wood splinter from his sword arm and threw it to the ground. Then he drew a sword of his own and came straight at them, his face filled with rage. Wilder stood protectively between Santiago and Bonnie and her dad, his own sword raised for battle.

"Take your dad and go! Go!" Reed yelled at Bonnie as he fended off a series of vicious blows from Maks.

Every urge in her body told Bonnie to stay and join her friends in the fight, but looking at her bloodied and beaten father next to her told her otherwise.

"Come on! We gotta get you out of here," Bonnie said to the sheriff, rousing him from his stupor as Wilder engaged with Santiago a few feet away.

"No. Go without me! Save yourself!" he protested.

"Yeah. That's not happening. You stay. I stay," she said, matching his stubbornness.

He saw it was useless and willed himself to rise. He was so weak she had to help him to his feet. They started for the cutter—Bonnie half carrying him, half dragging him across the sand.

On the way, they passed Hashpipe and Luz, who were engaged in hand-to-hand combat with Clegg. He had obviously regained his senses because he was putting up a vicious fight that took all the strength and expertise of both the young corsairs.

"Get the girl!" Bonnie heard Maks yelling to Clegg as she passed him. Hearing this, Bonnie tugged at her father's shirt, urging him forward. They had to get out of there. Now!

Clegg rallied enough brute strength to backhand Luz across the face, and simultaneously subdued Hashpipe with a debilitating side kick to the knee that elicited a horrible snapping sound! Clegg peeled himself away from both of them and gave chase to Bonnie.

By this time, Bonnie had gotten her father aboard the cutter and was halfway on herself when Clegg appeared behind her. The brute pulled her off the boat. They both tumbled backwards into the surf and a wrestling match ensued. Bonnie's head was pushed under water and she had to knee Clegg in the stomach just so that she could surface for air.

Back at the fireside, two battles raged on. Wilder was holding his own against the one-eyed, one-armed Santiago, but Reed was in dire trouble. Despite being spectacular with his blade, he was starting to tire. He could see that he was able to parry Maks's attacks just a split second later than when the fight had begun. Problem was, Maks could see it, too. Not only was he an accomplished swordsman himself, but he was twice as strong and three times as vicious. He grinned and advanced on Reed with fury.

"Think you're something, worm?" Maks said between crushing swings of his machete. "So did your old man!"

A feeling of shock ran through Reed and he was able to parry the blow only at the last moment.

Maks smiled and circled to Reed's left. "He wasn't bad with a blade, bein' honest. Left this calling card on my cheek." The pirate touched the large scar on his face. "Just before I ran him through."

Reed's face flushed blood red at the horrific revelation. Maks laughed maliciously and swung his machete backhand at Reed, adding with pleasure, "The bastard bled out on the deck of his ship, knowing full well that his little wifey was next. It was a glorious kill. The both of them!"

Reed said nothing, but the ferocity in his attack doubled with such force that it sent Maks back on his heels! The edge of his blade caught Maks on the forearm, drawing blood. The cocky smile disappeared from Maks's face. "Oh. You're gonna pay dearly for that, boy," Maks said and launched a relentless counterattack.

Back at the beach, Bonnie emerged from the ocean, Wilder's dagger in one hand. Clegg, who was vomiting water and bleeding profusely from his thigh, lay helpless at the edge of the surf.

She looked back at her friends. Luz was just regaining her senses next to Hashpipe, whose leg was broken at an excruciating angle. Luz nodded to Bonnie that they were okay. But they both saw that Reed and Wilder were in big trouble. Wilder was on the ground, Santiago on top, throttling him hard. Luz rushed over and jumped on Santiago's back, punching at his head as Wilder scrambled to extricate himself from beneath the pirate.

Meanwhile, Reed was buckling, too, as Maks advanced, slashing wildly with his machete. He spun and got under Reed's defense, and then brought the handle of his weapon up hard under his chin, forcing the sword out of Reed's hand and knocking him senseless to the ground. Maks raised his machete up to finish the job when—

"No!" Bonnie raced to the rescue, sunk the dagger deep into Maks's shoulder and pulled it quickly out again.

"Slag!" Maks yelled out in pain as he whirled on Bonnie and somehow brought his left hand up in time to grab Bonnie's wrist, and stopped her from bringing the dagger down again. Maks grabbed her other wrist and she struggled to tear away from him.

"Your boyfriend ain't nearly his father yet," Maks said, smiling a greasy grin at Bonnie. "Lucky for both of us, you came back to help him out." He then delivered a vicious head butt that had her seeing stars. She dropped her dagger. Everything went gray at the edges, and Bonnie felt herself starting to lose consciousness.

Maks grabbed the dazed Bonnie and threw her over his shoulder and ran full speed toward the far end of the beach where the pirate's dinghy was tied. He paused to pick up the birdcage with Crossbones in it.

Wilder, who was now free from Santiago, finished him off with a vicious kick to the face. Wilder whipped his head around to witness Maks about to toss the barely conscious Bonnie into the dinghy like a sack of potatoes.

"Bonnie!" he shouted. He found Clegg's gun in the sand and went to aim it.

"Don't! You might hit her!" yelled Reed, who was standing now, wobbly and bleeding profusely from the mouth and nose. He grabbed the gun from Wilder.

Just then, the outboard motor of the dinghy roared to life. As it did, Maks deliberately took the cage with Crossbones and flung it far out into the deep surf, the parrot squawking madly as it hit the water.

Reed retrieved his sword and turned to the badly beaten Wilder. "You gonna make it?"

"Can't not," Wilder responded. "Let's go get our girl."

Before they ran off, Reed tossed Luz the gun. "The other one's further down the beach. You got things covered here?"

"Just go! Either of these *pendejos* makes a move, I'll put a bullet in his head!" Luz said, digging her boot into Santiago's throat, eliciting a choking sound.

With that, Reed and Wilder ran at top speed for the cutter and jumped on. In their desperation to get to Bonnie, they had forgotten about the sheriff, who was lying bloodied and battered on the cutter.

"Come on, Sheriff. Let's get you on shore! Luz and Hashpipe will get you to a hospital," Reed urged.

"No, I'm coming," Bobby insisted. "She's my daughter. I'm coming."

Reed saw the dinghy rapidly putting distance between them and didn't have time to argue.

"Hit the water! Go! GO! GO!" he commanded. And he and Wilder pushed the cutter into the water. As it made it past the waves and into the open ocean, they passed the birdcage, which was bobbing on its side, almost three quarters submerged in the surf, with a panicked Crossbones clinging to the exposed edge, screeching as he tried to keep his beak above the surface. Wilder used his sword to fish the cage from the water and whipped it high into the air toward the beach, causing it to shatter when it hit the sand. Now free, Crossbones fluttered erratically toward the forest, his broken wing barely keeping him aloft.

"Hold on!" Reed swung the sail into position and it snapped in the blustery wind, sending the cutter off at high speed onto the sea. And though it was a moonless night, the sound of the motor from the dinghy told Reed which way to go.

Bonnie and Maks were a good five hundred yards ahead of their pursuers when Reed saw they were headed right toward the pirate ship, the *Dark Star,* anchored in the waters of the sound.

Reed and Wilder watched in alarm when, upon reaching the ship, Maks handed Bonnie off to the crew on board and climbed onto the ship himself. The ship's engines started up and soon it was headed due south at a good clip.

"They're getting away!" yelled Wilder. And he was right. No matter how good their sailing skills were, there wasn't enough wind to close the gap between them and an engine-powered ship like the *Dark Star.* Plus, Sheriff Maynard was still weak from his beating, so he was essentially dead weight for the boys at this point.

"They're heading to the inlet," said Reed, surveying the course of the ship. "At least the *North's* there to stop 'em."

"Uh, yeah. About that…" said Wilder, pointing to the south.

A dark blot appeared against the star-filled sky before it came into view, revealing that it was… the *True North*! Under full sail, it glided directly into their path.

"Damn Tanner," Reed growled.

"Ahoy!" called Tanner Prescott from the deck of the *True North* as it approached the cutter. "Fancy seeing you dudes out on the water tonight!"

"Tanner, what the hell? You guys are supposed to be blocking the inlet!" yelled Reed as Wilder guided the cutter alongside the *North*.

"And we were!" Tanner replied. "Until the mute over here started freaking out!" Tanner pointed at Malachi, who was now staring calmly off into the distance toward the *Dark Star*. "Dude kept yelling about danger and demanding we go to Tuscarora!"

"Since when do you listen to Malachi?" Wilder asked.

"Well, pardon me for saving your sorry asses," Tanner said indignantly as he helped Reed and Wilder get Sheriff Maynard over the edge of the *North*.

"It's not *our* asses you're under oath to save!" yelled Reed. "They've got Bonnie and they're getting away!"

Working under engine power, the *Dark Star* was indeed widening the distance between them and the *North*.

"Oh shit," Tanner said, realizing what he had done. He whirled around and screamed out to the crew. "Don't just stand there, Brigands! Follow that vessel! Micah! Yeun! Trim the mainsail and let's tack to port! Wendell, I need that foresail in position now! Go! Go! Go!" He turned to Malachi and said quietly, "And see if I ever listen to you again."

Malachi just stood at the rail, his eyes still fixed on the *Dark Star*, with an icy stare that seemed to know something the others did not.

Chapter 37
On the Water

On board the *Dark Star*, Bonnie was unceremoniously stuffed into a cabin below deck by a muscle-bound, snarling, bald guy with an earring who looked like Mr. Clean from the cleanser commercials. She had regained her senses just as they were loading her onto the *Dark Star*, but decided it would be to her advantage to pretend otherwise. The moment the cabin door locked, her eyes flew open and she assessed her situation.

She looked out the cabin window and saw the *True North* behind them. The *North* was supposed to be ahead of them, positioned in the narrow inlet to stop the *Dark Star* in case of just this situation. *What the hell happened?* Bonnie didn't have time to ponder that question. For once the *Dark Star* hit the vast expanse of the Atlantic, it would be the end, both of the Brigands' pursuit and, shortly thereafter, of her.

Having peeked through one slightly open eye while being lugged across the ship, she'd made a quick head count of the pirates. There was old Nine-Fingers himself—Maks—and Mr. Clean, and then five other guys for a total of seven. Rough odds, but possibly doable if the rest of the Brigands were around. However, the *Dark Star* was moving too fast for the *North*, which had only wind power to propel her. Bonnie had to level the playing field, and fast.

"We're losing them!" yelled Wilder, who had scaled the mainmast of the *North* and positioned himself in the crow's nest to get a better look at the rapidly moving ship ahead of them.

"The wind is giving us all she's got!" Reed yelled back.

"Don't give me that. We're supposed to be masters of the freaking sea or whatever! There's gotta be something we can do!"

All the Brigands looked expectantly at Reed.

"Tack a skosh to port, Mister Prescott, and we'll be at running speed!"

"Dude, serious?" Tanner started doubtfully. "That thing's a Slocum 2000, man. Gotta be cranking 300 HP under the waterline easy, probably with a variable pitch prop, too. Ain't no way we—"

"Make it so!" Reed snapped.

Tanner shot Reed a quick *"Are you frickin' kiddin' me?"* look before turning from the wheel to his crew. "Corsairs! Broad reach for this tack! We go on my call!"

"We're lit on my end!" Yeun called back.

"Don't forget to mind the running backstays!" Tanner urged. "One of those bitches breaks, we lose the mainsail!"

"Aye! Aye!" Yeun called as he and Daya worked the winch perfectly as a team, their weeks of training together with Zephyrus serving them well.

Though the crew executed the maneuver to perfection, Reed scowled as he looked through his spyglass. The *Dark Star* was barely visible now in the darkness of the moonless night. His experience told him what everyone but Tanner was still too green to see.

Short of a miracle, Bonnie was lost.

Back on the *Dark Star*, Bonnie stood in the crew cabin holding a wrench she'd found in a toolbox. She felt the whir of the ship's engine underfoot. From the faint aroma of fuel, she could tell it was a diesel engine, and they must be running at full capacity. She might not be up to fighting off armed pirates on her own, but thanks to all the time she'd spent hot-wiring repos, she knew if she could get to the engine, she could disable it.

There was a galley table and underneath an access panel over the spot where the engine hum was the loudest. She got on her knees and gave the metal handle on the panel a mighty yank and the hatch came open.

In the space below, she saw a familiar sight that had greeted her under hundreds of car hoods. Everything was situated a little differently, but a combustion engine was pretty much the same no matter what it was pushing. The pistons chugged along inside, and a long shaft that led to the propeller was turning rapidly. Bonnie knew that if she just loosened the right bolts, she could separate the shaft from its source of fuel, leaving the engine running, but not moving the ship. Her little trick could go unnoticed for enough time to give the *True North* a chance to catch up.

Lying on her stomach, she bent at the waist and put her head and shoulders through the hatch. She felt her wrench grip tightly on a huge bolt in the center of the engine block. She tried to turn the wrench. *Nothing.* Her odd angle and the encrusted bolt combined to thwart her. *Torque*, thought Bonnie, *I need more torque!*

She scrambled back to the toolbox, grabbed a second wrench, and then leaned down further into the engine compartment. She was half into the compartment now and connected the second wrench to the end of the first. It was an old repo trick she'd picked up in Arizona for when she was working in tight spaces. She smiled with satisfaction as she felt the bolt on the drive shaft turning. *That scumbag Clint Krokel was finally good for something*, she thought.

"The hell are you doin'?!"

It was Mr. Clean! His hairy hand grabbed at her belt loops and tried to pull her out of the compartment. Bonnie started kicking hard at him, all the while turning the wrench.

"Oh, no you don't, little hellcat!" Mr. Clean snarled, and she was violently yanked out of the compartment without finishing her job on the engine.

BAM! She reflexively smashed him on the side of the head with the wrench. Mr. Clean yelped in agony and Bonnie scrambled back toward the engine to finish the job. But just as she got there, Mr. Clean tackled her. He straddled her and pinned her down with his weight, his hands locked tightly around each of her wrists.

He looked at her triumphantly, and she returned the look with one of defiance as she loosened her grip on the wrench and let it drop into the engine below.

SCREECH! The drive belt screamed as the wrench jammed its path. BOOM! The lights flickered momentarily. Then the engine went silent and Bonnie felt the ship shudder and slow. Smoke billowed from the hatch.

The explosion from the engine compartment brought Maks tearing below deck to investigate. Furious, he ordered Squid—a fat-gutted pirate with disgusting teeth—to fix the engine ASAP.

"Cain't," Squid said finally, spitting tobacco on the floor. "She done too much damage. Gonna hafta take her in."

Maks turned to Bonnie, who stood in erect defiance to the side, and slapped her with such force that she thought she felt her teeth rattle in her skull. "You stupid little bitch!" Maks spat at her, then turned to the others. "Take the sow on deck and strap her to the mainmast so I can personally see to it she don't pull no more fast ones!" Maks stormed up to the deck and yelled to the other pirates. "We move under sail this very moment! Bartholomew! Two-Tone! I need my sheets up now! Lorenzo, Oskar, you man the backstays!"

Oskar, a strapping platinum-bearded Swede, and Lorenzo, a swarthy Italian with a ponytail, took positions at the backstays while two other pirates scrambled to hoist the sails on the open water.

"She'll be a bitch in this wind!" yelled the lanky Bartholomew.

"I need more line!" screamed Two-Tone, a burly Jamaican with some kind of skin condition that left half of his face a shocking albino white.

"As soon as you secure the girl, I need all hands workin' the sails!" Maks screamed. "There ain't a moment to be lost! We can still outrun 'em if we can beat 'em to open water!"

"Hey! They're in sight again! Way to go, Ballister! You guys did it!" shouted Wilder down to the deck of the *True North*.

"No. Not us. Bonnie. They're hoisting sails!" Reed said, incredulous, having witnessed the very miracle they'd been needing. "She must have gotten to the engine!"

"Woo!" cried Daya. "That's my homegirl!"

"You wan' me to ready the cannon now, Captain?" asked Wendell.

"Not yet!" Reed yelled. "Tanner! Tack back to starboard three degrees and we can get full blow! Let's do this, Brigands!"

A CHEER went up! The crew of the *North* was working like one organism now, responding to the commands of Reed in the same way that limbs respond to the messages of the brain. They had the *North* taking full advantage of strong coastal winds. Though the *Dark Star* was a more modern ship crewed by more experienced seamen, the *North* was a lighter and sleeker vessel, a marvel of the magnificent engineering of a bygone era, and it practically skipped across the water as they began to close the gap between themselves and the pirate ship.

The *Dark Star* started to make the turn around the end of the island as it headed through Tuscarora Inlet toward the open waters of the Atlantic.

Still lashed to the mainmast, Bonnie struggled violently against the ropes. But Mr. Clean had tightened them to the point where they were digging into Bonnie's flesh.

"'Bout a mile through this inlet!" Maks yelled to his men as they worked the sails. "Twenty miles after that, we hit the Gulf Stream, and we'll be on our way to deliverin' this package to its destination."

He sneered at Bonnie and she shuddered.

Chapter 38
Heavy Artillery

"We're gaining on them!" yelled Reed, peering out over the open water.

"We still gotta get Bonnie off that tub!" shouted Wilder from the crow's nest. "That's gonna be near impossible while it's still under sail."

"Then we've got to make sure it *isn't* under sail. Micah!" called Reed. "Retrieve the carcass! Wendell, you and Malachi swing that cannon to the starboard rail and prepare to fire!"

"WOOT WOOT!" Wendell whooped at the prospect of finally getting to use the explosives he'd been drooling over all summer. With the help of Malachi, he dragged the massive cannon across the deck and secured it with wooden blocks and sandbags.

Meanwhile, Micah rushed to the hold below the quarterdeck to retrieve the carcass—the hollow cast iron ball they'd first seen in Blades & Daggers class. Stuffed full with such misery-inducing ingredients as sulfur, saltpeter, and turpentine, it would burn fiercely when it hit its target. Micah flung open the doors to the hold and grabbed the carcass from the floor there, revealing, crouched inside, the bespectacled Barnaby Chisolm!

"I guess I took a wrong turn on my way to the toilet," said Barnaby sheepishly.

"Reed!" Micah yelled. "We have us a stowaway!"

Reed turned and saw Micah dragging Barnaby up the steps to the quarterdeck. "Barnaby! What are you doing here?!" he asked angrily.

"I wanted to help," Barnaby said.

"We're moving within range, Cap!" shouted Tanner.

"I'm sorry, Barnaby, but right now, all you are is in the way. Micah, hurry and get that carcass in place! Mistress Cepeda, escort Mister Chisolm below to the crew deck." Hurt and angry, Barnaby had no choice but to go below deck. As Daya locked the door behind him, Barnaby stood at the base of the steps, listening with envy to the scuffling and shouting sounds of the rest of the crew scrambling overhead in preparation for battle.

"What's happening up there?" a voice from the darkness startled Barnaby, and he turned to see Bobby Maynard lying in a crew hammock. He looked pale and disoriented, but he willed himself to sit up. "Did they get Bonnie back?"

"Not yet, Sheriff," Barnaby said as he strode over to a barrel resting against the hull, climbed onto it and pushed out the wooden cover to one of the gun ports that led to the exterior of the ship. Barnaby proceeded to squeeze himself backwards and feet first through the port until all that was visible was his head and hands. He paused a second and fixed his gaze on the sheriff. "But don't worry, sir, we're working on it." And with that, he disappeared, the cover banging closed with finality.

Despite his pain, Bobby had to shake his head and smile. "A true Brigand if I ever saw one," he said to himself.

Back on deck, the Brigands were so preoccupied with their approach to the *Dark Star* that they did not see Barnaby pull himself up a rope, over the rail, onto the deck, slither belly first beneath the ladder leading up to the quarterdeck, and, when he was certain the coast was clear, slip back into the weapons hold, quietly closing the door behind him.

"Mister Noble!" Reed yelled to Wendell. "Prepare to fire as soon as we're within range. Mister Prescott! Give me everything you got!"

"Aye!" Tanner yelled back. "Yeun, I need more foresail! Zion! Steady as she goes on the jib!"

"On it!" Yeun called, as he and Zion maneuvered their sails into position.

P-tew! P-tew!

"*Puta madre!* Those are gunshots!" cried Daya.

P-tew! P-tew! P-tew P-tew!

Everyone on deck dropped to their knees as the bullets flew over their heads. Wilder, still up in the crow's nest, could only press himself up against the mast and hold on for dear life.

"They're not in range of our cannon yet!" Wendell said in a panic. "What are we gonna do now?"

"Nothing we can do," Tanner responded, "except sail our way into a barrage of freaking gunfire."

"There's a reason Brigands are taught the old ways, Mister Prescott," Reed retorted calmly, bounding up to the forecastle deck. "Observe and learn." He strode to the masthead lantern and extinguished its flame.

"Put out those other lanterns as well!" he commanded. "This ship is going dark!"

Tanner smiled in appreciation, immediately understanding what Reed was up to. The *Dark Star*, still illuminated by battery-powered lights, was visible in the distance. On the other hand, once the *North* had put out its handful of lanterns, it would become effectively invisible on the moonless night.

"Swing us around to that vessel's starboard side, if you please, Mister Prescott!"

Tanner shook his head, smiling. "Dude, you got some balls on you, man."

"As do you, Mister Prescott," Reed said, tying his scabbard around his waist. "Now let's see if we can make a contest of this."

Back on the *Dark Star*, Two-Tone and Mr. Clean peered out into the blackness, guns at their sides.

"Why'd you stop firin'?" Maks shouted. "I gave no such order!"

"Ain't sure what to shoot at no more," Two-Tone explained. "They-they disappeared."

They've gone dark, Bonnie thought and smiled. *Way to go, Brigands.*

"They're out there somewhere! Just keep shooting!" Maks demanded. "And get this bloody tub out to sea already!"

The gunfire from the pirates' ship started up again, but this time it was way off the mark, sailing harmlessly off the ship's starboard side. Thanks to Reed's maneuver, the Brigands had bought themselves some time.

"Be at the ready, corsairs," Reed urged. "Once we get close enough to fire, we'll also be close enough to be seen!"

Everyone responded with their "readies."

"Reed!" yelled Tanner, pulling hard on the wheel. "We're coming up alongside. Go time!"

"Fire at will, Mister Noble!" Reed commanded.

Wendell, who had been waiting for this moment his whole life, eagerly lit a match and applied it to the touchhole, then hit the deck, yelling, "Fire in the hole!" Everyone braced themselves for the explosion.

But nothing happened.

"Fire, I said! Fire now!" Reed shouted.

"What the hell, Wendell?" Micah crawled over to Wendell to see what was going on.

"She's not lighting, Captain!" Wendell shouted, desperately trying to ignite the charge. "Gunpowder might be damp! Let me get some more—" He rose to retrieve some more gunpowder and when he did...

P-TEW! P-TEW! P-TEW! The gunfire renewed with ferocity.

"We can't stay this close! We gotta move away or we're sitting ducks!" Tanner yelled.

"Tack back full to starboard, and we'll try to make another pass at 'em on the opposite side!" agreed Reed.

Tanner spun the wheel, veering the *North* toward safety.

Reed called out, "Mistress Cepeda! Get to the weapons hold and see if you can find Wendell some dry powder!"

As Daya crawled across the deck to retrieve the gunpowder, a call was heard from overhead.

"Bonnie!" Wilder shouted from the crow's nest, for he had spotted her through his spyglass, tied to the mainsail mast of the *Dark Star*.

Hearing that name, Malachi Maguire rose to his feet.

"Malachi!" his brother grabbed at him to keep him down, but didn't have the strength to hold him back. Amid a rain of gunfire from the *Dark Star*, Malachi lumbered toward the mouth of the cannon. With his long arm, he retrieved the carcass from the bore and picked up the slow match that Wendell had dropped. Bullets showered down all around him, splintering wood in every direction, but Malachi walked on unscathed.

"The hell is he doing?" Daya asked as Malachi walked purposefully toward the quarterdeck, carcass in hand.

"I think he's gonna throw it off the back!" Micah marveled.

"Is he nuts? We're moving too far away, too fast!" Zion shouted as a fresh hail of bullets hit the ship.

Malachi touched the match to the carcass. Smoke and noxious fumes gushed from the weapon's holes.

"Go for the mainsail, Malachi! The mainsail, brother!" shouted Micah.

"Wait! No!" shouted Wilder. "Not the mainsail! Bonnie's tied to the mast!"

But it was too late.

"BRIGAAAAAAAAAAAAANDS!!!!" Malachi screamed at the top of his lungs as he heaved with all his might and sent the carcass airborne.

The corsairs watched in awe as it flew across the night sky. Now fully engulfed in flames, it streaked toward the enemy ship.

"Holy shit," Wendell said in awe. "It's actually gonna make it!"

"Holy shit," Wilder said simultaneously, in horror. "It's actually gonna make it."

"Incoming!" screamed Lorenzo aboard the *Dark Star*.

"Those gutter-crawlin' worms!" Maks cursed as everyone around him took cover.

Bonnie made the same distressing realization that Wilder had already made from his perch on the *North*. *That ball of flame is headed straight for me!* She watched helplessly as the carcass hit squarely in the middle of the mainsail. The mast bent with the weight of the iron ball, which set its sail on fire before dropping to the deck—sending a plume of toxic fumes spewing every which way as it rolled.

"Woo-hoo!" Bonnie could hear the distant cheers of her shipmates on the *North*. Bonnie would have celebrated along with them, but she had a more immediate problem: she was still tied to a mast whose sail was now completely ablaze.

"Oskar! Chuck that thing overboard! Squid, hurry, untie the girl and move her to safety!" coughed Maks through the smoke. "Bartholomew!" he yelled. "Strike the mainsail!" Oskar and Squid hopped to their tasks, but Bartholomew hesitated.

"But… the bloody thing's on fire!" he objected.

"Do it!" screamed Maks. "Or we'll all surely perish!"

Reluctantly, Bartholomew climbed up the mast over Squid, who was still trying to undo Mr. Clean's elaborate binding around Bonnie.

"Release the main lines!" Maks called to Mr. Clean. Now the sail was flapping freely in the breeze as Bartholomew shimmied further up the mast to deal with the sail cord that was tangled at the top. He reached the top of the mast and attempted to undo the tangle. Suddenly, a gust of wind! And the flaming sail changed direction. It was on top of Bartholomew!

"He's trapped!" yelled Squid.

"Bumboclaat!" yelled the nearby Two-Tone in his Jamaican dialect, which roughly translated means something along the lines of "Holy crap, my shipmate is tangled up in a flaming sail!"

Bartholomew screamed in agony. He flailed with one arm to get the sail off of him while with the other he clung to the mast for dear life. Bonnie, still bound to the mast, could do nothing but watch as the man struggled above her.

Bartholomew made one last swing with his arm to push the sail away from him, but he misjudged the distance between him and the sail. He could no longer hold on to the mast.

"Aieeeeeeeee!"

Bonnie watched horrified as Bartholomew, wrapped in the burning sail and fully engulfed in flames, dropped like a crate of anvils into the ocean.

"Dammit!" yelled Maks as he marched to the port side of the *Dark Star* and fired his gun wildly toward the *True North*. "You're all nothin' but putrid little crib-dwellers! Bring the *Star* around," Maks ordered the others. "Squid! Make sure those knots on the girl are still secure! No call to move her now."

"What about Bartholomew?" Squid asked.

"No mercy on the sea!" spat Maks. "And that goes for these urchins, too!"

On the deck of the *North*, the Brigands watched with great relief as the flaming sail of the *Dark Star* came loose from the mainmast and crashed into the water.

"Tack full to starboard!" Reed called out.

"Dude, they may not have a sail, but they still got guns!" Tanner objected.

"Full to starboard, Mister Prescott!" Reed repeated forcefully.

"Tanner's right," said Micah. "If we try to board her, we're no match for those rifles with dagger and swords."

"Leave that to me, Mister Maguire," Reed said with steely confidence. "I've got a plan…"

Chapter 39
The *North* Is Boarded

Bonnie's shock turned to dread as she saw the *North* was circling back toward the *Dark Star*, and she knew the Brigands were now spoiling for a fight. They were actually going to engage the pirates. And probably die. And it was all her fault.

The two ships rapidly closed the distance between one another.

"The second they engage, hit 'em with everything we got!" Maks commanded to the other pirates who stood at the rail, locking and loading a frightening amount of firepower among them.

"No. Please don't!" Bonnie screamed. "I'm what you wanted! Take me and go!"

"Shoulda thought of that before you wrecked the engine," snarled Maks. He turned to the pirates, "Give no quarter! Kill all aboard. And take the ship for our own."

But as the *North* drew closer, there was no sign of engagement. Nothing. Rather, the ship seemed to be on a collision course with the *Dark Star*.

"Bollocks," Maks murmured as the *North* continued to approach, not veering from its course. "They're comin' straight for us! Tack full to port!"

The *Dark Star* barely avoided colliding with the *North* as it sailed past on the Cuffee Island side of the inlet. The two ships were just feet apart when the ambient glow of the *Dark Star*'s navigation lights revealed… an entirely empty deck.

"Ghost ship," muttered Squid superstitiously.

"Seize her!" Maks commanded. "Don't let her by!"

The pirates threw grappling hooks across to the passing *North*. There was a great PULL and JERK as the ropes went taut. The *North* TILTED and GROANED as it slowed and succumbed to the weight of the heavier ship. Once the *North* was under control, the pirates began pulling the ropes hand over hand, bringing the two ships closer to each other, until they were lashed together, bobbing in unison upon the swells of the inlet.

Maks and the other pirates stood at the rail, scanning the deck of what appeared to be an abandoned schooner.

"Looks like they jumped ship," Two-Tone assumed.

Bonnie's eyes closed in dread. She knew her fellow corsairs would never have come this far just to give up the fight.

"Little chance of that," Maks replied, as if reading her thoughts. "Those little bastards are up to somethin'. Board her!" Maks commanded. "And watch yourselves."

Maks stood near Bonnie and they both watched as the other pirates boarded the *North*, guns at the ready. They split up; Squid and Two-Tone went toward the bow with Lorenzo. Mr. Clean headed astern with Oskar. They circled the ship and met up again in the middle.

"Nothing on deck," Squid called to the *Dark Star*.

"Well, they wouldn't exactly be hidin' *on* the deck, now would they, idiots! Check below!" Maks yelled back across to them.

Mr. Clean nodded to the door leading below deck. Squid nodded back.

"Ahoy! We know y'all are down there! Best come out. You're only making it worse for yasselves!" Squid shouted. He tried the door but it was locked. Squid smiled knowingly back at the others.

"Blast it off its hinges," Mr. Clean said. Squid stood back from the door and fired several rounds until the door fell open. He peered inside and saw only an empty hammock slowly swinging back and forth.

"No one here!" he shouted across to his boss.

"That ain't poss—" Maks started to say when—

A SAVAGE YELL cut through the night and… all hell broke loose. Brigands appeared from everywhere. Skittering, sliding, swinging, and springing from every nook and cranny of the *North*!

Bonnie watched in awe. The melee that followed was as epic as it was swift. Caught completely flatfooted by the deception, the pirates were overwhelmed by the Brigands. Reed swung across the deck from a rope, Wilder slid down another from the crow's nest while Micah, Malachi, and Zion vaulted onto the deck from where they'd been hanging off the side of the ship. Daya, Yeun, and Wendell appeared simultaneously from under overturned barrels. Before the pirates had a chance to turn around and take aim, they found themselves disarmed by a flurry of kicks and punches that would have made Wicked Pete proud.

No sooner had the pirates lost their weapons than—

"BRIGANDS! *Póg an talamh!*" Tanner Prescott's voice rang across the ship. He suddenly emerged from a giant coil of ropes, using the command Wicked Pete had taught them—the one only Barnaby recalled on the day of the parrot attack. Only this time, they all stopped and immediately hit the deck. Tanner swung his sword down, slicing through the stays that held the main boom in place. He leapt into the air and grabbed onto the boom with both hands. The force of his weight combined with the strong wind to turn the boom into a battering ram. And Tanner Prescott, the boy who hours earlier had wanted nothing to do with the rescue, was now flying across the deck of the ship directly into the mouth of danger. While the boom arm sailed harmlessly over the heads of the Brigands, the pirates had no time to evade it. The boom sent them all toppling to the deck, with Tanner's boot landing a savage blow to Squid's face. Tanner let go of the boom and barrel-rolled to safety. The blow to the pirates gave Daya and Wilder just enough time to scoop up the enemy weapons so that once the pirates had gathered their senses, they were staring down the barrels of their own guns.

Having been temporarily thrown by the Brigands' ruse, Maks quickly regrouped and pulled an automatic pistol from his holster, aiming at the rival ship.

"Wilder! Watch out!" Bonnie yelled from the *Dark Star* when she saw Maks aim his pistol at Wilder. Maks's first shot went wide of the mark. Just as he was about to take another, Bonnie did the only thing someone with no use of her hands could do—she steadied her right leg against the mast and swept up her left in a modified roundhouse kick that connected hard with Maks's knee. She heard a bone-crunching CRACK! Maks yelped in pain and grabbed his leg, dropping his gun as he did.

Maks struggled to his feet and looked at Bonnie with unbridled hatred. He pulled a machete from his belt and held it up high, murder in his eyes. *This is the end*, Bonnie thought. But instead, he brought his blade down on the rope that tethered the two ships together.

"Looks like this is a cruise for two from now on, luv," he sneered, cutting loose the remaining ropes and moving toward the ship's wheel. The *Dark Star*, hobbled as it was, still had a functioning foresail, and under its power, the ship pulled away from the *North* and headed back out to the mouth of the inlet, now visible ahead through the mist.

Chapter 40
A Father's Love

Bonnie struggled violently against her bindings as Maks expertly trimmed his lone remaining sail and prepared to make off with her. The *North* was so close. If she could somehow get loose...

And just like that, she felt her hands come free! She turned and saw kneeling behind the mast, none other than Barnaby Chisolm!

He held a finger up to his mouth. Then pointed to the sword he'd brought with him. It was her own sword! Siobhan! Her hands now free, she reached for the sword but suddenly a boot kicked it out of her reach.

Maks, his machete in hand, looked down at Barnaby, who was defiantly pointing his serpent-handled dagger at Maks, no match for the pirate's longer blade. Maks took a violent swing at the dagger, sending it flying from Barnaby's hand and leaving the boy utterly defenseless.

"You pigsty mongrels don't give up, do you?" Maks said as he raised his machete, ready to bring it down on Barnaby.

Bonnie quickly rolled, scooped up her sword, and jumped to her feet between Maks and Barnaby. She felt the familiar vibration and reassuring hum of Siobhan and it filled her with courage. "The only way to him is through me."

"If that's what it takes," Maks said. And to Bonnie's surprise, Maks swung the machete at her. Only her fast reflexes saved her from injury as she brought up her sword to block the blow. And then they were off, metal against metal.

Back on the *North*, Micah pointed and shouted, "Hey! He's leaving with Bonnie!"

Everyone looked and saw that the *Dark Star* was drifting apart from their ship even as the sword fight raged on deck.

"Yeun! Tie the jib arm back down," Reed barked. "Tanner, tack full to starboard and get back after that ship!" Then he indicated the pirates, "Zion, Malachi, see to it those men are bound and stowed below."

There were "Aye Captains" all around as everyone hopped to and the *True North* began to pull away so that they could come around and make another run at the *Dark Star*.

What happened next happened so fast, no one could stop it. And there was much debate afterwards about how things might have turned out if someone, anyone, had been able to do so.

There was a reason Squid had found the crew cabin empty when he had searched it. Sometime during the chaos, Sheriff Maynard had secretly slipped out of the crew quarters through the loading hatch. And upon seeing the two ships starting to separate, he pulled himself up onto the railing. No one knew where his strength came from, given how badly beaten he was and how much blood he'd lost. Later Winnie would say that it had been the most immutable, innate and all-powerful love in the universe, the love of a parent for a child.

Just as the bow of the *Dark Star* was about to clear the stern of the *North*, Bobby leapt! It was an impossible distance—ten, twenty-five or even fifty feet, depending on which version of the tale one heard around campfires in the years to come. There was a collective gasp from the Brigands when it seemed that Bobby wasn't going to make it. And another gasp when he had somehow, despite a missing finger, managed to grasp the loose line that hung from one of the cleats. There was a third gasp when Bobby slammed against the starboard side of the pirate ship and everyone thought for sure he would lose his grip and fall to the unforgiving water below.

But somehow he held fast to the rope, his feet gaining purchase on one of the portholes. He hung precariously off the side of the *Dark Star* as it receded into the blackness.

"I need this vessel turned around, Mister Prescott!" Reed commanded. "NOW!"

"Go, Barnaby! Hide!" Bonnie shouted to the boy cowering behind her on the deck of the *Dark Star*. Bonnie's arms quivered as she was doing all she could to fend off the vicious thrusts of Maks's blade. Even Siobhan seemed to falter, its hum growing fainter with each brutal blow the sword absorbed. There was only so much longer that her strength could hold out.

"I'm not leaving you!" Barnaby said.

"Go! He can't kill me. But he WILL kill you!" In Barnaby's attempt to protect her, she found herself in the position of trying to protect him. Fighting off exhaustion, Bonnie redoubled her efforts, launching attack after attack at Maks, all of which the wily pirate was able to parry. Then, an inspiration. The Palermo Maneuver! It had worked against Tanner in the barn, why not here? She dodged Maks's blade and pulled her own sword up toward the machete in a sweeping backhand motion.

It worked! Maks was thrown off balance. Bonnie immediately advanced. She lifted Siobhan and came across her body with a forceful diagonal attack. In one swift movement, she slashed the tip of her sword across Maks's face, in the opposite direction of the scar he already had. The pirate now looked as if he had a big "X" half written in blood across his cheek, thus completing the mark that Reed's own father had begun years earlier. Maks blinked, staggered back, putting his hand to his bloody face. His face contorted in fury, Maks HOWLED, revealing gums and teeth through the deep gash in his cheek.

"You slag!" Maks screamed in pain. "You filthy little slag! I'll kill you!"

Maks advanced and his machete sliced across Bonnie's right forearm, knocking the sword out of her hands. It skittered all the way across the deck, far out of her reach. Bonnie looked down in surprise at the blood on her arm. Maks lifted his boot and kicked Bonnie in the stomach with such force that she flew back hard against the rail and crumpled to the deck. Dazed and out of breath from the brutal blow, she struggled to her knees.

Maks started after her when—

"Leave her be, Maksymillian!" shouted a familiar voice.

Through the fog of her pain, Bonnie looked up and saw, jumping down from the railing with a cutlass in his good hand, Sheriff Bobby Maynard!

"I should have ended you when I had the opportunity," Maks snarled.

"Here's your chance. Unless you prefer fighting children," Bobby replied.

"DIE!" Maks screamed as he went for Bobby, blade raised high.

What followed was a fierce sword battle between two seasoned warriors. And in the brief time it raged, Bonnie saw in her father the Brigand that he had once been—fighting with elegance and surety that left no doubt that he was corsair through and through.

With attack and counterattack, Bobby Maynard quickly had the pirate on the defensive. Maks began to buckle beneath the blows as Bobby relentlessly pressed his advantage.

But at that very moment, the *Dark Star* finally hit the open waters of the Atlantic. Having cleared the protection of the inlet and with no one at the wheel to guide her, the ship was buffeted until it crashed back down hard onto the surface of the ocean. That was all it took. Bobby lost his footing for a split second, which was all the opening that Maks needed. The pirate curled his lip with satisfaction as his blade sliced across the back of Bobby's leg. Bobby dropped to a knee in agony. Sensing his opportunity, Maks turned back to Bonnie and stormed at her with his machete. "Whatever hell I have to pay with Jack will be worth it for the pleasure of runnin' you through!" he snarled as he brought back his blade.

Bonnie instinctively covered Barnaby, and stared into her executioner's eyes, prepared to take the blow. If she was to die tonight, it would be as a Brigand of the Compass Rose should die, showing no fear, valiant in the face of death.

But just as Maks went to deliver the fatal blow, Bobby Maynard lunged between his daughter and the machete. There was a sickening thud as the machete plunged into his chest instead of hers.

"NO!" Bonnie screamed. Seeing her father lying on the deck, blood gushing from the deep wound, something overtook Bonnie. Something so primal and so fierce that she felt she was channeling it from… somewhere else. Somewhere beyond herself, even perhaps some *time* beyond herself.

And then, as if by divine intervention, it happened. The ship hit another swell, which sent her sword spinning back across the deck toward her, coming to a stop at her feet. And without the slightest hesitation, Bonnie brought the heel of her boot down on its hilt. The sword flipped once, twice, up and up over her head and she reached out and plucked it from the air as it came down, and, in one fell swoop she brought it down hard on the pirate's machete, still dripping with her father's blood.

Maks staggered back and back and back to the stern of the ship, stunned by the strength of the blows coming from the skinny girl before him. One of them grazed his torso, and a line of fresh blood seeped through his shirt. He was cornered. And no matter how he tried to bring his machete up in retaliation, all he could do was hold it before him defensively, barely able to keep the girl's razor-sharp blade at bay. Blue sparks shot from Siobhan with each blow. The hum grew and crescendoed until it was deafening. Bonnie's fury seemed to connect with the sword. She felt a power blast through her and with incredible force, she knocked the machete out of Maks's hand and into the sea.

The unearthly fury did not stop and she brought up the rose-handled sword in preparation for the kill. Then something else deep inside her, the young girl who had never before taken a life, screamed NO! in horror at what she was about to do. But she pushed back all doubt and swung Siobhan with all her might.

It had been only a nanosecond of hesitation, but it was more than enough for Maks. He threw himself backwards off the ship as Bonnie's blade whizzed over his head, missing him by a hair.

She rushed to look over the rail. All she saw was foaming wake and endless sea. The pirate was gone, claimed by the black waters of the ocean.

She whirled her head around. In the distance and closing fast, she saw the *North*.

As quickly as the fury had come on, Bonnie felt it drain from her—in its place was panic as her thoughts turned to her father. She rushed over to where she had left him. Bobby was lying on the deck. Barnaby was next to him, pressing his small hands on the gaping wound in Bobby's chest, trying and failing to stanch the flow of blood.

Please be alive, she thought. She knelt next to him and replaced Barnaby's hands with her own, doing only slightly better at holding back the blood loss.

"The *North* is coming up on us. Take the wheel and bring us around. And get on the radio in the cabin, call for help," she told Barnaby, who nodded and was off.

Bobby's eyes fluttered and a moan escaped his lips. Bonnie was flooded with relief.

"Bonnie?" Bobby whispered. "You're okay. Thank God."

"Yeah, Dad. I'm fine. We're gonna get you some help…"

"Dad…" he said weakly. "First time you called me that. Sounds nice. Real nice…"

"Get used to it," she said. "You're gonna hear it a lot from now on. It's gonna be just like you said. We're gonna find mom and we're gonna be together forever."

"My strong, beautiful girl. So brave," he smiled, looking into Bonnie's face. "So like your mother. She would be so proud. So very…" he took in a ragged and labored breath that alarmed Bonnie.

"Dad?"

"When you see your mom, tell her I never stopped loving her." A soft rush of air escaped his lips, his smile slowly faded, and his eyes closed. Bonnie felt her father's body go limp.

"Daddy?" Bonnie cried, tears flowing. "DADDY!"

Chapter 41
A Hero Laid to Rest

When Bonnie Hartwright would think back on it in the days to come, the hours that followed the death of her father were little more than a jumbled haze. She vaguely remembered the jubilant hugs upon their return, but the mood turned somber when Reed reported that while the Cove had indeed been saved, it had been purchased at such a dear price.

Grandma Winnie openly wept when she heard the news of Bobby Maynard's death.

"He'll be buried with full honors in the Field of the Fallen," Captain Ballister proclaimed, his own voice thick with emotion.

In the midst of her bottomless grief, Bonnie clung to this morsel of comfort, knowing that her father would be laid to rest in the churchyard reserved only for Brigands who had died in service of the cause. The same churchyard that Bonnie had been drawn to by her dreams when she first arrived.

Meanwhile, in the aftermath of the sea battle, the *Dark Star* was seized by the authorities, the stolen property discovered in the ship's hold, and its crew taken into custody. During an exhaustive search of the waters off Cuffee Island, authorities turned up the body of Bartholomew, tangled and floating in the partially burned sail. The scar-faced Maks, however, was not to be found and was presumed drowned. The body of Deputy Wayne washed up just outside the marina later that week, and he too was honored for his valor in fighting the "yacht burglars," for the truth would remain locked in the heart of Tanner Prescott, the only living witness to his aiding and abetting Charley Eden and the pirates.

As for Charley Eden himself, ever since word of Bobby's death spread through town, he had disappeared. This led to conflicting speculation among the locals that Eden had either been involved with the crime ring, been a victim of the thieves' treachery, or both. In any case, the way Captain Ballister laid it out to the authorities, Bobby and Deputy Wayne had been killed following up the lead that the kids had provided them, nothing more. The kids had stumbled upon the sheriff at Corsair's Lair, where they confronted the criminals and the sea battle ensued. The captain told the story in a way that was sort of true, but a total lie at the same time, as he was silent about the most important fact: that Bobby Maynard was Bonnie Hartwright's father and he had died protecting his daughter from a 300-year-old curse.

In the end, the Brigands were deemed local heroes as well, and for the first time in decades, the Cove was finally safe. There was even interest among some of the big city papers in Charlotte and Raleigh to do a feature story on the brave teens who'd risked their lives against modern-day pirates, but Captain Ballister declined all such requests. The Brigands would deal with this episode as they had with everything else in their history, as far from the spotlight as possible.

*   *   *   *   *

On a misty afternoon two days after the battle, Bonnie sat with Reed and Wilder in the back seat of Wicked Pete's truck as he followed the hearse bearing her father back to Cormac's Cove for burial. They'd just come from a public memorial service at the Highcross Civic Center. Bonnie was wearing a simple black dress Winnie had brought out of storage. It had been her mother Brigid's, worn only once, at the funeral of Reed's parents years before. The civic center had been packed for the service. It had moved Bonnie profoundly to see that her father had been so loved and respected by the community. Speaker after speaker said Bobby was a decent, honorable, and brave man. Bonnie knew that, for she had seen it firsthand. And that thought squeezed her heart until she felt it would cease beating.

The mist had turned to a steady drizzle by the time the hearse passed through the main gate at Cormac's Cove. A few cars followed and came to a stop at the end of a narrow road that led to the side of the little white church on the hilltop that was to be the site of a smaller, private service... as well as Bobby Maynard's final resting place. Bonnie stepped out of the truck and took her place behind the hearse, joined by Wilder and Reed. She watched the pallbearers, Brigands who had come from far and wide, take the casket from the hearse and carry it into the small chapel. Many of these warriors Bonnie had heard of during the captain's stories of Brigand lore. Among them were Hart "The Ghost" Thorp, Fenwick "Handsome Fen" Nash and Dudley Carn, a large-gutted, red-haired man with a matching beard. As Carn moved away from the casket and took his seat in the chapel, Bonnie looked at him in amazement. He was the Ginger Santa Claus—the outbound counselor from Amargo Canyon who had signed the paperwork that had set this adventure in motion so many weeks ago. The guy was a Brigand!

Another of those legendary warriors who had gathered to pay their last respects was Barnaby's own father, Wakeman Chisolm, a regal-looking man who now sat in a pew near the front of the church, his arm proudly around his son. Barnaby had bravely held back tears when the casket passed by. Bonnie's other battle companions, battered but refusing to be broken, all sat together in the chapel. As she passed, they reached out to her and whispered condolences. Even Tanner Prescott, in whose eyes she saw genuine sympathy.

Bonnie was grateful to see Fati and Gam Gam among the mourners as well. She'd specifically requested that they be included in the private ceremony. As Bonnie walked toward the front of the church past the two women, Gam Gam nodded sadly, somehow "seeing" her just as she had seen so much. And Bonnie knew they were now an inextricable part of whatever was to come.

Reed and Wilder escorted Bonnie to her seat next to the Ballister family in the front pew. She felt a strong, reassuring hand on her shoulder as she sat and turned to see that it was Malachi, whose mismatched eyes conveyed so much without saying a word. She gratefully patted Malachi's outstretched hand and then turned back toward the front of the chapel. Grandma Winnie touched her cheek, tears swimming in her eyes. But Bonnie could only nod in reply.

What could one say? To have something snatched away from you so suddenly, the second after you had found it. The cruelty of it burned inside her. There was a time, not so long ago, that such overwhelming darkness would have led to despair, even to thoughts of putting an end to all the pain herself. But that had changed. For now she realized what such an act would mean to the world. How ironic that in order to see the value of her own life, she had to first discover that someone else wanted her dead.

Yet, that wasn't the only reason. She also understood what such a decision would do to people who loved her, people whom she had grown to love as well. And there is nothing that more binds one to life than the joy of loving and being loved. She knew that now. And that above all else, even above a pirate's curse, had delivered her at last from the dark thoughts.

*   *   *   *   *

As Father Foley, an old Brigand himself with scars to prove it, led the gathered in prayer, Reed and Wilder simultaneously took Bonnie's hands. Bonnie fixed her gaze on the baptismal font. It was here, in the water of this very font, that Calico Jack's chain of murder and violence toward her family began, and also here, she had learned, that she herself had been baptized soon after she was born. Somehow, it all came back to water. Water that could kill could also cleanse and heal.

"May the Almighty hold you in the palm of his hand," the priest concluded.

Captain Ballister stepped forward, put his hand to the casket, and addressed the group in a slow, deliberate voice.

"While it has been many years since Bobby Maynard was in our service, in the end he died in the name of the cause. Though I could never summon the grace to forgive him for his violation of vows, I understand now that what Bobby did, he did from a place of deep love." Ballister concluded, his voice full of emotion, "Today I welcome Robert Maynard back home. Today we lay him to rest, at Cormac's Cove, the place where he first met his one true love. May they be rejoined in the hereafter one day."

Captain Ballister's voice faltered when he said this last sentence. The thought of the long-lost Brigid was too much for him to bear. He shook his head and stepped away from the casket.

Jonesy stood with his accordion and began to play the old Irish ballad "*Mo Ghile Mear*" (My Gallant Hero) as the pallbearers moved forward to carry the coffin out of the chapel and to the graveyard. His voice was full of emotion as he sang, and others joined in one by one, soon filling the church to the rafters with lush harmonies. Bonnie could feel her own heart swelling with emotion as she listened in silence.

.   .   .   .   .

A steady rain fell as the mourners gathered in the Field of the Fallen around the freshly dug grave beneath a massive oak that gave some shelter from the weather. Father Foley spoke as the coffin was lowered into the ground.

"Receive our brother Robert, we pray, into the mansions of the saints. As we make ready his resting place, look also with favor on those who mourn and comfort them in their loss." The priest then nodded to Bonnie.

Bonnie knelt down to the pile of dirt next to the grave and took up a handful of earth. The rain had turned the dirt muddy and she felt it clump between her fingers. Bonnie rose and gazed at the headstone of her own father, just installed by the mason that morning, then down to the smooth lacquered wood of the coffin inside the grave at her feet. She felt a strange emotion coursing through her body. It wasn't grief anymore; it was something even deeper and more visceral. Her grief had been replaced by a mix of rage and quiet determination. She knew, just *knew,* that she would eventually come face to face with the author of all this pain.

And with that realization, she let the wet earth go. It landed with a sickening and final thud on the lid of the coffin.

Blinking back tears for the father that she would never get the chance to know, Bonnie whispered in a voice so low that none of the other mourners could hear.

"I will avenge you."

She turned away, and without speaking another word walked out of the churchyard and down the hill toward the main house. The other members of Boreas grabbed shovels and dutifully began to fill in the grave with the wet earth around them.

*   *   *   *   *

At the top of the windswept cliff in front of the church, Fati watched a solitary Bonnie walking down the path and shook her head.

"This is too hard," she said. "You see why I didn't want to get messed up in this business in the first place."

"Dis business done got messed up long 'fore we was here," Gam Gam said, "and so it will stay if'n nobody do nuttin'.'"

"Lord Almighty," Fati said, watching Bonnie disappear at the bottom of the hill. "What have you got us into, Gam Gam?"

"More den we kin hope tah guess," the old woman replied. "Bigger forces den you and me be at work now."

Chapter 42
The Wall of Investiture

Two weeks after Bobby Maynard's funeral, Bonnie Hartwright found herself staring into a roaring fire. She was sitting on the very same log in the center of the Cave o' the Four Winds where she had sat the night she arrived. So much had happened since that night that she could never have imagined. Not the least of which was making it here, to the Brigands' Induction Ceremony. As was tradition, the ceremony was held on the night of August's full moon—the Red Moon, so named for the reddish hue it takes on in the sultry haze of summer. To Bonnie it was just a reminder of the blood that had been spilled in recent days.

Bonnie looked around the cave at the others: her fellow corsairs who had survived the final cut. Rather than being jubilant about this special night, their demeanor was that of weary soldiers back from battle. In the end, the ceremony felt more like a confirmation of what they knew in their hearts than any kind of new beginning.

The newest Brigands were all adorned with the symbols of their new status as well. Around their waists they wore the swords they had adopted during their summer of transition and each bore the now-familiar Brigand tattoo in the shape of an eight-pointed star with roses... courtesy of Jonesy. Though unsteady in so many other ways, the one-eyed sailor proved a gifted tattoo artist, and all agreed that his work was exquisite: intricately detailed, with the deepest reds and goldest golds. And though tradition held that the tattoo would be on the sword-brandishing wrist, Jonesy made an exception in Bonnie's case. At her request, he put the tattoo on her shoulder blade, incorporating her birthmark into the design. The ugly Stain of Musangu had been transformed into a thing of beauty and in so doing, Bonnie had embraced both sides of her heritage.

Even Barnaby had gone through with getting his tattoo without a moment's hesitation. In fact, he had insisted on having his ear pierced as well, a request with which Bonnie happily complied. Now, sitting up taller than Bonnie had ever seen him, Barnaby looked utterly transformed, his new shiny hoop earring glinting in the firelight. There remained no doubt this boy had at last located his inner macho.

But Barnaby wasn't the only member of Boreas who had profoundly changed. Bonnie marveled at how the others too had grown from the first time they'd joined her around this fire. Wild boys, now all earnest young men. Micah Maguire was now twenty pounds lighter and strong enough to have pulled himself from the side of the *North* onto the deck to fight off pirates. And Malachi, who rarely spoke, never letting others get too near. Though he wasn't going to be joining the debate society any time soon, he now seemed comfortable among the corsairs, even allowing a congratulatory clap on the shoulder or a playful nudge here and there.

And, yes, even Tanner Prescott was there, his decision to stay now final. He said that he was doing it just to spite his father, but

Bonnie knew better. Beneath his cocky exterior, she could see a hint of the honor and pride felt by the rest of the corsairs. But even more than that, she could see a sense of belonging.

Finally, there was Wilder. The chocolate-eyed boy who had befriended her from the beginning. He had probably changed the most in Bonnie's eyes. Not just because he had become more self-assured, if that were even possible, but because of what he had come to mean to her. She now cared for him deeply, more deeply than she ever thought herself capable, though it would be some time before she knew just how much.

BLEEEOOOO! The sound of Jonesy's horn cut through Bonnie's thoughts. Everyone turned to Captain Ballister and Reed, who both stood at the head of the fire. Reed had changed too, Bonnie noticed. No longer the obedient, by-the-book Brigand she'd met at the gate that first night, he was now determined to choose his own path, even if it meant defying time-honored family traditions. He had an inner strength that she'd come to admire and a relentless devotion to her that moved Bonnie to her core. Reed looked at Bonnie and she felt her heart skip a beat. The captain nodded to him and he stepped forward.

"Corsairs!" Reed began, assuming the role that had until now been reserved for his grandfather. "Tonight is the night you've been preparing for all summer. In fact, your whole lives, though you did not know it. You initially came here because you were by fate born to the house of a warrior—descendants of the great corsair queen Mary Read."

The formal words sounded a little funny coming out of Reed's mouth, but at the same time, Bonnie felt he'd earned them. He'd earned the respect of everyone gathered there in ways they were all just beginning to comprehend.

"We have, by virtue of a trial by fire," he continued, "come to a place where we can freely pledge our lives to the sacred cause of ridding the world of Calico Jack Rackham!"

The pirate's name echoed and hung in the air for a moment before Reed spoke again. "So now, let us lift our swords in alliance! For no longer are you Boreas, Eurus, Notus and Zephyrus; those winds have all merged into the mighty gale that is the Brigands of the Compass Rose!"

The corsairs closed the circle, pulled their swords from their sheaths and brought them together above their heads.

"Brigands of the Compass Rose!" they all shouted as one.

And when the blades touched, a sudden powerful wind blew through the cave; there was crackling of electricity and blue sparks flew from their blades. Bonnie felt involuntary tears stream down her face. She could feel the devotion and camaraderie that emanated from all of them. Not just from those gathered in the cave that night, but from generations of Brigands who had served the same noble cause, a cause that would come to define each of their lives from this moment onward.

*   *   *   *   *

After the wind died down and the last spark disappeared, each of the newly anointed Brigands took a long stick from the fire and dipped the charred end into a mixture of pigments and animal fat that Grandma Winnie had concocted. Then, one by one again, they reached up and added their name to the Wall of Investiture.

Bonnie knew instantly where she wanted to put hers. Balanced atop the shoulders of Malachi Maguire with a torch in one hand and the writing stick in the other, Bonnie guided him until she was positioned under the spot where her mother's name was. She could see it clearly now in the steady torchlight: BRIGID BYRNE. Suddenly, she felt her breath catch, for the light revealed another name next to her mother's: ROBERT MAYNARD. *Of course it would be there*, Bonnie thought, imagining how in love they must have been on that night years ago. Bonnie instructed Malachi to shift his position slightly, and she began writing her name in the center, just beneath the two.

B-O-N-N-I-E she wrote, and her gaze lingered on the letters. But she paused before starting the last name. Then she wrote the name Hartwright.

Not Maynard, nor even Byrne for that matter, but Bonnie Hartwright. It was the name that made her who she was. It was the name of the baby abandoned in the church. The name of the girl who learned to live by her wits. The name of the girl who was marked with the Stain of Musangu. Changing her last name was not the best way to honor her father's memory. The best way to honor her father's memory was to find her mother.

With no trace of her former shame, she looked proudly at the word HARTWRIGHT on the wall.

And for a flourish, she dotted the "i" with a skull and crossbones.

* * * * *

Later, in the solitude of his office, Captain Ballister would open the Log of the Forebears to the family tree of Robert Maynard and Brigid Byrne. With his finest quill pen, he crossed out the name "Baby Girl Maynard."

Next to it, with trembling hands, he wrote "Bonnie Hartwright."

Once and for all sealing her fate.

Chapter 43
Friends

"Make a wish, Bonnie."

Bonnie looked down at the cupcake that Reed held out before her, a single burning candle planted firmly in its buttercream icing. She stood with him and Wilder at the bow of the *True North* as it bobbed up and down in the waters of Cormac's Cove. Perched next to her on the brass rail of the ship was the parrot Crossbones, which only that morning had finally managed to make the flight back to the Cove despite its still-damaged wing. The parrot eyed the cupcake with great interest as its candle flickered in the wind, protected only by Reed's cupped hand.

"If you don't blow out that candle quick, Curls, I think the bird is gonna call dibs on the frosting," Wilder urged.

Bonnie smiled. It was nearing midnight and the other corsairs were long asleep. It had been an exhausting day. But as fate would have it, not only was today the date of the induction ceremony, but it also happened to be Bonnie Hartwright's birthday. Her actual birthday—August 15th. Not the fake, guesstimated one in October that she'd been assigned by the state so many years ago. This real date she had learned from the Ballisters themselves as part of discovering the truth about her past.

Bonnie had insisted she didn't want a party. She had never really celebrated a birthday before. It never felt authentic. But now that the true date was known, the boys had insisted on at least acknowledging it with her. "Because after all," Wilder had explained, "it isn't every day you turn sixteen."

"Wonder how many of these I've got left," she said, staring into the flame.

Reed and Wilder both assured her there would be plenty, but they all knew how uncertain even their next day really was. Bonnie had just seen it herself. She thought of her father and his kind eyes. And of the possibilities that would never be. Then, she thought of her mother, out there somewhere on the run, alive but lost to her. She looked into the distance, far out over the ocean where heat lightning lit up the horizon, silently portending a coming storm. She could hear the roiling waters of the sound. Felt the thrum of the tides in her blood. And the fury of her bloodline in her heart. Whatever remained of her life—however many years she had before Calico Jack caught up with her—she knew what she wanted to do with them. *Exactly* what she wanted to do with them. She looked back to the cupcake in Reed's hand.

Then she closed her eyes, made her first-ever birthday wish, and blew out the candle.

The flame vanished. And only the three friends remained in the darkness.

As the waters of Cormac's Cove lapped gently against the side of the *True North*, Bonnie felt a swell of love and pride for these boys who had vowed to help her and to protect her, no matter what. And no matter what she had to face in the black hole that was her future, she knew that for the first time in her life, she would not be alone.

Epilogue

A thousand miles away, the Red Moon shone over the waters of the Sargasso Sea. Far from the prying eyes of civilization, four heavily armed men led a lone figure across the deck of the *Perdition,* a 1050 ft. cargo ship of Maltese registry. The figure, his face obscured by a hooded jacket, walked with a limp along the massive deck lined with freight containers. The leader came to a stop and knocked on one of the nondescript containers. In answer, a slit in the container slid back and two yellowy eyes peered out. Then, a small door opened up and the hooded figure was pushed inside. A hatch in the container floor was opened, revealing a metal staircase that led to the hold of the ship and to an entirely different world. Rows of high-tech monitors showing surveillance footage from all over the globe were spread around a huge command center, and a lighted map on the wall spoke of a vast worldwide empire.

The figure was led past the command center and down a long corridor, where one of the armed men stopped at a door at the end of the hall, pushed a button on the wall, and then stood in front of a retinal scanner. After the eye scan was complete, a buzzer sounded and the door slid open.

The hooded figure stepped into the cabin and seemingly back in time. The room was full of shadows, lit only by lanterns. A massive teak desk filled the wood-paneled room, and vintage swords and daggers hung from the walls, along with a tattered Jolly

Roger flag. A decorative glass decanter full of rum was open on the desk. A map of the world hung on the wall behind the leather-backed chair that was turned away from the visitor.

"She is back on the Cove then?" came a raspy voice from the chair.

The man in the hooded jacket stepped forward. A four-fingered hand moved to his face and lowered his hood to reveal the pirate Maks, the gash on his face from Bonnie's sword freshly stitched but still swollen and red.

"Aye, she gave us the slip, she did," he replied, trying to hide the fear that coursed beneath the surface. "It won't happen again, I swear."

The chair slowly swiveled around to face him. Looking back was the unmistakable face of Calico Jack Rackham. Appearing just as he had on the day of his execution as if frozen in time, the pirate radiated an unworldly vitality; his arms still rippled with taut muscles beneath the trademark calico fabric of his billowing shirt. The telltale scars from his hanging still lingered around his neck, visible beneath the pirate's meticulously trimmed goatee. And around that neck was a necklace, upon which hung leathery, ragged patches of skin, each bearing the Stain of Musangu—grisly trophies from three centuries of murder. Jack studied Maks with a steely gaze, his eyes black as coal.

"That I can guarantee," he said, the centuries having mellowed the pirate's harsh manner of speech. Then he motioned to the men, who roughly grabbed Maks and dragged him back out of the chamber.

"No! Nooo! I beg you!" he yelled in terror as he was being hauled away.

As the door slammed shut, Calico Jack leaned back in his chair.

"You're certain this plan can still work?" he asked over his shoulder.

A large African man in beads stepped forward from an anteroom. It was the shaman Salifu. "Aye, Cap'n. In many a way, even better so."

"Excellent," Calico Jack smiled, showing perfect white teeth. He held up his hand to the light, admiring the ring on his finger: two gold skulls with ruby eyes, wrapped around an hourglass... now close to full.

"So now..." the pirate said, "we wait."

Acknowledgments

Back around the time that we published our first novel, *Glitter Girl*, we were kicking around ideas about what to write about next. I think we were sitting around the community pool watching our daughters splashing around one summer day when the idea of writing a novel about "pirates" came up. "Sure, pirates!" we thought, "That will be a fun little trifle of a book that we can knock out in a few months." Little did we know the twists and turns that this little story would take before it would finally reach our readers' hands years later. But the journey is half the fun, and we are just so excited to be able to share the Brigands' first adventure with the world. However, we need to give a shout-out to those who helped us navigate the waters and bring this little ship into port. First and foremost, we have to thank our respective spouses, Randy and Junko, whose support and encouragement were vital to any of this happening. And of course, we want to thank our daughters Julia Runkle and Katrina Webb for being constant sources of inspiration. And to Bella De Vita for being a great early reader of the novel and giving us a "teen's eye view" of how the book was coming across. And, a big *muchas gracias* to Veronica Aguirre and her in-depth knowledge of colorful terms in Spanish. Special thanks to Jesus Santana and Rafael Rangel for helping us realize our vision for the cover art. We are also perpetually grateful to Carl Pritzkat and Tony Travostino, who planted the idea of our writing for young readers in our heads in the first place. And finally, a hearty pirate cheer to Reagan Rothe, David King, and the team at

Black Rose Writing for championing this project and seeing that it got to market safe and sound. It's great to work with a company that so values the independence of its creators. And heck, while we're at it, we might as well say thanks to each other, as it could have been very easy to "abandon ship" on this one at numerous points along the way. Here's to many more adventures, and many more ports of call for years to come!

About The Authors

Toni Runkle and Steve Webb have always loved telling stories. After becoming friends as graduate students at the USC School of Cinematic Arts, they worked separately in the movie and television industry for a number of years before coming together to write novels for young readers. Their first book, *Glitter Girl*, was called "...an empowering message about striving to be true to oneself..." by *Kirkus Reviews.* Toni loves scary movies, her garden, and trips to the beach. Steve loves baseball, not-so-scary movies, and a good cheeseburger. Both writers are married (not to each other because that would get weird) and live in Southern California with their respective families.

Note From Toni Runkle & Steve Webb

Word-of-mouth is crucial for any author to succeed. If you enjoyed *The Pirate's Curse*, please leave a review online—anywhere you are able. Even if it's just a sentence or two. It would make all the difference and would be very much appreciated.

Thanks!
Toni Runkle & Steve Webb

We hope you enjoyed reading this title from:

BLACK ROSE
writing™

www.blackrosewriting.com

Subscribe to our mailing list – *The Rosevine* – and receive **FREE** books, daily deals, and stay current with news about upcoming releases and our hottest authors.
Scan the QR code below to sign up.

Already a subscriber? Please accept a sincere thank you for being a fan of Black Rose Writing authors.

View other Black Rose Writing titles at
www.blackrosewriting.com/books and use promo code
PRINT to receive a **20% discount** when purchasing.

Made in the USA
Las Vegas, NV
09 October 2023